When the Night Ends

M J Lee has worked as a university researcher in history, a social worker with Vietnamese refugees, and as the creative director of an advertising agency. He has spent 25 years of his life working outside the north of England, in London, Hong Kong, Taipei, Singapore, Bangkok and Shanghai.

Also by M J Lee

DI Ridpath Crime Thriller

MJ LEE

WHEN THE NIGHT ENDS

CANELOCRIME

First published in the United Kingdom in 2022 by

Canelo
Unit 9, 5th Floor
Cargo Works, 1-2 Hatfields
London, SE1 9PG
United Kingdom

A CIP catalogue record for this book is available from the British Library.

Print ISBN 978 1 80032 779 5
Ebook ISBN 978 1 80032 778 8

This book is a work of fiction. Names, characters, businesses, organizations, places and events are either the product of the author's imagination or are used fictitiously. Any resemblance to actual persons, living or dead, events or locales is entirely coincidental.

Look for more great books at www.canelo.co

Printed and bound in Great Britain by Clays Ltd, Elcograf S.p.A.

For the lads: Dave, John and Pete.

February 21, 2018

Chapter One

Sergeant Tony Saunders glanced at the clock on the wall facing his desk.

3.24.

He stood up from his chair and stretched, yawning loudly as he did. Night shifts could be long and tedious as a custody sergeant if there wasn't much happening.

Outside the confines of Redbury Police Station, past the automatic doors, the night was as black as a pint of Chesters Mild and the wind howled through the trees. Sheets of icy rain sleeted down, flooding the roads in pools of water, battleship-grey under the neon street lights.

The last dregs of winter were blowing hard, scouring the estates and gardens and houses of suburban Manchester.

'Rather be nice and cosy in here than stuck outside in a car. This weather would sink the bloody *Titanic*,' he said out loud to the empty custody reception.

It had been a quiet night for him so far. After twenty-one years on the force, he really appreciated the peaceful times. It hadn't always been like that, of course. As a young copper, he'd been happy to volunteer for a Saturday night shift in the city centre, diving into the various rucks that formed as the pubs and clubs shut, giving as good as he got.

Now, in one of the suburban nicks at Redbury, he just hoped for a bit of peace and quiet.

He checked the custody board. Just two cells occupied. One DUI picked up on the M60 with a blood alcohol content level of 0.19 per cent, according to the breathalyser. The duty doctor was coming in later to take a blood sample from the driver. The other contained some thug who had beaten up a man in a pub.

He looked across at the CCTV monitors, each camera showing a different view of the cells, the station and the common areas. The pictures changed every five seconds, revolving through the bank of

CCTV cameras positioned throughout the nick. So different from when he had started. No cameras then, just more coppers in every station.

He missed those days. Life, and the police, had seemed so much easier.

He focused on the cameras in the cells. The driver was sitting on the concrete ledge serving as a bunk, his head in his hands, guilt stabbing through every bone in his body.

Serves the bugger right, thought Tony Saunders, he could have killed someone instead of being locked up for the night. Most nights he had a DUI in the cells and he had no pity for them. *Anybody who drinks and drives deserves everything the courts throw at them and more.*

The second cell, number four, was occupied by the thug who'd started a fight in a pub and then just waited for the police to arrive, slowly finishing his pint. His victim, a father of three, lay groaning at his feet with a broken jaw. When the coppers arrived expecting trouble, he'd just stood up and held his arms out in front of him, saying, 'You're taking me to Redbury, aren't you?'

He'd been quiet as a lamb when he was booked in, giving his name and address and asking politely to make a phone call to his solicitor. Expecting trouble, Saunders had put him in Cell 4, well away from the DUI. He was now in the cell with his back against the wall, staring into thin air.

'Can you go and have a look at number four, Terry?' Saunders used the intercom on his desk to ask the custody detention officer.

Terry Rodgers, an officer from one of the private security firms so often used these days, replied immediately. 'I only checked him half an hour ago.'

'Well, check him again. He's awake and I don't like the look of him.'

The CDO muttered something beneath his breath and pushed through the doors leading to the cells, now known with heavy irony as the custody suites. But to Saunders, they would always be the cells. He had lost track of the number of newsletters, emails, messages, pamphlets, refresher courses and quiet words in his ear he had received in the last six months on the latest custody guidelines from the College of Policing and his bosses. The last one had been about the use of language, of course.

Thugs were now detainees.

The cells were custody suites.

Lowlife were now customers.

It was almost as if his bosses were more concerned about the rights of the criminal than of the victim.

The door to the custody area reception slid open and two burly coppers burst in with a small, surly man sandwiched between them, his arms handcuffed in front of him.

'I'm telling you I want to speak to Detective Inspector Brett. Just call him.'

'What's up, Chris?' Sergeant Saunders asked the leading copper.

'We had a tip-off from a local he was dealing out of his car. We stopped him and had a look. Found these.' The young police constable held up a large evidence bag full of smaller bags, each containing a crystalline substance like rock sugar.

'Crack?'

'We think so, Sarge.'

'Has he been cautioned?'

'Yes, Sarge.'

Saunders stared at the small man in front of him. A stained leather jacket, scraggly goatee and eyes darting left and right like a rat looking for an escape hatch. The man looked familiar. Had he been here before?

'Just call Mark Brett, he'll sort it all out.'

Tony Saunders ignored him, addressing the police constable instead.

'Have you searched him and informed him of his rights?'

'Already done, Sarge.'

'No problems with the arrest?'

'He put up a bit of a struggle, but no real issues.'

'If you call Mark Brett, he'll sort it out,' the man said, speaking slowly and enunciating each word.

Tony Saunders turned towards the man. 'Never heard of him,' he said.

'He's National Crime Agency, just call him.'

The sergeant tapped his computer, opening up a new custody record. 'Name?'

'Mark Brett.'

'No, your name, pillock.'

The man closed his eyes and sighed. Finally, he opened them and said in a bored voice, 'Ben Holdsworth.'

'Date of birth?'

Another long sigh. 'January 12, 1982.'

Sergeant Saunders checked out the man. He seemed to be standing upright and his eyes were clear and focused. His answers were delivered quickly and without slurring. 'Address?'

'27 Church Street, Redbury.'

The policeman had begun filling in the boxes on the custody record when he realised the address was the same as the police station. 'Very funny. Address?'

The man stayed silent, simply shifting his weight from one leg to the other.

'I'll put down no fixed abode. Mr Holdsworth, are you feeling unwell, dizzy, or uncomfortable? Would you like to see a health professional?'

'No.'

'Have you taken drugs or any other substances?'

Another long sigh. 'No.' The man leant forward suddenly. 'Just call Mark Brett, will you?' He banged his handcuffed fists on the Plexiglas screen in front of Saunders.

The two coppers on either side immediately jerked him away from the custody desk.

'Right, Mr Holdsworth, I have reason to detain you under the 1994 Drug Trafficking Act with intent to supply a Class A substance.' The voice became a monotone as he recited the words he had said a thousand times before. 'I am going to repeat the caution to make sure you have understood. You do not have to say anything. But it may harm your defence if you do not mention now something which you later rely on in court. Anything you do say may be given in evidence.'

He paused, waiting for a reaction from the detainee. When there was none, he continued. 'You have the right to a legal adviser. If you do not have one, one will be appointed for you.'

The man remained silent.

'Is there anyone you would like to be informed of your detention?'

Again a sigh. 'Just call Mark Brett.'

'You are aware you will be under surveillance during your time in Redbury station. The details are set out here. You also have the right to consult the codes of practice.' He picked up the laminated sheet, delineating the various rights of detainees. 'Please read it and sign on the dotted line.'

Ben Holdsworth glanced briefly at the sheet before stating, 'I ain't signing nothing.'

Tony Saunders made a note of his refusal to sign on the custody record. He added the offence and the grounds for detention before finally asking, 'Would you like to speak to a solicitor or inform anybody of your detention?'

'Like I've said at least a thousand times, just call Mark Brett of the National Crime Agency. He's in Warrington.'

Saunders made a note of the request. 'As it is now 3.40 a.m., the National Crime Agency offices are closed. However, I have made a note on the custody record and the custody inspector will evaluate your request as soon as possible.'

'I want to call him myself. You have to let me call someone, and as you are not an inspector or higher rank, the right cannot be refused.'

Tony Saunders raised his eyebrow. 'We've got a right one here, Chris.'

'Knows his rights, does this one.'

Saunders narrowed his eyes. 'Been here before, have you?'

'Just let me call him.'

Saunders pointed to the telephone on the left-hand side of the custody desk.

The man picked it up and immediately called a number, waiting patiently as it rang. And rang. And rang.

'I'd like to try again.'

'Be our guest.'

Again, the man tapped in the number.

Again, no answer.

'I'd like one more call.'

'You've had two attempts already.'

'They didn't go through. I want to ring my mum this time. Let her know where I am.'

Tony Saunders sighed. 'Go ahead, but make it quick.'

Ben Holdsworth dialled a new number. After three rings the phone was answered.

Saunders could only hear one side of the conversation.

'Hi, Mum, I've been nicked... yeah... yeah... don't worry, I'll be out in the morning... yeah... yeah... sorry, Mum.'

He put the phone down, and, visibly deflated, shuffled back to face Tony Saunders.

'Isn't that heart-warming, Chris, a drug dealer who loves his mum?'

'Enough to make you weep, Sarge.'

'Would you like to make any other calls?' asked Saunders sarcastically.

Ben Holdsworth shook his head.

As if by magic, two muscular detention officers appeared on either side of the detainee.

'As you have been arrested on drugs charges, I am authorising a full body search.'

'You can't do that.'

Saunders tapped on the keyboard. 'I just have. Take him away, lads, and be careful to record his belongings. When you've finished put him in number three.'

Terry Rodgers grabbed Ben Holdsworth's left arm while the other detention officer, Lucas Harvey, took hold of the right wrist. 'Come this way, and don't give us any trouble.'

For a second, the man struggled before the grip tightened and he was led to the search room.

'We'll complete the arrest logs and let the duty inspector know, Sarge.'

'Thanks, Chris. Looks like a good collar.'

'Bit of luck. The stuff was on the front seat next to him. Bloody idiot.'

Sergeant Saunders checked the custody record twice, making sure every detail was correct, and completing the endless forms. These days, they could be pulled up for the slightest error. Better to be safe than sorry.

As he finished, he looked up to the CCTV to see the door of Cell 3 open. Ben Holdsworth was shoved roughly into the cell by the detention officers, stumbling forward before turning and shouting something loudly at the closing door. Luckily the CCTV in the cells didn't have sound – after all, what was there to hear except a torrent of abuse or a nightmare of snoring?

For a minute or so, the man banged on the door of his cell before turning, stopping, kicking his foot against the concrete floor and falling forward against the wall above his bunk.

Had he hit his head?

Tony Saunders leant forward to look more closely at the monitor.

The man lay on his bunk for a few seconds, before standing up, shaking his head and raising his middle finger towards the camera.

Tony Saunders remembered the fierce anger in the man's eyes.

Where had he seen him before?

His attention on the monitors was interrupted by the squawk of the radio on the desk.

'Hi, Sarge, this is Dan Hampson, we've just caught four kids trying to nick a BMW from outside a house. Homeowner saw them and called us in. They tried to do a runner, but ran straight into Jamie in the other car, stupid choughs, ETA nine minutes.'

'How old are they?'

'Young, boss. I reckon none of them are older than fourteen, plus one is a girl.'

'OK, I'll warn child services. We'll get the addresses and the parents down here when they come to the station.'

'Word of warning, they're a little feisty, Sarge. I reckon they're on speed or something.'

Through the radio, Saunders could hear Dan Hampson talking to one of the kids.

'Keep still or you'll be cuffed.'

'Don't touch me, copper, or I'll have you,' one of the young lads snarled.

'What's this?' Another copper's voice. 'What are you doing with this relay amplifier?'

'Science project at school, you arse.'

'What's up, Jamie?' Saunders asked.

'Looks like they've got a relay transmitter and an amplifier, boss. Obviously they were going to nick the car.'

'Didn't nick anything, you tosser.'

'They're using relay transmitters? How old did you say they were?'

'I'd guess about fourteen, but they could be younger, Tony.'

'OK, thanks for the heads-up. If they're on drugs, I'll check when the duty doctor can get here.'

Tony Saunders scratched his head, feeling the thinning hair between his fingers. He seemed to be losing more and more every day. After twenty years on the job, his hair was starting to feel the pressure. He put it down to wearing the helmet for all the time he was on the beat. Bloody thing never did fit properly.

The radio squawked again.

'Sit still or you'll get a backhander.'

'You and whose army, copper? And you can't hit us, we're underage.'

Tony Saunders sighed. He had a feeling it was going to be a long, long shift.

What he didn't realise was that the night was going to end with a death.

November 1, 2021

Chapter Two

'Gentlemen, I'd like to remind you this is a Coroner's Court, not a court of law. We are holding a preliminary hearing to rule on a request, by the legal counsel for the police, regarding anonymity for all police witnesses in the inquest into the death in custody of Mr Ben Holdsworth on February 21, 2018.'

From the back of the courtroom, Ridpath watched as Mrs Challinor set the scene. In front of her the solicitor for the family, Ronald Davies, sat behind a desk. Next to him, three legal counsels for the police plus two assistants were arrayed behind a similar desk. Unlike in full inquests, the rest of the court was empty. There was no jury, no reporters, no witnesses waiting to be called and no observers.

Ridpath had only just returned from holiday with his daughter, Eve, late last night, having spent a wonderful week with her walking in the Lake District during the half-term holiday. Blencathra, the Langdales, Grasmere and the charms of Ambleside had all succumbed to their hiking boots. They had read *Swallows and Amazons* together, walking in the footsteps of the Walker and Blackett children, following their adventures. It had been an amazing week but here he now was, back in court watching the coroner do her job.

She had called him late last night asking him to attend at nine a.m. He had dropped off a grumpier than usual Eve at school and then rushed over to the court, arriving just in time.

'What is it you are requesting, Mr Hargreaves?'

The barrister representing the police slowly rose to his feet, adjusted the papers on the desk in front of him and grasped the lapel of his jacket with his right hand. 'Thank you for the opportunity to present to you today, Coroner. We appreciate the tightness of your schedule but would like to aver that this matter has serious repercussions for the conduct of the inquest and its impact on my clients.'

'Yes, yes, Mr Hargreaves,' Mrs Challinor said impatiently, 'but what are you actually requesting?'

The man rose to his feet slowly again. 'During the inquest, we request all the witnesses from the police be allowed to give their evidence anonymously, and from behind screens whilst in court, or off screen if the evidence is given by way of video transmission.'

'And why do you make this request, Mr Hargreaves?'

'In the interests of fairness to my clients, ma'am...'

'Please call me Coroner or Mrs Challinor, Mr Hargreaves.'

'As you wish, Coroner. As I was saying, the request comes from a desire to show fairness to my clients. There has been a great deal of interest in this case from the beginning. My clients feel their safety would be compromised if their identities and faces were revealed as witnesses during an inquest.'

'Have there been any threats made against them since the death in custody of Mr Holdsworth?'

Mr Hargreaves consulted with one of the solicitors. 'No specific threats we are aware of, Coroner, but police work is by its nature a difficult and dangerous occupation. Anything, or any procedure, making the work more difficult or dangerous should, in the interests of criminal justice, be avoided.'

The coroner made a note on her legal pad. 'Anything else, Mr Hargreaves?'

'In addition, Coroner, this case has already been investigated by the Professional Standards division of GMP and the Independent Office for Police Conduct. In both these organisations, their reports agreed not to name the witnesses but to use code numbers instead.'

'Why was that, Mr Hargreaves?'

A whispered consultation with the police solicitor. 'These men and women are still serving police officers, Coroner. Both the PSD and the IOPC felt no public interest could be served by revealing their identities to the world.'

'Thank you, Mr Hargreaves.' The coroner adjusted her position to face the solicitor for the family. 'Mr Davies, have you anything you wish to say on behalf of the family?'

'I do, Coroner. The family oppose this petition.'

'On what grounds, Mr Davies?'

'On three grounds, Mrs Challinor. Firstly, as my esteemed colleague has just confirmed, there have been no threats against the safety of any of the officers who will be called as witnesses. My client, the mother of the deceased, is an old woman who simply wants to know why her son died in police custody in the early hours of February 21, 2018. She is hardly likely to pose a threat to the police.'

'And secondly, Mr Davies.'

'Secondly, the inquest is not a court of law, Coroner. It is an attempt to find out what happened when somebody died, why the death occurred and to prevent similar deaths from taking place in the future. Anonymity for police witnesses does not serve that cause in any way, shape or form. In fact, it may act to prevent the truth being known.'

Before the coroner could question this statement, the solicitor continued on. 'Thirdly, the importance of an inquest is that it is open and transparent. The proceedings must be seen, and seen to be performed in a fair and equitable manner. Hiding witnesses behind opaque screens is the antithesis of openness.'

Mr Hargreaves rose to his feet. 'It is not hiding them behind screens, Coroner, it is protecting their identities for their safety. We should not add to the danger of their jobs by making their identities known to the wider world. The evidence they give will still be heard by the court and they will still be questioned and cross-examined by my esteemed colleague.'

'But their testimony will not be seen by the court. As my colleague, the esteemed barrister Mr Hargreaves, is well aware, a witness's testimony is not merely his words but his whole demeanour: the body language, the way he sits, the way he presents himself to the coroner. Why would we not allow openness when such transparency is most needed?'

'I think my esteemed colleague mistakes openness for justice...' said Hargreaves.

'And I think you mistake secrecy for security. It doesn't—'

The coroner slammed her hand down hard on the table in front of her, interrupting the legal counsel. 'I will remind you once again, gentlemen, this is a Coroner's Court. It is not adversarial, rather it seeks to find the truth and nothing but the truth. I will take your presentations under advisement and let you know my decision shortly. However, I must remind you that the inquest will begin in seven days, on November 8. You must be ready to move forward with the witnesses on that day in whatever way they present their testimony. Thank you, gentlemen.'

She closed her files and stood up. 'Mr Ridpath, I will see you in my chambers as soon as the courtroom is cleared, thank you.'

Chapter Three

'Good morning, Mrs Challinor, you wanted to see me?'

'Good morning, Ridpath, come in and sit down.'

The coroner looked as perfect as ever: well-tailored black suit with a crisp, unfussy white shirt and simple make-up. The top of her oak desk complemented the neatness of her clothes; the three files she was working on were placed to her left, an appointment diary and her laptop to her right. In between was a pristine white pad with the day's date written at the top. The one element that looked out of place was her hair, a nest of grey corkscrew curls held in place by a red hair band.

'How was your holiday?'

'Great, a week of walking and relaxing. I always love the Lakes in the last days of autumn.'

'And the weather?'

'Surprisingly dry for one of the wettest places in England. And even when it rained we could do the literature bits Eve loves.'

The coroner's eyebrows rose slightly.

'Visiting Wordsworth's cottage, Ruskin's house and Hill Top...'

'Peter Rabbit, Squirrel Nutkin and all that?'

'I was worried Eve was too old but she lapped it up.'

'My daughter loved Beatrix Potter when she was growing up too.'

'We all do, there's a timelessness to the stories which works across the ages.'

Mrs Challinor pulled across the top file on the left and got straight down to business.

'Anyway, glad to have you back. We are very busy, so you will have to catch up quickly. You know from this morning's meeting, we have the inquest into the death in custody of Mr Holdsworth coming up on the eighth?'

He nodded slowly, wondering what was coming.

'While you were away, Jenny, Sophia and the locum coroner's officer from Derbyshire, Mr Jennings, arranged for all the witnesses to attend. They were chosen based on the testimonies given to the Professional Standards branch and the IOPC. The jury has been empanelled and we will begin at ten o'clock in precisely a week's time. I believe there are only a couple of witnesses who have not replied, one of whom is Sergeant Saunders. I will write a note to his solicitor in a moment ensuring he attends.'

'The hearing I attended this morning...?'

The coroner waved her hand in the air as if brushing away an imaginary fly. 'I had to schedule it at the last moment after the solicitor for the police requested anonymity during the proceedings. I've decided not to grant his request.'

'Why did he ask for anonymity?'

'He feels the safety of his clients would be compromised by having their names revealed in court.'

'But somebody leaked the CCTV footage of Holdsworth being booked in to the custody suite to the press, showing him well, healthy and responsive.'

'I'd like to know who leaked it – and even more, why they leaked it?'

'You know how it is. Somebody wants to earn a little extra on the side, or keep a favourite reporter sweet by doing favours.'

'The cosy relationship between the police and the press has always bothered me, but that's not why I'm denying the request.'

Ridpath stayed silent, waiting for her to tell him. She brought her long fingers together as if praying. 'I believe the strength of the Coroner's Courts lies in our transparency, our openness. We are here to represent the dead in the land of the living. Our job is not to assign blame but to find out how, when, and why a person has died. Our proceedings are open, the files are available for everybody to see. In the case of a death in custody, a case which we are mandated by law to investigate, this transparency becomes even more important.'

'But will transparency be upheld by knowing the name of the police officer?'

'As ever in law, it's all about balance. It is no coincidence that the statue on top of the High Court in London is of blind justice with a set of scales in her hand. There are three tests I have to apply.' She held out the fingers of her hand. 'The first is weighing the risk to life of the witness. Is it real and immediate? The second is fairness. Would making the witness anonymous ensure a fair inquest was held? The third is the respect for privacy and family life. Would naming the witness affect their personal life or that of their family?' She held up her other hand. 'On the other side, I have to balance the fundamental principle of open justice. The law must be done, and more importantly, must be seen to be done.'

Ridpath shrugged his shoulders. 'A difficult choice.'

'In these Jamieson inquests...'

'Jamieson?'

'Sorry, coroner's shorthand. The name comes from a Humberside coroner and refers to inquests where the coroner will consider whether a lack of care or common law neglect by any agents of the government, including the police, has led to the cause of death of the deceased. How can a jury issue a verdict if they don't know who was involved in a death? How can they judge a witness if they can't see their body language as they are testifying? A bereaved family must have the opportunity to see and hear a witness explaining their actions and being held to account.' She paused for a moment. 'Most importantly, the bereaved families and the public must have confidence in our process. They must have confidence the inquest will reveal the truth. Calling someone Policeman A and hiding them behind a screen may grant anonymity, but it doesn't reveal the truth. And the truth may be that there was personal animus or professional misconduct on the part of a government officer.'

'You will be challenged on this judgement.'

She smiled. 'I know. Luckily, I have a recent High Court ruling by Mrs Justice Jefford in 2019 to support me.'

Ridpath was silent for a while, turning over the case in his mind. 'But as I understand it, the facts in this case show no negligence by any particular officer and no negligence on behalf of the police as a whole. Didn't the PSD and IOPC investigations come to that conclusion?' Then the penny dropped for Ridpath. 'But you are not so sure...?'

Mrs Challinor tapped the file in front of her with a red-painted nail. 'I've been through all the reports and...'

'You aren't happy with some of the findings?'

'I don't want to prejudice your investigation, but I'd like you to go through the witness statements, the documents and the reports yourself. See what you think.'

'Didn't the coroner's officer do it while I was on holiday?'

'Mr Jennings did, and he agreed with the findings of the IOPC: the death was an unfortunate accident. But…' a long pause, 'I'm still not so sure. I'd like to be certain that the custodial systems used by the police are fit for purpose and that all individuals followed the procedures correctly.'

'To prevent such accidents from possibly happening again?'

'Precisely, Ridpath, that's why I need you to investigate. I want to make certain we get to the truth in this case. Is there anything the police could do better?'

'But as I understand it GMP's Professional Standards Department, the IOPC and the CPS have all ruled there is no case to answer.'

Mrs Challinor closed her eyes and exhaled slowly. 'Luckily, the coronial service is independent of those three branches. We're not here to blame anybody, or to protect the police or the justice system. We are here to represent Mr Holdsworth and find out the truth. What really happened in the early hours of February 21?'

'I understand, Coroner.'

'I must ask you a few questions, Ridpath.'

'Ask away.'

'Do you know Sergeant Saunders, or have you ever worked with him before?'

'I am aware of the name but I've never worked with him.' Ridpath leant forward. 'You're asking me if there is a conflict of interest here. A policeman investigating another policeman?'

'You're still employed by MIT…'

'I don't think there is. As you said, our job is to find out the truth, not to assign blame. My employment by the police should not affect that at all.'

'Exactly.' She closed the file and sat back, taking a moment before saying her next words. 'But I have to tell you, I asked Claire Trent while you were away and she doesn't want you to take the case.'

Ridpath frowned. Claire Trent was the head of MIT and his boss. 'Why?'

'She wasn't clear, but I get the impression she doesn't like the perceived conflict of interest. So I have to ask you again if you want to take the case. If not, I will bring in a coroner's officer from another jurisdiction.'

Ridpath shook his head. 'No, I'll do it.'

'You're sure?'

'Positive.'

'There is one other thing you need to be aware of.'

Ridpath frowned. 'What's that?'

'One of the reasons I need you to look into this is that I have to be able to ask the right questions.'

'What do you mean?'

'A recent ruling at the Hillsborough trial has muddied the waters regarding the police legal team's duty of candour in an inquest.'

'What does that have to do with our investigation?'

'If you remember, the solicitor for the police allegedly altered the statements of the policemen before they were presented to the inquiry into the Hillsborough tragedy.'

'I remember, they stupidly sent out the actual statements as well as the altered ones.'

'The judge ruled at the criminal trial that a public inquiry was not a court of law. Even worse, the police solicitors had no duty of candour to the inquiry as their duty was to their clients, South Yorkshire Police.'

'But how does it affect coroners' inquests?'

'The judge's views were unclear, but the same altered statements were then used in the inquest into the deaths of the Liverpool fans. According to the judge, this didn't pervert the course of justice as they were originally presented to an inquiry, not a court. It's a circular argument which ends up with the law vanishing up its own backside.'

'But that undermines the whole coronial system.'

'Putting it bluntly, the police and their legal counsel are not required to tell me the truth of what happened. They cannot lie, but they do not have to tell me the truth. What this means is I have to be able to ask the right questions if I am to find out the truth rather than simply accept what the police want to tell me.'

'And you want me to discover the questions?'

'You have it in one, Ridpath.' She passed the file over to him. 'Good. Personally I know you'll be fair, but I would counsel you that your colleagues might not share your beliefs.'

'I understand, Coroner. I'll do my job as best I can.'

'I couldn't ask for anything more, Ridpath.'

Chapter Four

Sophia Rahman, his assistant, looked up as soon as he returned to his office. 'Welcome back, stranger.'

'I've only been away for a week.'

'A lot can happen in a week.'

Ridpath placed the file down on the desk he shared with Sophia. 'So I've just found out from the coroner.'

'The Holdsworth inquest?'

'How did you know?'

'You forget I spent the last week helping Brian Jennings arrange the witness roster.'

'How was he?'

'Jennings? Slow and slightly hard of hearing. I got the impression he was already dreaming of his slippers, nice warm fires and cups of cocoa in the evenings.'

'Close to retirement?'

'I think he'd already ordered his watch.' She pointed to his chair. 'He didn't move much from there and left at four o'clock every day. Long drive back to Buxton apparently.'

Ridpath touched the file he had just put on his desk. 'That's why the coroner has asked me to take a look at this.'

'Can I help?' She pointed to her laptop. 'I'm stuck on statistics for the chief coroner. You know there has been a growth in misdiagnoses or failures to diagnose since GPs were asked to use Zoom rather than see patients in person?'

'Doesn't surprise me. It would be like interviewing a suspect on a laptop; you'd miss the little cues showing somebody is lying. The slight shift in position on a chair. The touching of the nose. The failure to look somebody in the eye. Or even staring at someone too much.'

'You and my mother would get on well. She always knows when I'm lying too.'

'So you're not busy?'

'I didn't say I wasn't. But I need something to get my teeth into a job and death statistics is not it.'

He sat down behind his desk. 'Right, you can help me with this.'

'I was hoping you'd say that.'

'What did you do with Brian Jennings?'

'I helped him create a witness list. We went through the statements given to the PSD and the IOPC investigations, calling anybody who they had interviewed. All the police witnesses had aliases like Police M or Police W. Luckily they also gave us a list of the real names and addresses with the corresponding aliases. I've changed all the documents for you. The notices were sent out last Wednesday. So far, everybody has replied except a Sergeant Saunders and one of the custody officers, Lucas Harvey.'

'Mrs Challinor is following up on Saunders with his solicitor. Can you find Harvey?'

'Will do.'

'Did you interview the family and the witnesses?'

She shook her head. 'Like I said, Brian Jennings was more of a desk jockey. We just used the witness statements and he never went to see the family.'

Ridpath began to roll up his sleeves. 'Right, first thing to do is let me read these statements and then we'll start seeing the witnesses and checking their testimony. But before then, you need to do me a couple of favours. Send copies of this post-mortem and the pictures to Dr Schofield; I'd like a second opinion. You two are still talking?'

'Why wouldn't we be?' came the tetchy reply.

Sophia and Dr Schofield had dated each other briefly but the relationship had quietly fizzled out.

'Sorry, I just meant—'

'I'll send them across right away,' she interrupted. 'And the other favours are?'

'Who have you been dealing with at the police?'

'One of the public relations people, Angela Dexter; she's not been very cooperative.'

'Why does that not surprise me? Can you arrange for me to visit Redbury nick; I'd like to see the place.'

'You've never been there?'

Ridpath shook his head. 'It's one of those small suburban stations. Stuck out in the middle of nowhere.'

'Anything else?'

'Can you call the family? I'd like us to go to see them as soon as possible. Today would be great.'

'Us?'

'You and me?'

'You want me to go?'

Ridpath looked around the office. 'That's generally what *us* means. You've cleared all your other work?'

'All done and dusted... now.'

'Make the call and we'll be on our way.'

'Don't forget you have your weekly meeting at Police HQ this afternoon.'

Ridpath's eyes rolled into his head. 'Try to arrange it before then if you can.'

'I saw that,' said Sophia, smiling. After a few moments, the smile vanished and she said, 'You know this case is going to attract a lot of attention? The death was in the papers three years ago – demonstrations on the streets and outside the station where it happened, allegations of police brutality. Even more news last year when the CPS decided not to prosecute.'

'We shouldn't let those sorts of pressures affect our work. The coroner wants us to dig deep before the inquest and make sure we do a fair job for the family and for the police. Let me go through the file and work out a plan of action.'

He opened the case file. It seemed very thin. The usual biographical details. Ben Holdsworth was thirty-six years old when he was detained, born in Middleton but resident in Cheetham Hill. Two previous arrests, one for possession of a small amount of cannabis, the other for driving without a functioning brake light. Separated from his wife, Rosie Holdsworth, two kids, Danny and Audrey. He turned the page expecting to see more but it was blank.

'Is that all?' he said out loud.

'What?' asked Sophia.

'Nothing, just talking to myself.'

'The first sign of madness, I've been told.'

'Nah, the first sign of madness is when you hear an answer.'

He took his notepad out from his jacket pocket and wrote HOLDSWORTH CASE in block capitals followed by the date.

Beneath he scrawled:

Victim's bio? More details?

Followed by:

Old arrest logs? Where? Check with Chrissy.

Chrissy was the civilian researcher he often worked with at Police HQ. She would have access to the Police National Computer and Crime Database.

He turned over the page and saw a photocopy of the custody file for Ben Holdsworth signed by Tony Saunders.

CUSTODY REPORT

Name of Detainee: Ben Holdsworth
D.O.B.: 12/01/1982
Race/Sex: IC1 MALE
Place of Birth: MANCHESTER
Address: NFA
Date/Time of Arrest: February 21, 2018. 03.10
Arrest Number: 3659/19
Also Known As (Alias Names): NA
Scars, Marks, Tattoos: NONE
Nearest Relative Name: MOTHER: MAUREEN HOLDSWORTH
Hgt Wgt: 181 cm, 82 kilos.
Occupation: NOT GIVEN
Hair Eye OLN and State: GOOD
Skin Tone/Consumed Drug/Alcohol: GOOD. NONE CONSUMED.
Calls Made: TWO. DETAILS IN PHONE LOG.
Custody Rights: EXPLAINED AND UNDERSTOOD.
Arresting Officer Name/ID Number: PC CHRIS CARTER 4349
Place Confined: REDBURY STATION

Narrative: Mr Holdsworth was arrested following a local tip-off he was dealing drugs from his car. PC Carter found the drugs on the front seat of a Mini Cooper S driven by Mr Holdsworth. The said drugs have been bagged as evidence and are held at 7689/19/342.

Mr Holdsworth was arrested and brought to the station after being advised of his rights. I am certain his arrest was in accordance with the standards set by the College of Policing and have detained Mr Holdsworth pending further investigation.

Charges: 1994 DRUG TRAFFICKING ACT, INTENT TO SUPPLY. HELD PENDING FURTHER INVESTIGATIONS.
Detention Confirmed: 03.40
Date/Time Released:
Arresting Officer Signature/ID #: CHRIS CARTER PC 4349
Date/Time Submitted: 03.45
Custody Supervisor Signature: SGT TONY SAUNDERS 3975
03.45 21/02/2018
Arrestee Signature: REFUSED

Case Status:
Further Inv. Inactive

Case Disposition:

Notes:
1. ORDERED STRIP SEARCH OF DEFENDANT BY CUSTODY OFFICERS, RODGERS AND HARVEY. NO DRUGS FOUND.
2. PLACED IN CELL 3 @ 03.50.
3. CELLS 3 AND 4 CCTV CEASED OPERATION @ 04.35. ORDERED HALF HOURLY MONITORING.
4. DETAINEE SEEN ON FLOOR OF CELL BY CUSTODY OFFICER HARVEY. UNRESPONSIVE. 06.30. ATTEMPTED CPR. STILL UNRESPONSIVE.
5. DUTY DOCTOR CALLED 06.35.
6. AMBULANCE ARRIVES 06.43. DETAINEE TAKEN TO SALFORD GENERAL ACCOMPANIED BY HARVEY.
7. PAUSED CLOCK ON DETAINEE'S DETENTION TIME PENDING RETURN FROM HOSPITAL.

Ridpath read through the file twice, making sure he understood it. To him, everything looked kosher. In many ways, Tony Saunders had been too accommodating with Holdsworth. If he were in charge, he wouldn't have allowed him to make a second call, but Saunders had. Doing a strip search in a drugs case was also standard operating procedure.

He turned the page and began reading the witness statements from Saunders, the two custody officers, and the arresting officers.

Again, everything looked straightforward and all the detention procedures had been followed. The description from Tony Saunders matched that of the two custody officers.

> At 06.30, I was called by Custody Officer HARVEY to an incident occurring in Custody Suite 3. I went immediately there and found the deceased stretched out on the floor with the custody officer standing beside him. I immediately began to give CPR in the correct way and ordered Custody Officer HARVEY to get the duty medical officer who was then examining the teenagers who had been arrested earlier for joyriding.

> The medical officer, Dr BOURKE, arrived at 06.35. After applying CPR again, the detainee remained unresponsive. Dr BOURKE called for an ambulance using his mobile phone. The ambulance and emergency responders arrived eight minutes later at 06.43.

> Mr Holdsworth was placed on a gurney and removed from the station at 06.50. I entered a log of the event into the Police Station Management System and paused the timing on his custody records.

The copper in Ridpath was impressed. Saunders had paused the clock, meaning if Ben Holdsworth had been returned to the station, the police would still have twenty-four hours minus the time he had already spent at the nick to investigate his case. However, it was a little cold-hearted given he had been giving CPR to the man just twenty minutes earlier.

Ridpath continued reading.

> I received a phone call from the victim's mother at 07.20 and told her he had been taken to Salford General Hospital. I was unaware of his condition before my shift ended.

Interesting the mother had called. Had Holdsworth made one of his calls to her? Otherwise how did she know her son had been detained?

The next page was a brief note from the hospital. According to their reports, Holdsworth had arrived in A&E at 07.04, but despite their best efforts, they were unable to save his life. He was pronounced dead at

07.36. His body was transferred to the mortuary and a post-mortem was performed at 13.10 the same day.

That was quick. Ridpath checked the name of the pathologist.

Statement of Dr Harold Lardner, BSc, MB, BS, MRC Path.
Age of Witness: 54
Occupation: Greater Manchester Police Pathologist
Address: Forensic Pathology Services, Oxford Road, Manchester.

Ridpath closed his eyes and his shoulders sagged.

Why did it have to be him?

Chapter Five

He was sure they were waiting in the car outside his house.

Two of them, big blokes who looked like they had to share a brain cell in order to function.

He'd seen them when he came home from work this morning. It had been a long hard night shift at the slaughterhouse, getting the carcasses ready for Christmas. Pigs, chickens, turkeys all had to be killed, hung, dressed and packed. He'd worked a couple of hours overtime too, time to get saving if he wanted to pack the job in and go to Thailand in the new year.

God, he hated this time of year. For everybody else it meant starting to plan the Christmas Day feast. For him, it meant working long hours as the days grew shorter. Sometimes he didn't even see daylight, going to work when it was dark at seven in the evening and getting home while it was still dark and sleeping through the daylight hours.

He'd started working there over three years before when he'd moved into the area. It was a job nobody else wanted, and nobody cared who you were or where you came from. Which suited him perfectly.

He'd arrived home at nine that morning, after taking the bus from work, getting off at his usual stop and walking back to the cottage.

That was what the grasping estate agent had called his rented two up, two down back-to-back without a hint of irony and even less truthfulness. But he needed a place to live far from his usual stomping grounds and this was available right away. It was right next to the only cotton mill still operating in England. It always amused him that, in a region built on cotton, he could still hear the sound of yarns being spun.

He'd come home that morning, walked past the mill, turning onto his street. As usual, the light at the corner was out of action, but parked beneath it was a black SUV with its lights off and two large, dark shapes sitting in the front seats.

He hurried across the road, deliberately walking past his house without going in.

What was he going to do?

Had they finally found him? Finally worked out where he had gone? But they'd had an agreement. As long as he disappeared they would leave him alone.

All his stuff was in the house. His passport, clothes, laptop, all the things he needed to get away again.

He'd planned for this moment, knew it was going to happen one day, just not when. Now, he'd been caught short.

He turned right at the end of the road, casually glancing back to the SUV. The men were still sitting in the front. Had they noticed him walking past them? Were they waiting for the lights in the house to go on before knocking on the door? Or had they not recognised him with his new shaven head?

What was he going to do?

The ginnel leading to the rear of his house was on his right. Or he just could run away, take a shortcut through the park, past the crematorium and back into Manchester.

He told himself not to panic. Perhaps they weren't after him at all. Perhaps they were waiting for someone else.

Besides, how could they have found him? He had changed his name, got a new passport and driving licence, left his old life and his friends behind.

He thought for a moment. Had Elaine dobbed him in?

A week ago, shopping in Tesco, he'd bumped into her with her three snot-nosed kids.

'Fancy meeting you here. You're living close by, are you?'

He'd been surprised seeing her and had mumbled some inaudible reply.

'You're going to have to speak up. When you have kids they make you a little deaf, my mum says. She should know, she had six of us.' A nervous laugh.

'I said I live nearby.'

'Oh, great, we can be neighbours then. I married Terry. Remember him from school? Got four kids now, one's with my mum. What are you doing?'

'This and that.'

'And a bit of the other, I'm sure. You were always a bit of a flash one.' She'd nudged him in the ribs playfully. 'How's your mum? I used to like your mum when we was courting. Proper lady, she was.'

'She died four years ago.'

'Oh, I'm sorry to hear it. God rest her soul.'

'Anyway, I've got to be off,' he'd said, desperate to get away.

She'd paused for a moment before saying, 'I missed you, you know. You were my first real boyfriend.'

Another long pause as she waited for him to respond. When he didn't, she carried on. 'Terry's a lorry driver, he's away a lot. We should go for a drink one night; Mum'll look after the kids. Be like old times...'

He'd mumbled another non-committal answer and then escaped.

Had she mentioned meeting him to somebody, and that's why two thugs were sitting in a car outside his house? Or was he over-reacting, and they were waiting for somebody else?

He couldn't take the chance.

He nipped down the ginnel and climbed over the wall behind his house. There was a spare key hidden on the ledge above the rear door. He reached up for it, praying it was still there, feeling for it with his fingertips.

He touched the rough metal outline of the key, taking it down and slowly opening the door. He stood in the entrance for a second, letting his eyes adjust to the darkness inside.

Was somebody waiting for him in the dark?

He listened carefully for the sound of breathing or the rustle of cloth against the fabric of a seat. His whole body was tense, holding his breath, ready to run at the slightest sound.

Nothing.

He stepped inside, stopped and listened again, before slowly closing the door.

He finally breathed out, relaxing for a second.

'Long time, no see, mate,' came a voice from the shadows.

Chapter Six

Ridpath stared at the first page of the post-mortem report.

Lardner's scrawled signature was at the bottom. A name from the past now staring at him from the pages of the present.

Ridpath had arrested the pathologist in his first case working for the coroner. The man was a serial predator, the Beast of Manchester, killing women brutally and without mercy. For years, he had hidden in plain sight, investigating his own crimes and covering them up, driven by a compulsion to cause pain. He was now locked up safely and securely in Ashworth high-security psychiatric hospital near Liverpool.

After their last meeting, Ridpath had hoped he wouldn't have to see him again. But here he was again, turning up like a bad smell from an old midden.

Ridpath scanned the report quickly, jumping to the most important section at the end. Lardner's voice spoke to him in every line, the ironic, slightly mocking tone present even in official documents.

CONCLUSIONS

This man died from a subdural haematoma to the brain, caused by striking his skull on the wall of the cell. CCTV evidence shows him falling and hitting his head. (Attached stills from CCTV in Appendix 3.) This injury would not have been obvious to an untrained observer, but should have led to increasingly erratic behaviour such as an inability to stand, shaking of the head, lack of coordination of the motor functions and dizziness.

The discovery of the man on the floor of the cell is not surprising. The subdural haematoma would eventually lead to his inability to maintain his normal motor and perceptual functions and cause a final collapse.

I would conclude the deceased struck his head from a fall in the cell.
Death followed three hours later.

Category 3. Accidental death.

Signed Harold Lardner, Pathologist. 4.30 p.m. February 22, 2018.

He saw the time and date written next to the signature. Both GMP and the pathologist had worked incredibly quickly on this case, even to the point of getting stills from the CCTV to the mortuary before the pathologist had completed his post-mortem report. No doubt the demonstrations outside Redbury nick had encouraged them in their efforts.

Ridpath read through the document one more time. Lardner was clear in his conclusion regarding the demise of Ben Holdsworth.

Death had come from a subdural haematoma: bleeding on the brain, invisible to the naked eye as it occurred within the skull.

Attached to the report were over twenty separate envelopes containing photographs of the cell and those taken during the post-mortem.

He hesitated for a moment before opening any of them. Looking at dead bodies and close-ups of human livers was not something he enjoyed. It reminded him far too much of his own brush with mortality. His diagnosis with myeloma, cancer of the bones and bone marrow, almost five years ago. For a while it had been touch and go, but he had pulled through after nine months of hell, otherwise known as chemotherapy, and was now in complete remission. Now, despite being totally lacking in superstitions, he self-consciously touched the wooden top of his desk.

He opened the first envelope. It was a close-up of a man's face, eyes closed, head lying against a stainless-steel background. The skin was white and the pale lips drawn slightly back to the reveal the teeth. On the back a name was written in red biro. BEN HOLDSWORTH. YZ 4643/18.

Just as he was about to look at the other pictures in the envelope, Sophia spoke.

'The mother, a Mrs Maureen Holdsworth, has confirmed the meeting at one p.m., Ridpath. She said she's been waiting for over three years for the inquest.'

'Thanks, well done.'

'And Angela Dexter was full of excuses why you shouldn't go to Redbury. The station was too busy, the cells were occupied. A dog had eaten her homework. You know the sort of stuff.'

Ridpath knew it well.

'But I finally got her to agree a visit for thirty minutes tomorrow at eleven a.m.'

'Great.' He glanced at the clock. 12.30. 'If we are going to see the mother, we should leave now and grab a sandwich on the way.'

'How about a Greggs sausage roll? Should do my diet a world of good.'

He would have to save the dubious pleasure of reading the post-mortem report fully and seeing the pictures of naked livers for later this evening, after Eve had gone to bed.

All in all, everything seemed to be above board. Just a terrible accident at a police station. The witness statements correlated with each other. Sergeant Saunders had followed the custody procedures to the letter. And everything else had been correctly documented. The only possible criticism of the police was in the design of their bunks and the walls behind them, but he couldn't see how any force could be held accountable if a detainee tripped and fell in his cell.

Even when all procedures are followed, accidents will still happen. Ridpath closed the file and stood up. 'Where does the mother live?'

'In Redbury, less than two hundred yards from the station.'

He gathered up the file. 'Let's get going. She deserves some answers.'

They both walked out of the coroner's office and down the stairs to Ridpath's car parked across the road. As he stood with his car keys in his hand, a thought struck him.

Why had they completed the post-mortem so quickly and produced a report with CCTV pictures only a day later?

Before he could finish the thought, Sophia spoke. 'Earth to Planet Ridpath. Are we going to Redbury or not? I mean, I like standing next to your car, but unless we get inside and start the engine, it's not going to take us anywhere.'

Ridpath opened the door and threw his briefcase onto the back seat. Why *had* they completed the post-mortem so quickly?

Chapter Seven

'You've not been easy to find, mate. Mind you, we haven't been looking too hard. No need, not until now. You can switch on the light by the way. Though I did enjoy sitting here in the dark, suits my personality.'

He switched on the light. The man was at his breakfast table, a mug of tea sitting close to his right hand.

'You really are going to have to get some fresh milk, though. That stuff is nearly off.'

'Sorry, Mr Delaney.'

'And so you should be, mate; fresh food is necessary for a person's health and well-being. I noticed your fridge had nothing but a few rashers of bacon and a bit of moody cheese. Vegetables, you need fresh vegetables, mate, no wonder you're looking so peaky.'

'I was going to the supermarket.'

'But you met Elaine. She told me she'd seen you. Always a clever girl, was Elaine. Acts dumb, but is street smart. Shame she married Terry. A waste of time, he is. He seems to have one talent, and that's to get her pregnant. Don't just stand there, come and sit down.' Delaney pushed the chair away from the table. 'Don't be shy. We've known each other for such a long time.'

He didn't move.

'I'm sorry, Mr Delaney.'

'Sorry for what, mate, have you done something wrong?'

'I... I...'

'I've changed my mind.' Delaney pushed the mug of tea away. 'I'd like a cup of coffee. Do you have any?'

He moved quickly, opening the cupboard doors. 'There's some Nescafé here somewhere.'

'Don't you have any real coffee?'

'Sorry, Mr Delaney, I don't think so.'

'There you go apologising gain. Well, Nescafé is going to have to do. What are you waiting for? You expect me to make it myself?'

He grabbed the kettle and filled it with water before lighting the gas with a match. His hand shook as he held the flame close to the burner.

'First sign of Parkinson's, that is.'

'What is, Mr Delaney?'

'Your hand shaking. You should go down to the MRI, get your brain scanned in one of those machines. I did it last year and you know what they found.'

He shook his head.

'Nothing. My brain is as fit as a butcher's dog. They said they'd never seen anything like it. I said it was because I had a clear conscience. Do you have a clear conscience, Garry?'

'I… I… don't know, Mr Delaney.' He spooned a measure of coffee into a clean mug and placed it next to the kettle.

'Aren't you having one?'

'One?'

'A coffee. I don't like drinking on my own. Nobody likes being alone, do they, mate? Even when I was in Cyprus, I always had a mate to have a few gallons of zivania with.' He looked around, taking in the house. 'Except you. Why did you come all the way out here to Dukinfield?'

'I wanted a change.'

'A change? We all want a change sometimes, but beggars can't be choosers, can they?'

'I thought we had an agreement, Mr Delaney.'

'And what agreement was that, Garry?'

'If I left your manor, you'd let it be between the two of us. Let sleeping dogs lie.'

'But I did, Garry. Haven't bothered you for the last couple of years, have I?'

'No.'

'Have I made life difficult for you?'

'No, Mr Delaney, you've left me alone.'

'And even though you beat up one of my best mates, I haven't so much as touched a hair on your little head.'

'You haven't, Mr Delaney, because I kept my side of the bargain. Left the manor and didn't return, not once. I kept our agreement.'

35

'The problem is…' There was a long in-sucking of breath, '…somebody, I won't say who, but just understand he's a very good friend of the organisation, has decided you need to be punished.'

'What have I done wrong, Mr Delaney?'

'I don't know, and I don't really care, Garry. Ours not to reason why, ours but to obey orders and all that crap. Unfortunately, he's decided this needs to be a terminal punishment. You've come to the end of the line, Garry.'

The kettle whistled loudly, causing him to jump.

He turned to pick it up, burning his hand on the metal handle. He grabbed a tea towel and gripped the handle again.

'Normally, I'd let the lads outside do it. They need the exercise. But this time, the instruction came from somebody very important, so I decided to do it myself. You should be happy, Garry, I don't often do the business myself any more. Bit of a privilege, in my book.'

He heard a pistol being cocked behind him.

It was now or never. He gripped the handle of the hot kettle as hard as he could and swung it round in a wide arc, connecting with Delaney's head just above the temple.

The look of surprise in the man's eyes as he saw the kettle swinging towards his head would stay in his mind forever. As would the slow topple of the body as it fell off the kitchen chair and slumped heavily to the floor.

The kettle shuddered as it struck home, hot water spilling all over his hand.

He winced, dropping the kettle to the floor. A sharp stab of pain shot through his arm, followed by a burning sensation all over his skin.

Ignore it, you need to get out of here. He looked down at the man lying at his feet. Should he hit him again just to make sure?

Then he remembered the thugs waiting in the car outside. Had they heard anything?

He stopped and listened.

No sound.

Delaney's inert body lay at his feet, blood oozing from a cut on the side of his head. Had he killed him?

He looked more closely. The man's chest was still rising and falling slowly.

Get out of here. Now.

He ran to the drawer where he kept his stuff and some spare cash, packing them in a gym bag lying next to the dresser.

There was a quiet knock on the door.

'Sorry to disturb you, Mr Delaney, but can we get anything for you?'

A gruff voice. A thug's voice.

Got to get out of here.

He grabbed a jacket from behind the door.

Another knock, louder this time. 'Are you there, Mr Delaney, can we help you?'

Silence.

Followed by the heavy thump of a shoulder against a door.

Got to leave. Forget everything else. Get out of here.

He opened the back door and ran down the stairs, taking a quick look over his shoulder as he heard the front door collapsing.

Got to run, but where?

He pulled open the rear door to the ginnel, stopping for a second to decide which way to go. Back towards the main road, or out through the back street, across the park and behind the crematorium?

A shout behind him in the kitchen.

He ran down the alleyway, kicking over a bin somebody had left there.

Got to get away from here.

Now.

Chapter Eight

Ridpath didn't think this sort of housing still existed any more. It was like a throwback to the 1930s. A row of terraced houses, each with its front step freshly donkey-stoned in a variety of colours: pink, mauve, camel, some even a bright maroon.

Around the area, a forest of high rises stood over the street like guards at Buckingham Palace, their flame-encouraging cladding grey in the damp of the Manchester mizzle.

As Ridpath knocked on the door, a woman came to a neighbouring entrance, folded her arms across her chest and stared at him.

'Do you know if Mrs Holdsworth is in?'

'If you're the police, you're not welcome round here.'

'We're from the coroner's office.' Ridpath deliberately avoided mentioning he was still a copper. 'We're here about the inquest into the death of her son.'

'No need for an inquest. They killed him, no two ways about it. She hasn't been the same since he went, poor woman.'

The door opened. In front of them stood an old, frail woman wearing a housecoat with her grey hair imprisoned in a hairnet.

'Who are you?' she asked.

'Mrs Holdsworth?'

'Who wants to know?'

'We're from the coroner's office. We need to explain to you the procedures for the inquest into the death of your son.'

'Ben? He's a long time gone. They killed him, you know.'

Ridpath glanced across at Sophia. There was something about the woman suggesting she wasn't of this planet. A faraway look in her eyes as if focusing on something in the distance but not quite seeing it. He'd seen pictures of soldiers in the First World War fresh from the trenches with the same look. Against the eyes, her skin was a bright yellow. Did she have jaundice? Or perhaps she simply never left the house? She looked like she wasn't long for this world.

Ridpath felt an immediate empathy for her, as he always did for those who were obviously ill. A function of his own bout with cancer, he knew. Losing her son in such a tragic way couldn't have helped her health. Had it been the final nail in the coffin?

He coughed twice. 'Can we come in? We won't be long, but we do need to explain to you what will happen at the inquest.'

She stood aside. 'The coroner, you say? It's taken you long enough; he's been dead over three years now.'

'We have to wait for all the other investigations to close first before we can proceed.'

'Come in then. I suppose you'll be wanting tea?'

Sophia was about to say no but Ridpath interjected. 'That would be great, I'm parched.'

'PG Tips will have to do and I don't have any biscuits left; I ate them all.'

She showed them into a front parlour. It was obviously hardly ever used. Kept for best was what Ridpath remembered.

'Sit yourselves down, I won't be a moment. Tea's already stewing.'

She left them alone. Ridpath looked around the room. It seemed like it hadn't been changed since the 1950s. A flock of plaster geese climbed up one wall next to a starburst mirror. The wallpaper was brown and faded, the furniture lumpy in all the right places. A fireplace laden with pictures of people long gone.

'Bit of a time machine, this is,' said Sophia. 'A lot of this stuff is coming back in fashion. Retro is in.'

'Give me IKEA any day of the week.'

'No style, Ridpath, that's your problem.'

He noticed a picture on a mahogany dresser. A young man was smiling shyly into camera, his hands stuffed in his pockets, standing next to a BMW. The shot was obviously taken outside the front door. 'That's Ben Holdsworth. Looks slightly different from the man lying on a stainless-steel table in the post-mortem pictures.'

'Not a bad-looking chap,' said Sophia.

'Not everybody is a possible dating opportunity, Sophia.'

'Tell that to my mother.'

As she spoke, the door opened and the woman bustled in, laying the tray on a small table next to the fireplace. 'I see you've found his photo. It's how I'll remember him. He was always a bit shy, was Ben, a quiet lad. Milk and sugar?'

'Just milk for me,' said Sophia.

'Same for me, milk no sugar,' added Ridpath.

'Watching your figures, are you? You won't want any of these digestives I found at the back of the cupboard? Don't know how long they've been there.'

She handed round the plate and both Sophia and Ridpath took one each.

Ridpath stared at the tea. It was a dark, rich mahogany brown as if it had been brewing in front of a fire for a century or more. He took a careful sip. It was like drinking creosote.

'Mrs Holdsworth, I'd first like to say how sorry we are for the loss of your son.'

'Not half as sorry as me.'

'Did he live here with you?' asked Sophia.

'He'd moved back. She'd thrown him out again and he had nowhere to go so he came back here. He always came back, did Ben, not like his sister.'

'There was a mention of a wife on his details, but the only address we have is yours.'

'She married again and went back down south not long after Ben died. I think she'd been carrying on with her fancy man behind his back. Not that he'd ever know, stupid he was with women.' She took a large slurp of tea.

Ridpath looked down at his cup and decided he couldn't face another drop. 'Do you have her address? We have to make her aware of the inquest.'

She shook her head. 'But the police will have it. She came to see me, you know, before she went down south. I didn't let her through the door.'

Another slurp of tea.

Ridpath took a deep breath, pausing for a couple of seconds as Mrs Holdsworth crunched down on one of the digestives with her false teeth. 'I need to explain to you about the inquest,' he finally said after she had finished chewing and taken another slurp of tea.

'You have to hold one when a person dies in custody. I presume it will be in front of a jury?'

Ridpath raised his eyebrows.

'I may be old, but I'm not stupid. And I've got a good solicitor. Mr Davies told me all about it.'

'Could we have his address?'

'His card is on the dresser.'

Sophia stood up and found the card. 'This one?'

'That's him. You can take it; he always gives me a new one every time he comes.'

'The tentative date for the inquest is November 8, next week. Your family is invited to attend and you may be called as a witness.'

'Why?'

'To testify about Ben's character. What was he like, by the way?' Ridpath tried to sound as nonchalant as possible.

'Like I said, shy. A bit soft if you ask me, not like his dad.' She pointed to another picture of a man in a white shirt and braces obviously taken at Blackpool. 'Used to do a bit of boxing, his dad. It was how I met him, down at a fight one night. I was just nineteen and stupid. Worst mistake I ever made was marrying Ben's dad.'

'Where is he now? Mr Holdsworth, I mean.'

'He passed away twenty years ago. Came out of the pub one night and walked straight across the road into a ten-ton lorry. Best thing ever happened to me.' She took another sip of tea. 'Ben missed him though. All boys miss their father, don't they?'

'Did Ben ever get into trouble with the police when he was younger?'

'Of course, they all do round here, can't be helped. They closed the playgrounds so the kids can only play with the police. You just get used to them coming around.'

'He was arrested twice?' Ridpath left the question open, hoping the old woman would give him some details.

She gave nothing away. 'Something like that.'

'Can you remember why?'

The old woman shrugged her shoulders. 'This and that and a bit of the other. They like nicking people, gives them something to do, otherwise they wouldn't have a job, would they? The police only stopped coming round when he went down south.'

'Oh?'

'Left for a couple of years. Met his fancy woman down there and had a couple of kids. He came back with her about six months before he died. Right snotty bitch, she were, stuck-up cow. Threw him out of the place they were renting and then ran back down to the south.

Didn't like Manchester. I suppose I can't blame her, being a southerner and all.'

The old woman obviously didn't like her daughter-in-law. 'Where was he in the south?'

'London, I think, or somewhere round there.'

'And he came back with his wife about six months before the incident at the police station?'

The long-distance stare from the woman returned.

'Mrs Holdsworth?'

'Didn't last long though, within a month he was back here living with me and she'd gone home. Good riddance to bad rubbish is all I can say.'

Ridpath decided to change the subject. 'The night he was taken to Redbury station, he was arrested for possession. Do you know anything about it?'

She shook her head. 'All I know is he rang me in the middle of the night to say he'd been nicked.'

'He called you?'

'From the station. I called later and they told me he'd been taken to hospital. Most calls I've ever made on that thing.'

She pointed towards the hall, where an old-fashioned phone sat on its own on the table.

'How did they get the number?'

'I dunno. When they said it was the police, I thought Ben had given it to them. He was inside again for something or other.'

'Did they pick him up often?' This was Sophia asking the question. She received a nod from Ridpath.

'Used to, but I hadn't seen them since he came back. That was why I was surprised to get the call.'

'So what happened next?'

'I rang the hospital and they told me he had already died.' She stared into the fire glowing in its grate. 'I rushed over there and saw his poor body lying in casualty.' Another long pause as she relived the time. 'I think I was the only person who cared about him in the whole world.'

'And so you went to identify your son?'

'Not that day, three days later. Mr Davies picked me up and took me to the mortuary. I'd never been in one of the places before. Don't want to go again.' She paused for a moment before adding, 'Suppose I will though. It's where everybody ends up, isn't it? Our final destination…' Her voice trailed off before continuing, 'The poor wee boy was cremated two weeks later at Southern Cemetery. Do you know what it's like watching the body of someone you love go through those doors and into the fire?'

Ridpath did know what it was like. He coughed and changed the subject. 'As I said earlier, the inquest will take place on November 8. We'll get in touch with Mr Davies and let him know all about it.'

'He's very good, is Mr Davies, he's been a real help to me.'

Ridpath stood up. 'Thank you for your time, Mrs Holdsworth, and once again I am deeply sorry for the loss of your son.' He took his card out of his wallet. 'If there is anything you need to ask, please don't hesitate to call me. Ms Rahman will liaise with your solicitor on the times and dates.'

He walked towards the door and then stopped as if remembering something. 'Just a thought, Mrs Holdsworth. Did anybody contact Ben before he was arrested by the police?'

The old woman shrugged her thin shoulders. 'I don't know. He would sometimes get these calls and rush upstairs to take them. I never heard what he was talking about. I learnt long ago from his dad not to poke my nose in where it wasn't wanted.'

Chapter Nine

A sharp rap on the door was followed by Detective Sergeant Alan Butcher popping his head around. 'You wanted to see me, boss?'

Detective Chief Inspector Paul Turnbull raised his glistening bald head from the rows of overtime costs. 'Yeah, come in, Alan. Just give me a minute while I finish these.'

His finger traced the numbers across the page, his lips moving as he mouthed the sums spent on each investigation.

'You going through the numbers, boss?' said Butcher, taking a seat.

Turnbull held his finger up for quiet and continued scanning the costs. They were high, too high. Anybody looking at these would see they were spending far over budget.

Finally he finished and raised his head to look at his subordinate.

'You wanted to see me, boss,' the young detective reminded him.

Turnbull stayed silent. He loved moments like this, when he imagined what was going through his subordinate's head. Silence was the perfect weapon. Letting the tension build as he watched Butcher's face parade through an arc of emotions: anticipation, concern, worry, terror. Right now, the man was probably imagining he was going to get a bollocking for some real or imagined error.

Sometimes, silence worked so well they admitted to a cock-up he knew nothing about. This time, however, the detective sergeant simply said, 'Boss?'

'How are we for this afternoon, Alan?'

'The weekly meeting? Fine, boss.'

'No screw-ups? No surprises? No unforeseen developments?'

'None I know, boss.'

'"None you know"? Not good enough, Alan. Today has to go as smooth as a baby's bottom, understand. Claire Trent is away and I'm in charge. Everybody is watching and the new chief constable is looking for results. Our new mantra is to investigate and solve crime, quickly.'

'Got it, boss.'

'So?'

'So, what?'

'How are we this afternoon?'

'All sorted, boss.'

'Better, because we may have an observer with us.'

'Who?'

Turnbull touched the side of his nose, suggesting he had information that was only on a need-to-know basis, and Alan didn't need to know. A whisper from the sixth floor. 'So have you remembered the six Ps?'

Paul Turnbull had been doing one of those personal management development courses online and was now equipped with a whole new series of acronyms and idioms to bewitch and bedevil his subordinates.

'Six Ps?'

'Proper Preparation Prevents Piss-Poor Performance. So are you?'

'Am I what?'

Butcher was a good copper, but not the sharpest knife in the box. However, like a good bloodhound, he was loyal and, for Turnbull, loyalty counted for a lot.

'Ready. For. The. Meeting.' He enunciated every word slowly, making sure Butcher understood.

'Of course, boss. Everything is tied up neatly.'

'Make sure nobody mentions the amount of overtime we are burning through.'

'Twenty-four-hour surveillance costs money, boss.'

'I know, just make sure nobody talks about it at the meeting.'

Butcher frowned. 'OK, boss, whatever you say.'

'How are we on the Rochdale case? Ready to charge him yet?'

'Not yet, boss. He's still denying stabbing his girlfriend and then setting light to the body. No forensics tie him in to the scene.'

'What about his phone records? Have we tracked his movements on the day she died through his phone?'

'Still waiting on the techs, boss.'

'Still waiting!' Turnbull roared. 'We've got a suspect in custody and we're still waiting? Kick them up the arse and get them moving, Alan. I want him charged, remanded and the decision to charge approved by CPS before Claire Trent gets back from her course. This is my collar and I want to make sure the new chief sees it was me and me alone.'

Butcher sat back in his chair. The blast from Turnbull had unnerved him. His boss's bad breath even more so. 'I'll make it happen, boss, trust me.'

Turnbull seemed to be appeased by his answer, so Butcher decided to press on. 'There's a bit of a rumour going around Claire Trent may be moving on to bigger and better things, boss. One of the new chief super jobs at a division is what people are saying.'

'Rumours are rumours, Alan. You just do your job,' replied Turnbull, careful not to discount the rumour with a denial. If the lads in MIT thought he could be their new boss, it would help focus their minds on their jobs. 'I want results over the next couple of weeks. Everything signed, sealed, delivered and tied up neatly like one of the Great Train Robbers' mail bags. Understand? We're about results now. Old-fashioned coppering is back in style – we stick the baddies in jail and throw away the key.'

'Right, boss.'

'Well, what are you waiting for?'

Butcher looked at him with a raised eyebrow.

'A pat on the back? The Queen's Police Medal? A bloody raise? Get out there and do your job.'

The detective sergeant jumped up out of the chair. 'Right, boss.'

As he opened the door to leave, Turnbull raised his voice. 'One more thing, before I forget.'

Butcher stopped, holding his breath. He'd nearly escaped without a bollocking. Had Turnbull found out about the missing binoculars?

'Ridpath. Have you heard anything from him?'

He breathed out. 'Nothing, boss, but I know he's coming in for this afternoon's meeting.'

'A little bird tells me he's going to be investigating Tony Saunders and the team at Redbury.'

'What? I thought they've been cleared by Professional Standards and the IOPC.'

'Apparently, it's not good enough for our coroner. She wants an independent investigation.'

'The lads won't be happy, boss; Tony Saunders trained a lot of them. He's well liked.'

'Shame to see a good copper like him spending his life doing data entry because we've got a shit computer system.'

Butcher shook his head. 'He should be back running a station, not being investigated… again.'

'Just thought I'd let you know, Alan.'

'Thanks for the heads-up, boss.'

'Now get back to work. I want those telephone records before this afternoon's meeting.'

'Right, boss.'

Butcher closed the door. Turnbull smiled to himself. Knowing his subordinate's predilection for gossip, the news about Ridpath would be around the department within five minutes.

He'd hated Ridpath from the moment he'd set eyes on him. Too cocky, too self-assured and too smart for his own good. Even worse, Ridpath wasn't loyal to anybody. Hadn't he dobbed in the former head of MIT?

Couldn't have disloyal members of a team; they were like a cancer that needed cutting out before they infected everybody else. Investigating another copper was the last straw. How can you turn on your own kind?

It just showed how disloyal Ridpath was.

To him. To the team. To the force.

Investigating a good copper like Saunders wasn't going to make Ridpath a popular bunny with the rest of MIT. It was just the opening he needed to get rid of the man before Claire Trent returned.

DCI Paul Turnbull smiled and rubbed his bald head.

While the cat is away, the mice will play.

Chapter Ten

Driving to Police HQ, Ridpath thought about the interview with Ben Holdsworth's mother.

The old lady had been a strange mixture of sharpness and distraction, as if she was in the room but not there at the same time. He needed to check up on the solicitor, though. Why had he contacted Mrs Holdsworth so quickly, and more importantly, who was paying his fees?

He made a mental note to ask Sophia to go through the newspapers and read up on the protests and demonstrations outside the station. Who had organised them?

He stopped at a crossroads, the red light shining weakly through the rain sheeting against his windscreen. People with their umbrellas held almost horizontal against the wind crossed in front of his car like figures from a Lowry painting, while a couple of feral kids leant against a wall not even wearing coats or anoraks.

His mind drifted back to his own bout with cancer, almost five years ago now. Eighteen months of hell for himself and Polly: chemo followed by a long bout in hospital and an even longer bout at home with nothing to keep him company during the day except the inane chatter of *Bargain Hunt* or *Homes Under the Hammer*.

At least his cancer seemed to be in full remission now. The doctors had even pushed his check-ups back to once every three months, but he wondered if it was due to his recovery or simply because they were so backed up during the pandemic. Luckily, it seemed to be under control now. Like every other key worker, Ridpath had his jabs and the bit of paper to prove it. But if he never had to go into a hospital for the rest of this life, he would be more than happy. Hospitals scared him; they were full of sick people. Full of people like he had once been, hoping against hope for a recovery but fearful it would never come. He never knew why his cancer, Bert, as Polly used to call it, had chosen him. None of the doctors had an answer. It was just there, trying to kill him in the sneakiest way possible.

But he had beaten it.

These days he just took one tablet of Revlimid every morning, saying a prayer to the NHS as he did so. Each tab cost over £160 but for him it was free except for prescription charges. A life to live free and watch his daughter grow up.

The lights turned green on Oldham Road. He put the car into gear. Why was he feeling so unsettled?

Was it because with the latest case he would have to investigate his colleagues?

No copper liked investigating other coppers. It broke the bonds of the camaraderie, the mateship, built up after years of grinding away on the beat or working cases.

He could have said no; perhaps he should have done. But Mrs Challinor had asked, and it was part of being a coroner's officer. There was a statutory duty to investigate all deaths in custody or in contact with the officers of the law.

His examination of the case documents had left him feeling slightly uneasy. There was nothing he could put his finger on, but it was all too perfect, too wrapped up. A detainee dying after a fall in the cell – a convenient solution.

It was almost as if he wasn't reading between the lines properly, wasn't understanding what wasn't being stated.

Sometimes, reading official documents, it was important to see what they were avoiding as well as what was being said. The ability to lie by omission had been honed for countless years by every bureaucracy. You had to be adept at seeing what wasn't there, as well as what was.

Then he smiled to himself as the words of Charlie Whitworth, his old boss, came back to him. 'Don't overthink it, Ridpath. Remember Occam's razor.'

'The most obvious answer is usually the right one, Charlie.'

'Right first time, Ridpath. So when a wife dies...'

'It's usually the husband who did it.'

'We might make a copper out of you yet.'

Perhaps he was overthinking it. The pictures showed the man falling and hitting his head. The fall had caused a bleed on the brain and he had died later in hospital.

QED.

After all, wasn't it what both the IOPC and Professional Standards had concluded? And the science of the post-mortem backed the conclusion.

CPS and the Ministry of Justice were satisfied, and so was everybody else.

Except the family, of course.

An image of the old woman's brown-spotted hand with its paper-thin skin shaking as she poured the tea flashed into his mind.

She needed to know the truth, even if he had to tell her it was all just an unfortunate accident.

He turned into the car park beside the HQ and switched off his motor.

He wasn't looking forward to this investigation.

Not like him.

Not at all like him.

Chapter Eleven

Ridpath walked into the weekly meeting and immediately noticed a chill in the air. People weren't looking him in the eye. In fact, exactly the opposite.

Even the two people he liked most in MIT – Chrissy Wright, the civilian researcher, and Detective Sergeant Emily Parkinson – both avoided greeting him.

As soon as he looked in their direction, they deliberately glanced away as if finding something fascinating in the grey skies louring over Manchester on that cold November afternoon.

He placed his coffee down on the table next to two detectives he didn't know. They took one look at him and then stood up, moving to seats on the opposite side of the room.

Only Harry Makepeace approached and sat down next to him. 'How's it hanging, Ridpath?'

'Same old, same old, Harry. How've you been?'

'Not bad, just got back from Leeds five minutes ago and rushed up to this meeting. Haven't even had time to get something to eat. It's steak and kidney pud in the canteen today too.'

'What you been working on?'

Harry touched the side of his nose. 'Liaising with the National Crime Agency for the last two weeks in Yorkshire; God, they're slow, it's like working with treacle.'

At the front of the room, Detective Chief Inspective Paul Turnbull banged on the desk. 'Right, you lot, let's be having you. I want this meeting over and done with in thirty minutes. No longer, right?'

He scanned the room, checking on all the detectives before stopping at Harry.

'Well, if it isn't Detective Inspector Makepeace. Long time no see, Harry. How was sunny Yorkshire?'

'It's still there, gaffer.'

'Have we closed the case yet? And if not, why not?'

Harry rolled his eyes. 'Not yet. We've been watching the head of the child sex ring for the last couple of weeks, but he hasn't put a foot wrong. Almost as if he knows we're on to him.'

'Why don't you pull him in anyway? I thought you had enough to put him away for a good ten stretch.'

'The NCA want it all tied up neatly with a bow before they take it to the CPS.'

Turnbull nodded his bald head slowly. Ridpath could see the vein in his temple throbbing.

'I'll say this once and once only, people.' His bottom lip came up to cover the top one and the muscles on his jawline clenched. 'I want results. No more pussy-footing about, waiting and watching and running up overtime so you lot can enjoy two weeks in Ibiza with the missus next summer.' He slammed his fist down on the table. 'Results. Got it.'

He scanned the room, making sure every detective nodded his agreement.

'But, gaffer...'

'No buts, Harry. You put pressure on whoever is in charge of the NCA this week to get his finger out of his arse and make an arrest. Jesus, this was a done deal a month ago.'

'It's a woman, boss. Detective Chief Inspector Watkins.'

'Well, tell her to get her finger out of her arse. I want a result, Harry, and I want it yesterday. Understood?'

'Yes, gaffer.'

'Alan, how are you getting on with the stabbing in Bolton?'

'The guy was charged yesterday. CPS have agreed he has a case to answer. We should have the papers to them by the end of the week.'

'Done and dusted?'

'Done and dusted.'

Turnbull clapped his hands. 'Well done, Alan. Listen, people, be more like Alan. Offence committed on Monday. Perp arrested and charged on Tuesday. Papers to CPS by Friday. A case cleared and off the books by Saturday. Efficient use of resources and time and one more idiot off the streets. Well done, Alan.'

The rest of the meeting continued on in the same vein, Turnbull alternatively cajoling, frightening, encouraging and demeaning but with one underlying message.

All that mattered was results.

'Right, we're done.' He glanced across the detectives who began to stand up. 'But… we've forgotten our little coroner's officer, Detective Inspector Ridpath. What do you have for us?'

Ridpath pulled out his notepad and checked the figures given to him by Sophia before he left. 'It's pretty quiet at the moment. Just a hundred and twenty-seven deaths last week and only three from Covid. We've noticed an increasing occurrence of deaths in the home as GPs are performing Zoom consultations rather than seeing patients in person. Not their fault, though, as it was a government directive. The coroner has raised a number of Section 28s with the health authorities.'

'Please explain to us mere mortals what a Section 28 is, Ridpath?'

'It's a notice of concern. If a coroner raises one, local health authorities have to respond in writing to her and to the chief coroner. It's to prevent similar deaths from occurring.'

'Do Section 28s also apply to the police force?'

Ridpath's eyes narrowed. He knew where Turnbull was going with this. Was that why he felt like persona non grata at this meeting?

'They do, if the police have made an error in procedure.'

'Are you investigating any cases for the coroner at the moment involving us?'

There was a smirk on Turnbull's face as he asked the question.

Ridpath could see no way of answering this except with brutal honesty. If all else fails, tell the truth. 'There is an inquest into the death in custody of Ben Holdsworth in Redbury station coming soon.'

'Wasn't Tony Saunders the custody sergeant?' This was Alan Butcher asking.

Ridpath nodded.

'He's good police, Tony. I was trained by him.'

'And so was I.' Another copper jumped in. Ridpath didn't know who he was. There were so many new people brought in by Turnbull, he had difficulty keeping track.

'The coroner has a statutory duty to hold an inquest when there is a death in custody.' Ridpath could hear the weakness in his voice.

'But I thought Tony had already been cleared by Professional Standards and the IOPC; why are you investigating again? He's been on office duties for the last couple of years. A good copper like him should be out working, not stuck filling in forms for the bloody computers.'

There was a murmur of agreement in the room.

'As I said, the coroner has a statutory duty to investigate all deaths in custody.'

Turnbull held his hands up. 'Enough, gentlemen, I'm sure Ridpath is just doing his job...' A pause for three seconds, '...investigating good coppers for the coroner. As the chief said last month, *our* job is to solve crime and arrest criminals. I want to see those results and see them quickly. Get it? Now get out and get them.'

The meeting was dismissed. Ridpath closed his notepad and put it back in the inside pocket of his jacket. He couldn't help but notice the disdainful glances of the other detectives as they left the room. Chrissy Wright and Emily Parkinson still hadn't spoken to him.

'Chrissy, have you got a second?'

The civilian researcher looked sheepish for a moment, glancing left and right, before finally walking over to him.

'Can you run something through the PNC for me? I'm looking for the files on the arrests of this man, Ben Holdsworth.'

Chrissy took the paper from him. 'Sure, Ridpath, I'll do it now.'

A hand came in and took the paper from her. 'No, you won't. You're to give no help to this man when he's investigating other coppers, is that clear, Wright?

The imposing figure of Turnbull loomed over her. He screwed up the paper and threw it in the bin.

'I'm still an officer in MIT, Turnbull. I've asked Chrissy to check some files for me.'

'It's Detective Chief Inspector Turnbull to you, Ridpath. And I decide how the resources in my department are being used, is that clear?'

Ridpath stood up. 'I'll do it myself then.'

'All the computers are being used at the moment. Important MIT business,' Turnbull said with a smirk. 'And I'm sure there is a conflict of interest with you investigating another copper. Chief Inspector Boyle at Professional Standards will want to take a look at what you're doing.'

Ridpath exhaled. 'As I said, it's part of the statutory duty of a coroner to investigate all deaths in custody. It's got nothing to do with Professional Standards.'

'If I remember correctly, wasn't a coroner's officer investigated in Cheshire for writing a report on my old force?'

'It was her duty to make people aware of a possible connection in deaths amongst old people the police may have missed.'

'But her duty to whom, Ridpath? The coroner or the police? Where did her loyalty lie?'

'Her loyalty was to the truth, Chief Inspector Turnbull. It's always to the truth.'

'My loyalty is to the people who pay my salary. Who are you employed by, Ridpath?'

'You know the answer.'

'You're paid by MIT, not the coroner. Until you remember investigating other coppers is not your duty, then you're not welcome here.'

'You can't do that, Turnbull.'

Another little smile. 'I just did.' He turned to look through the open door of the meeting room. 'Alan,' he shouted. 'Come here and escort Ridpath out of this office. He's not welcome any more.'

'With pleasure, boss.'

Chapter Twelve

On his way out, Ridpath spotted Emily Parkinson perched over a standing ashtray, exhaling a long stream of blue smoke into the air.

'You really have pissed them off this time.'

'You couldn't even look at me.'

'What do you expect? You know how it is. I have to work with these bastards every day of my life.' She glanced towards the main building. 'If Turnbull caught me talking to you now, I'd be out of MIT as quickly as Ronaldo scores goals. I'd probably end up in some dreary basement somewhere updating iOPS for the rest of my life.'

Ridpath stood downwind of Emily, not so passively inhaling her smoke as she expelled it from her lungs. He had promised Eve he would stop smoking. So far, he had kept to his promise, but a whiff of second-hand smoke didn't count, at least in his eyes.

'When is Claire Trent due back?'

Emily shrugged her shoulders. 'Who knows? Officially she's on a course. Unofficially, the scuttlebutt is she's going for one of the new chief super posts in a division. And you know what that means...'

'Turnbull will probably take over MIT.'

'Right first time.' She paused for a second, taking another long drag from her cigarette and then lighting a new one with the fag end of the old. 'One day, I'll give these up, but at the moment they are the only things keeping me going.'

'That good, huh?'

'Worse. Turnbull's making my life a nightmare. Nothing I can officially complain about, but it's the usual constant low-level hostility.' A deep breath. 'I've had enough, Ridpath; it's time to put in for a transfer.'

'Where will you go?'

'I don't know. Anywhere out of MIT. And now it looks like the divisions are becoming more important.'

Ridpath smiled. 'Our new task. Stop crime. Arrest criminals.'

'Yeah, why did we ever move away from the basics? What else is a police force for?'

'Providing a safe refuge for terminally incompetent managers?'

'That's too cynical even for me.' Emily held up her pack of Embassy. 'You still not smoking?'

'The last one was four months, three days and ten hours ago.'

'Like you're not keeping count.'

'One day at a time.' He felt his hand drift towards the packet.

She quickly put it back in her pocket. 'Sorry for even tempting you.' She changed the subject. 'How are you going with the death in custody?'

'Just started. The inquest is next week so I'm a bit pushed for time. I have to interview witnesses and work up a timeline for the coroner.'

'You're not investigating Tony Saunders?'

'Not directly. Our job is to work out why and how Ben Holdsworth died, and to see if anything can be done to prevent such deaths happening again. It's not to apportion blame.'

'It's not how they see it.' She stabbed her cigarette in the direction of the HQ building. 'They think you're out to get him.'

'What do you think, Emily?'

She paused and put the cigarette in her mouth, inhaling and then exhaling slowly. 'I was trained by Tony Saunders. He was my first sergeant at Cheadle Hulme. He's a good copper, Ridpath. A copper's copper.'

'Like I said, the coroner just wants to find out what happened and why. Nothing more, nothing less.'

'What are your next steps?'

'Go to the nick, check out the scene, talk to the coppers involved, build a timeline.'

'You're going to see Tony Saunders?'

'Of course.'

She grimaced, trying to hide her face, whispering, 'Well, you won't have long to wait. He's walking towards us now.'

Chapter Thirteen

He didn't know how long he'd been running.

His legs hurt. His chest was heaving. A stitch stabbed him in the side.

He glanced backwards.

Nobody following him.

He stopped running but carried on walking as fast as he could. *Don't stop now.*

Where was he going to go? Where was he going to stay?

He couldn't go back to Redbury; they'd get him in ten minutes. The rental house in Dukinfield was a no-go too, not any more, not with Mr Delaney's body lying on the kitchen floor.

He smiled to himself. It was good feeling the kettle strike the man's head, though. The satisfying crunch of metal on bone. And then watching him topple off the chair and collapse on the floor was priceless.

He shouldn't have done it, just as he shouldn't have beaten up the man in the pub, but sometimes he couldn't help himself.

Now he was in trouble though. Big trouble.

Where to go?

He wracked his brain for an answer.

Find a hotel. Nothing fancy, just some place where he could stay for a couple of days and nobody could find him.

But Delaney knew his new name; wouldn't they be able to track him?

Not if he stayed out of sight. And it would only be for a few days, less than a week. Afterwards, he could head down south and hide himself in the Smoke. He'd have to bring forward his trip to Thailand, though – England wasn't safe any more. Eventually somebody would recognise him and Delaney would be on to him in a flash.

He shuddered to think what would happen to him if he were caught.

What was it Delaney had said? Somebody wanted him dead? But why? He'd done as he was asked, left the area and not gone back, kept his nose clean and stayed out of trouble. He'd never even had a visit from the law.

So who wanted him dead? And why?

A tram station up on the left. He'd get on and go into town, find a cheap hotel and hide out there.

They wouldn't be able to find him if he didn't go out.

Mr Delaney was not a man anybody crossed lightly in Manchester. And he had just hit him with a heavy kettle full of boiling water.

He smiled to himself again. He shouldn't have done it, but it felt so bloody good. Three years of hell put into one swing of a hot kettle.

He'd do it again in a heartbeat.

Sod Delaney.

Sod his thugs.

He was getting out of this horrible city and going to Thailand for some sun, sea and sand.

Sod 'em all.

Chapter Fourteen

'Hiya, Emily, still smoking the coffin nails? Bad for your health.' Sergeant Tony Saunders stood close, his bulk imposing itself on the conversation.

'Hi, Tony, smoking these is better than breathing in Manchester's air. At least these have a filter. How are you?'

Saunders ignored the question, squaring his body and demanding, 'Are you Ridpath?'

'It's Detective Inspector Ridpath, Sergeant. You might want to show some respect, if not for me at least for the rank.'

'Respect? For a copper investigating other coppers? Give me a break. As for you, Emily, I'm surprised you're talking to a ponce like this.'

'I've worked with Ridpath before, Tony, he's a good copper.'

Saunders snorted. 'And he's investigating me?'

'All deaths in custody have to be investigated, Sergeant Saunders.'

'So far I've been questioned by Professional Standards, the College of Policing, a whole team of investigators from the IOPC and the bloody CPS. All have cleared me of any wrongdoing. I've been on desk duties for over three years, sitting in some basement with nothing but a bloody computer for company. And now you come along too?'

'It's my job.'

'Just what the police needs, another jobsworth,' Saunders sneered.

'The inquest is next week, Sergeant. I don't think we should be talking like this. I need to send you a notice for a formal interview, and you may want to have your union rep or solicitor attend.'

'Bugger off, I don't have to talk to you.'

'I'm afraid you do.'

'You're just a coroner's officer.'

'Who can subpoena you to testify at the inquest and arrest you if you fail to turn up. Do you understand?' Ridpath softened his tone.

'Let's not make this confrontational, Tony; the coroner just wants to discover the truth.'

'Don't we all. But I've had enough. I think you're going to need a subpoena to talk to me.'

With those parting words, he strode away, up the steps and back through the main doors of Police HQ.

For a moment both Ridpath and Emily Parkinson stood there watching the man vanish into the depths of the building.

Finally, Ridpath spoke ironically. 'Nice to meet you too, Tony.'

'I think he's had enough. Remember when the demonstrations happened outside Redbury nick, he was the one who had to carry the can. How would you feel if you'd spent the last few years on restricted duties?'

'I went through it all, remember? Look, I understand how he's feeling, but it doesn't change the coroner's statutory duty. There has to be an inquest, I have to investigate beforehand and produce a report for her. In the end, though, a jury will decide the verdict, as it always does.'

'It's just not good optics.'

'Bugger the optics, Emily. It's my job. I'm here to represent the family and the police. What if there was a procedural error leading to more deaths?'

'Have you seen any evidence Tony Saunders did something wrong?'

Ridpath shook his head. 'Not yet. He seems to have followed the rule book to the letter.'

'See, I told you he was a good copper.'

'But I still need to look into it. The inquest is going to happen, like it or not. It has to happen by law.'

Emily stabbed her cigarette out in the ashtray. 'I have to get back, Ridpath. You be careful, you hear? This one could bite your arse. Turnbull is whispering behind your back.'

'He doesn't worry me.'

'He should, Ridpath, he should.'

Chapter Fifteen

After the talk with Emily, Ridpath returned to his car and rang Sophia. 'How's things?'

'All quiet on the Stockfield front. Mrs Challinor has left for a council meeting; she won't be coming back. Everything else is running smoothly. John is going over the post-mortem report as we speak. He'll get back to you as soon as he can.'

'It's John, is it?'

'Ridpath, you're being annoying. *Dr Schofield* will get back to you. I'm just going through the newspaper reports of the death of Ben Holdsworth. There's nothing really new in them except somebody leaked the conclusions of the post-mortem and images from the CCTV of his fall. They appeared only a couple of days after he died.'

'Somebody wanting to earn a little money on the side?'

Sophia sucked in air through her teeth. 'It doesn't feel like it. I'll email them over to you so you can decide.'

'But what do you think?'

'Looks like an official leak to me.'

'To take pressure off the police?'

'You could think that; I couldn't possibly say.'

Ridpath laughed. 'You've been watching too much old television, Sophia. I thought *House of Cards* wasn't really your style.'

'It isn't, but anything is better than listening to my mother prattling on about eligible bachelors.'

Ridpath checked the clock on his dashboard. 'I'm not coming back. If I hurry I can pick up Eve after her music class. She's in the school orchestra.'

'What does she play?'

'The ukulele.'

Sophia laughed. 'Better than me. I was given the triangle. Can't go wrong with the triangle, but I somehow did. The teacher kept saying I was always coming in late. Story of my life.'

'I'll go through the files and the witness statements again later this evening and work out an investigative strategy. Something's bothering me, but I can't put my finger on it. See you tomorrow.'

'Call me if you need anything.'

'Will do.'

Ridpath turned off his mobile phone and drove to Eve's school in Altrincham, listening to one of his favourite groups from the seventies, The Sensational Alex Harvey Band. A great blues singer, shame he died so young.

Stopping at a traffic light, a young woman in the car next to him gave a strange look as he screamed out 'Next...', singing along to one of the songs. She accelerated quickly away from the lights.

Eve was surprised to see him as she came out, carrying her ukulele in its bag on her shoulder. 'Dad, what are you doing here?'

'Just thought I'd pick you up today.'

Eve turned away from him to say goodbye to Maisie before turning back. 'You don't normally come on a Monday. I was just going to get the tram.'

Ridpath shrugged his shoulders. 'Can't a dad pick his daughter up from school? How was your day?'

'Same old, same old. Maths followed by double English and then PE.'

'Was it good to be back?'

She shrugged her shoulders.

'How was the school orchestra?'

'OK.'

'What else did you do?'

'Why the inquisition, Dad?' she suddenly snapped. 'I'm not one of your suspects, am I?'

He frowned. 'Sorry for asking.' He put the car in gear and they drove home in silence.

As soon as they entered the house, he asked her what she wanted for dinner.

She responded by sighing loudly. 'Enough with the questions, Dad. I'm not hungry.' Then she ran upstairs to her bedroom, slamming the door loudly.

Ridpath wondered what he had done wrong. Should he have gone to pick her up at the school? Perhaps she was looking forward to getting the tram with Maisie. Or perhaps she had just reached the age when it was no longer cool to be picked up by, or even seen with, her dad.

He remembered her days at primary school, when she used to run out of the school gates and wrap her tiny arms around his legs she was so pleased to see him.

He climbed the stairs and gently tapped on the closed door to her bedroom. 'What do you want for dinner?'

'Go away, Dad.' The voice from inside was tired and exasperated. 'Leave me alone. I'm not hungry.'

'You've got to eat something.'

'I. AM. NOT. HUNGRY.'

Had he done something wrong? They'd had such a great time together on holiday, but now they were back in Manchester she seemed really annoyed with him.

'Look, if I've done something wrong, just let me know. Let's talk about it.'

'Not everything is about you, Dad. JUST. LEAVE. ME. ALONE.'

He stood for a second outside the door, wondering whether to continue or walk away. Eventually, he decided it would be better to leave her for a while.

He went downstairs and warmed up a pizza in the oven, eating a couple of slices sitting alone at the kitchen table.

He left most of it for Eve in case she was feeling hungry and decided he could either watch TV or go through the documents in the case one more time.

The case won out.

He read through the reports and witness statements, seeing no discrepancies in any of the papers. It all seemed clear and above board. Everything Tony Saunders did as a custody sergeant was to the rule book, his notes were well kept and his interaction with the detainee was a textbook example of how to deal with somebody fairly and firmly. Emily Parkinson was right: Saunders was a good copper.

All the other witness statements from the coppers, the custody officers and the duty doctor backed up Saunders' account. No wonder Professional Standards and the IOPC could find nothing wrong. Perhaps Ridpath was overthinking it.

He would report to Mrs Challinor tomorrow, telling her it seemed an open-and-shut case to him: an accidental fall in a cell.

He'd have to check on the witnesses for her before the inquest, but that was just a formality.

He was about to close the file when he decided to take one more look at the post-mortem. With Eve upstairs, he could look at the pictures without the risk of her seeing them. Such images would give her nightmares; they had the same effect on him.

He picked up the post-mortem report, turning to the first page.

STATEMENT of WITNESS

Statement of Dr Harold Lardner, BSc, MB, BS, MRC Path.

Age of Witness 54
Occupation Greater Manchester Police Pathologist
Address Forensic Pathology Services

This statement, consisting of 9 pages signed by me, is true to the best of my knowledge and belief and I make it knowing, if tendered in evidence, I shall be liable to prosecution if I have wilfully stated in it anything I know to be false or do not believe to be true.

POST-MORTEM REPORT. YZ 4643/19

February 22, 2018.
Mr Ben Holdsworth – date of birth: 12/01/1982.
Time of Death: 07.36 on 21/02/2018.

At 13.10 on February 21, 2018, at the request of Greater Manchester Police, I performed a forensic post-mortem on the body of Mr Ben Holdsworth, who had died at Salford General Hospital at 07.36 after being found unconscious in a custody cell at Redbury Police Station.

POST-MORTEM EXAMINATION

The people present were

Kate Brady: Mortuary Technician
Alfred Timms: Forensic Photographer

The identity of Mr Holdsworth had been confirmed by his mother at the hospital prior to the transportation of the body to the mortuary.

Mr Holdsworth's body was received in a white, signature-sealed bodybag and wrapped in a black plastic sheet. Head and hand bags were in place.

External examination

He was of medium build, weighed 82.2 kg and was 181 cm tall. His hair was dark and cut short to the head. There were no visible tattoos or any other body markings.

An outer examination of the body revealed signs of a sharp force injury to the side of the head, causing a Traumatic Brain Injury. A TBI is defined as 'an insult to the brain caused by an external force that may produce diminished or altered states of consciousness, which results in impaired cognitive abilities or physical functioning' (National Head Injury Foundation, 1988).

There is no skull fracture present but there is reddening of a wound in the temple area indicating it happened ante-mortem. Bruising to the left side of temple and parietal scalp approximately 4 cm above and 2 cm behind the right ear. No subdural haemorrhage in this location.

There is also a deeper wound at the rear of the skull with superficial bruising on the scalp. On examination of the brain, a subdural haematoma was found corresponding with this location indicating a closed head injury (CHI) occurred.

CCTV (stills attached) provided by GMP shows the subject falling accidentally in his cell and striking his head against the wall.

Abrasion marks to both wrists consistent with the application of handcuffs by officers on arrest.

Injection mark on inside of right elbow with bruising. On examination of the rest of the body i.e. inside of thighs, right inside elbow, between toes, no other injection sites were seen, indicating use of drugs a one-off event rather than long-term usage.

Toxicology samples of blood and stomach contents taken and sent to lab. Hair samples also dispatched.

The hands and arms showed no signs of defensive injuries.

Internal examination

The brain was removed and weighed. No abnormalities (other than the subdural haematoma previously cited) were observed.

All other bodily organs – liver, lungs kidneys and heart – were within the normal ranges of a healthy adult male aged 36 years old. No evidence of scarring on the lung tissue.

Stomach contents indicate the subject ate pizza at least six hours before death.

Toxicology

Still awaiting results.

Heart

Normal for a 36-year-old man. Inspection of the myocardium showed no pallor in the fossa ovalis. Ventricular dimensions were in normal parameters as were the pericardium, aorta, major blood vessels and the valves.

Attached is a list of the organ weights. Appendix 2.

Ridpath was a little lost given all the technical language. He turned the page and re-read the conclusion.

CONCLUSIONS

This man died from a subdural haematoma to the brain, caused by striking his skull on the wall of the cell. CCTV evidence shows him falling and hitting his head. (Attached stills from CCTV in Appendix 3.) This injury would not have been obvious to an untrained observer, but should have led to increasingly erratic behaviour such as an inability to stand, shaking of the head, lack of coordination of the motor functions and dizziness.

The discovery of the man on the floor of the cell is not surprising. The subdural haematoma would eventually lead to his inability to maintain his normal motor and perceptual functions and cause a final collapse.

I would conclude the deceased struck his head from a fall in the cell. Death followed three hours later.

Category 3. Accidental death.

Signed Harold Lardner, Pathologist. 4.30 p.m. February 22, 2018.

He opened the first envelope and took out four photos. The first was the one he had seen before: a picture of Ben Holdsworth's face as he lay naked on a mortuary table. The second showed a close-up of the side of the head, bruising evident on the shaved skin. The third picture showed the brain, still resident in the skull, with blood clots nestling in between the fissures at the rear. The fourth showed the brain, now out of the skull cavity, sitting in the middle of a stainless-steel tray.

He put the pictures down on his desk. God, he hated looking at these, but knew he had to do it.

Gingerly, he opened another envelope. It was a printout on photographic paper of a series of stills from the CCTV. The camera was positioned above the victim, looking down on him. Ridpath saw Holdsworth enter, gesture to the detention officers as the cell door closed, bang on the door for a minute. As he turned away, he lost his balance and fell towards the concrete wall behind the bunk, striking the side of his head on the wall. Then he told up, shook his head and gestured up towards the camera, his middle finger raised, anger clouding his face.

'Nice man,' said Ridpath out loud.

For the next hour he went through the rest of the envelopes, opening each in turn. The post-mortem had been extensively documented. There were five envelopes of printouts from the CCTV of the sequence of events leading to the fall and afterwards, showing the prisoner walking around the cell.

Somebody, probably a scene of crime officer, had added more shots of the interior of the cell, even indicating a small dent on the wall where Holdsworth may have struck his head.

Only one envelope remained. Ridpath opened it and found the final toxicology report from the lab.

Trace elements of Ambien were found.

No alcohol present.

High amounts of diamorphine (1200 mg) sufficient to cause an overdose were found in the man's blood.

No trace elements of any drug found in the hair samples.

Ridpath frowned. As far as he knew, that amount of diamorphine was a massive dose of street heroin, probably in a pretty pure form, enough to kill a small horse.

Had Holdsworth died of a drug overdose, or from a fall?

His question was answered by a note from Lardner appended to the toxicology report.

> Despite the relatively large amount of diamorphine present in Mr Holdsworth's body, I am still confident my initial conclusions were correct. This man's cause of death was a subdural haematoma caused by striking his head as he fell. The presence of diamorphine may have contributed to the fall but it did not cause his death.
>
> Signed Harold Lardner, forensic pathologist
>
> 11.04.2018.

Ridpath noticed the date of the note was six weeks after the death. Why had the toxicology report taken so long? Holdsworth had already been cremated by the time it was released.

The floor creaked loudly above his head.

Was Eve still awake? She still hadn't eaten anything. Perhaps she'd try some pizza now. He placed the toxicology report on the table and climbed the stairs as quietly as he could, tapping on her door.

There was no answer.

He pushed the door open and popped his head around. She was fast asleep, a book, *Harry Potter and the Half-Blood Prince*, open on the floor beside her bed and the light still on.

He walked in and closed the book, placing it on the nightstand. She slept on her back, her mouth slightly open revealing strong white teeth, but no sound coming out.

A silent sleeper, exactly the same as Polly.

He pulled up the bedclothes around her shoulders. She was still wearing the Peppa Pig pyjamas he had bought her last Christmas as a joke. One year, when she was three, they had driven all the way from Manchester to spend a day in Peppa Pig World, staying overnight near Winchester and returning to the park again the next morning. She had loved every second of it, queueing for one ride again and again and again.

He still had a picture somewhere of Polly being hugged, rather too energetically in his opinion, by an incredibly frisky Daddy Pig.

He took one last look at Eve's sleeping face and switched out the light.

God, how he missed that three-year-old child. Why can't we frame these moments in time, preserved forever so we can visit them again and again?

A time when Eve was young and Polly was still alive and laughing and happy and joyful.

He stayed for a minute longer before creeping out of the room and closing the door as quietly as he could. It was time to return to the real world, where young men died on the floor of police cells. A world in which he spent far too much time. Should he just recuse himself now from the investigation? Was it worth all the hassle with Turnbull and the rest of the detectives at MIT?

Mrs Challinor had suggested she could get Jennings back from Derbyshire to finish doing the work. It would be easy to go to her tomorrow morning and tell her he couldn't do this job. He was sure she would understand.

But then the image of Ben Holdsworth's mother crept like a burglar into his head. 'I think I was the only person who cared about him in the whole world.'

He stood there for a moment, outside Eve's room, resting his head on the door. Somebody had to care, somebody had to do the work. Wasn't his job to represent the likes of Ben Holdsworth and his mother? People who could no longer defend themselves in a world where nobody cared.

He gritted his teeth. Sod them all. He was going to finish this job, whatever happened.

He owed it to Ben Holdsworth and his mother.

But above all, he owed it to all those out there who couldn't defend themselves.

He could still remember the words of the oath he had spoken on the day he graduated from training. 'I do solemnly and sincerely declare and affirm that I will well and truly serve the queen in the office of constable, with fairness, integrity, diligence and impartiality, upholding fundamental human rights and according equal respect to all people; and that I will, to the best of my power, cause the peace to be kept and preserved and prevent all offences against people and property; and that while I continue to hold the said office I will to the best of my skill and knowledge discharge all the duties thereof faithfully according to law.'

For him, they were more than words.

They were his creed.

Chapter Sixteen

Garry Abbott found a cheap hotel to stay at in New Islington. The area had a trendy London name but was actually an old mill district next to the Ashton Canal. It was close enough to the city centre if he needed to go there, but far enough away to be safe. A tram stop was nearby and a convenience store downstairs.

Perfect. He could hide here for at least a few days.

The room itself was as dreary as any interior designer could possibly make it: a bed, small TV, basic bathroom, a six-inch desk permanently attached to the wall in case anybody tried to nick it and a wardrobe that was just a horizontal steel pole with hangers.

It was safe, and it would do.

He hung out the DO NOT DISTURB sign on the door. He didn't need some stupid maid to go blabbing about the strange man in room 324.

He lay down on the bed, hearing the springs pop beneath his weight.

Should he call Phil?

He had to find out how bad the damage was. He switched on his mobile and waited for it to boot up. He was sure Delaney couldn't track him while he was using this. Only the police could do that, couldn't they? But it didn't do to underestimate the man's reach. Anyway, he had to make the call, so time to get it over and done with.

'Phil, it's me.'

'What you done, mate? Delaney's goons are all over Manchester looking for you.'

'Have they been to see you?'

'Of course, the missus was right pissed off.'

'What did you tell them?'

'Nothing, mate. Haven't seen you for ages, have I? Last time was three years ago.'

'Did they believe you?'

'Well, I'm still here, aren't I? And I still have most of my teeth. Delaney has a thing about pulling teeth. I've heard he has a complete set of dental pliers. Doesn't use any anaesthetic, though.'

'Listen, Phil, I need some help.'

There was a long silence on the other end of the line.

'...I don't know, mate. If Delaney finds out...'

'He won't. All I need you to do is go to my safety deposit box in Mason Street. Inside, you'll find a bag. Just bring it to me.'

'Where are you?'

He sensed a tension in Phil's voice. 'I'll tell you later. Can you do it?'

'But will they open the box for me?'

'I'll call them and let them know. Just take some ID.'

'Well...'

'I really need your help, Phil. Don't do it today, though. Wait a few days, till it all calms down. Thursday would be the best day to go.'

'I really don't know, mate, I like my Newtons. If Delaney finds out...'

'I'm in a mither here and all you can think about is your teeth!' He took a couple of deep breaths. 'Who's gonna tell him? Not me, that's for sure.'

'Er...'

'There's a few bob in it for you.'

'How much?'

'A couple of hundred.'

'Make it five and you're on.'

'You're taking the piss now. Three max.'

'Sorry, mate, it's five or nowt. If Delaney finds out what I'm up to, I'm toast and you know it. Call it danger money.'

He knew Phil wasn't going to do it for nothing and he needed the spare passports and the cash. 'OK, you're on. Cash on delivery.'

'When?'

'On Thursday. I'll call you to let you know when to go.'

'Right, you're on. See you Thursday. But mate, I wouldn't go out much until then. Delaney isn't well chuffed with you at the moment.'

He hung up the phone, switching it off and taking out the battery. With Delaney on his case, there was no point in taking chances.

He switched on the TV. *Escape to the Country* was on.

'Just what I need,' he said out loud to the empty room.

Chapter Seventeen

Back downstairs, Ridpath read through the post-mortem report one more time. The more he looked, the more he noticed a few concerns.

Why had the post-mortem been completed so quickly?

Why had they sent the CCTV footage to the pathologist?

Lardner stated that the mother identified the body at the hospital, but she'd told Ridpath she had done it three days later, after the post-mortem. Surely by then it would have been in no condition to be viewed.

Why had the toxicology report taken so long to produce?

But most importantly, if such large amounts of heroin were in Holdsworth's bloodstream, why had none of the custody officers noticed slurred speech or the condition of his pupils? Saunders had booked him, while Harvey and Rodgers had strip searched him.

Strange.

Had Holdsworth taken the drugs when he was in the station, perhaps before they searched him? He would have to ask one of the custody officers. If so, perhaps procedures should be tightened up when a suspected drug trafficker was arrested.

Of course, the toxicology report may not have been correct. Had an error been made, and that's why they took so long to produce their results?

There was nothing anybody could do now. If the body had been cremated, then the only evidence they had to work with was the report written by Lardner. Would Dr Schofield agree with his fellow pathologist?

Ridpath wrote a note for himself to push for an answer tomorrow. He needed to clear these concerns before he went any further in this investigation.

And then the thought struck him. The report wasn't the only evidence they had. Lardner was still alive. Should he be interviewed?

A shudder ran down Ridpath's spine. The last person he wanted to meet again was Harold Lardner.

His thoughts were interrupted by the beep of his phone. Ridpath put down the file and checked who it was from.

Chrissy.

It was past midnight and she was still up. She couldn't still be at work, could she?

> Sorry I haven't been in touch sooner, Turnbull was watching me like a hawk. I rescued the paper from the bin so here are the cases you asked for. Two arrests. One for possession of a small amount of cannabis. The other for driving a car without a functioning brake light. Neither ended up in custodial sentences. Don't know why they bothered with the charges rather than issue a warning. Maybe they needed to make their stats look better?

Attached were the case files for Ben Holdsworth. Ridpath typed back immediately.

> Thank you, Chrissy, but you shouldn't have. Turnbull will not be chuffed if he finds out.

The response was immediate.

> Sod him. You know the whole team is still working? He's really pushing for quick results, cutting corners like it was going out of fashion.

> Still, be careful, but thanks for this.

> Let me know if you need anything else. Love Chrissy.

Ridpath opened the first file. A minor arrest for cannabis possession after a stop in the street. The second even less serious: a traffic stop for a broken brake light. Both cases had led to minor fines.

Ridpath scanned down to the end of the file, checking the signature at the end of the page.

His eyes widened. In both cases, the arresting officer was Sergeant Tony Saunders.

November 2, 2021

Chapter Eighteen

The next morning it was like sitting opposite Cousin Itt from the Addams Family.

Eve's hair was hanging down in front of her face, covering her eyes and cheekbones, while she shovelled muesli into her mouth through the gaps.

She had not spoken to him when he had called her for breakfast, simply stomping down the stairs and bustling into the kitchen.

They were both sitting at the kitchen table. Outside the weather had the strange undecidedness of late autumn. Was it going to rain? Or was the watery sun going to shine in a vain attempt to warm the cold bones of the city?

The day didn't know, and neither did Detective Inspector Thomas Ridpath.

He sipped his coffee and watched his daughter. With the smoothness of an automaton, the spoon scooped up the rabbit food and milk. This was her latest breakfast choice, a habit acquired from the hotel buffet on the holiday in the Lakes. Gone were the scrambled eggs on toast and the toast and jam. Now the rage was for 'healthy' food. Having tasted the sugary sweetness of this German brand – a mere £3.50 for a small box from Waitrose – Ridpath couldn't see what was 'healthy' about it. But his daughter had decided this was what she wanted, so who was he to argue? Next week it would be all change again anyway. Perhaps frogspawn with a side helping of chicken liver would be the latest choice?

He glanced at his watch. 'We need to leave soon, Eve.'

'Hhmrph.'

Ridpath couldn't work out whether that was an answer or if she was merely chewing her muesli. He tried again. 'We have to leave soon.'

'Hmmrh, hmmrrhh.'

He stood up and placed his cup in the sink, hoping she would get the hint, trying for a third time. 'We need to be off now if you don't want to be late. Remember what Mrs Snodgrass said about your lateness.'

'She said it was your fault.'

At last words came out from the mass of hair.

'Precisely, so we should leave now.'

The spoon was thrown into the bowl and Eve stood up sharply. 'OK, OK, I get it. You don't have to go on.'

With those words, she ran out of the kitchen and stormed up the stairs.

Ridpath was expecting the inevitable temper tantrums of the hormonal soup otherwise known as a teenager. He'd hoped they would hold off for at least a couple of years, but Eve had apparently decided to start early.

They had been so great together during the holiday. Why had she changed so suddenly when they returned?

Not for the first time, he wished Polly were there. At least he could have discussed it with her. She would have understood what was happening in the tiny mind of his thirteen-year-old daughter.

Was she missing Polly? Had the holiday just emphasised her absence and, now they were back, that absence was being felt even more strongly?

Of course, since Polly's death, Eve had been through the mill of therapists, each one stating she had done well to accept the fact of her mother's death. But Ridpath wondered if she secretly blamed him for what had happened. He understood if she did. He blamed himself too.

He could hear the tap in the upstairs bathroom running as she washed her face and combed her hair.

Should he talk to the therapist again? Ask her to resume the sessions they had stopped over the summer? It would cost, of course, particularly as he was trying to save to take her away somewhere special next year when it became easier to travel.

He went out into the hall and put on his jacket. Just as he was about to shout up once more, she appeared at the top of the stairs.

'My period's started,' she announced calmly.

Chapter Nineteen

He parked outside the coroner's office in his favourite place. Favourite because it was free, not for any other qualities.

He'd taken Eve to school that morning after asking her typical dad questions.

'Is there anything I can do?'

'Anything I can buy?'

'Do you want a day off school?'

Finally, she had rolled her eyes and turned to him in the car. 'Listen, Dad, it's no big deal. It's a period, not the end of the world. And no, I don't need anything. Maisie had hers three months ago and she gave me some pads, so don't worry. Can we listen to Olivia Rodrigo now?'

She took his phone and linked it to the car stereo. Soon the piano sounds of 'Drivers License' filled the car.

Ridpath had been totally blindsided by this news. Of course, he knew it was going to happen someday, but he hadn't expected it to be so soon. Didn't girls normally get their first period around fourteen years old?

He realised then how little he knew about periods and what girls went through. And not for the first time wished Polly were still there to handle it.

'Right, Dad, we're here.' She leant over and kissed him on the check. 'Listen, it's no big deal, OK? We've covered all the details in biology so I know what's going on with my body.' Then she giggled like the young girl he had once known. 'Just enjoy a few mood swings for the next couple of years. Till all the hormones settle down.'

Now, as he walked up the stairs to the coroner's office, he realised he'd better google what was happening to his daughter pretty quickly. Either that or ask somebody who would know. But who?

'Morning, Ridpath.'

Sophia was sitting at her desk, holding out a Starbucks cup for him. 'A latte with an extra shot. I know you like it a bit stronger.'

'Thanks, how much do I owe you?'

'Forget it, you can buy this afternoon. And don't worry.'

'What?'

'About Eve getting her period.'

Why did he always feel he was surrounded by women who knew more about what was going on in his life than he did?

'How do you know?'

'She texted me before she went into school. Said you weren't handling it very well. "Looked a bit lost" were her exact words.'

She'd texted Sophia? When did those two get in touch with each other? 'I'm handling it fine and don't look at all lost,' he said defensively.

'Don't worry, my dad wouldn't know what a period was if it shook his hand, did a curtsey and said how do you do. I've asked her to call me if she needs anything. I hope that's OK?'

Ridpath relaxed. 'Great, Sophia, it would be good for Eve to have another woman to talk with rather than a...'

'Clueless dad?'

He smiled. 'Exactly.'

'And Mrs Challinor would like to see you before her inquest starts.'

'Did she say why?'

Sophia shook her head. 'Perhaps Eve has been texting her too?'

Did everybody know what was going on except him?

Chapter Twenty

'If it's about Eve, I think I've got it under control.'

Mrs Challinor looked at him quizzically.

'Her period. She got it this morning.'

'Oh, really? It's no big deal. Get her to call me if she needs any advice. No, I want an update on the Holdsworth case.'

The coroner was already sitting behind her desk, her pen poised above an empty white pad.

Ridpath sat down. 'I'm afraid the investigation may not be as straightforward as I hoped.'

The coroner elegantly raised one eyebrow. 'Oh?'

'The police statements and those of the custody officers all seem consistent as to what happened and when it happened.'

'And what was that?'

Ridpath checked his notes from last night. 'Holdsworth was brought to Redbury station at 3.25. He was booked in and strip searched...'

'Why?'

'It's normal in drug cases. Addicts or dealers find the strangest places to hide their merchandise. After the search, he was placed in Cell 3, but he tripped up and hit his head on the bunk, causing a subdural haematoma. He collapsed in the cell and was found at 6.30 in the morning.'

'Why wasn't he discovered earlier?'

'Apparently the CCTV in the cell failed at 4.35.'

'So he should have been regularly checked.'

'The duty sergeant ordered those checks and, according to the duty log, it was during one of them he was found unconscious on the floor.'

Mrs Challinor was quiet for a while. 'Subdural haematoma can take a few hours to produce a reaction. The victim is usually not aware of any pain, and they normally become dizzy and increasingly confused before collapsing. Is this the conclusion of the pathologist?'

'Exactly. In his words, death was the result of a subdural haematoma caused by a fall.'

'So what's the problem?'

'There are two. Firstly, the pathologist was Harold Lardner...'

Mrs Challinor's eyes rolled. 'I thought we'd seen the last of Mr Lardner.'

'...and there was a toxicology report showing a large dosage of diamorphine in Holdsworth's bloodstream.'

'How did it get there?'

'Nobody knows.'

'Didn't the custodial sergeant or officers notice he was under the influence?'

'There is nothing in their reports.'

'Check it out and get a second opinion on the post-mortem. With Lardner involved we can't be too careful.'

'Already done. I've asked Dr Schofield to give an opinion. There is another problem, though. Holdsworth's body has already been cremated...'

'So the report is the only record we have.' The coroner was as sharp as ever. 'Any procedural problems with the custody operation?'

'None I can see. The procedures seem to have been followed to the letter.'

'Good, we will call the officers as witnesses.' She glanced at her watch. 'Anything else?'

'I went to see the family yesterday. Or at least I met the mother. The wife has apparently remarried and left to live in the south.'

'Follow up on her, Ridpath. Make sure she is aware she can attend the inquest if she wants.'

'Will do, Coroner. But I understood from Mrs Holdsworth that his wife was already estranged from her husband before the incident at Redbury station. He had been living at home for about six months before his death.'

'Nonetheless, she should be given the option to attend.'

'I'll follow up.'

'How was the mother?'

'Obviously missing her son. She has retained legal counsel, or at least legal counsel has been retained for her.'

The coroner opened the file. 'The legal counsel is a Mr Davies?'

'Correct.'

'He represented the family during the preliminary hearings. He has already been in touch with me numerous times regarding anonymity of police witnesses, the post-mortem findings, the dates for the inquest and a whole host of other issues. He's nothing if not persistent. He even called me this morning complaining you had been speaking to his client without informing him.'

'We were merely advising Mrs Holdsworth on the procedures of the inquest...'

Mrs Challinor held up her hand to stop him speaking. 'Just let him know from now on. I have a feeling this case is going to become even more difficult.'

'Why?'

'Late yesterday evening, a Ms Angela Dexter called me from the public relations department of the police.'

'I'm meeting her this morning to take a look around Redbury nick.'

'Not a pleasant woman. She was questioning your appointment to investigate the case.'

'But I'm the coroner's officer...'

'And also a serving police officer.'

'But most coroner's officers are also serving police. Does that mean we should never investigate if mistakes are made by a force?'

'I thought it would not be a problem, but apparently I was mistaken. I have scheduled a call with the assistant chief constable for operations this morning. The force has said the old days of a lack of transparency are over. We'll see if they deliver on their words.'

'Can you also ask him about cooperation with my investigation? Sergeant Saunders has already told me he is not interested in being a witness.'

'Doesn't Sergeant Saunders realise we can subpoena him to appear, arresting him if necessary?'

'I'd see it as a last resort, Coroner. I'd like to make the investigation more informal at the moment. Everybody seems so defensive about what happened that night.'

'I'll talk to the ACC. But there is one other thing, Ridpath.' She paused for a moment, considering her words. 'If you would still prefer to recuse yourself from this investigation, I will understand. It is unlikely to make you any friends within GMP.'

Ridpath thought about his meeting yesterday with Mrs Holdsworth. Once again her words came back to him. 'I think I was the only person who cared about him in the whole world.'

'That's fine, Coroner. Somebody has to discover the truth in this case. I'd rather it was me than anybody else.'

'I was hoping you'd say those words, Ridpath.' She glanced at her watch. 'I have to prepare now for the inquest.'

Ridpath stood up.

'Let me know how you proceed. Something tells me this is going to be one of our more difficult cases.'

Chapter Twenty-One

Sergeant Tony Saunders flashed his card at the policeman on duty and walked through the security gates.

Another waste of a day.

Three years he'd been doing this. Clocking on every morning and working through the day before going home at six p.m. on the dot.

Down the stairs, to his basement room, joining the other lads who, for one reason or another, were on restricted duties.

At first, he'd been collating crime statistics for the police divisions. Number of burglaries, car thefts, assaults, rapes and every other transgression of the law. It had been routine but boring work. And then they'd introduced iOPS, the new police operations system, and for the last two years he'd been doing data entry by hand, transcribing arrest details, criminal information and ongoing investigations into a computer system that steadfastly refused to accept it.

It was like pushing shit uphill.

Even worse, they could never catch up. The backlog was just too great and the amount of new information arriving every day just added to the total sense of bewilderment.

How could they have got it so wrong?

Idiots.

And here he was, one of the best sergeants in the force, stuck behind a desk in a basement, staring at a flickering light on a computer screen.

He worked for a couple of hours until his eyes began to hurt from staring at the lines.

'I'm going for a fag, Dennis. I'll be back when I'm back.'

The fat sergeant on another table just nodded his head. He was reading the *Racing Post*, probably working out how he was going to lose his salary.

Saunders put on his coat, walked back up the stairs and out through the front door into the fresh air. Or what passed for fresh air in Manchester: a combination of car exhaust, rotting vegetation, decaying leaves and damp.

He turned right, past the roundabout, and left on Church Lane into Moston Vale, hands deep in his pockets, head bowed looking down at the ground.

He often came here. A bare, windswept heath sandwiched between industrial estates. Rubbish from fly-tipping was strewn on the left that wasn't there yesterday. Must have dumped it last night. It would be easy to find out who, just check the security cameras. But nobody could be bothered; it was just too much hassle.

Three years he'd been doing this walk. Nobody ever noticed he wasn't there, nobody cared he was gone. Three years walking the bare paths of this heath, waiting for the bosses to announce his restricted duties were over.

He'd been through a Professional Standards review, an IOPC investigation, a decision by CPS in York and passed them all with flying colours.

All because some drug dealer had died in a cell in 2018.

What a joke.

His performance that night had been exemplary. Professional Standards had told him before they'd written their report exonerating him of any wrongdoing.

Now, some pillock from the coroner's office was checking up on him. Even worse, he was a copper. Three years and there were still more investigations going on.

Well, he'd put Ridpath in his place. He still had friends, even if they hadn't been a great help so far. Time to call a few favours in.

All he wanted was to get back to work, doing what he loved.

Being a copper.

Well, Mr Arsehole Ridpath, you don't know what's going to hit you; a ton of shit is coming your way.

Enjoy the ride.

He pulled up his mobile and made the call.

Chapter Twenty-Two

Redbury nick was not the prettiest police station on earth. It had been built in the 1990s, when function had triumphed over form in police circles. Constructed out of the reddest of red brick, it stood out like an inflamed boil against the white pebble-dashed houses of the rest of the suburb.

Ridpath parked at the back of the station and, as he didn't know the code for the rear door, walked around to the main entrance to get in.

A sergeant was behind the desk and a young couple sat in the lobby, obviously waiting for a relative or friend to be released after a night in the cells.

'I'm here to see Ms Dexter from the PR department.'

'And you are?'

'Thomas Ridpath, from the coroner's office.' He'd decided to use this title rather than his police rank as he was working for the coroner on this case.

'Right-o, she's with the inspector at the moment. If you want to sit down, I'll give her a tinkle.'

Ridpath sat next to the couple, hearing their whispers as he waited.

'Do you think they found the stuff?'

'I dunno, probably, otherwise why arrest him?'

'What if he gives us away?'

'He won't, Nick is straight, he won't say a word.'

The man noticed Ridpath was listening and stared at him. 'Oi, big ears, keep your nose out, OK?'

Ridpath ignored him.

'I was talking to you, big ears, you gone deaf or something, mate?'

'Listen, I'm not your mate, and I'm not big ears. Unless you'd like to add assault to the charge of drug dealing, I'd keep my mouth shut.' He whirled his hand to indicate the police station around them, pulling

out his warrant card. 'Not the best place to assault a police officer…
mate.'

The man went pale and turned away. At the same time, the
door opened and a woman's face appeared in the entrance. 'Thomas
Ridpath?'

He stood up.

'If you'd like to come through, I'll show you around.'

The woman didn't offer to shake his hand or introduce herself.
Instead, she clasped her clipboard to her chest and walked ahead of
him to enter the police station.

'I believe you want to see the custody suite where the incident
occurred, and the custody reception?'

'It's where I'd like to start. I'd also like to interview the head of the
station, Inspector Bob French. I think he was the duty inspector on
the night of the death in custody.'

'I'm afraid he's not available. Operational issues.'

They passed an open door with a uniformed man sitting at a desk.
For a second he glanced up, and then looked down again.

'This is the custody area. It's not the most modern but it's not the
oldest in our portfolio. There are the usual facilities: a holding room,
a medical examiner's room, a booking suite and behind that door, the
cells themselves.'

'I am acquainted with custody suites, Ms Dexter.'

She looked at him out of the corner of her eye. 'You are a serving
police officer, aren't you, Detective Inspector?'

Was she reminding of his rank and position in the force?

'It wouldn't do to rock the boat too much, would it? Career-wise
I mean.'

He ignored her, consulting his notes instead.

'So according to the files, in the early hours of February 21, 2018,
Ben Holdsworth was booked in here by Sergeant Saunders at 3.25,
taken to be searched at 3.40 and placed in Cell 3 ten minutes later?'

The woman looked at the clipboard. 'That seems to be correct.'

'Sergeant Saunders noticed the CCTV in the cell had failed at
approximately 4.35, ordering manual checks on Mr Holdsworth.
There is no record of these checks taking place until 6.30, when the
detainee was found to be unconscious and lying on the floor of his cell.
The medical officer was summoned and found him unresponsive. An

ambulance was called which took him to Salford General Hospital, where he was declared dead at 7.35.'

She glanced up from her clipboard. 'Those facts seem to tally with my timeline.'

'What was the exact time the CCTV in Cells 3 and 4 failed?'

She shook her head. 'I don't have that information.'

'Did the CCTV fail elsewhere in the station?'

'Sorry, I don't know.'

Ridpath frowned. 'Where is the CCTV equipment kept?'

'I don't know that either.'

'Well, can you give me a copy of all the CCTV recordings for the evening?'

'I'm sorry, those are the property of GMP. I believe they are now with the Professional Standards Department.'

'I'd like to see them.'

She smiled briefly. 'Not my department, I'm afraid. You'll have ask them.'

So that was going to be the tactic. Stall, stall and stall again.

'Can I see Cell 3?'

'It's this way.' She keyed in a code on the number pad on the wall. The door buzzed and she pushed it open. Inside, the civilian custody officer came out from the search room. Ms Dexter walked past him without acknowledging his presence and pointed to a long row of heavy, blue-painted doors on either side of a lined corridor. Each door had its number in yellow and a small window for looking inside.

Throughout the place, the stench of stale human sweat hung like a shroud. No amount of cleaning or mopping could ever remove that smell; it was imprisoned in every nook and cranny, injected into each brick.

'There are ten cells in this facility. Two are currently occupied. Cell 3 is on the left...'

Ridpath glanced into Cell 1. A young man was sitting on the concrete ledge that passed for a bed. His head was in his hands and he looked drained. On the walls around him people had scrawled graffiti. In the corner, an old, stained toilet could be seen.

Ridpath turned back to talk to the custody officer. 'Were you on duty in February 2018?'

The man shook his head. 'I've only worked in this nick for six months.'

Ms Dexter interposed herself between both of them. 'Mr Ridpath, you are only allowed to view the custody facilities, not talk to any of the officers. If you want to interview anybody, a request must be put in writing to my superior.'

'Or I could give them a subpoena.'

She smiled again. 'You could do that, but I wouldn't advise such a course of action.'

'When I want advice from a PR person, I will pay for it, Ms Dexter.'

'Thank you. You still cannot talk to any of the officers in this facility.'

'But I can see the cells?'

'No, you can see Cell 3.' She stuck out her arm, pointing him towards the cell.

'The door is open,' said the custody officer, 'and I cleaned it this morning.'

Ridpath walked to the cell and looked inside. It was almost perfect. There was no graffiti; the concrete ledge serving as a bed had a thin blue mattress that looked brand new. The toilet was clean and unstained. In the top corner, a small camera showed a red light indicating it was working.

'Is this how the cell looked on the night of the death?'

'I believe so.'

'It hasn't been changed?' He walked over and touched the walls. The paint and plaster work looked brand new. 'Has it been painted?'

'I don't have that information.'

He bent down and examined the wall above the concrete bed. There was no indent in it. Again, it had been freshly plastered and painted. 'The deceased, Mr Holdsworth, struck his head against this wall. The pictures taken at the time showed a depression in the plaster. Yet this wall has none.'

'I have no information on that subject.'

He pointed at the camera high on the wall. 'Is it the same camera, or has a new system been installed?'

'I have...'

'...no information on that subject.' Ridpath finished her sentence for her.

'If there is nothing else, Mr Ridpath, I need to return to my office. It's a very busy time for us, what with the arrival of the new chief constable.'

'A new chief, but the same old behaviour.'

'I don't know what you mean.' Her phone rang and she checked the screen. 'I need to take this, it's the assistant chief.'

'Say hello to him from me.'

She turned away and walked out of the cell. Ridpath could hear her voice become softer, more emollient. 'Good morning, Assistant Chief Constable, how can I help you?'

Ridpath checked the cell. The visit had been a waste of time. It had obviously been completely renovated since 2018. No doubt the argument would be that it was the normal updating of facilities. He wondered if the renovation had happened before or after the investigation by the IOPC.

Ms Dexter's voice was loud and clear in the hallway. 'Of course, Assistant Chief. I will. Yes, I do understand. Thank you for calling.'

There was silence for a long time.

Finally, she appeared in the doorway of the cell.

'That was the ACC.'

'So I gathered.'

'I'm to help you in any way I can. Give you every assistance necessary in the matter of Mr Holdsworth's death in custody. There is to be full disclosure to the coroner's office.'

Mrs Challinor must have made her call already.

'I thought that had always been the case,' Ridpath said archly.

Chapter Twenty-Three

'What would you like to know?'

Ridpath smiled. 'First, I'd get out my pen and pad. Ready? I need all the CCTV footage from February 21 and the day before, plus the name of the company who installed and maintained it.'

'Like I said, the footage has already been sent to Professional Standards.'

'But you kept a copy, didn't you?'

She paused for a moment, her pen hovering over the pad. 'I'll have to check.'

'Next, I'd like a list of everybody who was in the station that night. Detainees, staff, everybody.'

She nodded, scribbling furiously on her pad.

'And I'd like you to arrange interviews for me with the duty inspector, Sergeant Saunders, and the custody officers on duty.'

'Saunders won't do it. He's already informed us he has had enough of the investigations.'

'If he doesn't, the coroner will subpoena him. It won't look good on his files to be dragged kicking and screaming to an inquest.'

'I'll let him and his union rep know.'

Ridpath leant forward and said quietly, 'Please tell him I'm here to help. I just want to find out what happened. I'm not here to hang him out to dry.'

'Anything else?'

'I want all the files from the evening: charge sheets, duty log, timelines, rosters, everything, all the documents not in the IOPC file sent to the coroner.'

She nodded. 'Is that it?' She held up her notes. 'All this will take time to collect.'

'You didn't do it for IOPC?'

'Not really, they never asked.'

'Did they even visit the station?'

She shrugged her shoulders. 'Perhaps, I don't know.'

Ridpath stared into the cell. It would have been a pointless trip anyway. The cell had been refurbished extensively since the death. Why didn't they do the other cells too?

'Anything else?'

'No, that about covers it, but if the duty inspector is available right now, I'd like to have a chat with him.'

'He wasn't here that night. Didn't come in until 7.30. Holdsworth had already been taken to the hospital.'

'No matter, I'd like to see him.' Ridpath smiled. *Time to wind up, Ms Dexter.* 'Tell Bob it's Ridpath. I'm sure he'll see me.'

'I'll go and check.'

She wandered off, leaving Ridpath alone in the corridor leading to the cells. The custody officer was still standing there.

'You know Terry Rodgers, the custody officer that night, hasn't worked for GMP since.'

'Since?'

'The death in the cell.'

'You know him?'

'He's a good man. We used to do the same shifts together. He liked working nights because he was kept busy.'

'Do you know where I can get hold of him?'

The man nodded.

Ridpath reached into his jacket pocket. 'Give him my card and ask him to call me?'

'He's been told not to talk to anyone about the night. We all have.'

'Told? By who?'

'The company.'

'Get him to call me. Do you also know the other custody officer, Lucas Harvey?'

The man nodded. 'Not well, though. He won't ever talk to you.'

'Why not?'

'He's dead, in a car crash.'

Angela Dexter arrived back and the custody officer moved away. 'He has ten minutes between meetings. He'll see you now.'

Ridpath followed the woman out of the cells, turning back just as he was about to go through the security door to talk to the custody officer.

'Just one more thing. Does the CCTV fail often?'
The man shook his head. 'It never fails. The system is new.'
'When was it installed?'
'Last year, I think. Before my time.'

Chapter Twenty-Four

'Hello, Bob.'

The uniformed inspector looked up from his desk. It was as tidy as Ridpath expected.

'Hi there, Ridpath, long time, no see.'

Ridpath held out his hand and Bob French stood up, shaking it warmly. They had both been on a sergeants' course together at the training centre in Edgeley Park. Ridpath had liked Bob's sardonic humour. He didn't seem to take the job too seriously. Probably his way of coping with the pressures.

'I heard you were busy. Operational issues.' Ridpath stared pointedly at Ms Dexter.

'Nah, same shit, different day. Always happy to see you.'

Ms Dexter had the decency to blush vividly.

Bob French pointed at the seat in front of him. 'How can I help?'

Ms Dexter hovered nervously behind them. The head of the station stared at her. 'Why don't you get yourself a coffee from the machine?'

'I'm supposed to be here with Inspector Ridpath all the time.'

Ridpath noticed she was suddenly using his proper title. The ACC must have read her the riot act.

'Don't worry, myself and Ridpath are old mates. Go and get yourself a coffee.'

It was said casually, but Ridpath could hear the command behind the words. Ms Dexter heard it too. She held up her phone. 'Call me if you need me.'

'I won't... need you. Close the door on your way out.'

French watched as the woman left.

'You know, I remember the days when we didn't have corporate shills hovering over us constantly, making sure we toed the party line.'

'I don't think you were ever very good at it anyway, Bob.'

'Probably why they sent me out here to the arsehole of the world.'

'How long have you been here?'

'Six years, last Monday. The lads gave me a cake and a get out of jail free card. They've got a sense of humour... allegedly. How have you been? Still inspector too? What happened? Who did you rub up the wrong way?'

'Nobody. I got ill.'

French looked at him. 'I heard it was cancer.'

'Myeloma, to be exact. Cancer of the bone marrow. I'm in remission now, though, don't even have to go to hospital for check-ups any more.'

'Probably safer, what with Covid and all that malarkey.'

'How's Helen?'

Ridpath liked French's wife. A no-nonsense Yorkshire woman who called a spade a shovel and had an infectious laugh.

'We divorced four years ago. She's moved back to Leeds with the kids.'

A silence descended on them. Ridpath didn't want to ask why; he knew the answer already. The job wasn't the best advert for marriage. Few couples could withstand the strain of the long and unpredictable hours, shift work, and the constant uncertainty.

'I heard about Polly.'

Ridpath nodded. He didn't want to go there. Not here, not now.

'A lovely woman. A shame. How's Eve handling it?'

'Pretty well, too well – she's a good kid.'

Another silence slipped between the two of them. It was like the past was both present in the room and gone forever at the same time.

French suddenly sat forward. 'But you're not here to chat about old times, Ridpath, are you?'

'Not really.'

'I've been told to cooperate with you fully. Ask away.'

'You know I'm working for the coroner now?'

'I had heard.'

'There's an inquest into the death of Ben Holdsworth.'

'February 21, 2018. Not a date I'll forget.'

'You weren't on duty?'

The man shook his head. 'I was on call in case something happened, but I wasn't at the station.'

'When did you learn about Holdsworth's death?'

'Tony Saunders called me at roughly 6.50. The log will give you the exact time.'

'And you came in?'

'As quickly as I could, but Holdsworth had already been sent to the hospital. The duty doctor arranged the ambulance.'

'Who went with him?'

'Lucas Harvey, one of the custody officers.'

'What did you do?'

'I followed procedure. We cordoned off the cell to preserve the scene, checked the other prisoners were OK and reported the incident up the chain of command.'

'Other prisoners?'

'There were two other men in the cells that night.'

Ridpath frowned. Why had nobody mentioned this before?

'Who were they?'

Bob French sat back, opening his arms wide. 'Give me a break, Ridpath, it was over three years ago. I can't remember every lowlife we bang up in the cells.'

Ridpath chuckled. 'Yeah, sorry, stupid question. It will be in the arrest logs, won't it?'

'Probably, we keep good records here. Remember what we were taught. Cover your arse...'

'Or somebody will kick it for you.'

'Charlie was the best, wasn't he? Another one gone to the great beat in the sky.' Bob French stared out of the window for a long time.

Ridpath changed the subject. 'And after you cordoned off the cell?'

French seemed to come back to life. 'You know what it's like. Everything was taken out of my hands. I gave a statement to Professional Standards and the IOPC later but neither followed up on it.'

'What do you mean?'

'I mean I was asked once about the timeline of events, but that was all. You know the IOPC investigators, none of them have worked in the police, the questions were fairly basic. Professional Standards weren't much better.'

'For example?'

'Same as you asked. What time was I called? When did I arrive? They seemed more concerned the events were properly documented than anything else. And when the post-mortem revealed he had died from a bang on the head, they went through the footage and found the moment when he fell against the wall in the cell.'

'I saw the still pictures in the post-mortem report.' Then something occurred to Ridpath. 'You said the CCTV was checked after the post-mortem report?'

'I think so.'

'So why were the stills with the report?'

French shrugged his shoulders. 'I guess they must have sent them to the pathologist.'

'Who is "they"?'

The inspector shrugged his shoulders. 'I dunno, I was kept well away from the custody suites.'

'I don't know either, Bob.' Ridpath chewed the end of his pen. 'One last thing. The procedure for checking the cells was once every thirty minutes if the CCTV wasn't working. Why wasn't this followed?'

'You'll have to ask Tony Saunders or the custody officers. All I know is the CCTV was working when I got to the station at 7.30.'

'What?'

'The CCTV in Cell 3 was working; I checked the monitor myself.'

Chapter Twenty-Five

Ridpath decided to grab a very late lunch, more of an afternoon tea, before his meeting at 4.30 in the morgue with Dr Schofield.

He headed into town and one of his favourite cafes on Deansgate. He'd discovered it years ago when he was a young PC in the centre of Manchester. Now, whenever he wanted some comfort food, Katsouris was where he went.

It was located in one of those old Victorian buildings which used to be so common in Manchester but were now becoming a rarity. Inside, the building was nothing particularly notable, but as soon as he wrapped his mouth around the Italian Special, he knew it was worth making the trip.

Not the half-heartedness of the half sandwich for him. Rather, he went for the full Monty – spicy pepperoni salami with roasted red peppers, mushrooms, tomatoes, topped with melted cheese – knowing it would take him a while to fight his way through the whole thing but he would love every second of the assault on his tastebuds. Finish it off with a Greek latte and sit back afterwards, hands clasped across extended stomach safe in the knowledge all was well with the world.

Even if it wasn't.

He allowed himself half an hour of bliss and another latte before his mind turned back to the case. He'd hated interviewing Bob French this morning. Somehow, it felt like he was betraying an old friendship, calling into question those bonds of camaraderie built up over years of struggling in the fight to hold back the darker side of the human psyche.

True, he hadn't seen him for years, didn't even know he was divorced, but the ties that bind were still there.

It seemed that after the post-mortem result came in, everybody just went through the motions. Professional Standards. IOPC, even the CPS accepted the findings of Harold Lardner without question.

Maybe because it absolved them of all blame. But why hadn't they checked up on the toxicology results? Why had none of the custody officers spotted Ben Holdsworth was as high as a cloud?

And what about Tony Saunders, why was he so defensive? Did he know Ben Holdsworth? He'd arrested him twice already. But the duty log and the custody record showed he acted according to the rules and procedures designed by the College of Policing.

Was he hiding something, or was he just tired of the constant investigation of the events of one night three years ago, and of living under a cloud ever since?

The CCTV was another problem. According to Saunders and the custody officers, it had malfunctioned. But Bob French said it was operational when he arrived at the station. Surely it wouldn't stop working and start again for no reason?

He wrote his next steps in his notebook.

Talk to Dr Schofield re. post-mortem.

Follow up with Angela Dexter.

Interview Tony Saunders. Detailed timeline of the events?

Interview CCTV supplier. Why had it stopped working?

Interview the custody officer, Terry Rodgers. Why hadn't he noticed Holdsworth was on drugs?

Interview duty doctor, Bourke. What did he see?

A lot of interviews to conduct. Then it struck him.

He flicked back through his notes. Were there other people in the cells? Had anybody spoken to them? And if not, why not? He wrote one more note.

Find the other detainees and question them.

For a moment, a strange feeling washed over Ridpath. There, in a crowded cafe in the middle of a bursting city, he felt totally and hellishly alone.

He was certain nobody would lift a finger to help him in this investigation.

He was on his own, and it wasn't a good place to be.

Chapter Twenty-Six

The morgue was as unwelcoming as ever.

Not that Ridpath ever wanted a warm welcome from such a cold place; it was almost a contradiction in terms. But he would have liked something, anything, to soften the glacial sterility of the place.

Instead everything worked to emphasise it. The strong smell of disinfectant with a top note of decay suffused the place, seeping into every wall. The walls themselves were white-tiled and shiny as death, reflecting back light tinged with ineffable sadness. The furniture, in Scandinavian blonde woods devoid of personality and exuberance, was the very essence of joylessness.

But it was the people who worked in the place Ridpath found the hardest to handle. It was as if they floated rather than walked, their long white coats hiding any sense of shape or form, their pasty skins absent of colour, as if being born albino was a prerequisite for employment.

Only Dr Schofield with his high voice – the result of a boyhood encounter with hypogonadism – possessed any real life.

He was approaching Ridpath now, his plastic apron covered in blood and gore. 'Detective Inspector, how nice to see you.'

'I wish I could say the same.'

He laughed. 'I forget you don't enjoy my office.' He twirled his hands, removing his plastic gloves. 'Not everybody appreciates the need for cleanliness. I must admit I find it rather soothing.'

'It takes all sorts.'

'It does indeed. Now, if you'll follow me, we can discuss the post-mortem Sophia sent me yesterday evening.'

He pushed his way through the double doors leading to the mortuary itself. Two gurneys covered in green sheets with vaguely human shapes lying on them were parked in the corridor.

'It would seem the mortuary is full at the moment. We're still getting deaths from Covid, you know, even though the government insists the danger from the disease is over.'

'Never trust what politicians tell you, my mother used to say. If their lips move they are lying. And if their lips aren't moving, they are thinking about lying.'

'A dark view of our politicians from your mother, but not without an element of truth.'

They approached a small office. Schofield sat down behind his cluttered desk and switched on his computer. The top of the desk was covered in files, notes, a model of a human hand, more files, a plaster skull with the word FRED written across the forehead, articles printed from specialist pathology magazines and the remains of yesterday's sandwich.

'Right, where is it? Here we are. A post-mortem carried out by my famous, or shall I say infamous, predecessor, Dr Lardner.'

'Did you notice anything unusual about the post-mortem, Doctor?'

Ridpath asked a neutral question – or at least neutral in terms of conclusions; merely asking about something unusual suggested it may have existed. It was the only hint Ridpath would give.

'Other than the speed with which it was performed – just over five hours after the demise of the deceased – the post-mortem seems pretty straightforward. A man suffers a subdural haematoma, apparently from a fall, lapses into unconsciousness three hours later and dies in hospital, but...'

'But what?' Ridpath leant forward.

'There are a couple of things that seem... unusual.' A long pause. Dr Schofield always enjoyed the dramatic side of revealing his findings. He would have made a fine Richard III. 'We have still images of the fall.' He pressed a few keys on the computer and the stills from the post-mortem appeared. 'See, here he appears to stumble, falls across the bed and strikes his head on the wall, sitting upright moments later and shaking it.'

'But...?'

'But I'd like to see the CCTV footage, rather than a series of still images. I have no sense of how hard his head struck the wall, nor of his behaviour immediately afterwards.'

'I have requested the footage from GMP. I'll send it to you as soon as I receive it myself.'

'Perhaps I should wait to see it before voicing my concerns.'

'Please tell me now, Doctor; it could save time in my investigation.'

'The position of the blow to the head as a result of the fall seems wrong. If one looks at this still image, he seems to strike his head on the pterion just above the ear.' He picked up the skull marked FRED and pointed to an area on the cranium. 'But he also indicates another mark on the skin over the occipital bone, around the small protrusion called the external occipital protuberance, just about... here.' He prodded FRED's skull at the back of the head. 'Now, it is here Lardner indicates he found the subdural haematoma, in the occipital lobe. There seems to be no haematoma in the frontal or limbic lobes. These haematomas do not necessarily have to occur in the same place as the blow, but it is rare for them to travel so far to a completely different part of the brain.'

'What are you suggesting, Doctor?'

'I wonder if there was another cause for the subdural haematoma, rather than striking his head.'

'What do you mean?'

Dr Schofield paused for a long time and then held out his arms. 'You must understand this is a hypothesis only, Detective Inspector. Without the body to examine, we will never know. There just seem to be inconsistencies in Dr Lardner's notes, almost as if...'

'Go on, Doctor...'

'As if he had reached his conclusion before performing the post-mortem examination.'

Ridpath thought about what the doctor had just said. Had Lardner decided it was an accident before the post-mortem? Why?

'There is one other thing leading me to this conclusion. The toxicology report produced six weeks later showed the presence of diamorphine, heroin probably, in the victim's system. From the concentration of the drug, it may have been the cause of death.'

'But Lardner stated quite clearly he thought the heroin may have affected his behaviour, but was not the cause of death.'

'I believe he got it the wrong way round. I believe the drug over-dose was the cause of death and the subdural haematoma a symptom of toxic brain syndrome rather than a reaction to striking his head.'

'Toxic brain syndrome?'

'When a person overdoses, there is a possibility of a cardiac arrest, or the brain reacting to the level of drug in the system.' Dr Schofield checked his notes. 'In this case, 1200 milligrams. Enough in my experience to kill a man.'

'But I thought addicts can get used to high doses, their bodies adapt to the drug.'

'But Lardner's post-mortem states he found no evidence of long-term drug use. No needle marks in the arms, thighs or between the toes and no trace elements in the hair samples. The only possible injection site was in the crook of the elbow.'

'Let me get this right. You think the heroin was the cause of death?'

'At these levels, I do.'

Ridpath made a note in his book. He then paused for a long time before asking the next question. 'If the levels were so high, wouldn't they have had an effect on the man's speech and his demeanour?'

'Most definitely at this concentration.'

'But nobody noticed he was under the influence of drugs.'

'Strange, I would have thought the effects would have been obvious: dilated pupils, slurred speech, delayed reaction times, attention deficiencies. They should have been obvious to anybody, but particularly to a policeman trained to look for them.'

'According to the arrest report, nobody noticed anything when he was booked in.'

'Perhaps he injected the drug in the cell after he was cautioned?'

'He was strip searched before being placed in the cell, his personal belongings and clothes removed.'

'Even stranger.'

Ridpath couldn't think of anything more to ask. It was Dr Schofield who spoke next.

'In the absence of a body, though, my review of the post-mortem is just speculation based on my experience. Without actually examining the body, which is now impossible, I could not stand up in any court and make a definitive statement on the cause of death.' He held his arms out wide. 'Sorry, I will never be able to prove what I have just told you.'

'Thank you, Doctor. I think that's my job, not yours.'

Chapter Twenty-Seven

Eve was already home when Ridpath arrived back. He'd stopped off on the way to do some shopping.

'Hiya, how was your day?'

'Same old, same old. Maisie got detention again.'

'Why?'

'Being late for a class. There's one teacher who insists everybody is sitting at their desks with their arms folded in front of them before the class begins. Maisie was in the toilet and arrived late.'

'She needs to make her timing better.'

'You can't time a pee, Dad. Especially if all the cubicles are occupied. For boys, it's so much easier.'

Ridpath remembered his own days at school. Hanging out in the outside toilets sharing a fag with Ron and Andy. The smell of the place a peculiar mixture of damp mould, sour urine, harsh tobacco and body odour. He smiled.

'It's OK for you to smile; girls have it so much tougher.'

'I wasn't smiling at... I got you some stuff.'

He held out the shopping bag. 'Some Panadol – apparently there's a special type for period pains so I got you a couple of packs of those.' He passed the boxes over. 'Now, I didn't know whether to get Tampax or pads so I got one lot of everything they had in Boots.' He pulled out eight different boxes. 'Apparently, this lot have wings like angels.'

Eve hadn't said a word so he carried on.

'I also bought a hot water bottle because Google says it can help with the pain.' He held up a pink, furry bottle in the shape of a flat fish. 'This is the only one they had, sorry.'

Eve stood up and gave him a big hug. 'Thank you, Dad, but you shouldn't have bothered. You know you don't have to worry. I had a chat with Sophia and one of the teachers. It's all going to be OK.'

He smiled awkwardly. 'I know, dads are pretty useless at times like this. But if you ever need someone to go to the shops to buy your stuff and you don't feel up to it, just let me know.'

'Thanks, Dad, that's very sweet. You sure you won't be embarrassed?'

He shook his head. 'Not at all... well, a little bit, but I'll handle it like I did today.'

She kissed him on his cheek and he noticed how tall she was becoming. How had that happened?

'There is one thing you could do for me?'

'What is it?'

'I could do with eating. I'm starving.'

'What would you like?'

'Food.'

'Could you be a bit more specific? Lasagne from the freezer?'

'Too fatty.'

'A sandwich?'

'Too many carbs.'

He opened the fridge door. 'Three-day old spaghetti?'

'Ugh...'

'How about I order McDonald's?'

She pursed her lips. 'Sounds good.'

He looked at her out of the corner of his eye. 'You having the Happy Meal?'

'*Dadddd*...'

After the delivery man had come and gone, the Big Mac and the chicken salad devoured and the wrappers thrown in the bin, Eve went back to her room to finish her homework, and Ridpath sat alone downstairs.

The case wasn't going to be easy. Dr Schofield had raised doubts about the validity of Lardner's post-mortem findings. And, while it didn't cause any questions regarding police procedures, it did seem remarkable that nobody had noticed how high on drugs Ben Holdsworth was.

Even worse, though, it destroyed the narrative created by Lardner and accepted by Professional Standards, the IOPC and the CPS. Had Ben Holdsworth died from an accidental fall, or from a drug overdose?

It was his job to find the truth.

He thought about opening the file and going through the case documents once again. But tonight he couldn't face reading witness statements or staring at pictures of a dead man.

Instead, he just wanted to sit and think, work it all out in his head.

Outside, the rain was beating against the windows. Inside the living room, the old lamp in the corner threw a vaguely comforting light behind his head and the clock ticked on, counting out the seconds and minutes of his life.

On the mantlepiece, Polly's picture stood, a stark reminder of her absence.

'She's growing up, Poll,' he said out loud. 'Too quickly. I don't know how I can handle it. It's like I want to keep her as she always was. As she was when you were alive, but I can't. I know it's stupid, Polly, but in here, it hurts.'

The picture just stared back at him.

It didn't say a word.

Chapter Twenty-Eight

In the ugly confines of the hotel room, he was starting to go stir crazy.

He watched enough telly to give him square eyes. He finished the half-bottle of vodka he'd bought from the convenience store plus three bags of salt and vinegar crisps and a packet of Maltesers.

He now felt sick.

Sick of his life.

Sick of being scared.

Sick of being on the run.

Outside his window, a late tram rattled along the line going to Ashton-under-Lyne. Beside the canal, a man walked his dog, letting it run free, intoxicated by the smells left by other dogs. A cyclist, dressed in the tightest pink, white and green gear, hurried across the road against a red light.

And here he was, stuck in the ugliest hotel in Manchester.

He didn't have to hit the bloke that night. Now, he wished he hadn't. But the man had hit on his girlfriend at work and everybody knew. If he didn't sort out his own business, pretty soon he wouldn't be able to show his face around Redbury.

He'd given him a good going over, enjoying the look on the man's face when he walloped him from behind, relishing the feel of his Doc Martens kicking the man's body and face again and again. He'd thought about taking one of his knives and slashing the man. The pretty boy wouldn't be so pretty any more, but he'd decided against it. Too much blood.

After he'd done the business, there was no point in running; everybody knew who he was. So he sat there, waiting for the police to arrive, enjoying a pint, making sure he gave them no excuse to give him a kicking.

The problem was the man was one of Delaney's lieutenants. Of course, if he had known at the time, he would never have touched him. Just held his hands up and walked away. No woman was worth any sort of trouble with Mr Delaney.

The police had come to take him to Redbury nick. He thought he'd spend the night in the cells and get released the following morning when the man didn't press charges.

But it was the wrong place, wrong time, wrong nick.

Mr Delaney had visited soon after he was released. Told him in no uncertain terms to keep his mouth shut, leave Redbury and don't ever come back.

He had to move away from the girlfriend, his friends and his manor. He'd planned to work for six months and then go to Thailand. He had a mate there, Gerry Swift, who lived in Chiang Mai. Nobody would find him there and the money he'd saved would mean he could live like a lord. But then the bloody disease had come along and everything was in lockdown. Except his job, of course; abattoir workers carried on even at the height of the troubles, no home-working for him.

Well, everybody still needed meat, didn't they?

Weirdly, though, he felt safest during this time. Nobody was on the streets and he didn't have to constantly look over his shoulder to check if anybody was following him.

It was a good time, even a great time.

Now it was all finished. He had to escape again, away from Manchester, away from it all.

If Delaney or his thugs found him, he was dead.

He didn't know if he could last in this room until Thursday, but he had to. There was no other choice.

November 3, 2021

Chapter Twenty-Nine

The morning opened bright and clear, the recent rain forgotten in the light of a brand new day. Ridpath was up early; not working on the case last night had given him a new energy.

Today was a day to crack on and get to the heart of the investigation. He didn't have any time to waste. Last night had given him time to think, work out some new angles. He really needed to see the CCTV. Where had Ben Holdsworth struck his head? And how had the custody officers missed that he had injected heroin?

Eve needed to be in school early for some assembly or other. Waking her had been like stirring Rip Van Winkle.

'Eve, we're late. You can eat the toast in the car.'

She finally dragged herself down the stairs, hair bedraggled and school uniform thrown on and nearly missing.

'I've seen more life in a zombie. Let's go.'

'At least zombies don't have to go to school at 7.30,' she grumbled.

'Perhaps you could make a movie for them. *The School of the Living Dead*. How's that sound?'

'Sounds like a great description of most of the teachers.'

'How was last night, did you sleep well?'

'Not really, but the hot water bottle helped. Well, at least it did until it went cold in the middle of the night.'

'We'll have to buy a cosy for it.'

'A what?'

'One of those things that keeps it warm longer. My mum used to knit them. I could try to knit one for you.'

She walked into the hall to get her coat, shaking her head. 'Sometimes, Dad, you amaze me. You'll be taking lessons from Tom Daley next.'

'Nah, too old to start diving off high boards.' Ridpath closed the front door behind them.

Eve shuffled zombie-like down the path. She slipped into the front seat of the car and promptly fell asleep, waking just as he pulled to a stop outside the school.

'Bye, Dad.' She leant over and kissed him.

'See you this evening. What do you want for dinner?'

'Anything… as long as it isn't human, obvs. I'm on a non-cannibal diet this week.'

With that parting wish, she opened the door, hoisted her school bag over her shoulder and slouched into school.

He watched her walk through the gates. What had happened to his little girl? He put the car in gear and drove to Stockfield.

Ridpath was surprised to find Sophia already in the office when he arrived at 8.15.

'Morning, Sophia.'

'Is it? I hadn't noticed.'

Ridpath wasn't going to be fazed by the lack of energy of both his daughter and his assistant.

'Has Angela Dexter sent anything to us?'

Sophia checked her laptop. 'Nothing so far.'

Time to put a rocket under Ms Dexter. Despite the early hour, Ridpath picked up his phone.

'Good morning, Angela. Have you sent over everything I asked for yesterday?'

Ridpath could hear the sound of a car radio playing in the background. Was she driving to work?

'I can send across a list of the people who were in the station.'

'All visitors, police and those in custody?'

'Yes, but only those who signed in, not anybody sitting in the lobby.'

'And the other things I asked for?'

A slightly sheepish voice. 'Not yet.'

'When are they coming?'

'I told you, you've asked for a lot of things. It's taking time for me to put everything together.'

'Send me what you have. What about the CCTV?'

'We're still looking for it.'

'What?'

'It seems to have been lost in transit from Professional Standards to us.'

'You must have copies; you wouldn't have sent the original files to them.'

'We're looking for those.'

'This is not good, Angela.'

'I know, I'm sorry, Ridpath, I'm doing the best I can.'

'What about the interviews?'

'I've arranged for you to meet the custody officer, Terry Rodgers, this afternoon. You'll have to see him before he starts his shift at the Trafford Centre.'

'What?'

'He's working there now, on nights.'

'Right, give me the place and time.'

'Four p.m. in the Great Hall, under the video screen.'

Ridpath wrote the details in his notebook. He normally avoided the huge shopping centre on the outskirts of Manchester. It was a place where the air was heavy with the breath of thousands of demented shoppers.

'The other custody officer, Lucas Harvey, died in a car accident in Derbyshire a year ago.'

'So I found out yesterday. Why did nobody tell me before?'

'Did you ask?'

'No, but we have sent out a subpoena to his address requesting he attend the inquest.'

Sophia was holding the letter up in front of him.

'Sorry, I've just found out myself. You still have his statement, don't you?'

There was no point in blaming Angela Dexter. He would talk to the coroner and see if Harvey's statement could be read out if necessary. 'Nothing on Tony Saunders yet?'

'We're trying to find a time.'

'Don't bullshit me, Angela. The ACC said full cooperation, remember?'

He heard her take a deep breath. 'Between you and me, he's proving difficult.'

'Right, we'll handle it differently.' Ridpath opened his diary. 'Please inform him he is to attend a formal hearing with his union rep or authorised legal representative at the coroner's office in Stockfield tomorrow at noon. Failure to attend will result in a warrant being issued for his arrest. Understood?'

'Ridpath, I...'

'Understood?'

'I'll let him know. But I think...'

Ridpath put the phone down before she could finish her sentence. He'd had enough of being jerked around by these people. There was too little time to waste. The clock was ticking and he had to move this investigation forward.

'You were harsh.'

'Was I? Time for them to do their job.'

Fifteen minutes later, he glanced at his computer. 'It seems to have worked.'

An email had arrived from Ms Dexter with three attachments: a list of people who had been in Redbury station, the name of the company who had sold and maintained the CCTV equipment for the police station and a folder full of additional arrest reports and documents from Redbury station for that day.

Sometimes playing bad cop worked.

There was also a note attached. 'Still looking for the original CCTV footage. Apparently we did not keep a copy of it. Will appraise you when we find out where it is. Regards, Angela Dexter.'

Ridpath sighed. The loss of the CCTV was far too convenient. He didn't think Ms Dexter was lying, though. The ACC instructions had been clear: to give any and all help to Ridpath's inquiries. But without the footage there wasn't a lot they could do. They would have to rely on interviews.

'Sophia, can you contact Ben Holdsworth's wife? Make sure she knows the dates and times of the inquest. Also can you arrange a time for us to see this CCTV company today?'

'Do you want me to come with you?'

'If you want.'

'Please, I need a break from numbers and stats.'

'Deaths are rising again?'

She nodded. 'Trafford, where you live, now has the highest rate of Covid transmission in England.'

Ridpath frowned. 'How? It has some of the richest areas in Manchester.'

'And some of the poorest. The transmission seems to be in schools.'

Ridpath thought immediately of Eve. Was she at risk of catching it? But at least she was fit and healthy; it shouldn't affect her too much, should it?

'Ridpath… Ridpath…'

He realised Sophia was talking to him.

'I'd catch the coroner soon. She has a local council meeting at 10.30. Initial discussions on funding arrangements for next year.'

'Do you know everything that goes on here, Sophia?'

'Not really. But the stuff I don't know isn't worth knowing anyway.'

Chapter Thirty

Sergeant Tony Saunders had just settled behind his desk and switched on his desktop computer when the phone call came.

'Good morning, Sergeant Saunders, it's Angela Dexter.'

What did she want?

'I'd just thought I'd call this morning to let you know... er...'

He could hear the nervousness, the hesitation in her voice, but he wasn't going to help her out. Best to stay silent, listen to her struggling.

'...that Detective Inspector Ridpath, the coroner's officer for East Manchester, has been on the... er... phone, this morning... er...'

He remained silent, enjoying her discomfiture.

'...er... he has requested you attend an interview at the Coroner's Court in Stockfield at noon tomorrow.'

'I ain't going.'

'Sergeant Saunders, I don't think you realise the seriousness of this situation...'

'And I don't think you realise I ain't going. Doesn't he have to give me notice with a formal letter to my solicitor and my union rep?'

'Actually, he doesn't. As a coroner's officer, he can interview any potential witnesses at an inquest...'

'I'm still not going.'

'I think you need to let me finish. If you do not attend, he is able to issue a warrant for your arrest.'

'Arrest me. You think he's got the balls?'

'It wouldn't look good if you didn't voluntarily attend the interview.'

'I don't care how it looks. I care I have now been on restricted duties for over three years.'

'I understand how frustrated you may be...'

'No you don't, you don't have a clue.'

'…as I was about to say, the ACC has made it clear in no uncertain terms that he wants full and unlimited cooperation with the coroner's inquest.'

'If he's so keen, maybe he should do the bloody interview.' Saunders slammed the phone down and stood up.

'I'm off out for a fag, Dennis,' he said to the fat PC at the next desk. 'I'll be back later.'

'They giving you grief, Tony?'

'Shitloads of it.'

'I thought you'd already been cleared?'

'So did I, Dennis, so did I.'

He took his coat from the rack and headed upstairs and out into the daylight, pulling out his mobile just as soon as he was clear of Police HQ.

'Ridpath's hassling for an interview.'

'What's he got?' the voice at the other end of the phone asked.

'I dunno. How am I supposed to know?'

'Let me handle it.' A slight pause. 'But you may need to do the interview, if only to find out what he knows.'

'But you said…'

'Let me handle it. I've managed everything else, haven't I?'

Chapter Thirty-One

After a short meeting to discuss progress with the coroner, Ridpath went back to the office and started reading the documents from Redbury station that Angela Dexter had sent him.

The first detailed the staff, detainees and visitors to the nick on the evening of 20 February and until dawn on the 21st. Ms Dexter had been diligent. For the staff of the station, including serving officers, a name and ID picture was listed. There had been twelve coppers on duty. Just four had been based in the station, with the others out patrolling the area, and returning only as they made an arrest.

The two custody officers were both listed. At least Ridpath now knew what Terry Rodgers looked like before this afternoon's meeting. Lucas Harvey was younger than he expected, far too young to lose his life in a car crash.

Ridpath turned the page and saw the custody log for Ben Holdsworth. He checked with the one in the IOPC file and they matched exactly.

He turned the next page and stopped. What was this? Other custody logs? Two other people had been detained that evening. Their mugshots stared out at him from the page. One had been arrested for assault, one for a DUI.

'Sophia, have you requested witness statements from any of these people?'

He showed her the custody logs.

She shook her head. 'Who are they?'

'Garry Abbott, arrested for assault, and Neil Mallender, detained for a DUI. Apparently, they were in the cells at the same time as Ben Holdsworth. Abbott was right next door to Holdsworth in Cell 4.'

'First I've heard of them. They weren't on the witness list IOPC sent us.'

'Strange. Surely they would have interviewed the other detainees?'

'It would seem obvious. Perhaps they couldn't find them.'

'Or they didn't want to find them?'

He read through the custody logs for each of the detainees. Saunders had been as punctilious as ever. It was almost classic custody sergeant work.

He made a decision.

'Sophia, we have work to do.'

She picked up her phone and pressed a button.

'What are you doing?'

'Recording your instructions in case I forget anything.'

'Don't people just take notes any more?'

'Hello, welcome to the twenty-first century, Mr Luddite; why take notes when you can simply play back a recording?'

Ridpath was still old school, though. Taking notes was in his DNA. For him, the simple act of processing what he had to write was a filter that helped him sort the chaff of the obvious from the wheat of the interesting.

'I want you to track down these men. Find them and arrange an interview asap. We have to work out whether they should be called as witnesses.'

He handed over the custody logs from Redbury nick. 'The person I'd most like to meet is him.'

'Garry Abbott? Why him?'

'He was in the cell next to Holdsworth when he died. Neither Professional Standards nor the IOPC bothered to talk to him, which I find a bit strange. Plus the other one was drunk when they were arrested. His memory may be tainted.'

She leant over to check the names. 'Addresses but no phone numbers. I'll have to do a bit of digging.'

'See if you can find them. If not, I'll ask Chrissy to discover the phone numbers.'

'I'll have a go first.'

'Can you get on to Angela Dexter later? Check with her the interview with Sergeant Tony Saunders is confirmed for noon tomorrow. I'd like you to sit in if you can. We'll work together tomorrow morning to prepare.'

'Will do.'

'Can you also arrange for us to go to see the CCTV company?'

'Already done. It's at two p.m. in their offices in Eccles.'

'When did you do that?'

'While you were with the coroner. I figured you'd want to see them today. You can go on to the Trafford Centre afterwards, it's near there.'

'You have my life planned out for me.'

'Somebody has to do it.'

'Finally, can you get on to Lardner's high-security prison? I want to meet him again.'

'To ask him about the post-mortem?'

He nodded. 'All the inquiries stopped as soon as people read Lardner's conclusions. Dr Schofield has reached a different conclusion. The man may have died from a heroin overdose.'

'Not a fall?' She made a moue with her mouth. 'Anything else?'

'That's it. If I think of anything, I'll let you know.'

She pressed a key on her phone and sat back. 'See, it's all there when I need to remind myself. "His master's voice in the key of G."'

Ridpath shook his head. What happened when people could no longer use their technology? Would they lose the ability to write? He'd already noticed the short forms used in texts creeping into speech. Hadn't Eve this morning used the word 'obvs' to him?

'Right, Mr Dinosaur, what do you want me to prepare for the interview with Sergeant Saunders?'

Her finger hovered over the record button on her phone again.

Ridpath sighed.

Chapter Thirty-Two

'Listen, Tony, we can't get out of it.' DI Jack Cater, Saunders' union rep, was at his most wheedling. 'We have to do the interview whether you like it or not.'

Saunders was back at his desk in the basement, on the phone again.

'And the union has no say in this?'

'Not a lot. It's a coroner's inquest.'

'Doesn't he have to give me notice?'

'I've checked, apparently not. They can subpoena you to attend interviews and the inquest, ordering your arrest if you don't comply. Here's what I suggest...'

'What?'

'We accede to his request for an interview, but we make it at Police HQ, not at the coroner's office.'

'Why?'

'We can control the interview better, not let him take too many liberties. Plus you know what it's like in an interview...'

'...always control the environment. Make the perp feel he is out of place, on your turf, make him feel uneasy.'

'Exactly. We can't stop the interview, but we can make it work for us. Listen...' Cater's voice dropped a register, '...you're a good cop, Tony, who's been dealt a rough hand, I know you've been through this countless times over the last three years, but this is the last hurdle, I promise. Just get through the inquest and you'll be back at work sooner than you think.'

'You've got it in writing?'

'Don't be silly. But I've got the nod from somebody on high. One more week, that's all it is, and you'll be back on duty just as soon as the inquest is done and dusted.' A slight pause. 'What do you say?'

'OK, I'll do it, but on one condition.'

'What?'

'Ridpath can't get away with threatening to arrest a fellow copper. It just ain't right, Jack.'

'Don't you worry. Ridpath's card is marked. There's a shitload of pain coming down the track for him. He's toast.'

'I've a better idea. Maybe he should spend three years on restricted duties like I did. See how it feels. I'm sure iOPS will still need updating for a while yet. I see it as poetic justice.'

'Not a bad idea. I'll suggest it to a few friends. But for the next day or so, you should keep your nose clean. I'll arrange the interview for two p.m. tomorrow. Do you want to meet up for lunch in the canteen to go over a few points beforehand?'

'Won't be necessary, Jack. Everything I'm going to say about that night I've already said to Professional Standards and to the IOPC. Ridpath ain't getting anything more from me.'

'Suit yourself, it's your interview.'

'That's what I intend to do, Jack. It's what I've always done.'

Chapter Thirty-Three

The offices of Securilife Services Limited were in a modern office block in the centre of Eccles. Ridpath had worked in the area one summer, doing a job which involved carrying mail from one floor to another for a large insurance company.

He had hated every second of it. Most lunchtimes were spent in a local pub playing pool and spending his meagre salary on a wonderful jukebox; Bowie, Santana, The Sensational Alex Harvey Band and Free were all played endlessly.

He walked into reception with Sophia next to him, showing his coroner's officer card to the young woman sitting at the desk. 'Here to see Mr Fellows.'

'He's expecting you.' She issued them both with ID cards and showed them through the security barriers into the main office.

Steven Fellows was waiting for them. 'Hello, sorry for the security, but we must keep up appearances.'

He held out his hand and Ridpath took it, feeling a strong grip.

'Come this way to my office. I'm afraid you'll need your cards to go through two more doors.'

They went through the security obstacle course and settled in his spacious office with a view over Eccles itself. Unfortunately, there weren't any cakes to be seen.

'Now, Mr Ridpath and Ms Rahman, how can I help the coroner's office?'

Ridpath didn't remember introducing Sophia. 'Thank you. The coroner is holding an inquest into the death in custody of a Ben Holdsworth at Redbury Police Station on February 21, 2018...'

'I'm aware of the... incident. I think everybody is. It was well publicised.'

'We'd like to ask you a few questions about the CCTV system your company installed and maintained.'

'I'm happy to answer any of your questions, provided they don't impinge on any confidential or proprietary information.'

'Of course.' Ridpath ran his fingers through his hair. 'Is it true your company provided the CCTV system for the custodial area?'

'We provided them for the whole station, but the contract wasn't renewed in 2019. For some obscure reason one of the big multinationals was chosen, even though they have a record of screwing up everything they touch. I heard unofficially the death in custody was one of the reasons we lost the contract.'

Ridpath could hear the bitterness in the man's voice.

'As you may or may not know, we are a local Manchester outfit. We're small but very good at what we do...'

'And yet you lost the contract?'

The man shrugged his shoulders. 'Nobody ever got sacked for choosing IBM.'

'There is an indication the CCTV camera in the cell was not operating correctly that evening.'

Fellows opened a file in front of him. 'Not according to my information.'

'Oh?'

'We did receive a report of a malfunction in a cell, but when our technician visited Redbury at 10.35 that day, everything was working properly and every camera in the station was operational.'

'You managed the whole system?'

Fellows leant forward. 'The whole point of having CCTV cameras in all areas is to monitor those held in police custody, and where members of the public, like solicitors, health workers, have access. But even more, it is to protect the police themselves. We pride ourselves on our equipment being state of the art...'

'But all equipment goes wrong?'

'True, but we guarantee it will be repaired and operational within twelve hours of any reported malfunction.'

'So you sent a technician that morning?'

Fellows glanced at the file. 'He arrived at 9.15 and finished his check at 10.35. Everything, including all the cameras, was functioning normally.'

'But the cell where Holdsworth died should have been a crime scene; how could he have checked the camera?'

'It's not necessary to check each individual camera. He will have run diagnostics on the system as a whole and checked the feed at the central console.'

'Which is where?'

'Next to the custody sergeant.'

Ridpath was processing this information when Sophia asked a question. 'You said you provided a complete system for the station. How many cameras were used?'

Fellows checked the figures. 'A camera in each of the cells, cameras at the front and back entrances, vehicle docking bays, the entrance to the custody suites, the custody holding area and charge desk, the detainee property store, interview rooms, fingerprint areas and breath test room. As I said, it was a complete system. The only areas where we didn't put cameras were the shower rooms, the search rooms and the staff rest areas. The cameras were linked to the panic buttons and panic strips in the holding areas and the cells.'

'What do you mean linked?'

'If someone pressed a panic button, the feed to the screens would automatically switch to the nearest camera so the custody sergeant could see what was happening. We were quite pleased with the design of the system. It meant the whole operation could work with fewer officers.'

'Technology replacing people?' asked Ridpath.

'It's the way the world's going, Mr Ridpath. There will be a billion CCTV cameras in operation around the world by the end of this year. To meet the increasing demands on police forces to maximise cell availability and minimise the workload of the custody officer, our innovative custody systems integrate all cell electronic and communication services, providing a single-screen interface for management of police custody CCTV, prison cell cameras, intercoms, custody access control, affray alarms, fire detection and lighting.'

'That sounds like a sales pitch, Mr Fellows,' said Ridpath.

'Because it is.'

'But I'd like to ask who monitors the monitors?'

The man smiled at Sophia as she finished her question. He held out his arms. 'The world is now a safer place because of CCTV. How many crimes would go undetected without it? And if you ask people, they want more, not less. They feel safer.'

Ridpath couldn't disagree. The first thing any investigating officer did these days was to check the local CCTV.

'What happens with the images you capture?'

'They are stored on disk and in the cloud for thirty-one days and then erased.'

'Why?'

'Data protection laws. They can be held longer, but most police forces destroy the images after a month.'

'But they can be held longer?'

'If a designated officer decides to keep them, they can be downloaded onto a secure file.'

'Did this happen in the Holdsworth case?'

'I'm sorry, I can't comment on individual cases, but a log is kept of all downloads of CCTV images and the officers authorised to view them. It's a decision made by the police themselves.'

'Who can authorise a download?'

'The senior investigating officer will make a request to the nominated officer for the station.'

'And in Redbury's case, who was that?'

Fellows turned over a page on a file in front of him. 'An Inspector French.'

Why hadn't Bob mentioned it when they spoke?

'But you don't keep records of the images yourselves?'

The man paused for a second before answering.

'No, we don't.'

Ridpath pressed harder. 'Are you sure, Mr Fellows? Let me remind you, if we call you as a witness to the inquest and you perjure yourself, it is an offence according to schedule six, paragraph one of the Coroners and Justice Act 2009, liable to imprisonment of not less than seven years.'

The man blanched, his eyes flickering from left to right.

'Let me repeat the question. Do you keep records of the images?'

Slowly, reluctantly he nodded. 'In this case, we did. We were not supposed to, but when the investigating officer said to the press that the CCTV wasn't working, I felt my company had to be protected.'

'So you kept a copy of the CCTV feed for the day?' asked Sophia.

'We kept a copy of the feed on our server for the week, just in case it was needed.'

'I'll need to see the feed, Mr Fellows.'

'I don't think I can give it to you. The information is confidential and you should be able to get it from the police themselves.'

'They are saying it could be lost.'

It was Mr Fellows' turn to frown. 'How could they lose the footage? It's not possible.'

'Stranger things have been known to happen. Do I really need to issue a warrant for the images, Mr Fellows? The publicity might not be helpful for a company in the security business, where so much is dependent on trust.'

Mr Fellows' face went even whiter, if that was possible. He stared down at the file in front of him and made a decision. 'I'm afraid I can't give you the code to access our server, but I'll download the images for you and put it on a separate file for you to access.'

'Just the day of the incident will be fine to begin with, Mr Fellows.'

The man nodded without looking up from his file. 'I'll do it now, if you'd like to wait.'

'One last thing. If I wanted to disable a CCTV camera for a short while, how would I do it?'

Mr Fellows' eyes focused back into the room. 'Relatively easily. A laser pointer or even an LED torch can blind the sensor on a camera. But if I were to do it, I'd use a jammer to interfere with the feed.'

'But wouldn't I have to know the frequency?'

'Not necessary – we all use the same narrow frequency band to transmit; just jam everything.'

'But wouldn't every camera be affected?' asked Sophia.

'Not if the jammer was localised and short range.'

Ridpath began packing up his folder. 'Thank you for your answers, Mr Fellows; Sophia will download the footage later today.'

'Will I be called as a witness?'

'I'm afraid it's for the coroner to decide. We'll let you know before the end of the week.'

'You know this could destroy my company.'

Ridpath didn't know what to say. For him, the truth didn't destroy anything; it made institutions, companies and people stronger. 'We'll be in touch, Mr Fellows.'

Chapter Thirty-Four

'That was interesting.'

They both stood outside the office block after the meeting with Fellows. It was at such times Ridpath craved a cigarette. A moment when the inhalation of tobacco smoke seemed, in some intangible way, to aid the thought processes.

Luckily, Sophia didn't smoke.

'Wasn't it?'

'You were hard on him.'

'He deserved it. Firstly, he downloaded confidential police information when he wasn't supposed to. Secondly, he would have lied to us and at the inquest. There was one moment when he could have gone either way. Telling the truth or hiding his secret.'

'Would you have really charged him with perjury?'

'I could have, but proving it would have been difficult. If he had lied that he didn't retain the images, we would never have been able to find them without the help of a digital investigator, and even then my bet is the passwords and location couldn't be cracked.'

Sophia held up the server address and the code to the file. 'Now we have them.'

'I'd like you to download the images before he changes his mind.'

'OK, I'll go back to the office and get started.'

'How are you getting back?'

'I'll grab an Uber.'

'I could drive you.'

'I don't think so...' She glanced at her watch. 'Your interview with Terry Rodgers starts in an hour.'

'Where does the time go? Can you follow up on Garry Abbott and the other detainees? If a jammer was used to prevent the signal from the CCTV in the cell, then there is one person who may have heard something.'

'The person in the neighbouring cell.'

'Exactly, he becomes key. Call me when you find him. If you have a problem, I'll get Chrissy involved.'

'Will do.'

Ridpath stared off into mid-air. 'A couple of other things bother me too.'

'Like?'

'Why was Abbott never interviewed by either Professional Standards or IOPC?'

'The post-mortem cleared the police and suggested an accident.'

'But even so, why wouldn't you talk to the one man who may have heard what happened?'

She shook her head. 'It seems logical.'

'It also raises another question. If a jammer was used block the CCTV in the cell, then somebody didn't want images from it to be seen.'

'And?'

'Why? What would the camera have seen that was so important to keep secret?'

'The death of Ben Holdsworth?'

Ridpath looked off into the distance before finally saying quietly, 'Not only that, but more importantly, how he died.'

Chapter Thirty-Five

After saying goodbye to Sophia, Ridpath drove to the Trafford Centre, crossing over Barton Road Swing Bridge. He was tempted to stop off at All Saints' Church and look at Pugin's architecture. He didn't consider himself a Catholic any more; a combination of his mother and the monks had beaten a belief in the religion out of him. But he still loved the atmosphere, peace and reverence of a church.

He'd always promised himself he would return to this particular one. The last time he was here, he had been working with Charlie Whittaker on the murder of Phil Marsland, a Salford gangster's son.

It was only just over three years ago, but seemed an age and half a lifetime away. Charlie had died soon after. A good cop who believed the one and only job of a detective was to put the bad guys away. It sounded trite but he believed it with every fibre of his being. Funny how the force was finally returning to Charlie's way of thinking.

His ex-boss didn't have time for management jargon: 'customers', arrest targets, feasibility studies. He had a simple mantra. 'Gather the evidence, find the buggers, make the case and put the bastards away for as long as you can.'

Ridpath was still thinking about his old boss as he strode into the cavern-like main hall of the Trafford Centre. The design was supposed to be reminiscent of an elegant ocean liner from the 1930s, but instead it more resembled a cheap version of a Busby Berkeley nightmare. An array of fast-food outlets encircled rows and rows of tables. Above his head, a large LED screen blasted out music, news and adverts, the sound harmonising with the buzz of people's voices and the ker-ching of cash registers. It was like a retail version of the *Titanic* after the iceberg had been hit, with people drowning themselves in fast food.

Terry Rodgers was already waiting for him under one of the screens. Ridpath recognised him from his picture even though the man had put on weight in the last three years. He stuck out his hand, shouting above the noise of the giant screen above their heads, 'Mr Rodgers, my name is Ridpath, from the coroner's office.'

'What?'

'Ridpath, from the coroner,' he shouted, moving closer to Rodgers. 'Can we talk somewhere else? It's so noisy here.'

As he spoke the last words, the noise from the screen suddenly stopped and his voice carried halfway across the room.

An old couple, the woman nibbling her French fries, stared at him.

'Can we go outside to talk?'

Rodgers nodded.

They passed through a marble lobby, down some steps between two fake plaster columns, copies of those found at the temple of Karnak in Thebes, and into the open air.

Outside, it was one of those wonderful November days when the remaining leaves on the trees displayed all the russet colours of autumn and the sun gave off enough heat to warm the bones of even the most dedicated shopper.

They sat on a bench facing the centre.

'I don't have long; my shift starts soon. And I've already spoken to the bloody IOPC about that night.'

'I'm from the coroner's office. There will be an inquest next week. I will decide if you are going to be called as a witness. Did you get your letter?'

'You can't force me to go to court; I'll lose a day's pay.'

'Unfortunately for you, I can. It really depends on if you are open and accurate with me now.' Ridpath let the message sink in before continuing. 'What do you remember about the night of February 20, 2018?'

He started with a general question. Let Rodgers recount it in his own words. He could prompt the details.

'The night Holdsworth died?'

Ridpath nodded.

'Not a lot. I started my shift at nine o'clock as usual. It was a quiet night, just a couple of people in the cells. Sergeant Saunders asked me to keep a special eye on one of the detainees.'

'Which one?'

'Can't remember his name. He was in Cell 4.'

'Next to Ben Holdsworth?'

The man shrugged his shoulders. 'I think so. It all happened over three years ago.'

Ridpath tried to place the man's accent. Definitely not from Manchester. Somewhere in the West Country, Bristol perhaps?

'That man, his name was Garry Abbott, what was he like?'

'Quiet, just sitting on the edge of the bunk, staring at the wall.' He stopped for a moment. 'Being in the cells affects people in different ways. Some pace about endlessly, others go to sleep, even more cry their eyes out. He was a starer.'

'So what happened when Holdsworth was brought in?'

'I was called into the booking lobby by Sergeant Saunders and told to search him and afterwards put him in Cell 3.'

'What time was this?'

'I can't remember, it was too long ago.'

'Approximately.'

'Around 3.40 I think, but I can't be sure.'

His account tallied with the official timeline. 'You did the strip search with Lucas Harvey?'

Rodgers nodded. 'Lord save his soul. Dying in a car accident like he did. Poor man.'

'Was it normal to strip search prisoners?'

'No, not normal, but it happened, especially if the detainee was arrested for drugs.'

'So you searched Holdsworth. Did he resist? Did he try to stop you in any way?'

'No, he was resigned, like he was used to it. I guess he'd been in chokey before; he knew the score.'

The next question was important. 'Did he seem like he was on drugs, like he was high?'

'Not at all. He seemed like he was normal, a little pissed off at being arrested but who wouldn't be?'

'So not high, not out of it on drugs?'

'No, he kept saying to Sergeant Saunders he wanted to see somebody from the National Crime Agency.'

'Who?'

'Some inspector? Broad, Bright, some name or other. The sergeant let him make his call but whoever it was didn't answer.'

Ridpath glanced down at his notes on the custody log. It said the prisoner was allowed two calls; it didn't say who to. The other must have been to his mother.

'And what happened next?'

'After the search, we bagged his clothes and personal effects.'

'Did you find any drugs.'

'Nothing. Clean as a whistle.'

'What possessions did he have?'

'Not a lot. House keys, a wallet, a phone, some loose change, that was it.'

Ridpath stayed silent.

'We gave him an outfit to wear. He put it on and I escorted him to Cell 3.'

'On your own?'

'Yeah, he wasn't no trouble.'

'Did he go to the toilet?'

'No, straight to the cell.'

'So there was no time he was on his own.'

'None at all. We never leave the prisoners alone once the custody sergeant has given them to us.'

'And then?'

'I put him inside the cell.'

'That was all?'

'That's all.'

'You didn't give him a push when you put him in? A clout over the back of the head?'

'No.'

'And he was aware of his surroundings, answering your questions, responsive at all times?'

'He was just like you. Perfectly normal.'

Ridpath thought he was the least normal person he knew.

'And what happened next?'

'About three hours later, Lucas checked him and found him lying unconscious on the floor.'

'Not on his bunk?'

'No, definitely on the floor. He told Sergeant Saunders, who tried to give CPR. Anyway, that's what I heard.'

'You weren't in the cells?'

Rodgers shook his head. 'I was in with the doctor as he examined some young joyriders. Lucas came rushing in and asked the doctor to help with an unconscious detainee.'

'So what did you do?'

'I took the joyrider back to the holding room and then went to Cell 3.'

'When was that?'

'About 6.40. The doctor was giving CPR, then he stopped and called an ambulance.'

'This was about three hours after he was booked in?'

'Yeah.' He shrugged his shoulders. 'But it was too late. I knew he was dying as soon as I saw him lying on the floor.'

Ridpath thought for a moment, imagining the scene in his head. 'What about the prisoner next door?'

Rodgers frowned. 'Why are you asking about him? He wasn't involved.'

'But he was in the next cell, wasn't he? Did he hear anything?'

Once again, the man's eyes went up and left, recalling the evening. 'He was standing behind his cell door. I remember him asking what the hell was going on.'

'The DUI?'

'Slept through it all, I think. We released both of them at 8.30 without any charges. I suppose they'd been through enough.'

Ridpath looked at the timeline again. 'It says the camera feed to Cells 3 and 4 stopped at 4.35.'

'I wouldn't know anything about that; we can't see the camera feed. Only the duty sergeant can.'

'But didn't Sergeant Saunders ask you to check him out visually every thirty minutes?'

The man nodded. 'I think so.'

'So why didn't you do it?'

'Because I wasn't in the cells, Lucas was. Somebody pressed the panic button in the holding room. The four kids they'd arrested for joyriding were being difficult, acting up.'

Ridpath paused. That wasn't in the report either. 'Sorry, let me get this straight, you weren't in the custody area?'

'Like I said, I was called to help out in the holding room.'

'Called? By whom?'

'Sergeant Saunders. They needed help. Somebody had pressed the alert strip along the wall. When that happens, the duty sergeant will call for help if he thinks it's needed.'

'What time was this?'

'Around 4.15, I guess. I'm not sure.'

'How long were you away in the holding room?'

'Ninety minutes or so.'

'Why so long?'

'They were waiting for the parents or a responsible adult to turn up before the kids were booked for attempted theft. We won't put them in the cells if they are so young, so me and another cop babysat them in the holding area. Little buggers were on something. Speed or E, I think.'

'So Lucas Harvey was on his own in the cells during this time?'

'We only had three cons. He could handle them on his own. And anyway, Sergeant Saunders was there when I went back.'

'There?'

'In the custody cells.'

'What was he doing there? Shouldn't he have been at the front desk?'

The man hunched his shoulders. 'I don't know. On his break, I think.'

Ridpath frowned. 'Was he checking on the prisoners?'

'I don't know. He was chatting with Lucas when I got back.'

'And then what happened?'

'The bloody alert went off again. I'd only been gone a few minutes.'

'What time was this?'

His eyes went up and left as he recalled the information. 'Around 5.45. Myself and Sergeant Saunders rushed to the holding room. But the kids were sitting quietly, coming down from whatever drug they'd taken.'

'So what did you do?'

'I hung around and then took them to be examined by the duty doctor.'

'He'd arrived?'

'After six o'clock. He was checking them one by one when Lucas rushed in.' A sideways glance from Rodgers. 'Do I really have to give evidence at the inquest?'

137

'It looks like we will call you, I'm afraid. But it will be up to the coroner to decide.'

The man shook his head. 'I should have stayed at home that night. I wasn't even supposed to be working.'

'Oh?'

'The missus wanted a holiday in bloody Malaga, so I was doing all the overtime I could.'

'Bad timing.'

'You're telling me.'

'One final question. Why did you stop being a custody officer?'

'After Holdsworth's death, I was pushed out, wasn't I? I think they wanted a scapegoat. Now here I am at the Trafford Centre. Made it to the top, haven't I?'

The irony was heavy in the last sentence.

'We'll let you know the exact date you need to attend the inquest, but it will be sometime next week. I'll ask the coroner to call you early if she can.'

'Thanks, it would help.' He stood up. 'Time to start.' He glanced up at the immense building in front of him, with its green cupola standing out against the blue and white sky. 'God, I hate this place. It says a lot that I preferred working in a prison to working here.'

Chapter Thirty-Six

Ridpath thought about driving back to the Coroner's Court but one look at the traffic on the M60 and he decided against it. He took the back roads through Urmston to his home instead.

Eve was already there, sitting in the kitchen eating a piece of toast.

'At least you have your appetite back.'

'I'm starving, could eat a horse.'

'Sorry, we're out of horses. How about lasagne? I could microwave one for dinner.'

'Sounds good. Probably got horse in it anyway.'

Ridpath looked at her quizzically.

'The food scandal? Contaminated meat from horses and pigs found in supermarket frozen meals. A couple of years ago, remember?'

Ridpath shook his head.

'Really, Dad, you should keep up with the news.'

'I don't have time, I have a job... remember?'

'No excuse, the world's a mess and all people care about is what's happening on *Coronation Street*.'

This was a new, strident Eve. He went to the freezer cabinet and searched for the lasagne. 'When did you become so socially aware?'

'When I open my eyes every morning. Look, we have over forty thousand cases of Covid, stuff missing from supermarkets, electricity prices rising, life expectancy falling and topping it all, your generation have used and abused the planet so badly, there may be nothing left for me or my children.'

He popped the lasagne in the microwave and switched it on. The light went on and a discordant thrum filled the kitchen.

'You sound like whatshername, the Swedish girl...'

'Greta Thunberg? At least she's doing something. As she said, all we get from your generation is blah, blah, blah... All talk and no action.'

Ridpath smiled. He thought of himself at her age. All he knew about was football and telly and friends. Nothing else. She looked exactly like her mother when she ranted. At least she cared, too.

'Don't smile, Dad, it's not funny.'

He wiped the grin off his face. 'You're right, Eve, it's not funny, it's tragic, but what can we do?'

'Maisie's organised a leafleting of the shopping centre on Saturday morning. Can I go?'

'But you have Chinese lessons on Saturday mornings.'

Polly had been very keen for Eve to keep in touch with her Chinese, ensuring she at least spoke a few words of Mandarin.

'I know, Dad, but it's important, and it's just once. Can I go?'

The microwave pinged loudly behind him.

'All right, just this once, but you'll need to catch up on what you missed.'

'Thanks, Dad.' She rushed from her seat and wrapped her arms around him. 'Now can you do the trick with the lasagne?'

There she was, his little girl again. It was strange how she alternated between the two characters: the woman she was becoming and the girl she had been.

The trick with the lasagne was something he had shown her when she was five. It was just sprinkling extra grated Cheddar and Parmesan over the cooked lasagne and popping it under the grill for a couple of minutes till it was brown and gooey.

Her comfort food.

And his comfort making it.

Chapter Thirty-Seven

It was later in the evening when he received the phone calls.

Eve had already gone to bed. He'd gone upstairs to check and found her cuddling the rabbit she'd had since she was a baby. For a second, he stared at her, the child still there in the calmness of her face and the quietness of her breathing.

He returned downstairs to finish going through all the documents: the duty log and timeline, the investigation by Professional Standards and of the IOPC.

Once again, he was struck by how perfunctory and defensive both investigations had been. It was as if they'd already decided the outcome before they'd started looking at the evidence.

As he finished, Sophia called him.

'Hiya, I've just downloaded the CCTV from the station and put it on our server.'

'Where are you?'

'At the office.'

'Still?'

'I can't do this stuff at home. But don't worry, my mum is on the way to collect me. She's already rung four times.'

'Go home now, that is an order, Sophia.'

'Don't you start, Ridpath, I've had an earful from her already. Anyway, I took a look at the footage. It all seems pretty normal to me, but I guess you need to check it versus the timeline.'

'What about the CCTV from Holdsworth's cell?'

'It's fine until 4.35, then the cameras go off in both Cells 3 and 4. The images reappear at 6.46. Holdsworth is being taken out on a gurney.'

'OK, I'll take a look at it. Anything from Saunders or his union rep?'

'I had a message from Angela Dexter. They'll agree to the interview as long as it is held at Police HQ at two p.m. More convenient apparently. She didn't seem happy to give me the news.'

'Convenient for whom, I wonder? Send a message to her to confirm. I don't care how or where it's held as long as we actually talk to Saunders.'

'Will do.'

'Let's get in early to prepare. I'll go through the footage tonight and we can edit out the parts we'll need to show Saunders tomorrow.'

'OK, I'll bring my laptop in. See you at eight a.m.?'

'Perfect.'

'I've just heard a beep from my mum's car; I need to go. One last thing. I haven't been able to track down Garry Abbott. He seems to have vanished into thin air.'

'What about the DUI, Neil Mallender?'

'I found him. He's not keen to talk but I bent his arm and he'll meet you at nine a.m. tomorrow here. Apparently, he works nearby.'

'Great, but go home now. I'll get Chrissy to follow up on our missing detainee.'

Ridpath heard three loud beeps of a car horn in the distance.

'It sounds like she's getting impatient.'

'You don't know the half of it. I'm about to be scolded to within an inch of my life.'

'You deserve it.'

'Thank you for your support, and see you tomorrow.'

The phone clicked off.

He logged on to the server and found Sophia had separated and labelled all the feeds from the different cameras. There were fifteen in total, each showing the footage from that day.

He went back into the kitchen and made himself a strong coffee. This looked like it was going to be a long night. He had to review this footage before the meeting with Saunders tomorrow.

He returned to his table and was about to start on the file labelled 'Custody Desk' when his mobile rang again.

'I thought I told you to go home.'

'Did you, Ridpath? I don't remember. And anyway, I'm already at home.'

It was Chrissy's voice, not Sophia's.

'Sorry, I thought you were somebody else.'

'Easily done. Sorry for ringing you so late.'

'No worries, I'm still up and working. How can I help?'

She paused for a long time. 'It's more me helping you. I was sitting in the canteen and heard of couple of Turnbull's boys speaking. Your name is mud, Ridpath.'

'What's new?'

'But it's worse this time. They're actively out to get you. Investigating Tony Saunders is the last straw for them. It hasn't gone down well.'

'Can't be helped, Chrissy. He's going to be called as a witness; I need to know what he's going to say.'

'Or not say?'

'What do you mean?'

'I think he's going to go silent on you.'

Ridpath thought for a moment. If he refused to speak, then they would have to rely on the CCTV to check the timeline of events. It *was* going to be a long night.

'Thanks for the heads-up. I need a favour, Chrissy. I'm trying to find a man who was in the cells that night.'

'You want me to track his phone and find an address for him.'

'That would be great, but I don't want to get you into trouble.'

'No worries, I'll put him on another job we're doing as a person of interest.'

'His name is Garry Abbott, and I'll message you the phone number.'

'I'll get on to it when I get in tomorrow.'

'Thanks, Chrissy.'

He expected her to ring off, but she stayed on the other end of the line, hesitating for a long while before saying, 'There's one other thing you should know…'

'What? Turnbull doesn't like me?'

'That as well. But they were saying Saunders knew the victim before that night.'

Ridpath stayed silent as she carried on.

'Sorry, I just caught the end of their conversation and I think they saw me and stopped talking. But apparently, Saunders knew Holdsworth because of his daughter.'

'What's his daughter got to do with it?'

'Years ago she had a drug problem and apparently Holdsworth was her dealer. Saunders arrested him and brought him in.'

So that's why the sergeant's name was on the charge sheet for Holdsworth's earlier offence.

'Why isn't this in any of the reports from Professional Standards or IOPC?'

'I don't know, Ridpath.'

'Thanks, Chrissy.'

'One other thing. Saunders threatened to murder Holdsworth if he ever saw him again.'

'What?'

'They were laughing about it, Ridpath, like it was some big joke.'

Ridpath thought for a long time. This changed everything. Tomorrow's meeting had become even more important.

Was he investigating a death in custody, or a murder?

November 4, 2021

Chapter Thirty-Eight

By two a.m., Ridpath had only managed to watch footage from the camera covering the custody lobby and booking-in counter.

The camera was cleverly positioned above Saunders' head and slightly to the right, taking in both the sergeant and the detainee as well as the bank of security screens. A timer in the top left-hand corner ticked over unceasingly.

He watched as the night shift came on and Sergeant Saunders took charge. He followed procedure exactly, logging into the duty roster, checking the cells, scanning through the cameras and walking around the holding and medical rooms.

Bob French came in to check before he went home. This camera had sound attached.

'All set, Tony.'

'All good, boss. Anything I should be aware of?'

'Nothing much, NCA are running an anti-gang operation but they haven't sent me any details of action this evening.'

'Right-o. I'll give you a bell if anything comes up.'

'Good night, Tony, and don't sleep tight.'

'See ya, boss.'

Interesting, thought Ridpath. He checked the duty log and made a note on his pad.

> *Were the NCA running an operation? Who was it investigating?*

The rest of the evening went smoothly. Ridpath ran the video at double speed, stopping only to check when somebody approached the custody desk. Very few people did. It was as if Sergeant Saunders had a big sign above his head saying DO NOT DISTURB.

The DUI was escorted in by young cops, no doubt grateful to be out of the cold and into the warmth of the station. Neil Mallender was unsteady on his feet but Saunders was calm and patient with him, explaining what was going to happen slowly, sometimes twice, ensuring the man understood everything despite his befuddled state.

Ridpath checked the times of the arrest and the arrival at the station versus the duty log. It tracked exactly. Saunders was meticulous in completing his notes.

Next was the man placed in Cell 4. Garry Abbott. He had a sharp, pointed face and his hair was slick with rain. Ridpath wrote a note.

Check weather. Was it raining? Was it cold?

Throughout the booking-in process, Abbott was quiet and taciturn, answering the questions asked of him in a monosyllabic grunt. He didn't look like the sort of man who would assault somebody for no reason in a pub. Indeed, to Ridpath's eyes, all the fight had gone out of Abbott. He looked weak and insecure.

Again, procedure was followed to the letter; explanations were given, the man was offered a phone call, which he declined. He was told the charges and then, after having his fingerprints and photograph taken, escorted to the cells by Terry Rodgers and Lucas Harvey, who didn't even bother to hold his arms.

Ridpath fast forwarded again to 3.25 a.m.

Holdsworth was escorted in by two PCs, his arms handcuffed in front of him. He was wearing an old leather jacket and walked with a slight stoop but otherwise was perfectly capable of walking unaided. The constable on the right did all the talking.

Ridpath paused the video for a second, looking at the details of the scene. Everything seemed exactly how it should be; it was a scene that could have been shot in any police station in any force in the country any night of the year.

He turned the volume up to hear the conversation better.

'I'm telling you I want to speak to Detective Inspector Brett. Just call him.'

Ridpath paused the video and wrote a note to himself.

Who is DI Brett?

Why does Holdsworth want to talk with him?

He started the video again and the conversation continued.

'What's up, Chris?'

'We had a tip-off from a local he was dealing out of his car. We stopped him and had a look. Found these.' The young police constable held up a large evidence bag.

'Crack?'

'We think so, Sarge.'

In the video, the sergeant stared at Holdsworth, who shifted uneasily from one foot to the other. It was obvious to Ridpath that Saunders was assessing the detainee, checking out his mental and physical state as well as deciding what to do with him.

Finally, the man spoke again.

'Just call Mark Brett, he'll sort it all out.'

The sergeant ignored him, addressing the police constable instead.

'Have you searched him and informed him of his rights?'

'Already done, Sarge.'

'No problems with the arrest?'

'He put up a bit of a struggle, but no real issues.'

'If you call Mark Brett, he'll sort it out.'

The sergeant finally focused on the man in front of him. 'Never heard of him,' he said slowly.

'He's National Crime Agency, just call him.'

Ridpath made another note.

> *DI Mark Brett? NCA? Didn't Bob French say earlier they were running an operation that night? Check.*

The sergeant tapped his computer, opening up a new custody record. 'Name?'

'Mark Brett.'

'No, your name, pillock.'

The man closed his eyes and sighed loudly. Finally, he opened them and said in a bored voice, 'Ben Holdsworth.'

'Date of birth?'

Another long sigh. 'January 12, 1982.'

'Address?'

'27 Church Street, Redbury.'

The policeman had begun filling in the boxes on the custody record then stopped. 'Very funny. Address?'

The man stayed silent, shifting his weight from one leg to the other.

'I'll put down no fixed abode. Mr Holdsworth, are you feeling unwell, dizzy, or uncomfortable? Would you like to see a health professional?'

'No.'

'Have you taken drugs or any other substances?'

Another long sigh. 'No.' The man leant forward suddenly. 'Just call Mark Brett, will you?' He banged his handcuffed fists on the Plexiglas screen in front of Saunders.

The two coppers on either side immediately jerked him away from the counter.

Ridpath paused the video again, looking at the man's face. Why the sudden change? Was Holdsworth afraid? Or was he frustrated?

The two constables held the man firmly but he wasn't struggling and Ridpath could see he bore no marks of a fight.

'You have the right to a legal adviser. If you do not have one, one will be appointed for you.'

The man remained silent.

'Is there anyone you would like to be informed of your detention?'

Again a sigh. 'Just call Mark Brett.'

'You are aware you will be under surveillance during your time in Redbury station. The details are set out here. You also have the right to consult the codes of practice.' He picked up the laminated sheet, delineating the various rights of detainees. 'Please read it and sign on the dotted line.'

Ben Holdsworth glanced briefly at the sheet before stating, 'I ain't signing nothing.'

The sergeant typed something into the custody log before continuing.

'Would you like to speak to a solicitor or inform anybody of your detention?'

'Like I've said at least a thousand times, just call Mark Brett of the National Crime Agency. He's in Warrington.'

Ridpath made a note.

Mark Brett. NCA Warrington?

'As it is now 3.40 a.m., the National Crime Agency offices are closed. However, I have made a note on the custody record and the custody inspector will evaluate your request as soon as possible.'

'I want to call him myself. You have to let me call someone, and as you are not an inspector or higher rank, the right cannot be refused.'

'We've got a right one here, Chris.'

'Knows his rights, does this one,' the burly constable replied.

'Been here before, have you?'

'Just let me call him.'

Saunders pointed to the telephone on the left-hand side of the custody desk.

The man picked it up and immediately called a number, waiting patiently as it rang, tapping his fingers on the counter. 'I'd like to try again.'

'Be our guest.'

Again, the man tapped in the number.

Again, no answer.

'I'd like one more call.'

'You've had two attempts already.'

'They didn't go through. I want to ring my mum this time. Let her know where I am.'

Tony Saunders sighed. 'Go ahead, but make it quick.'

Ben Holdsworth dialled a number again. After a short while he began speaking. 'Hi, Mum, I've been nicked… yeah… yeah… don't worry, I'll be out in the morning… yeah… yeah… sorry, Mum.'

He put the phone down, and shuffled back to face Tony Saunders.

'Isn't that heart-warming, Chris, a drug dealer who loves his mum.'

'Enough to make you weep, Sarge.'

'Would you like to make any other calls?' asked Saunders sarcastically.

Ben Holdsworth shook his head.

On the right-hand side of the images, a white-shirted man, probably Lucas Harvey, took Holdsworth's arm and he was released by the constables.

'As you have been arrested on drugs charges, I am authorising a full body search.'

'You can't do that.'

Saunders tapped on the keyboard. 'I just have. Take him away, lads, and be careful to record his belongings. When you've finished put him in number three.'

Another custody officer, who Ridpath recognised as Terry Rodgers, came round to the other side of Ben Holdsworth, taking firm hold of the man's left arm.

'Come this way, and don't give us any trouble.'

Ridpath recognised Terry's slight West Country burr from this afternoon's interview. For a second, the man struggled against the arm before the grip tightened and he was led away, out of camera view.

'We'll complete the arrest logs and let the duty inspector know, Sarge.'

'Thanks, Chris. Looks like a good collar.'

'Bit of luck. The stuff was on the front seat next to him. Bloody idiot.'

Ridpath watched Sergeant Saunders check the computer screen for a long time before finally pressing enter. He was obviously making sure there were no problems and he had followed procedures exactly.

Ridpath exhaled and sat back in his chair. He ran his fingers through his thinning hair. Something wasn't right, but he couldn't quite put his finger on what it was.

And then it came to him in a moment of insight.

Quickly, he wrote a note before he lost the moment.

If Sergeant Saunders knew Ben Holdsworth, why is there no recognition between them? Surely one of them would have said something?

Chapter Thirty-Nine

Garry Abbott couldn't stand it any more. He had to get out of this place. Go for a walk, do something.

He fallen asleep earlier, the television still blaring, waking up in the middle of the night, freezing and alone.

He tried to turn down the air-conditioning but either the machine wasn't working or he'd broken it. He thought about calling down to reception to send someone up to fix it, but he couldn't draw attention to himself. Nothing would make him more memorable to hotel staff than complaining about the faulty air-con at three in the morning.

Instead, he put on his coat and paced around the room. Perhaps he could go out for twenty minutes, just get some fresh air. Visit the off-licence and get a bottle of something.

He walked over to the window and looked out.

Manchester was dead.

Nobody walked the streets. The trams had stopped running. The canal had ceased flowing. Illuminating everything was a dirty yellow light from the street lamps, giving it all the pallor of rancid butter.

The streets looked as lonely as he felt. A place where nobody lived any more, nobody enjoyed themselves. A sad place; a deserted city.

It would be safe to go out for just twenty minutes. Nobody would see him, would they?

Even if they did, they would give him a wide berth. Nobody but a nutter would walk the streets of Manchester at three in the morning.

He grabbed his key and his wallet. He'd sneak downstairs and out through the lobby. Nobody would see him. Just twenty minutes walking by the canal and then to the all-night offie for a bottle of Scotch. Something to keep him warm in the ice box they called a hotel room.

He was about to leave when he decided to check outside one last time.

A van had parked in front of the hotel now, its lights off, just sitting there.

Were there people inside?

He strained to look, then realised his face was silhouetted against the window. Anybody who looked up would see the one hotel room with a man standing there staring out into the night.

He quickly closed the curtains and sat on the bed.

Had they found him? Were they waiting until dawn to come up to his room? Were they calling Delaney now to bring his dental pliers?

He put his head in his hands.

What was he going to do?

Chapter Forty

Ridpath made himself a quick coffee and then began watching the footage again.

After booking in Holdsworth, the space had gone quiet, only to be suddenly filled with noise and activity ten minutes later as four young teenagers were brought in.

They were almost feral in their look. Short, crew-cut hair, thin haggard faces and aggressive postures. Ridpath could see immediately from the restlessness in their eyes they were on speed.

Saunders handled the situation well, calming down the offenders, making sure each was as comfortable as possible, detaining them in the holding room rather than the cells and calling for a responsible adult to be made available.

He'd followed the book to the letter. A textbook case of handling a difficult custodial issue with tact and firmness.

But within ten minutes of them going to the holding room, alarms rang through the station. Terry and two other coppers appeared in front of Saunders.

'Where's the alarm, boss?'

'Holding room, Terry, but treat them with kid gloves, no rough stuff, understand?'

Terry looked almost disappointed.

All three vanished towards the holding room. Saunders was monitoring the situation on the CCTV console. Again, textbook coppering.

At 5.22, Saunders stood up and, summoning another constable, said, 'I'm going for a break, Charlie. Look after the desk for me, will you? But give me a bell if anything comes in.'

'Anything expected, boss?'

'Nah, all quiet on the western front at the moment. But you know Redbury, World War Three could start at any minute.'

Saunders moved out from behind his desk and walked away out of the front door.

Ridpath made another note.

Where did he go? Was this when Terry saw him in the cells?

Twelve minutes later, at 5.41, Terry crossed in front of the custody desk's camera heading back towards the cells.

Look at 5.41 on cell corridor camera?

Two minutes later Saunders returned and relieved the constable, checking with him that all had been quiet.

There was just one more incident that evening until the death of Holdsworth. At 5.45, the alarms sounded. Once again, Terry Rodgers, Sergeant Saunders and one other copper arrived in front of the custody desk.

'It's kicked off again; you two go and quieten 'em down. Apparently, the parents and the responsible adult are on their way. The doctor will be here soon and he can take a look at them when he arrives,' ordered Saunders.

'Bloody kids, who'd have them, hey.'

The sergeant didn't answer.

At exactly 6.30 a buzzer on the internal phone system sounded. Saunders glanced at the CCTV screens and pressed the intercom.

'What is it, Lucas?'

'It's Cell 3, boss, he's on the floor, not looking good.'

'I'm coming.'

Saunders got up and ran around the desk. The place remained empty for twelve minutes, no one manning it or watching the CCTV. Then a blue-overalled paramedic ran in. Saunders appeared on the left and shouted, 'I called you. We've got an unresponsive detainee.'

The paramedic waited for a few seconds for his partner to arrive carrying a large bag and then both moved quickly through the open door guarding the cells.

The time in the corner ticked over to 6.50. An unconscious man on a gurney was being rolled out across the custody booking area and out through the front door.

The man was Ben Holdsworth.

Chapter Forty-One

Tony Saunders stared at the last dregs of whisky, burnt orange against the smoky crystal of the glass. The bottle lay empty on the table beside him. Another dead soldier gone to the great bottle bank in the sky.

Despite having drunk so much, he felt strangely sober.

Opposite him, the television flickered with one of the old black and white movies the BBC loved to show late at night. Jean Harlow was speaking but no sound came from her lips. He had the sound turned down, in case he woke the wife.

Another night sitting alone in his living room with only a bottle and a television for company.

His wife had gone to bed hours ago, complaining loudly he wasn't to come to upstairs drunk again. He'd promised he wouldn't, and then broken his word within five minutes, removing the wrapping from the top of the bottle, hearing the satisfying sound of the cork easing out, followed by the even more satisfying noise of the whisky gurgling into his glass.

The first swallows had been life-giving; everything afterwards just topped up his level of drunkenness.

At one point, he'd thought briefly about his interview with Ridpath tomorrow. He disliked the man intensely. How dare he investigate another copper? Was he so pure he'd never made a mistake?

Bastard.

But he mustn't think or worry about the interview. It was like Jack had said, just one more in a long line of bloody meetings to show that all the pen-pushers had used every bloody bureaucratic trick to cover their arses. Only one week to go and he'd be back on the job, everything would be back to normal. He'd give up the booze then, start to work out in the gym, get back to fitness.

'Bloody Ridpath and his bloody inquest,' he said out loud.

He thought about opening another bottle but he knew he'd finished the last one he'd hidden from the wife. After the interview tomorrow, he'd go to the supermarket and get a couple more.

'Bloody Ridpath and his bloody inquest,' he repeated.

Anyway, he'd set the dogs on him now. You don't work in the police for over twenty years without making a few mates along the way.

He drained the last of the whisky.

Outside in the garden he heard the loud hoot of an owl hunting prey in the darkness of the night.

He hoped the mouse escaped this time.

Chapter Forty-Two

The man he was cursing glanced at the clock above his mantlepiece. 3.10 a.m.

He rubbed his red eyes and stretched upwards towards the ceiling. He had finally finished going through the footage from the custody booking area. Each camera was taking a long time, mainly because he was stopping and comparing it to the duty log. So far everything had been accurate, but some details had been omitted.

Important details.

Like did Saunders already know Ben Holdsworth?

Was Holdsworth on drugs?

Did anything happen during the strip search?

Where did Saunders go during his break? Was it to the cells?

Why?

He would ask the sergeant at the interview this morning.

He thought about going to bed but decided not to. He had to watch the footage from the cell before the interview. There might be something important to ask Saunders.

He clicked the file marked Cell 3, fast forwarding through the footage of an empty cell until the door opened and Holdsworth was pushed in.

There was no sound this time so Ridpath created a timeline for himself with his notes.

> *3.50. Holdsworth in cell. Bangs on door.*
>
> *3.51. Stands staring at closed door. Turns suddenly, trips and falls, banging the side of his head on the wall. (Footage in post-mortem and IOPC report.)*
>
> *3.52. Stands up, shakes head and gives middle finger to camera. Walks around cell for eight minutes. Seems to be OK. Lips moving, but no sound.*

4.00. Sits on bunk. Puts head in hands.

4.02. Lies down on bunk. Curls up into foetal position.

4.18. Gets up and begins walking round cell again. Walk steady.

4.24. Begins exercising, doing squats and stretches.

4.25. Sits back down on bunk.

4.28. Goes behind screen to use toilet (not on camera).

4.31. Walks around cell.

4.35. Image goes blank.

6.46. Image returns. EMS attending to Holdsworth.

6.50. Holdsworth being wheeled out on gurney.

Ridpath checked when Saunders went for his break. 5.22.

Did he go to check up on Holdsworth? Did he talk with the detainee? And if he did, what did they discuss?

He doubled the speed of the video, but still the feed in Cell 3 was blank until suddenly it reappeared at 6.46. Medics were kneeling beside the body of Ben Holdsworth. An oxygen mask was placed over his face. Sergeant Saunders and the two custody officers were in the background.

Four minutes later a gurney appeared brought by one of the medics. Holdsworth was lifted gently onto it and wheeled out, followed by the custody officers.

Saunders was left alone in the cell, looking around and lifting up the thin mattress covering the bunk.

'What's he doing?' said Ridpath aloud. 'It's like he's looking for something.'

Chapter Forty-Three

It was six a.m. when Ridpath finally finished watching the footage from Cell 3 and taking notes. At least now he had some questions to ask Saunders.

He stood up and stretched, feeling his bones ache and the shirt stretch across his paunch. He hadn't exercised for ages; no wonder he felt so slow and sluggish.

Not having slept didn't help either. Time to get his head down for an hour. He set the alarm on his phone, slumped in the armchair and within a minute was snoring quietly.

At 7.15, the alarm rang like a klaxon to wake the dead. Ridpath reluctantly roused himself, rubbed his whiskered chin and stood up. For a moment he felt woozy, his body swaying. He stuck his arm out on the mantelpiece to steady himself.

'You're getting too old for this, Ridpath,' he said out loud.

He slowly dragged himself upstairs, feeling his bones complain at every step.

After a quick shower and shave he felt slightly better, almost human. He cooked scrambled eggs on toast for Eve and squeezed some oranges for fresh juice. For himself, he made a large pot of espresso. His stomach couldn't handle food in the morning.

Luckily, it only took three shouts up the stairs and two threats before Eve appeared sleepy-eyed and hair-bedraggled in the kitchen.

'What year is it?' she asked.

'You slept well, I see. Eat your breakfast quickly, I need to be at the coroner's office early this morning.'

She took a piece of toast and clamped it between her teeth, closing her eyes once more.

'Earth to Eve; come in, Planet Eve.'

'What happens to the time when you sleep?' she said without opening her eyes, still munching on her toast. 'One minute you are resting your head on the pillow, the next your dad is bellowing up the stairs for you to get up. I don't get it.'

'You won't get a lift unless you hurry and eat your eggs.'

She finally opened her eyes and stared at the nest of scrambled eggs in front of her. 'Sorry, possible chickens, Dad says I have to eat you.' She scooped up a large forkful.

'I was thinking…'

'It's bad for your health, Dad,' she said between mouthfuls of scrambled egg. 'Didn't the doctor warn you against it?'

'Like I was saying, smart arse, I was thinking we might visit your mum on Sunday.'

Eve's mood instantly changed. 'Yeah, we should, we haven't seen her for a while.'

'We could buy her some flowers and clean the grave. We haven't been there for a month.'

'Maybe some lilies this time. I think she'd like some lilies.'

'OK, and afterwards I can take you to see your grandparents. Paw Paw has been asking after you.'

'Do I have to?'

'You know it's our deal. Particularly as you're not going to Chinese classes on Saturday. You…'

'…have to keep in touch with the Chinese side. I know. I mean, duh, every time I look in the mirror I can see it.'

'The cultural side, not just the way you look.'

'I know, it's just…'

'Just what?'

She shovelled the eggs into her mouth and, still chewing, said, 'There's so many other things to do…'

'But this was important to your mum.'

'I know. I'll keep it up, promise.' She held out her hand with the pinky and thumb extended. 'You're supposed to do the same.'

Another teenage ritual. He intertwined his little finger and twisted. 'How's the other thing?'

She laughed. 'You can say the word, Dad. Period. How's my period?' She looked at him, encouraging him to speak.

Why was he embarrassed? It was a perfectly natural bodily function. Perhaps it was the way his own mother had sheltered him from such things when he was young. He vaguely remembered his mother and sister whispering to each other, making certain he couldn't hear. Maybe that's what they were talking about.

He took the plunge. 'How's your period?'

'Fine. The water bottle helped last night. Thanks.'

'So it's all OK?'

'I wouldn't say it's all mint, but I can handle it. You're gonna have to give me some money for next time, though, so I can buy some pads.'

'I don't mind buying them.'

'No worries, Dad, I have to work out which ones I need through trial and error. Different flow days and all that.'

Ridpath wondered what the 'all that' was, but instead of asking, simply said, 'Just let me know when you need the money. And there's one other thing...'

'What?' she said, finishing off the last of the eggs.

'You know you can be honest with me all the time. Tell me stuff, I'll understand.'

She put her hand on his. 'I know, Dad.'

A little moment passed between them before he said, 'Now get upstairs and get ready. We're leaving in five.'

'Yes, sir.' She saluted badly and ran heavily upstairs. It was like a herd of elephants had just discovered a hand of bananas and were all desperate to get there first.

He downed the dregs of his coffee, collected the dishes and placed them in the sink. The washing-up could wait until he got back this evening.

Suddenly, without warning, he leant on the side of the sink and began to weep. Seeing his empty coffee mug lying next to the used dishes had set him off. Polly had been useless without her coffee in the morning. It took two strong mugs before her brain finally kicked into gear. It was like starting a car on a particularly cold morning; eventually it turned over.

'Pull yourself together, Ridpath, you're just tired. Can't pull the all-nighters any more.' He straightened up and took a deep breath, wiping his eyes with his sleeve.

'Dad...'

Eve was standing at the door. Why hadn't he heard her coming down the stairs?

'Are you crying?'

'No, not really, tired, that's all.' He wiped his eyes again.

'Did you sleep last night? I went in your room and saw the bed hadn't been slept in.'

He could tell a white lie and say he'd already made the bed, but he decided after his lecture on honesty, he should tell her the truth. 'No, I spent the night working, checking some video.'

'You know it's not good for you, Dad, your health…'

'I know, it's just this case…'

'It's always just a case, Dad. But what would I do if you weren't around?'

'Sleep late every day?'

She hit his chest softly. 'Don't joke, I'm serious.'

'I know.' It was his turn to hold out his hand with the little finger extended. 'It won't happen again, I promise.' He glanced at the clock. 'Jesus, is that the time? Let's get moving, little lady.'

Chapter Forty-Four

At the coroner's office, Ridpath briefed Sophia on what needed to be done before the meeting with Saunders.

He had just finished when Jenny popped her head around the door. 'There's a Mr Mallender here to see you. I've put him in the interview room.'

'Thanks, Jenny.'

'You want me to come with you, Ridpath?' asked Sophia.

He shook his head. 'It's more important you stay here and finish the document deck for Saunders. The interview won't take me long.'

Neil Mallender had the slightly red-faced, podgy look of a drinker. He stood looking out of the window at the mean streets of Stockfield, turning back to face Ridpath as soon as he entered.

'How long is this going to take? I have to be at work soon.'

Ridpath ignored the question and gestured for the man to sit.

'It's Mr Mallender, isn't it?'

The man nodded.

'Neil Mallender?'

'Correct. What's this about? Your secretary called and asked me to come in, making it obvious I had no choice, but wouldn't say why.'

'Mr Mallender, my name is Ridpath, and I am the coroner's officer for the inquest into the death of Ben Holdsworth.'

'The man who died in the cells? But I thought it had been solved. He fell and hit his head, according to the news.'

'What do you remember of the night? You were in a nearby cell. Number nine, I believe?'

'I don't remember the number, don't remember much of anything.'

'Tell me what you do remember.'

'I'd been out celebrating with the lads from work. We'd just won a big account which was going to keep us in business for the next three years.'

'Where were you celebrating?'

'In Altrincham. Stupidly, I thought I was OK to drive and took the M60 home. I must have done something wrong because next thing I know I'm parked up beside this cop car blowing into a bag and doing sobriety tests.'

'They treated you well?'

'I've no complaints. It was my bloody stupidity.'

'What happened next?'

'They told me I was over the limit and then they took me to Redbury station. I was booked in by this sergeant.'

'How was he?'

'Fine. He explained everything, but the drink was starting to hit me. It must have been the adrenalin. Anyway, I think I signed some stuff, can't remember what, and was put in a cell. Not a pleasant place to be. Made me think long and hard about my life and the drink and everything. I've been going to AA since. Not as much as I want, but enough to keep me off the drink. Haven't touched a drop for three years now.'

Ridpath regretted his first impressions of Neil Mallender. 'Well done, it's hard to give up.'

'You're telling me. Hardest thing I've ever done.'

'What happened after you were put in the cells?'

'Not a lot. I remember curling up, pulling this smelly blanket around me and going to sleep. Next thing I know, they were waking me up the following morning and telling me I could go free.'

'They released you without charge?'

'Some inspector said he was giving me a verbal caution but next time they would throw the book at me.'

'What time was this?'

'Around 8.30 the following morning. There were lots of other cops there and these guys in the white suits. I found out later somebody had died in the cells not far from me.'

'You didn't hear or see anything?'

The man shook his head forcefully. 'Like I said, I slept through it all. One of the advantages of alcohol, it knocks you out. Wish I could sleep like that again, but I can't. Insomnia now, can't sleep at all.' He shrugged his shoulders. 'Swings and roundabouts, hey?'

'Just to be clear, Mr Mallender, you heard nothing?'

'Not a sausage. Out like a light I was.'

Ridpath closed his file and held out his hand. 'Sorry to have brought you in so early.'

'No problem, it's on my way to work. So I won't have to attend the inquest? Only your secretary suggested I might have to come here.'

'I don't think so, Mr Mallender. I think you are free to go.'

Within seconds the man had picked up his briefcase and was out of the door, leaving Ridpath alone in the room.

One possible witness was cleared. Now all they had to do was find Garry Abbott. Why was he so difficult to locate?

Chapter Forty-Five

When Ridpath went back to the office, Sophia was still editing.

Last night, Ridpath had noted the relevant time codes on the CCTV. Sophia was now copying the clips and putting them in separate folders ready to be called up when Ridpath needed them.

He sat down and wrote a rough script for the interview; the main point was to get Saunders' account of what happened. He added a few questions on the anomalies he had spotted in Saunders' duty log, showing them to Sophia so she could put the clips in the correct order.

The rough script was just a guide, however, as he realised the interview could take many directions once it had started.

Mrs Challinor came to see their progress. 'What time is the meeting?'

'Two p.m.,' answered Ridpath, looking over his shoulder.

'It's already 12.15, you should get a move on.'

'Nearly done.'

'Will Saunders come to the meeting?'

'He's said he would.'

'And are you all set?'

'I'd like to have watched all the CCTV, but we're ready for a first meeting.'

'Make sure it's documented, Ridpath.'

'A recording and transcript will be available to you, coroner.'

'You met somebody this morning?'

'A Neil Mallender. One of the possible witnesses who spent the night in Redbury station at the same time as Ben Holdsworth.'

'I don't remember the name from the file.'

'He wasn't in the file. Either IOPC didn't interview him or they didn't retain notes on the meeting.'

'Will we call him?'

'I don't think so, Mrs Challinor. He was drunk and slept through everything, having been arrested for DUI.'

'They didn't charge him?'

Ridpath shook his head. 'I think they wanted the cells cleared before the SOCOs went in. Understandable in the circumstances.'

'Right. At least it's one less witness for the inquest.'

'We're still looking for one other man who was in the cells that night.'

'Who was he?'

'A Garry Abbott, arrested for assault and battery.'

'Another name not in the files.'

'He doesn't seem to have been interviewed at all.'

'You'd better find him, and quickly.'

'We will do, coroner.'

'Good. And break a leg.'

'Mine or his?'

She smiled and left them alone to finish the preparations.

An hour later, they were in the car driving to Police HQ.

'Have you brought a laptop to record everything?'

Sophia held up her bag. 'Wouldn't be seen without one.'

'And the CCTV clips are cued properly?'

'I followed your script to the letter.'

'I may change the script.'

'I'll just follow your lead.' She laid her hand on his arm. 'You seem nervous.'

Ridpath took a deep breath. 'You realise what we are about to do? We're going to interview a copper with over twenty years under his belt. His union rep will be there looking for the slightest mistake on our part. We need to be buttoned up, Sophia, as tight as a penguin in an Arctic gale.'

'Not possible.'

He took his eyes off the road and stared at her. 'We have to be organised, no screw-ups.'

'I meant the penguins in the gale bit.'

'What?'

'There aren't any penguins in the Arctic. Only in the southern hemisphere.'

They both looked at each other and burst out laughing.

'A polar bear's bum works. As buttoned up as a polar bear's bum.'

'Well, whatever it is, we need to be on the ball. There's no second chances with this interview.'

On arrival at Police HQ, they set up in a room on the fourth floor. Ridpath checked the video and recording machines while Sophia connected her computer to the system.

At exactly two p.m., Sergeant Saunders walked in wearing full dress uniform, his long service ribbons prominently displayed, accompanied by his union rep in a suit.

'Let the games begin,' the sergeant said from the door.

Chapter Forty-Six

Sergeant Saunders and his union rep sat down across the table from Ridpath and Sophia without looking at either of them. The tension in the air was palpable.

'I'd like to thank you for attending this morning...' began Ridpath.

'It weren't my choice,' responded Saunders gruffly.

'Nonetheless, thank you for coming.' He nodded at Sophia, who started the tape and passed across the folders they had prepared.

'This meeting has been called to discuss the witness statement of Sergeant Tony Saunders before the inquest into the death of Ben Holdsworth.'

Saunders sighed loudly and prodded the file with his large thick forefinger. 'I already gave a statement to the other investigations, why am I here again?'

'As I said, we need to discuss your witness statement before the inquest.'

The union rep laid his hand on Saunders' arm. 'Sergeant Saunders has already provided a comprehensive account and written statement to both Professional Standards and the IOPC with regards to the events of the early hours of February 21.'

'I am aware of his statements, and they are included in the file. However, as you are aware, the coroner's inquest is a completely separate inquiry, and under the 2009 Coroners Act we have a statutory duty to investigate all deaths in Crown custody.'

Saunders rolled his eyes and sat back heavily. 'Waste of bloody time.'

Ridpath continued. 'For the tape, present at the meeting are Sergeant Saunders, his union rep...'

The man sitting next to Saunders leant forward and, in a heavy Manchester accent, spoke into the tape. 'DI Jack Cater.'

'DI Cater, and two representatives of the coroner's office, Thomas Ridpath and Sophia Rahman. Shall we begin? If you open the files in front of you and turn to page three, we will present the first image and revisit the events of that night.'

They all opened their documents.

DI Cater frowned and glanced at Saunders. 'I wasn't aware the coroner's office had been provided with CCTV images from the station.'

Ridpath ignored him and carried on.

'Document one is a screenshot taken from CCTV dated February 20. Please show it, Sophia.'

On the TV screen on the left, a picture appeared of Saunders in uniform, standing in front of the custody desk at Redbury station.

'Sergeant Saunders, is this you in the picture?'

DI Cater leant forward. 'Where was this image obtained?'

Ridpath ignored him again, pressing on. 'Sergeant Saunders, can you confirm this is you, and the date and time in the top right-hand corner is correct?'

Saunders glanced up from the table to the monitor. 'Yes. It's me at the beginning of my shift.'

'And you were the custody officer in charge on Redbury station on the night of February 20 and the morning of February 21?'

'Yes.'

'Document two in the files is the statement given by you to the Professional Standards Department regarding the events of the night. Is this correct?'

Saunders turned the page and looked at the statement. 'Yes.'

Ridpath stared at him. 'Sergeant Saunders, is there anything you would like to add to this statement?'

'No.'

'Would you like to take this opportunity to amend or qualify anything in this statement?'

Saunders sighed loudly. 'How long is this going to go on for? I need to get back to work.'

Ridpath continued. 'Would you like to amend anything in this statement?'

Saunders leant over and whispered in his union rep's ear.

'The sergeant has nothing to add,' said Cater.

'Moving on. We will now play video of the booking in of the deceased, Ben Holdsworth, at 3.40 a.m.'

'For the record, Mr Ridpath, I am not aware that any CCTV has been provided to the coroner's office.'

'Duly noted, and it's DI Ridpath, for your information, DI Cater. Please play the video, Sophia.'

Sergeant Saunders sat forward, staring at the screen, taking an interest in the proceedings for the first time. Jack Cater was messaging on his phone.

On the screen, a man was standing in front of the custody desk, escorted on either side by two constables. Behind the desk sat Tony Saunders.

'Is this the deceased, Ben Holdsworth?'

'Yes.'

'And you booked him into the station at 3.40 a.m.?'

'He'd been arrested for drug possession with intent to supply by Constables Carter and Dryden that evening. He was placed in custody under provisions of the 1994 Drug Trafficking Act.'

The CCTV continued on-screen.

Ridpath paused it.

'He keeps asking for a DI Brett of the National Crime Agency. Why?'

Saunders shrugged his shoulders. 'Why don't you ask him?'

'Mr Holdsworth is dead.'

'Then ask DI Brett.'

'Don't worry, I intend to, Sergeant Saunders.'

The CCTV continued, with Saunders taking down all the details and finally asking the detention officers to strip search Ben Holdsworth.

'Why did you request a strip search?'

Another long sigh. Saunders' voice took on the tones of an adult explaining the theory of relativity to a stupid child. 'In cases where illegal substances are involved, it is recommended all detainees be searched thoroughly before being placed in the cells, for their own safety as well as that of the detaining officers. Page three of the College of Policing's Code of Conduct for custody officers. I thought you would have known, DI Ridpath, being a copper and all.'

Cater leant forward, closer to Ridpath. 'Throughout the booking-in process, Sergeant Saunders followed the exact procedure as described in the handbook for custody officers. The Professional Standards Department called his conduct exemplary.'

Ridpath ignored the interruption and carried on.

'Throughout your interaction with Mr Holdsworth, did he in any way seem under the influence of drugs or intoxicants?'

'No.'

'Was he slurring his words?'

'No.'

'Were his pupils dilated?'

'No.'

'Did he do anything suggesting he was under the influence of any intoxicants?'

'No.'

'Please turn to document three, which is the post-mortem report written by Dr Harold Lardner on the deceased. You will see the toxicology analysis appended to the main document showed he had a large amount of diamorphine in his bloodstream.'

Saunders read through the passage from the report. 'So?'

'You still say he didn't display any signs of being under the influence of drugs.'

'Yes.'

Cater interrupted again. 'The post-mortem also states clearly that Ben Holdsworth died from an accidental fall in his cell. No police officers were present in the cell when he fell.'

'We have had a second opinion from another pathologist who challenges the validity of the work of Dr Lardner. He has stated that with the quantities of diamorphine in Ben Holdsworth's bloodstream he would have been unable to function. I need to ask you again, Sergeant Saunders, did you notice Mr Holdsworth was under the influence of drugs?'

'Sergeant Saunders has answered the question. Can we move on?'

'Were any drugs found in the strip search of the deceased?'

'No.'

'All the possessions of Mr Holdsworth were noted in his arrest record,' interrupted Cater again.

Ridpath knew what the union rep was doing: trying to break up the rhythm of his questions. He ploughed on regardless.

'When you found him on the floor of the cell, was a needle lying nearby?'

'No.'

'Are you sure?'

'The question has been answered.' Cater stared directly at the detective.

Ridpath made a note on his pad. 'Document four. You gave Mr Holdsworth the opportunity to make a phone call. Why?'

Another loud, long sigh. 'It's standard operating procedure. A detainee is allowed to make a phone call to a solicitor, family member or friend before being placed in the cells.' He turned to DI Cater. 'How long is this going on for? I've been through all this with Professional Standards and the IOPC. This… man… doesn't even know the standard custody operating procedures.'

'It's a fair question, DI Ridpath; how long is this going to continue?'

'Thank you, Sergeant Saunders, for your patience,' Ridpath answered emolliently. 'I am just trying to establish if there needs to be a review of the standard operating procedures in the event of an arrest for drugs. Of course, the coroner and the jury will make the final decision, but it helps if they understand your testimony as a witness.' He smiled at the end, as if apologising for putting the poor sergeant through an unfortunate process.

'It's just taking too long,' said Saunders finally.

'Shall we move on then? When did the signal from the CCTV in Cell 3 cease?'

Saunders frowned. 'I can't remember.'

'Let me help you. According to the custody log, you made a note at 4.37, but according to the CCTV images from Cell 3, it ceased at 4.35.'

'Just two minutes earlier,' interrupted Cater.

'As soon as I noticed it wasn't working, I made a note.'

'You didn't go to check it?'

'No point. Only the maintenance people can open up the camera. They're always going on the blink.'

'So it didn't worry you that it wasn't working?'

'No. I ordered the custody officers to check on him every thirty minutes. Standard…'

'…operating procedures. Did they do it?'

'As far as I am aware, yes.'

'Please turn to document five. This is the witness statement given to the IOPC by Lucas Harvey, civilian custody officer on duty. It reads, "The camera went on the blink and I was told by Sergeant Saunders to check on the prisoner every half an hour. Unfortunately, due to an incident, I didn't have time." What incident?'

'There was trouble with some kids we arrested for joyriding. Someone pressed the alarm and when that happens, everybody including the custody detention officers goes to the aid of the officer concerned. Standard operating procedure. But I sent Lucas Harvey back the first time as he wasn't needed, keeping Terry Rodgers to watch over the kids. They were on something.'

'The kids were on drugs?'

'Looked like it.'

'But you didn't notice Ben Holdsworth had over 1200 milligrams of diamorphine in his system?'

Saunders looked sheepish for a moment. 'No.'

'How many times did it happen?'

'What?'

'The alarm being pressed?'

'Twice.'

'And in each case, you sent Lucas Harvey back to the custody cells?'

'No, the second time he stayed in the cells.'

'Why?'

'I told him he wasn't needed.'

'Then why didn't he check Cell 3 as you had instructed him to do?'

'I don't know, you'll have to ask him.'

'He's dead.'

Saunders raised his eyebrows, but didn't respond.

Ridpath made a note and then carried on. 'Document six is a statement taken from the other civilian detention officer, Terry Rodgers. He says, "I returned from the holding room at 5.45 to find Sergeant Saunders in the cell corridor; he was standing outside Cell 3." What were you doing there?'

Saunders glanced across at his union rep. 'Checking on the detainee.'

Ridpath frowned. 'But there's nothing in your witness statement or the custody report about checking on Cell 3, or on Mr Holdsworth?'

'I must have forgotten. So much happened that night.'

'So you went to check on a man arrested for drugs in the cells?'

'Yes. Standard...'

'...operating procedure. I get it. Did you speak to Mr Holdsworth at all?'

Saunders looked flustered for the first time. 'I... I don't know.'

'You don't know if you spoke to the detainee?'

'I'm not sure... I can't remember.'

'But he was alive when you looked in on him at 5.45?'

'Yes.'

A long pause as Ridpath breathed in, quietening himself and glancing at his notes. This was going to be a difficult question. 'Sergeant Saunders, you had a daughter, Hannah, is that correct?'

Saunders' jaw tightened. 'What's my daughter got to do with it?'

'She had a drug problem and died from an overdose of heroin in October, 2017, four months before the incident.'

'Leave my daughter out of this,' Saunders growled.

'I don't see what relevance this line of questioning has to a man who died in police custody, DI Ridpath.'

Eve's face flashed into his mind. How would he feel if she died in some shooting gallery with a needle sticking out of her arm? His whole body shuddered with revulsion at the thought. He paused for a moment. Was he going to push this, or back off?

His job was to find out what had happened in the cells that morning. Nothing more, nothing less. His own personal emotions had no part in this interview. He decided to go ahead, tapping the desk in front of him lightly. 'Did you speak to the detainee, Sergeant Saunders? Is that why you were in the cells?'

'Of course I spoke to him. I had to check he was OK.'

'Where was Mr Holdsworth arrested?'

Again, Saunders glanced across at DI Cater. 'I can't remember.'

'Let me refresh your memory. It was on Quince Road, part of the Orchard Estate. Your daughter was found dead in one of the local shooting galleries, from a drug overdose.'

Suddenly, Saunders launched himself across the table towards Ridpath, trying to grab hold of his jacket. Sophia screamed. Cater grabbed the man's arms, holding him tight and dragging him back to his chair.

'Calm down, Tony...'

'He's talking about my daughter...'

'He's well out of order, but calm down.'

Saunders was visibly shaking. He gritted his teeth, pointed at Ridpath and snarled. 'This bastard… it's my daughter… she was only nineteen.'

And just as quickly as it had arisen, the anger left Saunders and his shoulders slumped. He held his head in his hands.

Ridpath had sat impassively throughout this time, looking at his interviewee.

'Shall we continue?' said Ridpath quietly. 'I will ask you once again. Did you speak to the detainee, Ben Holdsworth?'

'Of course I spoke to the scum. He was a drug dealer, trading in people's lives.'

'And what did you say?'

Sergeant Saunders took his hands away from his face and stared straight at Ridpath. 'I told him I would kill him if he ever sold drugs on my patch again.'

Cater laid his hand on Saunders' arm. 'I think we should take a break now. Mr Ridpath, your insinuations have upset my client.'

Chapter Forty-Seven

Garry Abbott was still pacing the room. Should he call Phil? Should he get him to pick up the stuff from the safety deposit box on Mason Street?

He'd been up all night, glancing out of the window every ten minute to check if the van was still parked outside the hotel.

It was, but he couldn't see if anybody was sitting in the front seat.

Around seven a.m. a man and a woman left the hotel and walked over to the van. The woman wore high heels and a micro skirt, tottering slightly as she opened the door and slipped into the passenger seat.

Garry Abbott breathed out, feeling his whole body relax.

It was just some one-night stand. Some two-timing husband who didn't want to go back home to his wife. The van didn't belong to Delaney or his goons.

For the rest of the morning, though, he couldn't sleep. His mind chased a world of possibilities.

What if he left today? Went to London without picking up the money and passports from the safety deposit box?

What if he booked a flight from Manchester instead? Just went to Thailand anyway? His mate in Chiang Mai would put him up for a while even if he had no money.

Or what if he went to Delaney and apologised for hitting him? Went down on his knees and begged forgiveness?

He rejected all these possibilities. Without money he could do nothing. Without the passports he couldn't build a new identity for himself. And he was sure Delaney would never forgive him. He was a marked man, that's what Delaney had said. Somebody wanted him dead, so dead was what he was going to be.

He racked his brains, trying to work out why.

Was it the night in the jail? The things he'd heard in the cell next door?

He hadn't told anybody about it. Well, nobody except Phil. He knew everything, but he would never grass him out to Delaney... would he?

He picked up the phone and dialled the number.

'Phil, it's Garry. You can go to the safety box company this afternoon. I'm going to call them now and give them your details. What ID are you using?'

'We've agreed I'm going to get five hundred quid?'

Abbott sighed. 'Yeah, as soon as I get the stuff, you'll get your money.'

'Right, I'll use my driving licence.'

'You need to get there before they close.'

'Where are you now?'

Again, the hackles on the back of Abbott's neck rose. Why was Phil so interested to know where he was? 'I'll tell you where to meet later.'

'We're meeting tonight?'

'Nah, tomorrow. It's not safe yet. Give me the number on your driving licence in case they ask.'

Phil said a long list of numbers and letters.

'Hang on, let me write it down.'

He repeated the number. 'Got it now?'

'Yeah, I'll call 'em straight away, you get yourself down there.'

'Will do. See you soon, Garry, take care of yourself.'

Abbott clicked off the call and made another to the manager at the depository, giving his password and issuing instructions that his agent, Phil Wardsley, would be along in the afternoon to open his safety deposit box and remove some items.

The calls done, a wave of immense tiredness suddenly swept over Garry Abbott. As he lay down to sleep, for the first time in a while he felt hopeful. The nightmare would soon be over and he could escape to the warmth and smiles of Thailand.

Not long to go now.

Chapter Forty-Eight

Ridpath started the tape again.

'The interview is recommencing at 2.45 p.m. on November 4, 2021. Sergeant Saunders, what did you do after speaking to Ben Holdsworth?'

Saunders was calm again now, self-composed. In a curt voice he said, 'I went back to my seat at the custody desk after checking out the holding room where the joyriders were kept.'

'Ben Holdsworth was still alive when you left him?'

'Of course he was.'

'And the CCTV in Cells 3 and 4 was still down?'

'As I noted in the duty roster.'

'But you didn't note your visit to him in your account of the night?'

'I must have forgotten.'

'You were the last person to see the detainee.'

Jack Cater leant in. 'I think we have already covered those events before the break, Mr Ridpath; can we move on?'

Ridpath turned the page in his document folder. 'The following video, document seven, is an excerpt of the second time the security alarm sounded that night.'

They all watched as on the custody desk camera, Terry Rodgers, Saunders and a single copper rushed in from the right. The beeping of the security alarm was loud on the screen. The time in the left-hand corner said 5.46.

'Who sounded the alarm?'

'I don't know.'

'What?'

'I don't know. I presumed the kids in the holding room had kicked off again.'

'That's why the officers responded?'

'Yes.'

'What did the security system tell you?'

'I don't know, I didn't look.'

'What?'

'I just presumed the alarm came from the holding room.'

'What did you do?'

'I went with the officers to the holding room.'

'Leaving the custody desk?'

'Yes.'

'Is that standard operating procedure?'

'No.'

'Isn't the desk supposed to be manned at all times?'

'Yes, but...'

'But what?'

'But the kids kept kicking off, I was going to give them one last warning.'

'And did you?'

Saunders looked down. 'No.'

'Because they were quiet. The alarm had come from somewhere else. Did you check where it was from when you returned to the desk?'

'No.'

'Why not?'

'I thought it was just a glitch. It happened quite a lot.'

'Security alarms going off?'

'Yes.'

'But there is no report of a fault in the duty log?'

'I didn't report it every time. No point.'

'How long is this line of questioning going to continue, Mr Ridpath? My client has now answered the question.'

'Let us move on to the death of the detainee. You received a message from Lucas Harvey at 6.28 that Ben Holdsworth was lying on the floor of his cell. What did you do?'

'I left the desk...'

'Unguarded again.'

'I left the desk to attend to an emergency.'

Cater had pulled out a booklet from his desk and began reading from it. '"In emergency circumstances, the office in charge may leave the custody desk to attend to the incident." Page twenty-four of the Operating Standards Manual for custody sergeants. I'll leave you a copy, Mr Ridpath.'

'That won't be necessary. What did you see when you went to Cell 3?'

'I saw the detainee lying on the floor. He seemed to be unresponsive.'

'The door was closed and locked?'

'Yes.'

'Where are the keys kept?'

'In the custody officer's room.'

'On the wall?'

'Yes.'

'What did you do next?'

'Lucas went to get the keys to open the door. He returned and we rushed in to see the detainee.'

'Was he responsive?'

'No.'

'So what did you do?'

'I commenced to give CPR, compressing the chest and giving mouth-to-mouth resuscitation.'

'Anything else?'

'I sent Harvey to get the doctor, who was in the medical room checking on the joyriders.'

'What time did the doctor arrive?'

'Six thirtyish.'

'6.35, actually, from the CCTV above the custody desk. It's not in the duty log.'

'I must have forgotten to note it.'

'So you sent Harvey to get the doctor?'

'Correct.'

'How long was he gone?'

'Gone?'

'How long did he take to get the doctor?'

'I don't know, a couple of minutes or so.'

'In that time you were left alone with the prisoner?'

'I was giving him CPR.'

'Alone?'

'What are you insinuating, Mr Ridpath?' asked Cater.

'Nothing. I'm merely establishing a timeline and the whereabouts of the personnel during the death in custody, DI Cater.' He turned back to face Saunders. 'So you were alone with the deceased for two minutes. What happened then?'

'Nothing happened.'

'I thought you were giving CPR?'

'I was, but I stopped.'

'Why?'

'The man was unresponsive, and I was waiting for the doctor to arrive. I tried again but...'

'He didn't move?'

'No.'

'Was he already dead?'

Cater leant forward again. 'I would remind you, Sergeant Saunders is not a medical officer. It is not his job to pronounce death.'

'True, DI Cater, but you've worked the job long enough, Sergeant Saunders, you know if somebody is dead, don't you? So, had he already died?'

The sergeant nodded, and then took a long time before answering. 'I don't know. I'm not a medical officer.'

Ridpath sighed loudly. 'When the doctor arrived, what did he do?'

'He performed CPR too, and then called for an ambulance.'

'Which arrived at 6.43.'

'I think so.'

Ridpath clasped his fingers in front of him. 'So how did you feel, Sergeant Saunders? A man died on your watch.'

For the first time, a fleeting smile crossed Saunders' lips. 'You want to know the truth?'

Ridpath nodded.

'You think you can handle the truth?'

'Try me.'

A hardness came into Saunders' eyes. 'I was happy. There was going to be one less drug-dealing lowlife in Manchester.'

Jack Cater's phone beeped as he received a message. He glanced down to look at it before standing up. 'This interview is terminated, Mr Ridpath. According to the force's public relations branch, the coroner's office has not been sent any CCTV images. The footage has been lost, and they are still trying to find it. They have no idea where this comes from. And, as there is no chain of evidence for these videos, there may be a potential offence under the Data Protection Act. Come along, Tony. We've wasted enough time here.'

'I still have questions to ask this witness, DI Cater.'

'You may do, but he doesn't have to sit here and answer them. Come on, Tony, we're off, time for us to go.'

'Sergeant Saunders, had you met Ben Holdsworth before February 2018?'

'No, never.'

'You don't have to answer, Tony.'

'Document seven please, Sophia. This document is a copy of an arrest made in 2016. The detained man is Ben Holdsworth. Can you tell me the signature of the arresting officer at the bottom of the sheet?'

Tony Saunders looked up at the screen. 'Not my signature. I'd never met Ben Holdsworth before.'

'Let the record show the signature is that of Sergeant Tony Saunders.'

'That's it, we're out of here.'

Jack Cater gathered the documents and, taking his client's arm, strode towards the door, stopping just before the exit. 'One more thing, DI Ridpath. As a serving officer, I will be reporting your conduct of this interview to Professional Standards. They will no doubt want to know where you obtained the CCTV of the station. It will be interesting to see how it feels when *you* are being investigated.'

Chapter Forty-Nine

After Cater and Saunders had left, there was a moment's silence before Sophia broke it. 'You were hard on him.'

'Was I?' Ridpath said absentmindedly, checking his notes from the meeting. There was something niggling him.

'What do you think about Saunders?'

'Too many inconsistencies in his testimony – saying he didn't speak to Holdsworth in his cell, and then admitting he did.' Ridpath screwed up his face. 'He's hiding something.'

'What?'

'I don't know. But we need to talk to the duty doctor asap. Why has nobody interviewed him before? There's no witness statement in any of the documents from public relations.'

'There's a lot of people they didn't interview. It's almost as if...'

'Say it.'

'...as if they didn't want to dig too deeply, frightened of what they might find.'

Ridpath stared at Sophia. He'd forgotten how astute she was. An old head on very young shoulders. She'd make a fine copper if she ever joined the police.

'It's been worrying me as well. Too many obvious leads avoided or ignored.'

'I'll find the doctor and arrange an interview.' She stared down at the table for a while. 'Aren't you worried about being investigated?'

Ridpath snorted. 'Cater? He's just trying to intimidate me. I would do exactly the same if the boot was on the other foot.'

But inside, Ridpath didn't feel so confident. Had he broken the data protection laws by using the CCTV? Perhaps he shouldn't have used the images, but without them, there was no proof of anything.

'Can you check something else for me, Sophia?'

'Sure.'

'See what we have on the death of Lucas Harvey. It strikes me as strange that the one man who can tell us what happened that night is no longer available for questioning. It all seems too pat…'

'I'll check with the other coroners and find out who handled the death.'

There was a loud knock on the door and Turnbull's bald head appeared. 'DI Ridpath, the boss would like to see you straight away. You've been a naughty boy, and she's not chuffed with you.'

Chapter Fifty

'You're here, boss.'

'And where else would I be?'

Detective Superintendent Claire Trent sat behind her desk, her hair swept back in a new short cut. Officially, she was still Ridpath's direct report, as he had only been 'seconded' to the coroner's office. The 'secondment' had lasted over three years now thanks to an agreement with Mrs Challinor.

'It's just… you weren't here at the last meeting.'

'I was on a course, Ridpath, remember those? Time you returned to Edgeley Park for a few refreshers.'

'I agree, boss.'

She looked down and seemed to be checking some notes.

'How are things with the coroner?'

Ridpath wondered if the two of them had already spoken that morning. 'Fine, busy as ever.'

'I hear you are looking into the death in custody at Redbury.'

He glanced across at Turnbull. The man had a smug smirk plastered all over his face.

'It's one of the investigations I'm working on at the moment,' Ridpath answered.

'Probably the most important, I should imagine.'

'It is taking up a lot of my time…'

'I also hear you interviewed Tony Saunders and his union rep this afternoon.'

'I did.'

'Good copper, Tony. I worked with him when I first started sixteen years ago.'

Ridpath didn't answer. Where was this going?

'But I'm sure you will do a good and fair job. Let me know if MIT can help you in any way.'

Ridpath stayed silent as she turned to Turnbull. 'I also hear Ridpath was denied help from MIT, Paul. As long as he is a serving officer with this department, he will receive the aid any other officer gets, is that clear?'

Turnbull's mouth opened and closed like a fish out of water. 'But... but... he was investigating another officer and working for the coroner...'

'It does not matter. We will help him whatever he is investigating, do you understand?'

Turnbull went bright red and the vein in his bald head pulsed. 'But...'

'Do I have to spell it out for you? The old days are done and dusted. It's history. The sooner we put it behind us the better. There will be no more cover-ups, no more hiding the truth behind a web of half-truths. The old policy of denying mistakes and sweeping them under the carpet has gone; the Inspectorate of Police report ended all that. If we have done anything wrong or our procedures are incorrect, we must use events like an unfortunate death in custody to improve our operational management. This was made very clear in the course I just attended. There's a new sheriff in town, and he's cleaning up our act. Do you understand, Paul?'

'I think so.'

A smile crossed her lips. 'The more cynical among you' – she glanced at Ridpath – 'may think it does help that this... event... happened over three years ago, before the arrival of the new sheriff. But, of course, that has nothing to do with it at all.'

Ridpath watched her with awe. She was such an accomplished political operator. He couldn't do what she did in a million years. On the other hand, Turnbull's mouth was wide open as if he'd just discovered Father Christmas didn't live at the North Pole and had previously been arrested for child abuse.

Claire Trent turned to him. 'So, Ridpath, in the interests of transparency and openness, let us know what you need.'

He wasn't going to lose his chance. 'I'd like Chrissy's help, boss, to find a missing witness. And Emily if she's free,' Ridpath added as an afterthought.

'You can have them both.' She sat back in her chair. 'Listen, both of you, the world has changed, the past is the past. We need to move on as quickly as possible. There is now one goal and one goal only:

to nick the baddies and stick 'em inside. The new mantra is openness and transparency...'

'As long as it's about stuff that happened in the past...' muttered Turnbull.

She frowned. 'Such negativity is not a character trait appreciated by the new management, Paul, nor by me. We focus on our jobs and nothing else.'

It was Turnbull's turn to stay silent.

'How is the investigation going, Ridpath?'

'It's early days, boss...'

'But?'

Ridpath wasn't going to say what he really thought. Until he had more evidence, he was going to keep his concerns as vague as possible. 'But something is off,' he finally answered. 'The CCTV, Tony Saunders' testimony, the post-mortem report, the IOPC investigation... it just doesn't feel right.'

Turnbull snorted. 'More of your feelings, Ridpath?'

The detective ignored him.

'But procedure was followed.'

'It seems to have been, boss, but...' He shrugged his shoulders.

'Next steps?'

'Interview the duty doctor called to Redbury nick and find the prisoner in the next-door cell, a Garry Abbott. Nobody ever interviewed him about what happened.'

She stood up, indicating the meeting was over. 'Right, let myself or Paul know if you need anything.'

Ridpath stood up to leave.

'But I also hear you've obtained some CCTV footage which you shouldn't have...'

'How had she found out so quickly?'

The surprise must have shown on his face because she answered, 'You forget how many friends I have on this force. It was professional courtesy to inform me that one of my officers was being investigated. But if you have broken the law, Ridpath, I cannot help you.'

'The new policy of openness and transparency, boss.'

'Exactly, the memo is just taking a little longer to reach some departments. That will be all.'

Chapter Fifty-One

'Hi, Chrissy, there's a couple of things I need you to do for me.'

'Sorry, Ridpath, I'll have to check with Turnbull, you heard what he said.'

'It's OK, it's been approved by Claire Trent.'

'The boss is back? Great, what can I do?'

'I need to find the current whereabouts of a man called Garry Abbott. Here's his address and number from three years ago. Can you find him for me?'

'I'll try, Ridpath. Luckily it's not such a common name. Anything else?'

Ridpath thought for a while. Sophia was going to find the doctor and she was checking up on the death of the custodial officer, Lucas Harvey. Best not to double up on the workload.

'Could you get the financial audit people to check these two people out for me?'

He wrote out the names.

Tony Saunders

Lucas Harvey

'Are you sure, Ridpath?'

'Yes, but could you ask them to be discreet?'

'Ask who to be discreet?'

Turnbull was standing behind him, trying to peer over his shoulder. Chrissy Wright quickly covered the paper with a file before he could see the names.

'Nothing, DCI Turnbull. I was just reminding Chrissy of the necessity to keep everything under wraps when we are investigating witnesses for the inquest.'

Turnbull leant in closer. Ridpath could smell and taste the man's breath. He spoke in a low voice so nobody else could hear. 'Don't you ever go behind my back to Claire Trent again, d'you hear?'

'I didn't.'

A finger began to prod Ridpath's chest. 'Just as soon as she is promoted to chief super and I am in charge, you'll be gone, Ridpath. I don't care where, Timbuktu as far as I am concerned, but you'll be out on your arse quicker than Ole Gunnar Solskjaer.'

Ridpath stepped back. He wasn't going to be goaded or prodded by this man.

'If you don't mind, sir, I have work to do.'

Turnbull stepped into his personal space again, leaning and hissing, 'Enjoy the moment, son, it won't last long.'

He sauntered off, whistling gaily, as if he had just had a pleasant chat with a friend.

'Ignore him, Ridpath, he's an arsehole.'

'Nah, worse, Chrissy, at least an arsehole is useful. One more thing, have you heard anything more on Saunders or his daughter?'

'Only what I overheard in the canteen. Apparently, he was pretty cut up by her death, took a month's personal leave to care for his wife.'

'She died in October, 2017, just four months before the death in custody of Ben Holdsworth...' Ridpath suddenly remembered something. 'One more thing. Have you ever heard of a DI Mark Brett of the National Crime Agency, based in Warrington?'

She slowly shook her head. 'Doesn't ring a bell, but you know what the NCA people are like.'

Ridpath nodded his head. 'Not great at sharing.'

'Like a five-year-old with a bag of his favourite sweets.'

'OK, ta, Chrissy.' He scanned the desks across the floor, most occupied by detectives. 'Have you seen Emily?'

Chrissy shrugged her shoulders. 'Probably gone for a fag, she's been doing it a lot these days.'

'Turnbull on her case?'

'On everything as far as I can see. She's getting all the worst jobs.'

Chapter Fifty-Two

Outside, Emily was leaning against the metal bars close to the smokers' corner round the back of the building. Here, all the reprobates gathered, eagerly puffing away as if their souls depended on it, each with a furtive air knowing they were doing something frowned upon even though it was legal.

'Ridpath, haven't seen you at HQ for a while. Avoiding the place?'

'Not really.'

'Avoiding Turnbull, then, can't say I blame you.'

She spoke in a loud voice, not caring if the other detectives heard.

'How's stuff, Emily?'

'Same old, same old. I finally put in for the transfer.'

'Heard anything yet?'

'Nah, it'll take time, you know what GMP is like.'

'Turnbull been hassling you?'

'When hasn't he?'

'Why don't you report him to HR, or Claire Trent?'

'Who's going to listen? A junior reporting her boss? What do you think that's going to do for my career? And anyway, there's nothing concrete, he's far too clever. You can't report an attitude.'

'Sorry it's come to this.'

'Not to worry, time to move on anyway.' She laughed to herself. 'You know the old trick...'

'Move on before your mistakes catch up with you...'

'Got it in one, Ridpath.'

'Another of Charlie Whittaker's sayings I'm surprised it's still hanging around the halls.'

'Now more than ever, Ridpath.' She took a long drag on her cigarette and lifted her chin to exhale the blue smoke. 'How do you handle it?'

'I keep my head down and do the work. You know, people like Turnbull are only temporary; they always get found out eventually.'

'But when? He seems to be getting stronger and stronger. Fancies himself as the next head of MIT when Claire Trent gets promoted and given a division.'

'Are you sure she'd take it?'

'What?'

'Well, look at it this way. Why would you swap a high-profile job in MIT, at the cutting edge of the new chief's mission, for all the bureaucracy of running a division?'

'Ambition? Promotion? More dosh?'

'Not her motivation. At least not yet – she's smarter, more political.'

'I hope you're right, Ridpath.' Another drag on her cigarette and then she spoke in a softer voice. 'You got anything for me? I'm going mental at the moment.'

'The main thing I'm working on is the death in custody of Ben Holdsworth.'

'That case? And I thought I had it hard.'

'It's not the easiest case, and something just isn't right. It smells funny.'

'So does rotten fish, and that's why I don't go near it. But in your case, I'll make an exception. If you need any help, let me know.'

'There is one thing. I'm looking into a DI Mark Brett from the NCA. They are being as forthcoming as the Home Office. Chrissy's checking up on him, but it would be good if you could ask around your contacts. Where was he previously? Where is he now? What's his background? Usual stuff.'

She looked across at him through a cloud of smoke. 'What's he got to do with a death in custody?'

'That's what I want to know. Holdsworth asked for him by name when he was detained, even rang his number, but got no reply.'

'Didn't the IOPC question him?'

'Apparently not. Or if they did, I haven't seen any witness statement.'

She stubbed the cigarette out forcefully into the standing ashtray. 'No worries, I'll ask around for you.'

He began walking away and held his hand up to his ear in the shape of a phone. 'Call me asap.'

'Will do.'

'And in the meantime, look after yourself, keep your head down.'

But Emily Parkinson had already turned her back and was walking back up the stairs to the main building, her shoulders hunched, like a snail dragging a heavy weight.

Chapter Fifty-Three

How dare Ridpath go behind his back and nobble Claire Trent?

When she had asked to see him, Turnbull had gone along expecting him to receive a right bollocking. Instead, he had been patted on his head and told he was a good little soldier.

What the hell was she playing at?

Even worse, he had been reprimanded and told to help Ridpath in any way possible.

Bastard.

Why should he help that toerag? Ridpath spent his life undermining him, making him look foolish in front of the lads, and she supported him.

Not any more.

Claire Trent had humiliated him for the last time.

He took three deep breaths, the vein in his temple pulsing.

His phone rang. He was tempted to ignore it but saw who it was from.

'Jack, good to hear from you.'

'You won't be so pleased when I'm finished.'

'Oh?'

'I've just made a formal complaint to Professional Standards about one of your lads.'

'Who?'

'A Detective Inspector Ridpath. He is on MIT's books, isn't he, but seconded to the coroner?'

'Nothing to do with me, Jack, you need to talk to Claire Trent.'

'I thought she was away on a course.'

'Not any more, she's back. But between you and me and the four walls, the more you complain about the little toerag, the happier I'll be.'

'It's like that, is it?'

'For me, Ridpath is a disloyal arsehole who's not fit to lick the boots of any copper here. The sooner he leaves the police, or is forced to leave, the better it is for all of us… but don't quote me.'

'Wouldn't think of it; thanks for the heads-up.'

The phone went dead. Claire Trent already knew about Jack Cater's complaint, and so she was protecting Ridpath, trying to speed up his investigation.

But he'd put a stop to that. *Put one step wrong and you're toast, Ridpath.*

A knock on the door.

'COME IN,' he shouted.

Alan Butcher popped his head around the door. 'I thought I'd bring you some good news from Harry in Leeds, boss. He says the NCA have finally given the green light to make the arrests. They are going in tomorrow morning.'

Turnbull's face fell.

'I thought you'd be happy, boss.'

Claire Trent was back now. She would claim credit for closing this case, despite all of Turnbull's work pushing the NCA to act.

He could see his chances of promotion vanishing quicker than a vindaloo on Curry Mile.

Bloody Ridpath, it was all his fault.

Chapter Fifty-Four

Back in the car, Ridpath started the engine and checked his watch. Time to go back to the coroner's office, or should he go home? A quick phone call to Sophia to check.

'Hi there, how is everything?'

'All good, I've found the medical officer.'

'So easily?'

'It wasn't difficult. I contacted the local office of the BMA. And get this, he's still on call for the police, but in a different station. I've set up a meeting for you tomorrow afternoon at his GP surgery.'

'Great, well done. Have you found anything about Lucas Harvey's death yet?'

'Give me a break, Ridpath, I've only just got back.'

'Sorry, getting ahead of myself.'

'It's the next job. You coming back?'

'I thought I'd go home and spend the rest of the evening watching the remaining CCTV. But if I need to come back I will.'

'And I thought you might be enjoying *Corrie*.'

'Fat chance. Still got a lot of cameras to work through.'

'Nah, no need to come back. The coroner was asking for an update, so I've arranged a meeting at nine a.m. tomorrow before she goes into court. I hope that's OK?'

'Sounds good. Quite a lot to tell her.'

'Don't work too late.'

'That's what I'm supposed to say.'

'Oh, and one more thing. Lardner has refused to meet you. According to him, "It would adversely affect his mental health." You do have an effect on some people, Ridpath. Are you going to subpoena him?'

'Difficult if he's claiming mental health issues. And his evidence as a witness would be worthless.'

'Is he playing the system?'

'Like a champion poker player.'

'What are you going to do?'

Ridpath went silent for a moment. Outside, the windscreen wipers on the car had started automatically as the rain that had been threatening all day finally began to fall. Another beautiful day in sunny Manchester.

'Let me think about it this evening and chat with the coroner tomorrow morning. Perhaps we can get away with not calling him as a witness and just accepting the original post-mortem as it is, with Dr Schofield calling it into question. At least we'll avoid two expert witnesses contradicting each other in court.'

'Sounds like a plan. See you tomorrow.'

'Call me this evening if anything urgent turns up.'

He switched off the phone. The windscreen wipers made another noisy pass across the glass in front of him, clearing the rain. Within seconds it was splattered again, with large gobbets of water distorting his view.

He realised the same was happening with this case. Things would begin to clear and then something would come along to make it all opaque again.

He put the car in gear. *Keep moving forward, Ridpath, that's all you can do. Just keep on going.*

Unless the past catches up with you first.

Chapter Fifty-Five

Eve was already at home when he got back.

'Hi, Dad, you're back early – wasn't expecting you for at least an hour.' In her hand she was carrying a strawberry jam and cream cheese sandwich. A strange combination, which, for some reason, was one of her comfort foods.

'How was your day?' he asked, looking at the sandwich.

'Not great. Double maths followed by double physics.'

'Sounds like double trouble to me.'

Her eyes rolled. 'Oh, Dad, you still tell the worst jokes.'

'What would you like for tea?'

She held up the sandwich.

'You need something more nutritious.' He remembered his research. 'Something with more iron. How about a nice piece of lamb's liver?'

She made a violent retching sound. 'Dad, bits of an animal, really?'

'You're not turning vegetarian, are you?'

'You don't "turn" vegetarian, you become one. And no, I'm not becoming a veggie. At least not yet. Just cutting down the amount of meat I eat.'

'Are you sure? How will you get your iron? A growing girl needs iron.'

'Green vegetables, kale, eating scrap metal. Loads of ways to get it outside of meat.'

'Scrap metal? What food group is that?'

He could see she was laughing at him as she bit into her sandwich.

'Seriously, what do you want to eat for tea?'

'How about pizza? I feel like something cheesy.'

He waited for the joke and when it didn't come, continued. 'The usual, Hawaiian?'

'Of course. Need my fruit too.'

'I'll order. You know real Italians would turn in their oven at the thought of putting pineapple on a pizza.'

She held up the sandwich. 'What about strawberry jam on cream cheese?'

'Conniptions.'

'Loads of hand gestures and *mamma mia*s.'

'Double conniptions.'

'Reminds me of a joke Maisie told me yesterday. A blonde went to buy a pizza. Chef asked her, would you like it cut into four or eight slices? The blonde replied, four please. There is no way I could possibly eat eight slices.'

He laughed. 'That's not funny.'

'But you're smiling, Dad... it's been a while since I heard you laugh,' she finally added.

There was an awkward silence between them.

'I'll call the pizza place,' he finally said. 'They'll take at least an hour even though pizza is supposed to be fast food.'

She walked towards the stairs. 'I'll get my homework started. Chemistry.'

'Give me a shout if you want some help.'

'It's on the elements and the periodic table.'

'Probably best I leave you to it, then.'

She nodded, smiling. 'And Dad, it's good when you laugh.'

Chapter Fifty-Six

'Tell me what you've heard, Alan.'

Paul Turnbull finished half his pint in one immense swallow. Spending his life shouting at the detectives in MIT was thirsty work. They'd finished late and had popped into the Gas Lamp for a swift half or three on the way home.

It was the sort of place he loved best. A subterranean bar with tiled walls, decent pints of craft ales on tap, no TV, a great selection of malt whiskies and not a goujon of chicken or an overpriced hamburger in sight. Even better, it stayed open till late so decent, hard-working men like himself could still get a pint after they had finished a shift.

'It's like this, boss. I was talking to a few of the lads down in the canteen and they weren't happy.'

Another large swallow of beer, followed by a sip of his whisky chaser. 'About what?'

'About Ridpath.'

'Tell me more.'

'They weren't happy about him investigating Tony Saunders. Said the man had already been cleared by Professional Standards, IOPC and the CPS, so why was there another investigation.'

'I hope you put them right.'

'Of course, boss, I told 'em it was a travesty. Tony Saunders was a good copper who should have been back on duty years ago.'

'Ain't it the truth.'

'But then Emily Parkinson came along and said Ridpath was just doing his job.'

'Did she?'

'Said the coroner had to hold an inquest as it was a death in custody. They had a statutory duty to look into what happened.'

'Is our Emily screwing Ridpath?'

'Not that I've heard, boss. I think she bats for the other side.'

'Really? Anyway, let me deal with Ms Parkinson.'

'You got to be careful, boss, you don't want her squealing to HR.'

'Don't teach me how to suck eggs, Alan.' Turnbull finished his pint in one long swallow, picking up the whisky chaser and downing it too. 'Don't worry about her, I know exactly how to deal with her sort. She'll soon be requesting a transfer to another department. Somewhere that appreciates her skills.'

'Where?'

'I don't know yet, Alan, but it'll be somewhere far away from MIT. And it's your round. Another pint, and a drop of Laphroaig to go with it.'

'But I got the last one in.'

'Rank has its privileges, Alan, and one of those is to be treated by the junior officers in the department. Unless, of course, you'd like to join Ms Parkinson in the Shit Squad.'

Alan Butcher went to the bar without another word, leaving Paul Turnbull to his thoughts.

As he was working out how to turn this information to his advantage, his phone rang. 'DCI Turnbull.'

He listened to the dispatcher's voice at the other end of the line. 'Right, I'm on it. Don't let anybody else know, OK?'

Alan Butcher arrived back with the pints and the whiskies.

'You can forget about those; we've got a job to do.'

'Now, boss?'

'Nah, next bloody year.' Turnbull stood up. 'On second thoughts, Alan, you stay here, it'd be a shame to let good beer and whisky go to waste. Wake up the lazy cow Parkinson. 'Bout time she did some work.'

'OK, boss, what's the job?'

'A jumper. Apparently, the brains are all over the pavement. Should make her night.'

Chapter Fifty-Seven

Later, after they had demolished the pizza and the garlic bread and a very large 7 Up, Ridpath sat alone in the living room as Eve finished her homework upstairs.

He would have loved to have just switched on the telly and spent a mindless couple of hours watching something instantly forgettable, like *Dinner Date* or *Celebrity Coach Trip*. Something requiring no active involvement from any brain cells.

Instead, he pulled out his laptop and began checking the remaining cameras on the CCTV. Were these images going to be a problem for him? He hoped not. Why had public relations held them back? Was it true they'd been lost, or were they just stalling for some reason?

No matter, he would handle it later if it became a problem.

He began with the camera overlooking the main entrance of Redbury nick. Again, he watched as people entered, some escorted by coppers, some on their own. Nothing seemed out of the ordinary.

Next he checked the cameras at the entrance to the custody lobby. Again, everything checked out. The timings and the appearances all duly noted in the duty log.

The holding room was next up. It was empty until the joyriders arrived at four a.m. with two coppers in tow. There was sound, so he could hear what they were saying. They were all wired and restless, continually swearing and goading the coppers with them. At one point one of them got up to leave.

'Where are you going?'

'Home.'

'Sit down.'

'Are you going to make me, fat man?'

There was a short scuffle and the alarm suddenly sounded as the copper hit the strip along the wall. Seconds later more coppers arrived, including the custody detention officers.

Terry Rodgers stayed in the room with the teens for over an hour. Gradually whatever they had taken wore off and a general lassitude and tiredness crept in.

Terry left, only to rush back ten minutes later as the alarm rang again. Ridpath checked the footage twice.

The copper hadn't moved; he'd gone nowhere near the strip on the wall. Who had sounded the alarm, then? And more importantly, where had it sounded?

He checked the witness reports from the custody officers and the police on duty. Everyone had heard the second alarm, but nobody had admitted pressing any of the buzzers or alarm strips.

Strange.

He went through the remaining cameras in the drunk's cell and the medical room. Nothing happened with the drunk; he slept through everything, only waking up after Holdsworth had been sent to hospital.

The footage from the medical room was empty until it showed the arrival of the doctor at 6.10. He was examining the joyriders with Rodgers in attendance when suddenly he was called to Cell 3 just after 6.30.

Nothing to see here, but it would still be useful to talk to him.

The final camera was perched above the rear entrance to the station, leading directly on to the secure car park.

It was a slow, drizzly night so Ridpath put the replay at 9X speed. He'd had enough of watching CCTV and was now desperate to sleep.

The lights of the arriving cars briefly blinded the cameras. The three coppers on night duty drifted into work, tapping the key code on the security pad to enter the station.

As the night wore on, the camera just showed a row of steps leading up to the door, empty except for a few drops of rain dripping off a broken gutter.

Ridpath glanced at the clock above the mantlepiece. 11.30 p.m. Where had the time gone?

He paused the playback, stretched and yawned. A glass of Glenmorangie to round off the night, or should he just go to bed and look at this tomorrow?

No, best get it over and done with tonight.

He stood up, stretched some more and poured himself a small tumbler of the golden liquid. It had been a while since he'd had a drink and the rich, honeyed taste of the alcohol struck home as it hit the back of his throat, followed by a long, golden aftertaste.

He pressed play again and sat back to watch the footage as quickly as possible. The only thing that changed was the lighting and the time code in the corner. Nobody came in or out of the station using the rear door.

He was about to give up and call it a night when something flashed across the screen. *What was that?*

He rewound the footage, watching the time code until it went back to 4.20 a.m., and then he pressed play.

It was just a copper using the back door to come in. Perhaps he had been out for a fag or something. The man keyed in the code and went straight through into the station.

Ridpath was about to put the footage back on to running at 9X speed when he stopped.

Something wasn't right. Why would a copper be using a rear door at that time of night? Surely he would have walked in the front?

'You're getting paranoid, Ridpath. He probably didn't want any of the sergeants to see him,' he said out loud.

He played the footage again anyway. The copper obviously knew what he was doing. He approached the door confidently and keyed in the code. Ridpath tried to see the man's face but couldn't because the peak of his cap shielded his eyes.

Just before he entered the station, though, there was a flash of light on his shoulder. The camera had caught the glint of something. Ridpath paused the footage, zooming slightly to see the man's ID number. 2568.

He went back to the list of coppers on duty.

Strange, there was no copper with the number 2568 listed. He checked it again.

Definitely not listed. Why?

Just as he was making a note on the pad, his mobile rang. He picked up the phone. The call screen said it was Turnbull. What did he want?

'Ridpath speaking.'

'Good to hear you're still awake.'

'Still working.'

'Good for you. And so am I.'

'What do you want, Turnbull?'

'It's DCI Turnbull to you, or sir. Whichever trips off the tongue most easily.'

Turnbull sounded almost jubilant. What did he want?

'How can I help you, *sir*?'

'That's better. A little common courtesy always goes far, Ridpath. I was just calling so I can inform you of an incident I've been called to.'

'What incident?'

'It's Sergeant Tony Saunders. He's been found dead. Looks like suicide. He jumped from the top of a block of flats.'

November 5, 2021

Chapter Fifty-Eight

The following morning Ridpath's head felt heavy, his body listless and a searing pain was shooting through his back muscles. He'd finally nodded off at two a.m., but it felt like he hadn't slept at all. Even in his dreams he had been going over the interview with Saunders in his mind.

Had he pushed too hard?

Why had the man killed himself?

Was his investigation to blame?

He'd asked Turnbull for details last night but the man had been tight-lipped.

'Sorry, Ridpath, we're still investigating and you're not part of the team.'

'At least tell me where it happened?'

'At Redbury House, not far from his station.'

Could he hear glee in his voice? Redbury was part of the coroner's area. 'Do you want me to come there now?'

'No, that would be a distraction, wouldn't it? Dr Schofield has already pronounced him dead. The body has been moved to the mortuary.'

'As coroner's officer, I should be there.'

'And as your senior officer, I'm ordering you to stay away. You... are... not... wanted. Understand?'

'At least tell me what time he died.'

But the other end of the line was already dead. Ridpath was tempted to ignore Turnbull and go anyway. Despite the lateness of the hour, he called Mrs Challinor and explained what happened.

'Stay away for now, but go tomorrow morning,' she advised. 'It will be better then. Fewer people around, and fewer distractions.'

'The death happened in our area. I should be there.'

'I agree, Ridpath, but treat it as you would any other suspicious death. If it were another suicide, would you go rushing off to the scene in the middle of the night?'

'No, but...'

'You would follow up the following morning with the duty medical examiner, leaving the police to investigate, wouldn't you?'

'Yes, but...'

'So follow procedure, Ridpath. If I were you I'd go to the scene in the morning and talk to Dr Schofield afterwards.'

He realised she was right. 'Yes, Coroner.'

'You're supposed to be updating me at nine on the progress of the case. I suggest you go to the scene instead. You can fill me in later, after I've finished in court.'

'Yes, Coroner.'

'And, Ridpath, don't blame yourself. It's not your fault.'

'But Coroner...'

'If this is a suicide, as you were told, there are many reasons why people end their lives. Perhaps rather than blaming yourself, you should be asking why? What drove him to take his own life?'

So he had spent the rest of the night going over the questions and looking for reasons. But, in the end, there could only be one answer.

Ridpath's interview had pushed him over the edge.

Literally.

At seven, he got up and stumbled downstairs, fixing breakfast for Eve. French toast with maple syrup. It was something to do to take his mind off the events of last night.

For once, Eve had woken up without him having to shout upstairs like a drill sergeant.

'Great, Dad, I'm starving,' she announced as she sat at the kitchen table, already wearing her school uniform.

'You're chirpy. Good dreams?'

'I slept well. By the look of you, you didn't.'

Ridpath saw his reflection in the window. It wasn't great. He looked gaunt and pale, his hairline receding further like the tide going out on a beach.

'You should eat something, Dad. A mug of coffee isn't a great start to the morning.'

'You're right, I just can't face food.'

'How about tomorrow I fix you breakfast instead?'

'You're going to wake up?'

She crossed her heart. 'Promise. What would you like?'

He thought for a moment. What would he really like to eat? A picture came into his mind. Of Polly at the stove, before his illness, before her death, frying eggs. The smell of her perfume mingling with the aroma and sound of the sizzling eggs.

'Fried eggs on toast.'

'Really?'

'Really.'

'Eggs on toast it is.' She held out her finger and thumb in confirmation of the promise. He took them both, feeling the softness of her hands. 'Oh, and Dad, can I go shopping with Maisie this weekend after handing out the leaflets?'

'Shopping?'

'I need some new things. Bras and stuff.'

He looked at her again. She was changing, growing taller, looking older. 'Sure. I'll give you some money. How much do you need?'

'Thirty quid should be enough.'

'I'll give you fifty, buy yourself something nice.'

'Thanks.' There was a slight pause. 'I'd still make you breakfast even if you'd said no. I wasn't trying…'

He stopped her speaking. 'I know, Eve, don't worry. Let's make it a tradition, you always make breakfast on Saturday.'

'A deal. But you have to do the washing-up.'

'Done.'

All the time they had been talking, she had been hoovering up her French toast as if she hadn't eaten for weeks. She popped the last piece into her mouth and said, 'That was good. You make a fine breakfast, Dad.'

She stood up and put her arms around his shoulders. 'Cheer up. You look like the end of the world has been announced.'

He forced a smile. 'It was, but you slept through it.'

'If it's the end of the world, I don't have to go to school, then, do I? I can spend the day watching old episodes of *Brainchild*.'

He shook his head. 'Nice try, little lady. Run upstairs and wash your face before I drive you to school. You've got icing sugar on your cheek.'

She quickly wiped it off with her sleeve before looking at him. 'Seriously, Dad. You need to cheer up.'

'I will, just an issue at work I need to sort out.'

'OK, but look after yourself; I don't know what I would do without you,' she whispered in his ear before running upstairs like a herd of hippos.

Ridpath was left in the kitchen nursing his coffee.

God, he missed Polly right now.

Chapter Fifty-Nine

The scene at Redbury House was quiet. He wouldn't have known Tony Saunders had jumped from the roof of the sixteen-storey block of flats except for the presence of a small white tent over a patch of concrete on the east side and a couple of people dressed in white Tyvek, moving in and out.

One of the people was Emily Parkinson. She saw him and walked over.

'You shouldn't be here, Ridpath.'

'I'm the coroner's officer for this area; it's my duty to be here.'

'Still, Turnbull told me to report you if you turned up.'

'Will you?'

She shook her head. 'Nah, sod him.'

'What happened?'

'Just working it out. We got a call from somebody at 10.30 last night saying a man had jumped from the roof. One of the responding coppers recognised the body and called it in.'

'You were on duty?'

'No, but Turnbull called me anyway.'

'Jumpers are always the worst.'

'And this one was pretty bad. I got here at midnight. We cordoned off the area but the body was still lying on the concrete area between the blocks.'

Ridpath looked across. 'Where the tent is?'

'Yeah, forensics have nearly finished, then we'll call somebody to clean the scene up. A lot of blood and bone.'

Ridpath stared at the tent and the block of flats towering over it. 'He's quite far out from the side...'

'We think he leapt out rather than just stepping off the parapet.'

'You've checked the roof?'

She nodded. 'Forensics have just finished.'

'Mind if I take a look?'

She rolled her eyes. 'Ridpath. I'm not even supposed to be talking to you. I'm supposed to report that you came here.'

'I'll be quick, nobody will know. You said forensics were done.'

He strode towards the entrance to the block of flats, past the tent, Emily Parkinson following in his wake.

'Ridpath... Ridpath...'

'I won't be long, Emily.' He strode through the open doors and found the one working lift.

Emily Parkinson squeezed in beside him just as the doors closed.

'You'll be the end of me, Ridpath.'

'Or the beginning, Emily. Could be either.'

At the sixteenth floor, the doors opened and Emily took a sharp left up some stairs. 'This way leads to the roof.'

'I'll get one of the forensics to do it.' She clicked her radio. 'Before you go, guys, can someone come up here and dust for fingerprints?'

Ridpath could swear he heard a groan coming through the loudspeaker. He bent down and examined the lock. 'Who has the key for this?'

'The caretaker who looks after all three blocks. He said the door was locked when he checked yesterday at five.'

'Just a normal Yale. Hasn't been broken but it could easily have been opened with a credit card. Any copper worth his salt could have done it.'

'That's what Turnbull said.'

'Where is he anyway?'

'He went home.'

'Leaving you to finish off?'

She shrugged her shoulders. 'He always gives me the good jobs...' she said sarcastically.

Ridpath stepped out onto the roof, taking it all in. A flat, pebble-strewn expanse with a lift motor room on the left and a forest of aerials attached to it. Surrounding the edge was a low, three-foot parapet. 'Where did he jump from?'

'Over there.' She pointed to the middle of the parapet on the right.

Ridpath walked towards it, hearing the pebbles crunch between his feet. 'Strange place to do it, isn't it? Why kill yourself here? Why not sit at home with a bottle of whisky and a handful of sleeping tablets?'

'We can't ask him, can we? Who knows why anybody takes their own life?' She paused for a moment as he squatted down and examined the pebbles near the parapet. 'Rumour is you were pretty rough on him during the interview...'

Ridpath ignored her, pointing to a cigarette butt lying against the low wall, partially covered by the pebbles. 'It looks fresh. Did Saunders smoke? I don't remember him having cigarettes. Can you get the forensics to bag it? And see, all around here, the pebbles are scuffed up. See, there's two lines leading back to the door.'

She squatted down next to him. 'I can't see it.'

'Get lower. See, there are two distinct lines, like somebody has been dragged across with their feet trailing behind them.'

She bent lower. 'Could have been from anything. Forensics, the doctor, even Turnbull was up here.'

'Check the CCTV cameras at the entrance.'

'Already done. They weren't working.'

Ridpath stood up, gazing over the city stretched out beneath him. Why had Tony Saunders killed himself? It just didn't make sense.

'Are you sure it was suicide, Emily?'

'It's what Turnbull thinks.'

'I interviewed Saunders yesterday afternoon, and I can tell you suicide was the last thing on his mind. He just wanted to get back to work.'

'A lot may have happened after the interview.'

'Like?'

'He may have felt guilty about something he did. Or thought the police were out to get him. May have believed *you* were out to get him.'

'I wasn't, Emily. I was just looking for the truth.'

'I believe you, Ridpath, but you've got to understand how it looks to the others. A copper kills himself a few hours after he was interviewed by you.'

'And what if he didn't die by suicide? What if he was murdered?'

'Where's your proof? Where's your evidence?'

A white-suited man appeared at the door carrying an examination case. 'You wanted me to fingerprint something?'

'It just strikes me as strange and out of character. If you were going to kill yourself, why would you bother to leave the door propped open behind you? And if there are other fingerprints on the brick, it would suggest somebody else was here with Saunders, he wasn't alone.'

Emily turned towards the CSI. 'Dust the brick, and there's a cigarette butt near the parapet you can bag.'

'You want me to test it?'

She stared at Ridpath. Turnbull was going to kill her when he found out. 'Check it for DNA,' she said, not believing the words as they came from her mouth.

'Thanks, Em. One last thing, can you check a PC 2568 for me? Find out who he is and where he's based?'

'Why?'

'I dunno, but his number came up on something I saw.'

Ridpath's phone rang.

'Get yourself here now, Ridpath.'

It was Claire Trent, and she didn't sound happy.

Chapter Sixty

Garry Abbott hurried to meet his friend. Phil had called him last night.

'I got the bag from the safety deposit place.'

'No problems?'

'Nah, it was easy, just showed my driving licence. You want me to bring it to you?'

Again, a warning light went off in Abbott's head. This was the third time Phil had asked him where he was.

'It's OK, tomorrow is fine.'

'It's no problem.'

'Tomorrow is good. I'll call you with the details of where we can meet tomorrow morning.'

'Am I good for the five hundred quid? Only I owe a bit to the bookies at the moment and they're starting to get a bit heavy.'

'You're good, Phil, and thanks, mate, you've saved my life.'

He'd called him that morning, arranging to meet at ten a.m. outside St Anne's Catholic Church in Crumpsall. This was just five minutes away from the hotel, so he was unlikely to be spotted by Delaney's goons as he walked there, plus the area around the church was clear. He'd be able to spot them a mile off and do a runner if Phil had betrayed him.

But Phil wouldn't do it, would he? They were best mates.

He stood outside the church waiting and rubbing his hands to keep warm. After he'd picked up the passports and the money from Phil, he'd go straight to the airport. There was a flight to Thailand leaving at 1.30. He'd buy a ticket and in thirteen hours he would be lying on a beach in Phuket, away from the mob and the cold and all the shit Delaney could dish out.

Around him the old women who had been at Mass were beginning to drift out of the church, chattering away in a variety of languages.

Was that Phil?

His friend was walking towards him carrying the bag. He waved his hand and Phil picked up his pace.

'Hello, mate, great to see you.'

'You checked nobody was following you?'

'Don't worry, mate, I took two trams like you said, changing at Piccadilly so nobody could follow me. You're getting paranoid, mate.'

'If Delaney was after you, you'd be paranoid too.' He put out his hand to take the bag.

'Sorry, mate, cash first. We agreed five hundred quid, remember?'

'The money's in the bag, Phil.'

'Right.' He handed the bag over.

Abbott felt the weight of the money. There was enough here to keep him in the lap of luxury for a good few years in Thailand. He opened the zipper. 'What the...'

The bag was full of bricks. What were bricks doing there?

He looked up. Behind Phil, three black-suited goons were walking from the same direction Phil had come.

'Sorry, mate, Mr Delaney's offer was too good. He said I could keep whatever was in the bag. You have been a busy little saver for the last few years, haven't you?'

A hand appeared on Abbott's shoulder.

'Garry, don't have a kettle today, do you?'

Abbott turned round. A bandaged Delaney was standing behind him, flanked by two thugs as broad as they were tall.

'You missed a lovely Mass; the lads enjoyed it, didn't you?'

'It was very interesting, Mr Delaney, all that stuff about All Souls,' one of the thugs answered.

Delaney ran his hand though his dark, Brylcreemed hair. 'I remember when I was an altar boy, I used to love the All Souls Masses, remembering all those relatives and dear ones who had passed away.'

A van screeched to a halt outside the church. As two muscular hands grabbed his arms, Garry Abbott looked around for someone, anyone, who could help him.

Everybody had vanished; all the old ladies had departed for home. He was alone.

'Who's going to remember your soul, Garry?' asked Mr Delaney.

Garry Abbott didn't know the answer.

Chapter Sixty-One

Stepping out onto the MIT floor at Police HQ, Ridpath was aware all the detectives' eyes were staring at him.

Nobody moved to speak.

Nobody said hello.

One copper, a Turnbull hire, stood in his way refusing to move. 'Should be ashamed of yourself,' he sneered beneath his breath.

Ridpath walked round him to knock on Claire Trent's office.

He heard a crisp 'Enter' and went in.

His boss was sitting behind her desk. 'Sit down, Ridpath,' she said in a cold voice.

He settled himself in the chair.

'What the hell is going on?'

'Boss?'

'Don't play dumb with me, Ridpath. A sergeant you just interviewed killed himself last night. Or aren't you aware?'

'I went to the scene, boss.'

'What? You were told not to go by Paul Turnbull.'

'I had to see it for myself, boss.'

She snorted and shook her head. Holding up some sheets of paper, she said, 'I have here a series of complaints about your conduct. Paul Turnbull says you've been insubordinate. And you have just admitted to me you have disobeyed a direct order from him.'

'But, boss...'

She held out her hand to stop him speaking. 'Secondly, I have a complaint from DI Jack Cater, who alleges you obtained footage from CCTV cameras placed in Redbury station. Apparently, he checked and you pressured the supplier of the cameras to release the footage. What do you have to say for yourself?'

'The force was supposed to give me the footage, but they said it was lost. I found out it had been retained by the CCTV company and asked for it.'

'Did you inform anybody you had it?'

Ridpath opened his mouth to say something, then simply shook his head.

'Did you share it with the force PR department?'

'No.'

'Did you inform your direct superior, DCI Turnbull, that you were using the footage?'

'No.'

'These are serious charges, Ridpath. What do you have to say for yourself?'

It was time to voice the concerns that had been swimming around inside his head since the death of Tony Saunders. 'Look, boss, something happened in Redbury nick on the night of February 20, 2018. There are just too many inconsistencies, too many half-truths.'

'And now a serving police officer of twenty years has killed himself after being interviewed by you.'

'I don't think he did, boss.'

'Did what?'

'I don't think he died by suicide. I think he was murdered.'

'What?'

'I don't think he jumped from the roof. I think somebody, probably more than one person, threw Tony Saunders from it.'

'Evidence, Ridpath?'

'The post-mortem, I'm sure it will show...'

'Motive?'

'I don't know, boss. Something happened that night...'

'Enough, Ridpath.' She sighed, placed the complaints against him back in a folder and closed the cover. 'Before I went on my course, I advised Mrs Challinor there was a conflict of interest in you investigating a serving police officer in the Manchester force.'

'All deaths in custody have to be investigated, boss.'

She slammed her fist down on the desk. 'DO NOT TEACH ME MY JOB, RIDPATH.' She brushed away a hair which had strayed over her forehead and fixed him with her blue eyes. 'I have spoken with the coroner this morning and, even though she seems to be unaware of your behaviour in this case, she is still supporting you and your role. However, I believe you have been fatally compromised by these complaints and your admission of insubordination towards a senior officer. I am therefore suspending you immediately and informing you the Professional Standards Department has opened an investigation into your behaviour and use of illegally obtained CCTV images.'

'But, boss—'

She held out her hand. 'Give me your warrant card, Ridpath.'

'But...'

'NOW.'

He reached into his jacket and pulled out his warrant card, placing it on her desk. 'Boss, you need to look into the death of Tony Saunders, it...'

'Enough, Ridpath. Go home, this interview is terminated.'

He sat in the chair facing her for a moment before standing up. 'Tony Saunders was murdered, boss.'

She ignored him, focusing on her computer.

He stood there for a moment longer before turning and leaving her room.

The walk from her office to the lift was the longest he had ever taken. The MIT floor, normally full of activity, was now silent, with all eyes on him. Everybody had heard the bollocking he had been given by Claire Trent.

It was an interminable walk of shame.

Chapter Sixty-Two

He was headed to the car park when he received the first text from Chrissy.

> Sorry to hear you've been suspended. Checked out Garry Abbott. His last known address was 27 Rochdale Terrace, Redbury. He's down on the database as a person of interest.

Quickly, Ridpath texted back.

> Why is he a person of interest?

> Doesn't say. Investigated for another crime? Want me to check for you?

> Thanks, Chrissy, please check. Anything on DI Mark Brett?

> Nothing so far. They are being tighter than City's defence. Will keep looking.

> Ta, Chrissy, you're a star.

He didn't know what he would do without Chrissy. What was Garry Abbott doing on the database? Was he wanted for another crime? And why was Mark Brett so hard to find?

He opened the door to his car and settled inside. Should he go home, as Claire Trent had told him, or go to the coroner's office and keep doing his job?

He tapped his fingers on the steering wheel. Eve would be pleased to see him. Perhaps he could take her out to Pizza Express, or the new Korean place in Withington.

For a moment, he thought about forgetting Tony Saunders, Redbury nick and the whole sorry mess. A wave of tiredness swept over him. Perhaps it would be better to just go home and sleep for years.

He started the engine. The radio came on and an old Bowie song was playing. How he missed this music. Mick Ronson's power chords. Woody Woodmansey's drumming. Trevor Bolder's bass line. And above it all Bowie's soaring voice, singing about Ziggy Stardust and the Spiders from Mars.

He'd read somewhere the band's name came from the UFO sighting in 1954, where a stadium crowd thought they had witnessed Martian spacecraft which cast off a thin filament material. They turned out to be migrating spiders. So it goes.

The windscreen wiper swept across the glass, wiping out the last drops of rain, revealing Police HQ in all its glass-covered transparent glory.

He wasn't going to give up. Not now, not when he was so close.

Had Tony Saunders killed himself, or had somebody murdered him?

Despite what he had told Claire Trent, he wasn't sure.

But he was going to find out, and neither she nor anybody else was going to stop him.

Chapter Sixty-Three

He turned on the speaker phone in his car, dialling Sophia's number.

'Hi there, Ridpath.'

'Is the coroner still in court, Sophia?'

'She won't be out until four, the Finnegan inquest is taking longer than she expected, bogged down in some procedural point is what I've heard.'

'OK, can you give her a message?'

'No problem.'

'Tell her I'll be in later to brief her.'

'You're coming in?' There was an incredulousness in Sophia's voice.

'Yes, of course, why not?'

'I heard you'd been suspended.'

News travels fast. 'From GMP, not from the coroner's office.' *At least not so far*, he thought without saying it. 'Can you text me the doctor's address, Sophia?'

'Will do.'

'Anything else I should know?'

'Not really. Except...'

'Except... what?'

'There were a couple of coppers here this morning who wanted to check your computer. The coroner was in court so Jenny told them to come back later with a warrant if they wanted to check anything in this office. They weren't happy bunnies.'

'Good for Jenny. Remind me to buy her a double-strength latte next time I see her.'

'Can they just barge in here and search our computers?'

'I don't know. They can certainly try, but there are questions of family confidentiality.'

'Just texted you the address.'

As she spoke his phone buzzed.

'Do you need me to come too?'

'I don't think so. It should be a straightforward meeting, better for you to guard the fort in Stockfield.'

'Circle the wagons?'

'Something like that. I've a feeling it's going to be rough for a few days. They may want to question you about the meeting with Tony Saunders.'

'It's all on tape.'

'It is, isn't it? Can you make a copy for me? I'll pick it up later.'

'I can just email it to you.'

'Better not. I think hard copies would be useful for the next couple of days. One last thing, can you check with John Schofield when he is performing the post-mortem on Saunders?'

'Are you planning to attend?'

'In my capacity as coroner's officer. I'll be in later; can you book a time with Mrs Challinor?'

'I'll let her and John know.' There was a slight pause. 'Look after yourself, Ridpath.'

'I intend to, Sophia. I'll be a spider from Mars.'

'What?'

'Nothing. I'm off to see the duty doctor. Bye.'

He switched off the loudspeaker and sat silently in the car for a moment. Outside, the drizzle had started again. Manchester looked grey and wet, the streets already slick with an oily sheen. Another beautiful Bonfire Night in bonny Manchester.

He checked the address and entered the postcode in the satnav.

It was going to be a difficult journey. And he wasn't talking about the potholes on the roads.

Chapter Sixty-Four

The doctor's surgery was in one of those detached Edwardian houses in Withington Ridpath had always loved to look at. The outside still had black and white painted wooden panels that harked back to a golden age of Tudor England, while the door retained its original stained glass: a picture of a sailing ship against a stylised sunset.

Inside, though, the smell was definitely the sharp tang of modern disinfectant, not the mellow polish of old England. An aroma which made his nose twitch and reminded him of the mortuary.

He noticed a sign in the entrance, asking people to wear masks. He dug his out from his pocket. These days it seemed to be so rare anybody took any precautions, despite the rising number of cases. Covid fatigue, he thought, everybody just wanted to live normal lives again. To go back to the time before the disease had ravaged the country.

A young receptionist in a white coat was standing behind a small hatch in the wall.

'Mr Ridpath, the doctor will see you in a minute; he's on a Zoom call at the moment. Won't be long, though, it's just a repeat prescription.'

How the world had changed. No longer did one have to queue to see the doctor. They would now come to your home – remotely of course. Unlike the *Daily Mail*, he could see nothing wrong with this. Anything that made the whole process more efficient was OK by him. In fact, if he never saw another doctor in his life he would be more than happy. Nine months of cancer treatment plus all the follow-ups had rid him of any desire to visit hospitals. These days, even his check-ups were done remotely. Five minutes answering a few questions and it was all over. Fine by him, as he was sure if anything was seriously wrong they would order a full examination quicker than a Manchester bus going back to the depot at the end of a shift.

He sat down in the waiting room and picked up a magazine dated March 2014. At least some things hadn't changed; the magazines were still as out of date as ever.

There were just three other patients waiting, all wearing masks. Nobody looked at each other. A clock ticked quietly in the corner, its sound loud in the silence, interrupted only by the occasional cough.

After a couple of minutes his name was called, which stimulated a bunch of coughing from an old man with a red face in the corner.

Poor bloke, he'd have to wait a little longer.

Ridpath knocked on the doctor's door and entered. A young man was sitting behind a desk strewn with the accoutrements of the medical profession. Pens with the names of drug companies, jars with wrapped tongue depressors like wooden lolly sticks, two metal trays with syringes in individual packets, a bottle of cotton swabs, an old desktop computer and countless patient files.

The desk looked a mess to Ridpath, but he was sure the doctor knew where everything was.

The man was just clicking off a Zoom conversation as he stepped in.

'Mr Ridpath, your assistant told me you were a coroner's officer. How can I help you? I hope one of my death certificates isn't a problem.'

The voice was strong and forceful, with a slight Liverpool accent. The last sentence was said jokingly but Ridpath could hear a touch of anxiety in the voice. Had this man been in trouble for his death certificates, or was he just worried he was going to be tarred as another Harold Shipman?

Ridpath decided to put him at ease.

'Nothing to do with death certs, Doctor Bourke. There will be an inquest soon into the death in custody of Ben Holdsworth at Redbury station in February 2018. I believe you were the duty doctor?'

Bourke immediately frowned, and his tone changed. 'I was... unfortunately, and I've received the notice I might be called as a witness. Not a night I'll forget.'

'Can you tell me what happened?'

'I was called at 4.30 to attend the station as I was on duty.'

'How does that work?'

'I don't understand.'

'The duty doctor. How are you chosen?'

The doctor made a moue with his mouth. 'The police had a contract with my NHS trust. I was on the list and it was my turn.'

Ridpath checked his notes and the timeline for the evening. 'You weren't called earlier to a DUI?'

'No, I remember it clearly, the call came in at 4.30. I was to check on some teenagers the custody sergeant believed were on drugs of some sort, but it wasn't an urgent request.'

'And you arrived at what time?'

'Roughly six o'clock. I'd started to examine the young lads when one of the custody officers ran into the medical room shouting I was needed.'

'And what did you do next?'

'I ran to the cells, where a man was lying on the floor being given CPR by the custody sergeant.'

'Given CPR?'

'He was doing it well. Compressing the sternum and counting, then giving mouth-to-mouth resuscitation. I stepped in and took over.'

'The man was still alive?'

The doctor nodded. 'All this is in my statement given to the IOPC.'

This was another statement Ridpath hadn't received. 'Sorry for going over it again, but as you know, an inquest is a separate judicial examination by the coroner.'

'Of course.'

'What happened next?'

'I checked the man. He was still breathing, but his heart rate was irregular and his pulse was weak so I asked the custody sergeant to call an ambulance. They arrived and took him away. I found out later he died in hospital.'

'What did you think happened to Ben Holdsworth?'

'I don't know, Mr Ridpath. I'm not a pathologist, just a GP.'

'But as a doctor you must have formed some opinion.'

'I was told the man had a subdural haemorrhage…'

Ridpath heard a tone of doubt in the man's voice.

'But…'

'But it struck me as strange. I was sure he suffered some sort of drug overdose. The custody sergeant told me he'd been arrested for possession earlier. So that's why I gave him ephedrine.'

'What?'

230

'I gave him a shot of ephedrine. I thought he was going into seizure from a heroin overdose, so I gave it to him. He responded immediately.'

'It wasn't in the witness statements.'

'The custody sergeant watched me do it.'

'Sergeant Saunders?'

'I think that was his name.'

'Was anybody else there?'

'Another custody officer.'

'Terry Rodgers?'

'No, the small one, I think his name was Lucas Harvey.'

Why had nobody mentioned this before? And why wasn't the presence of ephedrine noted in the toxicology report?

'Thank you, Doctor. Anything else you remember?'

The doctor shook his head, and then a memory lit up his face. 'There was one other thing. After I gave him the ephedrine, he came to for a short while and babbled something about brats or brads, something like that.'

'Could it have been a name? Brett?'

The doctor shrugged his shoulders. 'Could have been. I guess we'll never know.'

Ridpath closed his pad and put his pen back inside his jacket. 'Thank you for your time, Doctor.'

'Do I need to go to the inquest?'

'I'm afraid so.' Why was everybody so unwilling to take part in a coroner's inquest? 'Civic duty.'

'It's just we're snowed under at the moment, what with Covid and everything.'

'Life, and justice, goes on, despite Covid, Doctor.'

'Less life, Mr Ridpath, that's the problem.'

'Point taken, Dr Dourke. I'll do my best to schedule you early in the proceedings, but it is the coroner who will make the final call. Thank you once again for your time. You've been very helpful.'

For the first time, glimmers of understanding were beginning to lift the veil on this case.

He needed to look at the CCTV again.

Chapter Sixty-Five

Back in his car, he checked his phone and found a message from Sophia.

> Post-mortem debrief on Saunders at 4. I can come if you
> want. Haven't been to one for a while.

Sophia had attended post-mortems during her university course in anatomy. Personally, he found them unbearable. It wasn't so much the sight of human flesh such as hearts or lungs being weighed on scales, but it was the smell of disinfectant mixed with dead humanity which made him gag as a reflex. He'd taken to smearing copious amounts of Vicks under his nose but it hadn't helped much. Instead his fingers just stank of eucalyptus for days.

He messaged her back.

> No need. Will see you back at the office this evening.
> Need to chat.

> OK. 😊 Mrs Challinor will wait for you too. John's just
> messaged he's already started the PM. As a heads-up,
> Turnbull is there too.

Turnbull at a post-mortem? That was a rare event, the man usually avoided them.

He had two things to do before going to Oxford Road.

First was a quick SMS to Eve.

As soon as he sent it, he felt guilty. The last thing he wanted was for his daughter to become a latchkey kid, looking after herself while he was never around.

Did latchkey kids still exist?

He vaguely remembered the phrase from when he was growing up. Some of the national dailies had gone through one of those moral panics where the end of the world was nigh because a kid had let himself into his own house.

Tossers. They should look to their own kids.

He started the engine and turned on the radio. Bloody Ed Sheeran. He could do without his depressing nasal screeches on a wet Manchester day.

He called Chrissy. 'Hiya, any luck with finding Garry Abbott?'

'Not so far. He moved house to near Dukinfield in March 2018, split up with his partner according to the neighbours and was working in an abattoir. I found out the new address through a phone company. The neighbours haven't seen him for the last couple of days or so.'

'When exactly did he vanish?'

He could hear Chrissy turning pages as she checked her notes. 'Last Monday, on November 1, a neighbour saw him going out. I rang his work and they hadn't seen him since then either.'

Sophia and Brian Jennings had started to send out the witness notices the previous week. But he had never been interviewed and wouldn't have been called, so why suddenly vanish?

'Thanks, Chrissy, any chance of a mobile number for him?'

'I'm checking if a number was registered to his address. They'll get back to me soon.'

'Sit on them, Chrissy. Did you find DI Brett for me?'

'It's weird, couldn't find him on any staff listing for the NCA.'

Chrissy was almost whispering; he had to strain to hear her – either that or his hearing was knackered.

'Rang them and they were very cagey. Passed me from pillar to post and said they'd check it out. Hang on, Emily is talking to me.'

Ridpath heard muffled voices before Chrissy came back on the line.

'Emily rang her mate and he said Brett used to work at NCA but he moved on at the end of 2018.'

'After the incident at Redbury nick?'

'Emily's nodding her head.'

'Moved on where?'

Muffled voices again as the question was relayed.

Chrissy's voice again. 'Her friend doesn't know. Just moved on. He presumed it was to another NCA operation, probably in the south because that's where Brett was from.'

'He wasn't from Manchester?'

'Not according to Emily's source. Croydon, she thought, wherever it is. And the copper's number you asked her to check, 2568. She's saying are you sure it's correct?'

'It's right, why's she asking?'

'Because the number used to belong to a constable, but he retired in 2017 and is now living in Guernsey.'

'What?'

'It's what she said.'

So who was the man entering Redbury nick through the rear door at 4.20 in the morning?

'One more thing. The mob from Professional Standards have been here asking questions about you. They interviewed Turnbull.'

'Thanks for the heads-up, and keep your head down, Chrissy.'

He rang off. A copper with a number who retired four years ago, two people, Mark Brett and Garry Abbott, who had vanished and two more, Tony Saunders and Lucas Harvey, who were dead. Either this was all some big coincidence or something very strange was going on.

And Ridpath did not believe in coincidences.

Not in life.

Never in an investigation.

Chapter Sixty-Six

Slathers of Vicks beneath his nose hadn't helped. The nausea in the pit of his stomach was still there as he entered the mortuary. A feeling that would stay until he left.

Dr Schofield was bent over a body as he entered. He recognised the shattered corpse of Tony Saunders.

'Hello there, Ridpath, just give me a second and I'll take you through what we've found out so far.'

The doctor pulled out Tony Saunders' stomach and emptied the contents into a large jar, squeezing out every last drop.

'This man hasn't eaten for the last six hours, judging from the contents in his stomach, but check with lab later.' The doctor spoke to nobody in particular, knowing his words would be picked up by the overhead mike recording everything.

'What are you doing here, Ridpath?'

It was Turnbull's voice coming from the shadows.

Because of the bright lights focused on the corpse lying on the table, Ridpath couldn't see where he was standing or if anybody was with him.

'I asked you a question. You're suspended; what are you doing here?'

'In my role as coroner's officer, I am required to attend post-mortems.'

'Not this one, you ain't. Get out now!'

'Excuse me, Detective Chief Inspector Turnbull, I am in charge of this post-mortem, and I have requested DI Ridpath's presence. If you have a problem, I suggest you take it up with my superiors.' Despite its high pitch, Schofield's voice was firm and unyielding. 'Now if you two could shelve your animosity for a short while, I'll update you on my findings so far.'

Both Ridpath and Turnbull stayed silent.

'Good. As you can see from the condition of the victim, it took me a while to put the body back into a recognisable shape. But you are looking at a relatively healthy human cadaver. Heart, kidneys, and lungs are all in good shape. However, multiple fractures of the major long bones, tibia, fibula etc plus lacerations of the liver and internal organs are consistent with a fall from a considerable height. The skull and facial bones are all completely smashed, with most of the frontal cortex and lobes of the brain separated, suggesting the man landed head first on the concrete beneath the tower block.'

'Multiple fractures consistent with fall from height,' said Turnbull.

Ridpath could see the man now. He was taking notes while leaning against a wash basin in the rear of the examination room.

'In my experience, the complete destruction to the facial bones and skull is relatively rare.'

'What do you mean, Doctor?' asked Ridpath.

'Most people who kill themselves by jumping off a roof do so by simply stepping off the parapet and letting gravity take its course. This means the leg bones, hips and feet are often shattered but the head and face remain relatively intact. However, the opposite is true in this case. The face and skull are shattered but the leg bones are simply broken, not suffering compounded or compressed fractures.'

'Meaning?'

'This man landed head first.'

'But it is still consistent with suicide?' asked Turnbull.

'Yes, it is, just much rarer than other injuries sustained from a fall.'

'But it still happens, landing head first,' persisted Turnbull.

'Yes, it does, just not so common. There are a couple of other things you should be aware of. See the right and left wrists?' He pointed to the hands and arms lying next to the shattered corpse. 'There are indications he was bound at some point. See, there are rope marks on his left wrist where chafing occurred.'

'Maybe he liked a bit of S&M,' Turnbull chuckled from the back.

They both ignored him. 'How recent are the marks, Doctor?' asked Ridpath.

'Quite recent, within a day or so of the death judging from the bruising.'

'Couldn't the bruises have been caused from the fall?' asked Turnbull.

'The bruising could have been caused at that time, but the marks are from a rope, not a fall.'

'Did the forensic team find any evidence of a rope?'

'Not that I am aware of, Chief Inspector.'

'Did they find any rope on the roof?' asked Ridpath.

'Again, I am not aware of anything found there.'

For once, Turnbull stayed silent.

'You said there were two things you wanted to tell us, Doctor.'

'I did. If you look at the crook of the elbow there is evidence of a recent injection site. See the small puncture mark on the skin.'

Ridpath leant forward to look, feeling his head go woozy as he got closer to what remained of Tony Saunders. His eyes swam back into focus and he saw the small mark the doctor was describing.

'Would you like to come forward to see, Chief Inspector?'

'I'm fine back here, Doctor. Dead bodies up close are not my cup of tea.'

'Please yourself.'

'Could he have had a flu jab or a Covid booster recently?' asked Ridpath.

'All adult flu vaccines are given by injection into the muscle of the upper arm. A recent blood test or blood donation is a possibility. You will have to check his medical records. Of course, I will know more when the blood records come back from toxicology. Until then, we are just guessing.'

'I'll kick the lab up the arse so you get the results quickly. Anything else, Doctor?' said Turnbull.

'That's about it. You will receive my full report in the next day or so, Chief Inspector, or as soon as I get the screening from toxicology.'

'So you are happy to confirm this is a suicide, Doctor?' asked Turnbull.

The doctor sucked in air between his teeth, forcing the mask covering his mouth to press against his lips. 'It has all the signs of a classic suicide by jumping from a height, except...'

'Except what, Doctor?' asked Ridpath.

'Landing on the head worries me, plus the presence of rope marks on this wrist and the injection site in the arm.'

'But it's not unknown for people to land that way, is it?'

The doctor shook his head.

'And the rope marks could have come from sexual practices any time in the week leading up to his death.'

'No, the marks are more recent.'

'OK, sexual practices in the hours leading to his death.'

'It is possible.'

'Plus he could have given blood or had a blood test recently?'

'You'll have to check his medical records. We'll know for certain when toxicology comes back.'

Turnbull placed his notebook in the inside pocket of his jacket. 'Right, I'm off. And just a word of warning before I go, Ridpath. If you interfere in this investigation in any way, shape or form, it will be the end of you, understand? You may have to do your job as the coroner's officer, but it does not allow you to get in the way of an ongoing police investigation. Do I make myself clear?'

Ridpath didn't respond.

'Thank you for your time, Doctor. I'll be waiting for your report. Looks like a pretty clear case of suicide while the balance of his mind was disturbed.' There was a long pause. 'And we all know why that was, don't we, Ridpath?'

The last insinuation was too much for the detective. He strode towards Turnbull, clenching his fists. The chief inspector clumsily stepped back as far as he could, bumping into the wash basin behind him.

'Remember who I am, Ridpath.'

Ridpath kept advancing. He'd had enough. How dare this man insinuate he was responsible for the death of Tony Saunders?

'Gentlemen, gentlemen, remember where you are. Please show respect to the poor person lying on the table here.'

Ridpath stopped within two feet of Turnbull, his arms tensed at his sides, his eyes staring at the man in front of him.

'Gentlemen...'

It was the doctor's voice which stopped Ridpath. He reached out and gently brushed a piece of lint from Turnbull's protective suit.

'I think we're finished here, don't you, Chief Inspector Turnbull?'

Turnbull moved towards the door as quickly as he could, shouting over his shoulder, 'You're going to regret it, Ridpath. You wait and see, you'll hang for this.'

The doors were flung open and Turnbull rushed out.

A moment of silence passed between Ridpath and the doctor.

'It wasn't a very smart thing to do, Ridpath. It would be better not to antagonise him.'

Despite eighteen months of pain, Ridpath was apt to agree. 'Better perhaps, Dr Schofield, but not half as enjoyable.'

Chapter Sixty-Seven

Back at the coroner's office in Stockfield, Mrs Challinor was waiting for him. He'd gradually calmed down during the long drive, realising the pathologist was correct; it wasn't a very smart thing to do.

But the confrontation with Turnbull had happened, and he couldn't turn back the clock now. At least it hadn't escalated into a fight.

'Come in, Ridpath. You've been a busy man.'

He slipped inside Mrs Challinor's office. Despite a long day in court at an inquest, she still looked fresh and composed. He, on the other hand, looked positively bedraggled. One day he would find out her secret.

'Well, you seem to have annoyed most of the judicial system of Manchester. Professional Standards, Claire Trent and the CPS have all rung me this afternoon. I'm waiting for a call from the mayor next.'

'I'm sure he has better things to do.'

'I wouldn't bet on it.'

Despite her jocular tone, her face was deadly serious.

'The latest is a report of you assaulting a senior officer. Apparently, according to Professional Standards, who rang me five minutes ago, they have added it to your list of offences. DCI Turnbull is being treated in hospital as we speak.'

Ridpath's mouth opened wide. 'Treated? In hospital? But I never touched him. True, I advanced towards him and wanted to smash his smug face in, but I didn't go through with it. Not the smartest thing to do in the middle of a post-mortem, but I didn't touch him.'

'Apparently he has a different version of the events.'

'Dr Schofield will back me up; he was in the mortuary when it happened.'

'According to Turnbull, the confrontation happened near his car.'

'I didn't do anything, Mrs Challinor, I swear on Eve's life.'

'I believe you, Ridpath, but unless there are witnesses to what happened, it will be his word against yours. The word of a senior police officer.'

Ridpath shook his head. 'I didn't do it.'

'Right, well, Claire Trent has asked you be suspended as my officer as well as from the police. I have rejected her request simply because with the inquest less than three days away, it would be far too short a time to pull in somebody else from another district. You're it, I'm afraid, Ridpath. Now can you take me through your findings so far?'

Ridpath's head was spinning. He had hit Turnbull? The man was in hospital? Impossible. He had simply got in his car and driven straight here.

'I'm waiting, Ridpath.'

The detective focused his mind. 'Superficially, the custody log, CCTV pictures of the night's events and the post-mortem examination by Harold Lardner seem to confirm the accepted version of the events.'

'Which is?'

'Ben Holdsworth fell and banged his head on a wall in the cell, causing a subdural haematoma to form in his brain. The police and a doctor did their best to revive him, but unfortunately he died in Salford General later that morning. The custody officers may have been guilty of not checking on the prisoner more often, but even then the culpability would be limited. A subdural haematoma often produces the appearance of a man sleeping, especially when seen from afar.'

'You said this was a superficial explanation.'

'It might still be accurate, but there are sufficient anomalies to suggest a deeper problem.'

Mrs Challinor frowned. 'Go on…'

Ridpath counted on the fingers of his hand. 'First, the subdural haematoma isn't in the correct place, according to Dr Schofield. The CCTV shows him falling and striking just above his temple, but the haematoma and the bruising to the skull occurred at the rear of the head.'

'It could have been a delayed reaction. Quite often, the haematoma doesn't occur in the same area as the blow or the concussion.'

Ridpath had forgotten Mrs Challinor had a degree in forensic science as well as the law.

'But taken with the other anomalies, it begins to call the official account into question.'

'And they are…'

Ridpath held up his hand again, counting off with his fingers. 'Secondly, Lardner mentions an injection point on the victim's arm. The post-mortem toxicology suggests a massive dose of diamorphine was in his system.'

'He could have injected himself before he was arrested.'

'Then why weren't the effects of his drug use noticed by the arresting officers or the custody sergeant?'

'You know as well as I do, Ridpath, long-term drug abusers are well versed in hiding the effects of their drug use from others.'

'But his hair samples didn't show any residual evidence of drug use.'

'Perhaps he had stopped for a while and then recently started again. That would explain the reaction to the heroin. His body was no longer used to it, but he was still able to control his actions.'

'His mother says he had given up drugs after returning to Redbury.'

'Mothers always protect their young. I said the same about my own daughter for a long time despite the evidence being there in front of my eyes. And wasn't he arrested for possession of drugs? It hardly suggests he had given them up.'

'The custody officers should have spotted it, at least.'

'Perhaps he took the drug in the station? Was he allowed to go to the toilet?'

'Terry Rodgers, the custody officer, said he was accompanied at all times, and no drug paraphernalia was found in the station.'

'Flushed down the toilet?'

She had a point. 'I'll check.'

'Number three. The CCTV in Cells 3 and 4 stopped at 4.35 a.m. Saunders made a visit to the prisoner when the CCTV was off. We don't know what they talked about but the rumour is Holdsworth was the drug dealer on the same estate where Saunders' daughter had died in October 2017.'

'The answer could be as obvious as he was doing his job: checking on the condition of the detainee. What does the custody officer say?'

'Nothing. He's dead. And now so is Saunders.'

Mrs Challinor pursed her lips. 'How did the custody officer die?'

'A road accident, apparently.'

'Who was the coroner?'

Ridpath checked his notes from Sophia. 'North Derbyshire, a Mr Holden.'

'He's very good. Young, but detailed and smart. Do you want me to call him and ask for the details?'

'If you think it would help, Mrs Challinor.'

She made a note on her pad. 'The deaths of the two men are circumstantial, but not causal. There is no evidence to link the deaths to anything that may or may not have happened in February 2018.'

'But these anomalies are beginning to add up.'

'But it's all circumstantial, Ridpath, I've seen no proof so far. Anything else?'

'There are two more things, Coroner. There was a policeman present in the station who isn't on the duty log or the roster. A policeman with the number 2568.'

'Really?'

'He appears at 4.20 a.m. at the rear door of Redbury using the keypad to enter but I can find no record of his presence in the station.'

Mrs Challinor shrugged her shoulders. 'Somebody forgot to include him in the log? He didn't sign in?'

'I don't think so, Mrs Challinor, it's a small station. Plus the only record Emily Parkinson can find of the number belongs to a retired copper living in Guernsey.'

'That sounds strange, Ridpath. Have you spoken with Claire Trent?'

'I was going to, Coroner, but then I was suspended. There are two final areas we haven't followed up yet. When Ben Holdsworth was taken to Redbury, he kept asking for a DI Mark Brett of the National Crime Agency. I haven't been able to find him either.'

Mrs Challinor seemed unimpressed. 'Go on...'

'And the cell next to Holdsworth was occupied by a Garry Abbott. I can't find any record of him being interviewed or a statement being taken. He must have heard what happened. How could they have missed interviewing him?'

'Easy to do, particularly when Lardner's post-mortem was so conclusive with regards to a fall. Is that it, Ridpath?'

The detective sat back. 'It's all I've got so far.'

'It's not enough.'

Ridpath's shoulders sagged. 'I know.'

'Any barrister worth his fee would tear apart these "anomalies", as you call them, and explain them away in minutes. And I would agree with him, advising a jury to come to the conclusion the death was accidental.' She closed her pad. 'Sorry, Ridpath, but I wouldn't be doing my job if I wasn't honest with you.'

'I understand, Coroner.'

'What are your next steps?'

'With the death of Tony Saunders, I think there are only three. Find DI Mark Brett and ask him why Holdsworth wanted to get in touch with him. Second, discover who PC 2568 is and why nobody mentioned him. Three, talk to Garry Abbott, the prisoner in the cell next door.'

'You only have a few days left.'

'I know, Coroner.'

'Plus Professional Standards have begun their investigation, far quicker than usual, I might add.'

'I know that, too.'

'Jenny has already empanelled the jury. I'll ask her to start working out a witness schedule today. The process has to move forward, Ridpath.'

'I understand, Coroner.'

'I'll protect you for as long as I can, but it can't be forever.'

'Thank you.'

'Your use of the CCTV from the security firm was in breach of the Data Protection Act. They are out to get you.'

'It's obvious.' Ridpath breathed out heavily. 'But my instincts tell me something wasn't kosher about the events in Redbury nick. Something happened. I'm not saying it was a cover-up but it's like nobody wants to know the truth. They've found an answer that keeps everybody happy, and they are going to stick with it, come hell or high water.'

'Not everybody is happy, Ridpath.'

The detective stared at her.

'The solicitor for the family contacted me today. He'd heard the news about Saunders' death and was checking the inquest would be fair and impartial. We mustn't forget, somebody's son died in the early hours of February 21, 2018. Our job is to represent that dead man in the court of the living.'

'I know, Coroner.'

Chapter Sixty-Eight

Coming out of Mrs Challinor's office, Ridpath realised how much he still had to do.

As ever, she had spotted the flaws in the investigation instantly. All of his 'anomalies' could be explained away easily. It was the accretion of all these coincidences and accidents that set the alarm bells ringing in Ridpath's head.

Sophia was sitting at her desk staring at her laptop. 'Still here?' he asked.

'Better than home. My mother has arranged for me to meet a matchmaker this evening. Better I'm not there; I'll just lose my rag as she shows me pictures of "eligible bachelors" who look like characters from some ID line-up or FBI most-wanted list.'

'She's certainly persistent.'

'Aren't all mothers? My absence should give the matchmaker an indication of my willingness to participate. How was your meeting?'

Ridpath frowned, sitting down heavily in front of his desk. 'Not good, I still have tons of work to do and only three days to do it in.'

'*We* still have work to do. How can I help?'

Ridpath thought for a moment. What would be the best use of Sophia's time, and his own? 'Can you go through the footage again? The PC with the number 2568 on his shoulder enters the station at 4.20 a.m. Can you see if he appears on any other CCTV camera footage? He should be responding to the alarm call at least. See if you can give a timeline for him from the moment he enters. It may be just a mistake on the roster list.'

'No problem. Why's he so important?'

'According to Emily, that particular number belongs to a copper who retired to Guernsey four years ago.'

'Strange…'

'Can you get me a screenshot of the point when he enters the building? There's just one moment when he lifts his head and is caught on camera.'

'I'll look for it.'

'Also, have you found more on the death of Lucas Harvey yet?'

'Everything I know, I already emailed to you. A finding of death by accident possibly under the influence of drugs or alcohol. Nobody else saw the crash. He drove into a tree on the A6 outside Bakewell. Broke his neck, according to the medical examiner.'

'Another accident where a witness vanishes? A lot of it in this case.'

'Tell me about it. Anything else?'

'That's enough. Should keep you away from the mother for a while.'

'Nah, I need three tons of garlic, a silver cross, and gallons of holy water wielded by an irate Peter Cushing as well.'

'That bad?'

'She makes Dracula look like a saint; Christopher Lee in a salwar kameez.'

'Didn't know you liked Hammer horrors.' Ridpath remembered watching them late at night, sneaking down to the living room after his mother had gone to bed.

'My favourites. I love *The Brides of Dracula*. You can almost feel how paper-thin the sets are.' She paused for a moment, glancing down at the desk. 'What was your mother like?'

Ridpath didn't ever remember such a personal question from her. His mother flashed into his mind. 'Bouffant hairdos even though it was the nineties. A hard, red mouth, the scent of Estée Lauder. Not a warm person. Cold, distant, Catholic. She went to two Masses on Sunday and was always encouraging me to join her.' He smiled at the memory. 'I never did. She was always there but not there, if you know what I mean.'

Sophia nodded.

'Loved, me I'm sure, but like many of her generation, particularly those raised in Ireland, had difficulty showing it. Clashed constantly with my sister, two sides of the same difficult coin.' He glanced at this watch as if embarrassed by his honesty. 'I need to get back to see Eve. Are you sure you'll be OK here?'

'Mrs Challinor is still here.' She pointed to the light seeping under the door of the coroner's room. 'Perhaps she has a mother she doesn't want to see either.'

He put his jacket on, checking he hadn't left anything lying on his desk. 'Between you and me, I don't think the coroner ever had a mother. She was born exactly as she is today – the illicit child of a high court judge and a recorder.'

'I heard that, Ridpath.' Mrs Challinor's muffled voice came from inside her room 'Go, Ridpath, your daughter needs you.'

Ridpath put his finger across his lips and whispered, 'Call me if you get anything; I'm going to be working late too. I want to go over all the witness statements one more time. Something isn't right. I just can't put my finger on what it is.'

Chapter Sixty-Nine

Ridpath drove slowly home, part of his mind on the road, the rest turning over the case and the meeting with Mrs Challinor in his head.

This case seemed to be full of missing persons, accidents and suicides.

The copper who wasn't on the list, PC 2568, who was he? And why was he in the station? Had they simply left him off the roster by mistake? But his number had been retired from the force in 2017, so who was he?

DI Mark Brett had gone missing too; there seemed to be no record of him, and NCA were neither confirming nor denying he worked for them.

Finally there was the missing detainee from the next-door cell, Garry Abbott. Where was he?

Ridpath drove past a piece of open ground where a crowd had gathered around a bonfire. He'd forgotten it was Guy Fawkes night. He remembered when he was a kid how excited he had been going to a bonfire party at one of the neighbours' houses. Eating toffee apples, the smell of the wood burning, the heat of the flames, the swoosh of the rockets, the crisp hiss of the sparklers and the buzz of Catherine wheels.

These days, it just didn't seem very important any more. A sign of advancing age? Or was it because there were so many other distractions? The simple pleasure of a roaring bonfire no longer mattered so much.

He forced his mind to return to the case, turning over the details again and again. One conclusion stood out: three missing persons all in the same case, one accidental death and one suicide? It was far too much of a coincidence. In fact, it stank to high heaven.

Why was he the only person who could smell it?

And now he was being investigated by Professional Standards himself for a data breach of all things. Perhaps he shouldn't have used the CCTV in the interview with Saunders. But he had to put the man under pressure somehow.

He found himself outside his house, once again wondering how he had arrived there. Part of his brain must have been implanted with a satnav and autopilot. Perhaps it was a side effect of the Covid vaccinations he had been given?

Another conspiracy theory he'd read about in one of the redtop rags. How people reached these conclusions was beyond him.

Then it hit him.

Was he doing the same with the Ben Holdsworth death?

Taking a few coincidences and anomalies and building them into some vast conspiracy theory?

The thought stopped him for a moment, before he gathered his stuff and opened the car door.

From the outside he could see all the lights were on in the house. Despite being an ardent environmentalist, Eve still wasn't too keen on saving energy. He didn't mind, though; at least it meant she felt safe, particularly as the rest of the street seemed shrouded in darkness.

He gathered up his laptop and files and stepped out of the car, searching for his keys.

'DI Ridpath?'

A voice called to him from somewhere on his left. He scanned the area to see who it was but couldn't see anybody.

'DI Ridpath,' the voice repeated.

'Who's asking?' he replied.

'I hear you've been looking for me.'

He stared into the shadows behind the van. Was somebody there?

'Who are you? What do you want?' Ridpath glanced back to the illuminated house. 'How do you know where I live?'

A man stepped out from behind a van parked across the road but remained in the shadows. Ridpath could barely see his face.

'We know a lot about you, Ridpath.'

'Who are you?'

'It's DI Mark Brett. I hear you've been asking after me.' A dramatic pause. 'A word of advice. Don't.'

Ridpath put his laptop and files down on the roof of the car. He wanted his arms free just in case. What was this man doing outside his house? He'd obviously been waiting for him to return. He looked back towards Eve's bedroom.

'If you're wondering about your daughter, she's safe. Doing her homework, I think.'

Ridpath advanced towards him, fists clenching. 'What are you doing here?'

'Stop there.' The voice was soft, almost coaxing, but Ridpath recognised an order whatever the tone. He took two deep breaths. *Calm down, Ridpath, handle this.*

Off to the left, a rocket soared into the sky, exploding above his head, illuminating the night sky in a star of red, green and white sparks. The sudden flash of light revealed a man's round, smug face.

'Why don't you come out, where I can see you?'

'This is just friendly advice, one copper to another. Leave it alone, Tom. You don't know what you are getting yourself into.'

The use of his first name surprised Ridpath; nobody called him Tom. Perhaps this man didn't know him as well as he pretended.

'You want me to leave the Holdsworth case alone, to drop it?'

'Not drop it, just accept the findings of IOPC and Professional Standards. No need to rock the boat. You don't know what you're doing. Stay away from it, understand?'

'Why? Why should I stay away?'

There was no answer. Ridpath listened for a noise but there wasn't any. He ran towards the shadows behind the van, but the man wasn't there. The ghost had disappeared. The man who didn't exist had gone.

Was it Mark Brett? And why had he threatened him outside his house?

And then it struck Ridpath.

Eve. He had forgotten about Eve.

He ran to the door, fumbling in his pocket for his keys, finally finding them and pushing into the house.

'Eve, Eve!' he shouted as loud as he could.

She appeared at the top of the stairs, already dressed for bed in her Peppa Pig pyjamas.

'Hi, Dad, you're back. Why are you shouting so loudly?'

Ridpath recovered his breath. 'How are you? Is everything OK?'

She walked down the stairs towards him. 'Sure, why wouldn't it be? Just doing my homework. Maths, ugh...' She reached him at the bottom of the stairs. 'What's wrong? You look like you've just run a mile.'

He closed his eyes and took three deep breaths. 'Did you see anybody tonight? Anybody hanging around?'

She shook her head. 'Nah, been here since I got home. Made myself a sandwich, watched a bit of TV then started on my maths. Just a normal boring night in suburbia...'

A few more breaths. He focused on his safe spot high above the Derbyshire Dales. A calming technique he had been taught to cope with his PTSD. Should he tell her about the man outside their house? He decided against it. Why worry her unnecessarily?

'It's nothing, just worried about you. We've had reports of burglars in the area,' he lied, not so convincingly.

'What's here for them to steal?' She looked around the hallway. 'Duh...'

Ridpath realised she was right. There wasn't much there. He needed to buy some more furniture, make the place more homely, more lived in. The stuff Polly would have done without thinking.

He smiled. The 'duh' was so like her. 'You hungry?'

'As a locust.'

'How about I reheat the lasagne?'

'You mean melt it, don't you. It's frozen solid.'

'OK, melt the lasagne and then reheat it.'

'Sounds perfect.' A beat. 'And Dad, you shouldn't be so worried. I can look after myself even when I'm here on my own.'

But you shouldn't be alone, Eve, that's the problem, he thought.

'Shit.'

'What?'

'I've left my files and laptop on top of the car.'

Chapter Seventy

After Eve had gone to bed, Ridpath sat alone for a long time in the dark. His laptop and files had been sitting on top of his car where he had left them.

Untouched and unwanted by anybody.

He had been through all the witnesses' statements again and again. Read through the timeline and the duty log, even revisited the post-mortem report. He'd written a first draft of the case summary for the coroner but his mind wasn't really on the job in hand.

Instead, he kept asking himself the same questions.

Why had Mark Brett come to his house?

Why had he been told to leave the case alone?

Was it simply an organisation coming together to protect one of its own? Was it like the Catholic Church, who for decades had protected paedophile priests to the detriment of the young people it was supposed to protect?

Ridpath understood the siege mentality. There was always a sense of us vs them in the police. Us being the thin blue line that was society's bulwark against the forces of anarchy and lawlessness, them the great unwashed masses who, left to their own devices, would turn on each other like animals, allowing the strong to prey on the weak.

The police were a close-knit community like any other, with its rites and rituals, its codes and unwritten laws. One of those Ridpath had broken: you don't grass up another copper.

But what if these unwritten laws led to illegality? Where those tasked with defending the rule of law were also, at the same time, the people breaking it?

Had this happened in the early hours of February 21?

The official view was that it was just an unfortunate accident combined with a failure of the CCTV.

Ridpath had shown, at least to himself, that something else was going on here. Was Brett's visit and warning to him tonight designed to protect those who had broken the law? Or was there something else behind it?

Ridpath remembered the words the man had used. 'This is just friendly advice, one copper to another. Leave it alone, Tom. You don't know what you are getting yourself into.'

Friendly advice, or an unfriendly threat?

It all came down to the death of Ben Holdsworth. Had he killed himself with an overdose of heroin? Or had somebody killed him?

As this question and its implications rattled around his mind, the phone rang.

'Ridpath,' he answered immediately.

'Great, you're still awake.'

He glanced at the clock. 12.20. Where had the time gone?

'You're not still at work, Sophia?'

'Just about to go home, the Uber is on its way. Thought I'd call you first.'

What was she still doing at the coroner's office?

'Are you alone?'

'Yeah, Mrs Challinor went home a couple of hours ago.'

'Go home now, that is an order. You shouldn't be there on your own.'

'Why? I quite like it here when it's quiet.'

'Don't be silly. Go home now.'

'I am, the Uber is coming. And it is not silly to do my work.'

'But it is silly to do it alone, without any security.'

There was silence for a while before she answered. 'Point taken. Do you want to hear what I discovered in the CCTV?'

'Go on.'

'PC 2568 appears twice, fleetingly, on CCTV in the station.'

'Just twice?'

'Yep. I got the feeling he was aware of the cameras, avoiding being filmed properly. The first time was on the camera behind the custody desk. Sergeant Saunders isn't there, but I saw his shoulder and number standing beside the desk.'

'Did you see his face?'

'No. He's doing something at Saunders' desk but he has his back turned so we only see the back of his head.'

'And the second time?'

'He's near the cells, talking to Lucas Harvey. Here we see the side of his face for about thirty seconds.'

'What are they saying?'

'There's no sound on the camera, remember? I suppose we could ask a lip-reader to tell us? I've sent you both of the CCTV clips plus a screenshot of the man's face. I know I wasn't supposed to use email but...'

'No, you did the right thing, Sophia.' There was no point hiding the continuing investigation from the prying eyes of Professional Standards any longer.

On the other end of the phone, Ridpath heard two loud honks.

'My Uber is here. See you tomorrow, Ridpath.'

'Thanks, Sophia, and great work. Sorry I went on at you earlier.'

'That's OK, at least you care. Night. Or should I say morning?'

'Just say bye. See you tomorrow.'

'Bye...'

The phone went dead in his hand. He opened up his email, finding the clips she had sent. PC 2568, whoever he was, was in both of them, but it was the second which was most important.

Did the man know Lucas Harvey?

6 November 2021

Chapter Seventy-One

Eve cooked breakfast in the morning. Slightly charred toast, two fried eggs, one with the yolk broken and coffee with the taste and texture of mud.

'How is it, Dad?' she asked tentatively.

'Delicious.' He pointed to the clean, empty plate. It had nearly killed him but he had finished every single morsel. 'I would use less coffee next time, though. I think this pot contains the yearly production of Brazil.' He saw her face drop and quickly added, 'The eggs were great, though.'

'Same again, next week?'

He immediately said yes. It wasn't the food after all, it was the thought behind it. And watching her at the stove, with a spatula in her hand, had sent shivers of joy down his spine.

She really was her mother's child.

After breakfast, Ridpath dropped her off at the shopping mall where she was meeting Maisie to hand out the climate change flyers.

The bitter smell of bonfire smoke and gunpowder was heavy in the air, and a thick haze hung over the ground. The smell didn't seem to bother Eve, though.

'See you later, Dad.'

'Be careful. If you have any problems ring me immediately.'

He'd thought long and hard about letting her go to this after last night. It was a difficult decision but he reasoned she was safe enough as long as she stayed with her friends all day. The meeting last night was a warning, not a threat.

A warning for him.

'What sort of problems?'

'Nothing, just call me if anything comes up.'

Eve frowned, not really understanding. 'Don't worry, there'll be lots of us from school there.'

'Still...'

'I'm thirteen now, a big girl, I can handle myself. And besides, I'm going shopping with Maisie afterwards.'

Those two ideas had no logical link, but Ridpath didn't follow up on it. 'What do you want for dinner?'

'Can we go out? Somewhere like Nando's. I feel like a chicken thigh.'

'You don't look like one... boom tish.'

Her eyes rolled backwards in her head. 'Your jokes are becoming worse, Dad. You're not going to become one of those terribly embarrassing dads, are you? Telling fart jokes, failing miserably at handshakes and trying to be besties with my friends?'

Ridpath sometimes felt the adult in this relationship wasn't him.

'No fart jokes. No besties. No weird handshakes. Message received and understood.'

'Just being my dad would be enough. Anyway, see you tonight.'

She collected her backpack from the back seat and strolled off to the entrance of the shopping mall to find her friends.

'Call me,' he shouted.

She waved her hand without looking back. For some reason, the nonchalance of the gesture broke his heart. She was growing up too quickly.

He drove to Stockfield and parked in his usual place. He thought about going for another coffee to get his brain started but decided against it. He had to finish compiling a case review for the coroner. He'd started it last night, now it just needed polishing, then Sophia could attach all the witness statements, the custody and duty logs, and all the other papers into one file. It was normally the sort of bureaucracy he hated, but strangely he felt it might help here.

Sophia was already sitting at her desk when he arrived, perfectly dressed and made up. Did the woman never sleep?

'Morning, Sophia.'

'Morning, Ridpath. I brought you a coffee, double shot, thought you might need it. Did you look at the clips I sent over?'

Ridpath nodded. 'They were useful, thanks.'

'I've checked and there is a lip-reader available if we want to check what they are saying.'

How had she got so much done already?

'Great, let's do it.' They might just be talking about the weather, or it could be more interesting. They wouldn't know unless they tried. 'Go ahead and book her. I'd like to be there at the meeting when she sees the footage.'

'I thought you'd say yes, so she's coming in this afternoon at four. There's a couple of other things too.'

Ridpath shook his head. It was only 9.10 on a Saturday morning; how could things have moved so quickly?

'Harold Lardner has agreed to a meeting if you want to see him. It's short notice but he wants it at noon today.'

What had changed Lardner's mind? He didn't particularly want to see the former pathologist, but had to cover all the bases. Perhaps Lardner could have interesting information about the post-mortem on Ben Holdsworth. 'Say yes, I'll be there.'

'You want me to come?'

Ridpath shook his head. 'Better stay here. We need to take Jenny through the witness list so she can make a schedule, and finish compiling a case summary for Mrs Challinor.'

'I've already started collating the files for the summary, I hope that's OK.'

When did she find the time? 'Great. What would I do without you, Sophia?'

'Get into more trouble?'

'That as well.'

'Talking about trouble, Professional Standards are trying to arrange an interview.'

'Who's made the request?'

'A Detective Sergeant Morris.'

'Charlie Morris? I didn't know he was at Professional Standards.'

'Who is he?'

'One of the fast-trackers. Should have been an inspector by now. Must have done something to blot his copybook.'

'And the interview?'

'Remind them I need to be questioned by an officer of the same rank or higher. Plus it has to be held in the presence of my union rep. Should stall them for a while.'

'OK, I'll reply. What tone do you want?'

'Formal, official with a soupçon of disdain. Can you manage it?'

'With pleasure. Here are the screenshots of the man's face in the cell corridor. What are you going to do with them?'

Ridpath thought for a moment. 'I'll meet Lardner and afterwards pay a visit to Redbury nick again. Perhaps Bob French will know who he is.'

'Busy day.'

'We have just a few days left before the inquest and we still don't understand what may or may not have happened that night. There are things we know, things we know we don't know and, what worries me the most, things we don't know we don't know.'

'Too deep for me at nine o'clock in the morning.'

'As the police pointed out to me, they have no statutory duty to tell us what happened. To find the truth, we have to give Mrs Challinor the ammunition to ask the right questions. Witnesses won't lie, it would be perjury, but they won't volunteer information either.'

Sophia frowned.

'I spent a long time thinking about it last night,' said Ridpath.

'Should've slept instead.'

'Yeah, perhaps. Anyway, let's get Jenny in here and start planning the inquest.'

'So I'll confirm Lardner?'

'Please do, it'll be fascinating to hear what the man has to say for himself.'

Chapter Seventy-Two

After finishing the summary, Ridpath had given it to Sophia before driving down the M62 to Liverpool.

The usual security and identification procedures had proceeded smoothly and he was shown into the bare room which passed for an interview area at Ashworth high-security hospital.

A cheap table bolted to the floor, three plastic chairs which had seen better days back in the seventies and an empty cork noticeboard were the only furniture. A poster on the wall listed a dense set of rules and regulations printed in eleven-point type.

Ridpath read them briefly while waiting for Lardner's arrival but stopped after the first three. Apparently the only activity allowed in this room was breathing, but even that was regulated.

The morning had passed too quickly but at least the bureaucracy was now in place for the inquest. He knew he could leave the actual details to the combined efficiency of Jenny and Sophia.

The door opened behind him.

'What a pleasant surprise, Mr Ridpath. I have looked forward to meeting you again.'

Lardner stood in the doorway dressed in an orange jumpsuit. He looked fit and active despite having the sallow pallor which was endemic among prisoners. The colour of lukewarm porridge.

'Thank you, John, I'll call if I need you.'

On his dismissal, the prison guard simply nodded without saying a word and closed the door. Lardner was in charge even here. The arrogance of the man dripped from every pore.

'Why don't you take a seat, Mr Ridpath. Personally, I would have chosen a more salubrious meeting place, the Tea Room at the Midland for example, but unfortunately beggars can't be choosers...' He held his arms open while a smug smile spread on his face.

Ridpath sat down, followed by Lardner, the man acting as a host even in prison.

'Now, how can I help you? The note I received from your secretary...'

'My assistant, Sophia.'

He smiled again. 'Your assistant, Sophia. Interesting name, it has both Greek and Arabic roots. Means wisdom, of course. Is she as intelligent as she seems?'

Ridpath ignored him. 'I've asked for this meeting because one of your post-mortems will be presented at an inquest soon, and I have some questions about it.'

Lardner lit a cigarette and blew the smoke across Ridpath's face. 'A horrible habit, smoking, but one I seem to have picked up during my stay at Her Majesty's pleasure. But why Her Majesty gains any pleasure from me being in here, nobody has yet provided a satisfactory answer. One of life's imponderables, don't you think?'

The door opened and the prison guard popped his head into the room. 'I'm sorry, Dr Lardner, but you're not allowed to smoke in here.'

Lardner rolled his eyes, stubbing the cigarette out against the top of the packet. 'You're being very tiresome, John.'

The door closed again.

'If we could return to the post-mortem you performed...'

'Still focused on your work, Ridpath, so diligent. How is your wife, by the way?'

Lardner already knew the answer, he was just trying to unsettle Ridpath.

'Polly died eighteen months ago, Lardner. But you knew, so why ask?'

'Just making conversation. It is so difficult inside here to talk to anyone with an ounce of brain matter. The governor went to Sunderland University. Until I met him, I didn't know Sunderland even had a university.'

A regretful touch on the now-closed cigarette packet.

'Is it hard to raise a daughter on your own? My wife and I never had the pleasure of raising children. She was barren of course, and I had my little diversions...'

Lardner's 'diversions' had included murdering up to eight women over a period of twelve years after the death of his wife.

Ridpath tried to stay on track. 'About the post-mortem, it was on a man called...'

'Ben Holdsworth, a death in custody on February 21, 2018. Don't look surprised, Ridpath. We do get the newspapers in here, even though it is a prison. The governor has been very kind by arranging to have my pathology magazines and the *Daily Telegraph* delivered.'

'You carried out the post-mortem?'

'I did.'

Ridpath pulled out a copy of the post-mortem findings and passed it across to Lardner, who waved it away with his hand. 'I don't need it. I remember every detail of every post-mortem I ever carried out.'

'I just have a few questions...'

'You said that already.'

'You ascribed Mr Holdsworth's death to a subdural haematoma caused by striking his head after a fall.'

'I may have done.'

Ridpath pointed to the relevant passage in the report. 'I would conclude the deceased struck his head from a fall in the cell. Death followed three hours later.'

'I was so much more definite back then, wasn't I?'

'You mean you're not sure now?'

Lardner shook his head. 'I was merely making the observation that I was more certain at that time. The world has become less of a certainty these days. The days drift into one another, the nights dominated by the sounds of coughing and farting and the whispers of life outside these walls.'

Lardner wasn't answering his questions. Ridpath decided to push on regardless.

'We had your post-mortem re-examined by another pathologist...'

'The squeaky-voiced Dr Schofield, no doubt.'

'He did relook at your findings.'

'And what conclusion did the boy wonder come to?'

'The subdural haematoma was in a different place on the skull from the impact of the fall against the wall.'

Lardner snorted loudly. 'Is that it? Really, perhaps he should return to being a butcher, not a pathologist. Even a first-year medical student at No Hoper College knows a haemorrhage can occur anywhere, not necessarily at the point of impact. Schoolboy stuff to go with his schoolboy voice.'

'There was something else... the toxicology.'

Lardner's eyes narrowed.

'It reported high levels of diamorphine.'

'The man was an addict, what do you expect?'

'Do you think this could have caused the death?'

Lardner laughed. 'It could have been a contributing factor in the man's unsteadiness, but I doubt it was the actual cause of death. There are so many factors contributing to someone's death. In your wife's case, it was two bullets in the chest, was it not? But the bullets didn't cause her death. It was probably a result of the combined effect of loss of blood and shock. Am I right?'

Once again, Ridpath ignored the man.

'Did you examine Ben Holdsworth's heart?'

'Of course. As you know, in every post-mortem the heart is weighed and examined.'

'And...'

For the first time, Lardner hesitated. 'One heart is very much like another. It pumps blood and then it stops and you die.'

'But this particular heart...?' Ridpath persisted.

'Pumped blood until it stopped. Hard to know why...'

Lardner was playing with him. This was a waste of time.

'One last question before I go, Mr Lardner...'

'So soon, Detective Inspector? I was so enjoying our little conversation.'

'You performed the post-mortem five hours after the man's death and the report followed only a day afterwards. It was fast, wasn't it? Normally, you would wait for the toxicology to come back before pronouncing definitively on a cause of death.'

'Ah, what is normal, Detective? It is a question I have often pondered in my time in this place.'

'And why did the toxicology report take six weeks?'

He waved his hand as if swatting a fly. 'Labs these days, you can't get the staff.'

'And why wasn't the duty doctor's use of ephedrine on Ben Holdsworth mentioned in the report?

'Like I said, you can't get the staff these days.' The man scratched his nose and smiled teasingly. 'I have some news which might interest you.'

'What?'

'I may be allowed out soon. The doctors are pleased with my rate of recovery and believe I am no longer a danger to society.' A quick glance over his shoulder to the door. 'Between you and me, apparently I have discovered Jesus and am now a reformed character. But all the praying is awfully wearing on the knees. The release will only be for a day or so while they evaluate my progress, but it is a start, isn't it? I may even be able to begin lecturing again.'

'Over my dead body will you be released from here.'

Lardner stood up quickly. 'That can be arranged, Detective Inspector, don't tempt me.'

'I haven't finished asking you questions, Lardner, sit down.'

'But I have finished answering them.'

'Did you remove the ephedrine from the lab report?'

Lardner ignored him, strolling over to the door and rapping on the wood twice. It opened immediately. 'I'm ready to go, John.'

'Of course, Mr Lardner.' The guard almost tugged his forelock as he answered.

'One last thing, Ridpath. In answer to your question. I was asked by an old friend to provide a quick post-mortem report.' A long pause. 'And to make sure it was seen as an accident.'

And with these last words, he was gone, leaving behind a cloud of uncertainty in his wake.

Ridpath ran to the door, shouting, 'Who? Who asked you?'

There was no answer.

Chapter Seventy-Three

Ridpath couldn't wait to escape from Ashworth after the meeting with Lardner. His clothes stank of an unholy aroma of prison sweat, cigarette smoke and fear. Lots of fear – it oozed from the walls and dripped down on everybody who was forced to be in the place, even the warders.

Back in his car, he found his hands shaking as they rested on the steering wheel. Why had he allowed Lardner to get to him? The man was a psychopath who enjoyed manipulating people. He should never have agreed to meet him.

Lurking at the back of his mind was the feeling Lardner was playing him. Hinting at something darker and deeper than a rushed postmortem. Was it true, or was it just another one of Lardner's games? Who had asked Lardner to make sure it was seen as an accident?

It was the findings of the post-mortem that allowed the death to be brushed under the carpet. Just another accident rather than something more sinister.

He decided to ring Chrissy before going back to Stockfield.

'Hiya, I was hoping you'd ring. Just a minute.'

He heard the sounds of the civilian researcher getting up from her desk and stepping out into somewhere where her voice echoed. Probably the emergency stairwell at Police HQ.

'Sorry, couldn't talk, too many people listening. I managed to find Mark Brett for you. He's been seconded onto a special task force. One of those secret deals nobody is supposed to know about. But you know how coppers gossip...'

'What is it?'

'Operation Ventnor. It's all part of the fallout from the decoding of EncroChat.'

'EncroChat?'

'In short, WhatsApp for criminals. It was a totally legal service allowing over fifty thousand users around the world, and nine thousand in the UK, to communicate safe in the knowledge that none of their texts would be uncovered by law enforcement. Until, of course, the whole communication system was busted by the French police.'

'I remember now, but I thought the raids happened more than a year ago?'

'Apparently there's a new investigation into people missed in the original arrests after the investigation. It's run by the National Crime Agency and they are set up in a separate building with completely different reporting structures and computer systems.'

'What?'

'It's like a force within a force. Now get this...'

'Don't tell me... they are investigating links between organised crime groups and the police in the north.'

'Ridpath, that was going to be my big surprise.'

'Who's running it?'

'A superintendent no less, goes by the name of Ratcliffe.'

'Never heard of him.'

'Not surprising. *She* comes from the Thames Valley force.'

'How long have they been operating?'

'Sorry, my friend didn't know.'

'And what's the link to the death of Ben Holdsworth?'

'Don't know that either. But I do know where they are based.'

'Can you text me the address? Time to pay a visit to Mr Brett.'

'I wouldn't if I were you, Ridpath. You're in enough trouble as it is. Turnbull is saying you assaulted him. He wants to press charges against you. Claire Trent is trying to dissuade him and keep it an internal affair but he seems adamant.'

He hadn't touched Turnbull, but how to prove it? 'I'm in trouble, aren't I, Chrissy?'

'An understatement, Ridpath. You're up shit creek without a paddle, or a canoe, and the water's rising above your head.'

'That good, huh?'

'Worse.'

He thought for a moment. 'Where's Emily?'

'At her desk, keeping her head down, trying to avoid the shit flying around.'

'Could you get her? I'd like to have a chat.'

'Give me a sec.'

The phone went dead. Ridpath was in worse trouble than he thought. He'd been tempted to laugh off Turnbull's allegation but a charge of striking a senior officer was serious. He could get jail time for it or, at minimum, he could be dismissed from the force for gross misconduct. What would he do then?

'Hi there, Ridpath, you're in big trouble.'

'Thanks for reminding me, Emily.' He paused, taking a breath. 'I need you to do me a favour.'

'What is it?'

'I swear I never touched Turnbull. We were together at the post-mortem and had an argument, but then I left and drove to the coroner's office.'

'Dr Schofield has confirmed the dispute during the post-mortem but says there was no fight in his presence, simply a "healthy exchange of opinions", in his words.'

Thank you, Dr Schofield, I owe you a pint or three.

'But Turnbull says the fight happened outside the mortuary. You ambushed him on the way to his car. Verbally attacked him and then committed an assault.'

'It's a lie, Emily.'

'I believe you, Ridpath, but it's the word of a senior officer against yours, plus he was assaulted by somebody; you only have to look at his face.'

'It never happened, Emily, I swear on Eve's life.'

'As I said, I believe you, Ridpath.'

The detective stared through the windscreen of his car. Once again, rain was starting to fall. So much rain at the moment, seeping into everything, leaving a damp, muggy smell everywhere.

'I have favour to ask, Emily. Please say no if you don't want to do it. I promise I will understand.'

'What is it, Ridpath?'

'I need you to check the CCTV outside the mortuary. We left at roughly five p.m. yesterday. If you go quickly it won't be erased.'

There was silence at the other end of the phone, before she finally responded. 'If Turnbull finds out, it could be the end of my career. I'll be writing parking tickets for the next twenty years. Or worse.'

'I know, Emily. Normally I wouldn't ask but I'm in trouble, deep trouble.'

More silence.

Finally she spoke. 'OK, I'll check them out this evening. But you owe me big time, Ridpath. And Chrissy, you owe her too.'

'A curry for three in Rusholme?'

'And the rest.'

'Thanks, Emily, and sorry for asking.'

'No worry, Ridpath, but a bit of me would like it to be true.'

'What?'

'I wish you had punched Turnbull.'

Chapter Seventy-Four

After the phone call to Emily, Ridpath said a small prayer in thanks for friends. Polly's death had reminded him how precious they were, and during his PTSD counselling he had been frequently reminded of the meaning of gratitude.

It was never more important than today.

He sat back in the car, listening to the rain beat down on the roof. When would it stop bloody raining? It seemed as if the drizzle had lasted for a year and day. He imagined meeting a Mr Noah soon at B&Q buying up all the spare four-by-twos. No doubt he would live in Ark Avenue next to Sale Water Park.

Focus, Ridpath, concentrate.

Where to next?

He had planned on visiting Redbury nick again and having a chat with Bob French, showing him the picture taken from the screenshot. This man was key. What was he doing in the station and who the hell was he?

Or he could go and confront DI Mark Brett. His phone had already buzzed with a message from Chrissy. The address was Nexus House, in the centre of Manchester. What about doing both today? After all, he didn't have much time left and Professional Standards could make life difficult for him at any moment.

He slapped his forehead. Dinner with Eve. He'd promised to take her to Nando's this evening.

Shit.

He picked up his phone and messaged her.

> Sorry, Eve, will be back a bit late this evening.

Her answer came almost immediately:

> But you promised we were going to Nando's...

The text was followed by a long line of angry emojis. Ridpath had never got the hang of using these things. Wasn't English easier? He'd watched his daughter and her friends communicate entirely without words.

> Sorry, I'll try my best. Perhaps a late dinner?
> Better late than never.

The reply was instant again, if a little curt. This time there were no emojis.

He put the car in gear and decided to go to Redbury, reasoning it was on his way back to Manchester and it would be easier to park in the city centre later on a Saturday.

Bob French shouldn't take long anyway. He just needed to verify if PC 2568 was employed at the station.

Chapter Seventy-Five

'Never seen him before.'

'He's never been stationed here?'

Inspector French looked at the image of PC 2568 again. 'Was this taken at our rear door?'

'On the night of Ben Holdsworth's death. He entered the station at 4.20 a.m.'

A deep frown creased the forehead of the uniformed officer. 'Impossible, we change the code weekly at six a.m. on Wednesdays, and it's only emailed to serving officers on the intranet. It's not widely distributed. We don't want every Tom, Dick and Harry coming in.'

'So you've never seen him before?'

'Not at this nick, and I've been here six years. He should be easy to track, there's his number.'

'The number belongs to somebody who retired in 2017.'

'What?'

'The man lives in Guernsey now.'

'So who is this copper?'

'I think it's a better question to ask if he was a copper at all.'

Bob French leant forward. 'But if he entered the station at 4.20, it means he was here before the death of Holdsworth.'

'Correct.' Ridpath handed over the other photo of PC 2568 talking to Lucas Harvey, the custody detention officer. 'They obviously knew each other.'

The uniformed inspector's forehead creased again. 'But what's he doing there? Regs say he shouldn't be anywhere near there. When was this taken?'

'The time code is at the top. 5.55.'

'But Holdsworth was reported as lying on the floor of the cell just over half an hour later.'

'And the report was made by Lucas Harvey.'

French stared across the table for a long time. 'What are you trying to tell me, Ridpath?'

What *was* he trying to say? For a brief moment, it all coalesced in Ridpath's mind in a series of images. He'd have to check the timings, but he thought it made sense.

'What if, and this is only my suspicion, Bob, I don't have any evidence yet. What if Ben Holdsworth didn't die from a brain haemorrhage but instead was injected with an overdose of heroin?'

'I've been through those reports a thousand times. The postmortem findings were clear. Death was caused by a haemorrhage from a fall in the cell. None of the custody team reported Holdsworth was on drugs and he was body searched before he was placed in his cell. All the standard procedures were followed to the letter.'

'I think you are misunderstanding me, Bob. I said what if he were injected with an overdose?'

The penny dropped. 'You mean, he was murdered? By whom?'

Ridpath tapped the photo. 'My best suspect is him.'

French picked up the photo again. 'But that means somebody managed to get inside my nick and kill a detainee. I can't believe it, Ridpath.'

'It also means somebody must have colluded with him.' He picked up the second screenshot. 'They obviously knew each other.'

'This can't be true, Ridpath, you've totally lost the plot. No wonder Professional Standards were asking me about you.'

'When?'

'Earlier this afternoon.'

They were moving quickly. 'What did they ask?'

'Just had you been here. What questions were you asking people.'

'Are you going to report this conversation, Bob?'

'You know I have to.'

Ridpath nodded. He definitely had to interview Brett quickly.

'Are you all right? I heard you suffered from PTSD after Polly died. Is this case getting to you?'

'What? Why do say that?'

'It's just... you seem overwrought. Professional Standards were worried about your mental health. Attacking a senior officer, going round making accusations. And now you're in my office suggesting Holdsworth was murdered.' A long pause. 'I'm worried about you,

Ridpath. As a friend, I suggest you go home and spend time with your daughter. She needs you now.'

Ridpath stood up. 'Thanks for your time, Bob. Perhaps you could show those pictures to your team. One of them might recognise him. After all, he was in your station on the night somebody died in one of your cells.'

Chapter Seventy-Six

Professional Standards were moving quickly, far more quickly than he'd ever known them move before. He had to stay ahead of them, just for a few days more. He knew he was close to an answer now, he just needed time.

Ridpath drove as quickly as he could to Nexus House in the centre of Manchester, just off Deansgate. The building was one of those modern brick and glass nightmares shoehorned among the elegant Victorian and Edwardian properties lining the rest of the street.

It stood out like a criminal in an ID line-up with an 'I did it' sign above his head.

Luckily Ridpath found parking in front of the building, feeding the meter with all the change he had. It bought him fifteen minutes of time. It would have been cheaper buying gold bars.

The lobby of the building was empty. Ridpath checked the listing of tenants. The only space with no name next to it was on the fourth floor. He checked the address Chrissy had sent him. Fourth floor it was.

He took the lift up and entered a smaller lobby blocked by a security door. Above a keypad a small notice said, 'Please press for entry.'

He jabbed the button, aware the single eye of a security camera was watching him. The intercom squawked.

'Who is it?'

'DI Ridpath to see DI Mark Brett.'

The only answer was a loud buzz as the glass door unlocked.

Mark Brett appeared in the corridor. It was the same man who had been waiting outside his home last night.

'Ridpath, I see you've found me. I was wondering how long it would take you. Why don't you come this way?'

He followed Brett down a short corridor to another coded security entrance. Brett swiped a card and entered a code. The entrance opened out into a large open-plan room. A dozen people were sitting behind computers. Every one of them looked up as he entered. They obviously did not receive many visitors.

Brett spread his arms. 'Welcome to Operation Ventnor, not that we publicise it much. I think you're the first local officer we've ever had here. Let's have a chat in my office.'

The office was small but neat, with a row of files on the table behind a desk. The only other furniture was a couple of cheap chairs, a laptop and a lockable filing cabinet.

Brett noticed him looking at the cabinet. 'You can't be too safe. Our rule is all files need to be locked away securely every evening.'

Up until now, Ridpath hadn't said a word. 'Security is tight. What are you afraid of?'

'Everything and everybody. Why don't you take a seat and we can chat.'

Ridpath pulled out the chair and sat down.

'Right, what can I do for you?'

Brett's attitude was completely different from the previous evening outside Ridpath's house. Now he seemed affable, almost welcoming.

'You warned me off the case.'

'Well, that worked out well, didn't it? I told my boss it wasn't going to work, but he wanted me to try anyway. I know if somebody had warned me off it would only have piqued my interest even more.'

The accent was southern and educated, not London, though, more Home Counties.

'Your boss, Ratcliffe?'

'Somebody has been talking out of turn. Ventnor is supposed to be secret.'

'There are no secrets in Manchester. It's a village pretending to be a city.'

'Somebody told me that and I didn't think it was true... until today.'

'You're investigating the EncroChat communications and their links to organised crime?'

'Our official brief, yes.'

'And your unofficial one?'

Brett sat forward. 'What I'm about to tell you is confidential. You must promise not to repeat it outside these walls.'

'I can't agree. If the information impacts on the case, I am duty bound to reveal it to the coroner.'

'Ah yes, your other role as coroner's officer. Any conflict of interest?'

'Not until recently, when I started looking into the death of Ben Holdsworth.'

Brett stared into mid-air for a long time as if making a decision. 'Our other brief is to investigate links between north-west police forces and organised crime groups.'

'Links?'

'There have been some low-level prosecutions but nothing major so far. We want to find out how far police teams may have been penetrated by the OCGs.'

'And what have you found?'

'I can't divulge anything. Suffice to say, the investigation is ongoing, but there have been indications OCGs have penetrated senior ranks.'

Ridpath stayed silent.

Brett ran his fingers through his blond hair and exhaled. 'Look, the NCA has been investigating EncroChat since 2016. It was a secure mobile phone system providing command and control for organised crime groups across the world. We think there were about sixty thousand subscribers each paying about fifteen hundred quid every six months to chat with each other, order drugs, have video conferences, send encrypted messages, and arrange the auto-destruction of data.'

'I thought you managed to break the codes?'

'We didn't, the French did. They found the main server and placed malware in it.'

'You managed to read all their messages?'

'More than that, we could see all the data sent by the world's drug dealers, people traffickers, prostitution gangs and loan sharks. They didn't even use any code. It was like having an inside person in every leading organised crime group in the country.'

'I know you busted them eighteen months ago...'

'So far in Operation Ventnor in the UK, we've arrested 1384 suspects, charged 260 criminals with offences, seized 75 million quid, 165 firearms, 5.6 tons of Class A drugs and 8.7 tons of cannabis. But...'

'There's always a but.'

'...But we didn't bust all of them. At least fifteen of our targets, and probably more, did a runner the night before we went in. They were all over the north-west, not within any particular force's area.'

'Tipped off?'

'Definitely. Your work on the Ronald Barnes case was another red light.'

'The copper involved with people trafficking? But he was just a bad apple.'

'Was he? Too many coincidences for us, too may leaks. So Ventnor was set up to see if we could find the OCG moles.'

'Right, I get it. Sounds like something out of *Line of Duty*.'

'It's worse. What puzzled us was the thugs who were on their toes came from not just one of the criminal gangs, but from all of them. What the EncroChat bust revealed was that all the OCGs were working together. The Albanians, the Chinese, the Kashmiris, the Irish and the Manchester gangs in Moss Side, Cheetham Hill and Salford were in it. The closest analogy is the 1950s mafia when the five New York families all formed the crime commission.'

'That's big. But where does Ben Holdsworth come in? He was just some petty drug dealer working the Orchard Estate.'

'Ben Holdsworth was working the estate, and he was working for us. He was trying to infiltrate the crime groups to discover how EncroChat operated in Manchester.'

Chapter Seventy-Seven

Ridpath was done for.

He had him exactly where he deserved to be.

Isolated. Suspended. An object of hate.

He couldn't survive this. Even Claire Trent, his biggest supporter, had finally turned on him.

He'd played it wonderfully, even if he did say so himself. Righteous outrage at being assaulted, followed by being convinced, as a huge favour, to keep it an internal matter rather than press criminal charges.

In the subterranean light of the Gas Lamp, he finished off his pint and considered ordering another. He should have stayed at home, continued the pretence of being injured, but the temptation to celebrate was too great.

Professional Standards were on Ridpath's case, determined that, after the Tony Saunders affair, the man shouldn't be a member of this or any other police force any more.

The charges were going to be gross misconduct, which, after an investigation and professional tribunal, would lead to instant dismissal with all loss of pension rights.

Ridpath would have to resign first if he wanted to keep his money.

He ordered another pint and a whisky chaser, ignoring the boisterous set of women on a hen party on the other table.

Ridpath was going to be an ex-copper, and he had delivered the kick in the teeth.

The whisky arrived and he raised his glass. 'Good luck, Mr Ridpath, enjoy your new life,' he said out loud.

Now, the next one on his list was Claire Trent. Time to get rid of her too. Hadn't she indulged Ridpath, given him too much freedom, allowed him to become a law unto himself?

She was as guilty as Ridpath was. All he had to do now was make sure the powers that be could see the truth.

He was going to run MIT, not her.

It was his destiny, his calling, his promotion.

All he had to do was play the game properly. And Paul Turnbull knew how to do that. It was as if his whole life had been building towards this moment.

He saw Alan Butcher come down the stairs and raised his hand to let the detective know where he was. The man walked straight across to him, taking a quick glance at the hen party on his right.

'How are you feeling, boss?'

'Fine, Alan.'

'No hard feelings?'

'None at all. I enjoyed every second of it.' He finished the rest of the whisky in one swallow. 'It's your round,' he said, 'make mine a double.'

It was time to celebrate.

Chapter Seventy-Eight

'What?'

'Holdsworth was working for us as a confidential informant.'

'He was your CI?'

'Holdsworth had some troubles in Manchester and came to Guildford, where I was working at the time. He soon popped up on our radar and it was relatively easy to turn him and send him back to Manchester to report on the gangs and their activities, particularly who was using EncroChat.'

'He was selling smack on the estates,' said Ridpath incredulously.

Mark Brett shrugged his broad shoulders. 'Needs must. He had to prove his credentials to the gangs. On the morning before his arrest, he rang me to say he was onto something big. I had to go down to London so I arranged a meet for when I came back.'

'But he never turned up...'

'Because he was already dead.'

'What did he find out?'

'I dunno, he wouldn't tell me over the phone. Said it had to be in person.'

'Meanwhile, he's arrested and dies in custody at Redbury nick.'

'I was away two nights. A bit of a coincidence, don't you think?'

'I don't believe in coincidences.'

'Neither do I. Afterwards, a custody officer died and, since you started your little investigation, Saunders, the custody sergeant, has apparently jumped to his death.'

'More coincidences?' And then it suddenly hit Ridpath. 'Was that why the investigations into Holdsworth's death were so...' he searched for the word, '...superficial?'

'You may think that but I couldn't possibly say.'

Ridpath reached into his bag and pulled out the photos of PC 2568. 'Do you know this man?'

Brett shook his head. 'Never seen him before.'

'He was in the station the night of Holdsworth's death, but the inspector had never heard of him and the number belongs to a retired copper.'

Brett stroked his chin. 'Give me a second.' He pressed the intercom. 'Rich, can you come in for a minute?'

The door opened seconds later. 'You wanted to see me, boss?' The accent was definitely from London.

'DS Rich Holder, meet DI Ridpath.'

They both shook hands.

Brett held up the pictures of PC 2568. 'Do you mind?'

Ridpath shrugged his shoulders.

'Can you run these pictures through the National Crime Database? See if we can find a match.'

'Not great quality, boss, taken from CCTV? Never the easiest things to match.'

'Give it a go, Rich, we might get lucky.'

'Sure, boss.'

As Rich left, Brett asked, 'Do you have any more tricks up your sleeve, Ridpath? Any more CCTV? Or perhaps you would like to assault me?' It was said with a smile, but the eyes weren't laughing.

'I didn't assault anybody.'

'It's not what DCI Turnbull is saying.'

'He's wrong.'

'From what I've heard, he seems a bit of a tosser.'

Ridpath didn't answer.

'Right, I've told you as much as I know. Now it's your turn. Other than the pictures of matey, what else do you have?'

Should he reveal everything to this man? Someone who only last night was warning him off outside his house?

Ridpath decided he had nothing to lose.

'I believe Ben Holdsworth was murdered in Redbury station in the early hours of February 21, probably by the man you are now checking on the database.'

'Proof?'

'I don't believe he died from subdural haematoma at all. That was just an excuse concocted by the pathologist at the time, Lardner. I thought at first it might have been a cover-up, but it wasn't. Lardner was doing a favour for somebody.'

'Who?'

'I don't know.'

'So how did Holdsworth really die?'

'I believe he was injected with a massive overdose of heroin. It's there in the toxicology report if anybody cared to read it. Saunders was also injected in the same place before he died too. My bet is the toxicology report will show he also had massive amounts of diamorphine in his body. And I'd make one further bet – if we exhumed Lucas Harvey's body, we would find the same high levels of opiates.'

Mark Brett thought about this for a long time before asking, 'PC 2568, or somebody impersonating him, was in the station that night?'

'CCTV was off a full hour before Holdsworth died. 2568 is caught on camera, near the cells, talking to the custody officer, and nobody noticed him after Holdsworth's death was discovered.'

'So he had opportunity. Motive?'

'You've just given it to me. Holdsworth had information on the OCGs and was about to give it you. He had to be silenced. He's on record as asking for you the night he was detained.'

'I know. I didn't answer my phone.'

'Sometime that evening, PC 2568, whoever he is, disabled the CCTV, went into Holdsworth's cell, aided by the custody officer, and injected him with heroin. They probably waited fifteen minutes or so, giving PC 2568 time to get away before raising the alarm.'

'Where does Saunders fit in?'

'I don't know yet. Perhaps after Harvey died he worked it out. Or maybe Harvey told him. Or perhaps he wasn't involved at all. Whatever it was, when I started asking questions, he became a liability.'

'It's all very tenuous, Ridpath...'

There was a tap on the door and Rich Holder popped his head around. 'We've had a hit on the picture, boss, I've sent the file to your laptop.'

Brett swivelled around and entered his password, accessing his mail.

Ridpath craned round to see the screen. A man's mugshot appeared with a long list of offences.

'Well, that is interesting, Ridpath.'

'What is it?'

'You've hit the jackpot.'

Chapter Seventy-Nine

Emily Parkinson was standing outside the mortuary on the Boulevard near Manchester Royal Infirmary. It always struck her as incongruous that a few steps away from where most forensic examinations were carried out, there was a children's nursery.

Across the road was the car park in front of Manchester Royal Infirmary. Wasn't this where Turnbull said he'd been assaulted by Ridpath?

She'd agreed to do this as a favour for her friend, but regretted it now. If Turnbull found out, he would make her life even more miserable than it already was.

What if he blocked her request for a transfer?

What if made it impossible for her to ever leave MIT, just kept her there indefinitely doing the most menial jobs?

And if Claire Trent was promoted, he would probably take over. Her life would become a living hell. Perhaps she could switch to another force. Go back home to Preston and join the Lancashire Constabulary; they were probably looking for experienced detectives.

She walked across the road. The area was covered by multiple CCTV cameras. One of them must have captured the assault. For a second a feeling of déjà vu stopped her dead in her tracks. Hadn't she spent days checking CCTV for Ridpath during the killing of the kids in Chorlton Ees too?

She was tempted to just walk away, forget about it all. Leave Ridpath to sort out his own problems. After all, it had nothing to do with her. Why should she get involved in a fight between two grown men?

But something made her stop. Ridpath had always been straight with her. He'd always taken her side, even though sometimes it had been difficult to do. Now he was in trouble, shouldn't she help him out? She'd promised she would.

'Bloody hell, Ridpath, you're always getting me in trouble,' she said out loud.

Taking out her phone, she took a picture of the car park company's address and telephone number. She rang the number and it went to an answering machine.

'This is Detective Sergeant Emily Parkinson. I'm contacting you regarding an assault that occurred in one of your car parks. Please call me back.'

She'd contact them tomorrow if they didn't return her call and ask to see the CCTV footage.

A promise was a promise.

Even if it showed Ridpath was guilty.

Chapter Eighty

Ridpath leant across the desk to look at Brett's screen. PC 2568's face was displayed prominently in the right-hand corner of what was obviously a police intelligence file.

'This is Trevor Sinclair. Ex-British Army, ex-2nd Battalion of the Parachute Regiment. Served in Northern Ireland, Iraq, various outposts of the British Empire and finally in Helmand Province in Afghanistan. Since leaving the army, our Trevor has been employed by the Albanians as one of their hitmen. Not the type of man you'd want to meet in a dark alley on an even darker night.'

'Nor in the custody cells of Redbury nick. Anything else on him?'

'Last seen living in Wales, close to the Brecon Beacons. That's all we have.'

Ridpath sat back down. 'Isn't it strange, the Albanians employing an ex-British soldier to do their dirty work? I thought they'd use one of their own.'

'Equal opportunity employers, are our Albanians. And besides, if someone infiltrated the nick to kill Ben Holdsworth, it would be difficult to do if he didn't speak any English.'

Ridpath didn't speak for a moment, trying to get it all clear in his mind. 'But the question remains, how did he get a police uniform, and how did he know what the code was for the rear entry of Redbury nick?'

'You're jumping ahead of yourself. You still haven't proved he killed Ben Holdsworth. All you have is he was in the nick at the same time as the man who died. No proof, no evidence, Ridpath.'

'And conveniently the two possible witnesses, Lucas Harvey and Tony Saunders, are both dead too.'

Brett shook his head. 'It's all circumstantial, wouldn't stand up in a court of law.'

'Or an inquest.' Ridpath thought hard. 'There's one other possible witness: the man in the cell next door to Holdsworth. Nobody interviewed him and I've been trying to find him for the last week with no luck.'

'What's his name?'

'Garry Abbott.'

Brett returned to his computer and tapped a few keys. In seconds an image of the man appeared. It was the rap sheet it had taken Ridpath ages to uncover. 'This him?'

'Do you know where he is now?'

Brett stared at his screen. 'No, but it won't take Rich long to find him.'

Ridpath expected him to call in the officer as he had done before, but Brett just sat there, his arms folded across his chest.

'I need your help to find him.'

'You've done your work, Ridpath, leave the rest to us.'

'What? I've done all the legwork and now you're going carve me out just like that? What about the inquest?'

'Bugger the inquest. We're almost ready to take down an organised crime group who've infiltrated the police and all you can worry about is some inquest on a two-bit hustler-cum-drug dealer.'

'A man who was working for you.'

'A man who was informing for us to save his own skin. Do you think I'd risk the operation for him?'

'So that's why you did nothing when he died. Ben Holdsworth was expendable?'

'Don't be so bloody naive, Ridpath. You've been a copper for how long? Fourteen years? And you still think scum like Ben Holdsworth deserve a fair shake. He took a chance and it didn't work out.'

'What about his family?'

'What about his family? He was a nothing, they're better off without him.'

Throughout this conversation, Brett's voice had been getting louder. Then he closed his eyes for a second and when he spoke, the voice was softer, more emollient. 'Go home, Ridpath, you've done a good job. We now have Trevor Sinclair in the frame for three possible murders. Leave it to us, we'll make sure he's off the streets and charged. Just as soon as we have finished our investigation. That's what we're here to do. I've spent the last three years of my life working on this

– don't screw it up now. We're this close to putting the lot of them away for a long, long, time.'

'Ben Holdsworth, Lucas Harvey and Tony Saunders were all murdered by this man and you're asking me to trust you'll get round to arresting him just as soon as you're ready?'

'No, I'm asking you to trust that we will assemble the evidence to put him away for a long time.' Brett stared at him. 'You know I can't let you jeopardise this investigation?'

'Then don't. Work with me here. Help me find Garry Abbott. I think you've forgotten a policeman, Tony Saunders, was murdered.'

'A, we don't know that yet. And B, Saunders may have been a bent copper.'

'But he was still a copper. We should be looking to prove he was killed and find his killer. We need to find out what Garry Abbott knows.'

Brett didn't answer.

'Look at it this way. If he was working for the Albanians as you say, then couldn't you add a charge of conspiracy to murder to their rap sheet?'

'It's possible.'

'So help me find Abbott.'

Brett stared into mid-air, past Ridpath's head. 'I'll think about it,' he finally said. 'In the meantime, go home. Do not pass go, do not collect two hundred quid and most importantly, do not involve yourself with my case. We've worked so hard; don't screw it up now.'

'When can I expect an answer?'

'I need to talk to my gaffer.'

'When?' Ridpath persisted.

'Tomorrow at the latest. But don't get your hopes up, I don't think she'll go for it.'

Ridpath stood up. 'I won't.'

Brett held out his hand. 'Thanks for your work, and sorry for visiting you at home. The gaffer's idea, not mine.'

Ridpath glanced at the screen. PC 2568's face was still there, staring out like a gargoyle on an old building. 'Find him and we can put Trevor Sinclair behind bars for a long, long time.'

Chapter Eighty-One

Outside, Ridpath held his briefcase over his head to protect himself from the rain sleeting down like stair rods. He ran to his car, getting soaked in the process.

Once inside, he reached forward to start the engine, seeing the parking ticket tucked neatly under the windscreen wiper.

Bastards.

He opened the car door and snatched the ticket from beneath the wiper, getting soaked once again in the process.

He screwed the sodden mass into a ball and chucked it onto the floor on the passenger's side. He'd get a notice to pay in two weeks' time.

He started the engine, adjusting the air vents to clear the mist already forming on the windscreen and side windows.

He thought he knew what had happened now. Ben Holdsworth had been arrested, had asked to call the National Crime Agency and then had been killed before he could talk.

But as the pieces began to fit together, they raised other questions.

How had the killer known Holdsworth was in Redbury nick?

How had he responded so quickly?

Did the OCG already know Holdsworth was an informant?

And why take him out then? What had he discovered that was so important?

Either Lucas Harvey or Tony Saunders must have let them know what was happening. His bet was on Harvey. After all, had they been filmed talking together in the corridor outside the cells.

He picked up his phone and called Sophia.

'Hello, Ridpath, long time no see. The coroner is asking for you. She wants a briefing.'

'Now?'

'Tomorrow will be fine. She's already left, had some event she had to go to. Women in Business or something. She's giving a speech. I've got something for you.'

'Don't tease, what?'

'The lip-reader has taken a look at our film from the cell corridor.' Ridpath had forgotten all about the meeting.

'She could pick up most of it.'

'And?'

'It doesn't really make sense to me, so I've typed it out and sent you a copy.'

'I'll check it this evening. Anything else?'

'Not a lot. I've prepared a draft summary for the coroner. I've sent it to you too.'

'What would I do without you?'

'Not a lot.'

'Please go home, don't work late tonight.'

'Will do, I just need to help Jenny prepare the witness schedule and then I'm done for the evening. Mother wants me to meet someone.'

Evening? Outside Ridpath could see the street lights had already come on. What time was it? He glanced at the clock. 6.30. It had been light when he'd gone in to meet Mark Brett.

Shit. Eve. They were supposed to be going out for dinner.

'Great. Sorry, Sophia, got to go. I have a dinner date with Eve.'

'Mine is with some heating engineer from our home village. Yours sounds *sooo* much more fun.'

'It would be if I wasn't already thirty minutes late.'

'One day life will catch up with you, Ridpath.'

'Or I will catch up with it.'

Ridpath drove as fast as he could but the A56 was jammed. United were playing City in the Manchester Derby at Old Trafford. How could he have forgotten?

He eventually reached home at 7.30. There was a deadly silence as he opened the door, shouting hopefully, 'Hi, Eve, I'm home.'

She came out of the kitchen, dressed and ready to go out in new clothes he hadn't seen before. For the first time, there was no trace of the little girl she had once been.

'Sorry, love... work.'

'I guessed, Dad. At least you messaged... and you're here now.'

'Shall we go? Not the usual Nando's at White City, too many football fans. How about we go to Parrs Wood instead?'

'Sure, let's be adventurous.'

He wasn't certain if she was being sarcastic or playful, but there was something different about her. 'Are you wearing eye make-up?'

'Just a little. I bought it this afternoon. I hope it's OK. I was aiming for the "sophisticated woman of the world" look, but I think it's probably more like "here's someone who thinks a smoky eye is something you get on Bonfire Night". Do you know how hard it is to apply eyeliner?'

'Not one of my skill sets.'

'Not easy. I had to go on YouTube to work it out.'

Ridpath made a mock bow. 'Your carriage awaits, milady.'

Her back straightened and she stared down her nose. 'To Nando's, James. Our chicken is grilling and our stomach is growling.'

Chapter Eighty-Two

It had been a good night.

The food had been spicy and Eve had chattered on all about school, shopping with Maisie, leafletting outside the shopping centre and how great Greta Thunberg was.

For once, Ridpath didn't have to talk, just listen. He enjoyed sitting back and hearing all the gossip about her life and her friends and her school. The child was still there; she was just being taken over by the woman she was going to become.

But now, back at home, with a glass of whisky by his side and Eve safely wrapped up in bed with her hot water bottle, Ridpath had opened up his laptop.

The summary Sophia had produced was excellent: exact, concise, explaining the case and the witnesses' testimony for the coroner. What would he do without her?

The transcript from the lip-reader of the conversation between PC 2568 and Lucas Harvey was worrying, though.

> PC 2568: You going to open it or not?
>
> Harvey: What you going to do?
>
> PC 2568: (unintelligible, his face turned and I can't see his lips)... not your business, just open it up.
>
> Harvey: But I'll be blamed...
>
> PC 2568: It's all sorted... unintelligible... will handle it. Open the bloody door...
>
> (for the rest of the clip both men have their backs to camera).

Was this the smoking gun? Lucas Harvey had allowed this man impersonating a police officer, Brett said his name was Trevor Sinclair, to go into Ben Holdsworth's cell.

Was this definitely a murder, not an accident?

Had he injected the detainee with an overdose of heroin?

Was Tony Saunders involved?

Why go to all that trouble to get rid of one minor criminal?

The lip-reader's transcript seemed to raise as many questions as it answered. Who was going to 'handle it'? What did that mean?

There were only two people who could answer his questions.

Garry Abbott.

And Trevor Sinclair, the man who had impersonated PC 2568.

Both had to be found, and found quickly.

7 November 2021

Chapter Eighty-Three

Ridpath was up early the following morning. It was a bright, cold Sunday with just a few clouds scudding across the blue sky. A nip was in the air, though, as Ridpath found out when he went to put the trash in the bins.

He was surprised when he returned to find Eve already up, awake and dressed, and her hair combed.

'Good morning.'

'What time are we going to see Mum?'

Because he had been so busy on the case, Ridpath had forgotten his promise. 'Whenever you want,' he quickly improvised.

'I'd love some toast first, and a boiled egg. Then we should go. We can pick up some lilies from Tesco on the way. I know it's not the best place to buy flowers but Mum won't mind. It's the thought that counts. Afterwards, I'll go to Ah Kung and Paw Paw's place for lunch. She's always saying how skinny I look and how I need feeding. The old Chinese always show their love through food. Did you know the words for "hello" literally mean "have you eaten yet"?'

'You sound like you have it all planned.'

'And I guess because you have your inquest starting tomorrow, you'll need to go to work after we've visited Mum.'

'You know me better than I know myself.'

'Ain't it the truth.'

Ridpath ignored the last remark. 'Right, toast, boiled egg, orange juice on the side, coming up.'

He had just put the water on to boil and popped a couple of eggs in the pan when the doorbell rang.

Who could that be at this time on a Sunday morning?

'I'll get it, Dad.'

Memories of Polly answering the door flooded back into his head. The old woman standing there. The door opening. Him shouting no. Two loud gunshots. And in two short seconds, his world, his tiny world, destroyed.

'No worries, Eve, I'll get it. You just watch the eggs; they need to be boiled for five minutes.'

'I do know how to boil an egg, Dad.'

He went to open the door, seeing the distorted shapes of a man and a woman through the frosted glass. He hoped it wasn't the Jehovah's Witnesses.

He opened the door.

'Good morning,' the man said, 'are you Thomas Ridpath? Detective Inspector Thomas Ridpath?'

'That's right, who are you?'

The man held up a warrant card. 'Detective Sergeant Ian Worthington, and this is Detective Constable Shirley McCann.'

Ridpath frowned. 'What do you want?'

'We work for the Professional Standards Department, and we'd like you to accompany us to Police HQ for an interview regarding a misuse of confidential police data and an assault on a senior police officer.'

Chapter Eighty-Four

As she always did on a Sunday morning, Emily went for a run through the park. It was one of the things which gave her the most joy in life, the initial stiffness gradually replaced by a consciousness of her heart, legs, breathing and arms all working together as she ate up the ground. Later, as she relaxed into the rhythm of the run, her mind roamed free, thinking all those thoughts she was too busy to allow herself during the week.

After eight kilometres, it was time to stop and grab a long, hot shower.

Usually she had arranged a brunch with some friends or, if she was working weekends, would head into Police HQ. But this Sunday, she picked up the phone and called the car park company again; they still hadn't returned her call.

This time it was answered after only three rings by a young woman.

'MPT Car Parks, can I help you?'

'Hello, my name is Detective Sergeant Emily Parkinson, based at Police HQ. I rang you yesterday regarding an assault committed in one of your car parks.'

'I heard your message this morning, but Mr Hadley isn't in today. He's in charge of the CCTV at the car parks. Unfortunately, he's caught Covid and is isolating for a couple of weeks. He'll be back a week next Monday.'

'That'll be too late; I need the CCTV footage well before then. Can nobody else give it to me?'

'Only Mr Hadley is supposed to deal with these requests.'

'This is urgent; it could be a matter of life or death.'

She ummed and aahed for a moment. 'I suppose if it's so urgent, I could find it for you.'

'You're a star.'

'Which car park do you want?'

'The one in front of Manchester Infirmary.'

'I know it. And the dates?'

'On Friday, November 5, from four to six p.m.'

'Bonfire Night, it wasn't assault with a deadly sparkler, was it?'

'Not this time.'

'Right, let me check.'

Emily heard the rattling of computer keys. 'Yep, we've got it, the cameras are operational in the area. They go down so often, you know.'

'Great, can you send it to me?'

'We're not supposed to. You're supposed to view it here.'

'It's Sunday, and I can't get there until four p.m.'

'I finish at noon. You'll have to come tomorrow.'

'How about you just email me the CCTV footage from the car park. Then it'll save you working late and me coming in tomorrow. I promise I'll just keep it between us girls.'

Emily Parkinson kept her fingers crossed as she waited for the answer, hoping the appeal to female solidarity had worked.

'Well... I suppose it's OK, with Mr Hadley being off sick. What's your email?'

Emily gave her private address as she didn't want anybody, meaning Turnbull, to know what she was doing.

A note of concern entered into the woman's voice. 'That's not a police email. How do I know you work for the police?'

'It's because I'm working at home today, but let me give you my police email and you can send it there as well, OK?' She could erase the one to the police address later.

'I suppose so. It'll take me a couple of hours, though. These machines are a right bugger to work.'

'No worries, I'll wait for it.'

Emily put down the phone.

She hoped Ridpath realised how far out on a limb she was going for him. If Turnbull happened to check the emails on the server...

Her body shivered at the thought. It was as if somebody had just walked over her grave and then stomped on it three times for good measure.

She crossed her fingers and touched the wooden table for good luck. Turnbull was off; he wouldn't be checking incoming emails, would he?

She shook her head. Why the hell was she doing this?

Chapter Eighty-Five

'Are you placing me under arrest?'

'No, sir, not at the moment. We are simply asking you to come down to HQ to answer some questions.'

'Who is it, Dad?'

'Nothing, Eve, don't let the toast burn,' Ridpath shouted over his shoulder. 'As you can see, Detective Sergeant...?'

'Worthington, sir.'

'...Worthington. It isn't convenient at the moment. In a few minutes, myself and my daughter are going to Stretford Cemetery to spend time with her mum and my wife. You do remember my wife, don't you? She was shot because of my work as a policeman.'

'I am aware, sir, but I still would like you to come to the station with me now.'

'And I have explained it is not a convenient time, Detective Sergeant.'

Worthington glanced back at his fellow officer. 'Can we do this inside, sir? I don't want to embarrass you in front of the neighbours.'

The man moved to come inside the house. Ridpath stepped in front of him, blocking the entrance. 'You won't embarrass me, Detective Sergeant Worthington, only yourself.'

'Right, sir, you give me no option but to give you this.'

He pulled out a sheet of paper and passed it across to Ridpath.

'As you can see, this is a PR15 notice. You are being investigated for two offences. The mishandling of confidential police data and a separate offence of striking a senior office in the performance of his duty. Both offences could lead to a charge of gross misconduct, but those charges may be changed later if the evidence justifies that course of action. In both cases, a finding of guilty will lead to dismissal from the force. Have you read the PR15 and do you understand the notice?'

Ridpath smiled. 'I have and I do.'

'Then I must repeat my request you accompany me now to the station and answer questions from me regarding the charges laid down in this form PR15.'

'You really did choose the short straw this morning, didn't you, Worthington?'

The policeman's eyes showed surprise at Ridpath's answer.

'Did nobody tell you a police defendant requires fifteen days' notice of any interview conducted under a PR15?'

There was no answer.

'A defendant also needs to be questioned by an officer of an equivalent rank or higher. As a detective sergeant, you don't quite make the grade.'

'I—'

'And finally,' Ridpath interrupted before Worthington could answer, 'I require the presence of my union rep at any interview. In this case, my rep is Detective Inspector Jack Cater.'

'But... but...'

'But what, Detective Sergeant?'

'Jack Cater is one of the complainants about your conduct.'

'Now that is interesting. It opens up a world of difficulties regarding possible conflicts of interest, doesn't it?'

Worthington glanced once more at his detective constable. 'So I take it you are not going to accompany me to the station for a voluntary interview.'

'I see the penny has finally dropped, Detective Sergeant. I'm afraid I have better things to do. But I will expect your letter requesting an interview in fifteen days' time. Actually, I will look forward to it. Now, if you would excuse me, I can smell my daughter burning the toast.'

'This won't look good with the disciplinary board, Detective Inspector Ridpath.'

'Have a good day, DS Worthington.'

He closed the door, leaning on it and listening to the sound of their feet as they walked down the path.

He breathed out. Eve was standing in front of him.

'What did they want, Dad? Are you in some sort of trouble?'

He smiled. 'I'm not, but you will be unless you eat your breakfast and get ready to see your mother. She's waiting for you.'

As he followed his daughter back to the kitchen, he wondered how he was going to get out of this one. People were out to get him, and it wasn't just Turnbull this time.

Chapter Eighty-Six

After visiting Polly's grave, Ridpath dropped Eve off at her grandparents' and drove to Stockfield. For once Sophia wasn't in the office before him, but Mrs Challinor was.

He knocked on her door and received a sharp command to enter.

'Good morning, Ridpath.'

'Was it? I must have missed the memo.'

'You seem a little out of sorts.'

'Well, when you're visited by Professional Standards at nine in the morning and afterwards you listen to your daughter telling her mother's gravestone she really misses talking to her, it hardly makes for the best start to the day.'

'I'm sorry for Eve. I hope she's handling it.'

'Normally she does, it's just at times like this I realise how much she has buried deep inside her and it worries me.'

'If you need any help, please don't hesitate to ask, Ridpath. I think the world of Eve and would do anything to assist her. As for Professional Standards, they are out of my jurisdiction, but if you'd like me to recommend a good solicitor...'

'It won't be necessary, Mrs Challinor. If they were halfway competent I might need help, but not at the moment.'

'Be careful, Ridpath. Don't underestimate them.'

'I won't. Now, I presume you've read the case summary,' he said, changing the subject.

'It's very good, thank you for your work.'

'It wasn't me, Coroner, it's all Sophia.'

'She's doing very well, isn't she?'

'She's indispensable.'

A long exhale of breath. 'Just so you know, I am being pressured to cut costs. All the councils are suffering at the moment; too many jobs to do and too little money to do them all.'

'You're not suggesting we no longer employ Sophia?'

'Not at all, but we will have to shave costs in other areas to maintain our staffing. Training, external suppliers and so on. The mantra is to do more with less. I keep telling them, the only thing you do with less, is less. Anyway, enough of my issues. I have adjusted the order of the witnesses based on the summary you sent me.'

She passed across a sheet of paper.

Ridpath paused for a moment. 'Mrs Challinor, can I speak frankly?'

'Always, Ridpath.'

'I'm becoming more and more convinced Ben Holdsworth was murdered in his cell in the early hours of February 21. I think he was murdered by a man called Trevor Sinclair posing as a policeman. He—'

'Ridpath, I will stop you right there. It is not up to you or me to decide the result of an inquest. It is always the decision of the members of the jury. Our job is to find out who died, how they died, when they died and see if their death was due to any negligence on the part of the officers of the law. We simply present the evidence, question the witnesses and attempt to discover the truth for the jury. It is not our job to find out who committed a crime, nor to ask why they committed it. Nobody is ever found guilty or innocent at an inquest, and no criminal or civil liability is determined.'

'I understand, Coroner, but...'

'No buts, Ridpath, the policeman in you is speaking. As far as I see, having read the summary, there are two possible verdicts the jury can reach: accidental death or unlawful killing by a person or persons unknown. We will present the witnesses, question them to find out the truth and let the jury reach a verdict. That's how the system works...'

Ridpath was about to argue a verdict of accidental death would be a travesty in this case when his phone rang.

He checked the number. It was Mark Brett.

'Morning, Ridpath, do you want the good or the bad news first?'

'The good news.'

'We've found your witness, Garry Abbott.'

'And the bad news?'

'He's dead.'

Chapter Eighty-Seven

Garry Abbott's body was lying in a blue waste bin in Cotton Field Park, just across from what was now called New Islington Marina. The area had undergone massive regeneration in the last twenty years. Ridpath remembered it as the Cardroom Estate, an old council house area with more problems than most: no schools, no pubs, no parks, no jobs and far too many drugs. Nowadays, it was achingly hip and trendy with a design echoing the canal-side ambience of Amsterdam, or so the developers kept telling people.

Ridpath had signed in at the cordon surrounding the park and was led to where Mark Brett and the local CID were standing.

'Who found him?'

'One of the locals on the canal boats. He went to put his rubbish in the bin and saw the body.'

'What time?'

'Late last night, around eleven p.m.'

'And you didn't let me know?'

'Listen, Ridpath, we only found out ourselves this morning, when the discovery of the body was flagged on our computers. Rich Holder put two and two together and I called you.'

'How did he die?'

'No post-mortem yet but the medical examiner is still here. We'll ask him.'

Ridpath instantly recognised the small, slight figure of Dr Schofield walking towards them even though his face and body were hidden by an oversized white suit, cap and large face mask.

'Hello, Ridpath. North Manchester isn't your patch.'

'I was looking for the man you just found. His name is Garry Abbott and he was a key witness in a case I'm working on. Can you give me a heads-up on how he died?'

'Normally I wait for the post-mortem, but as it's you, I'll make an exception. As far as I can see, he was tortured viciously and then

305

given a lethal overdose of a drug. My bet is heroin.' Schofield held up an evidence bag with a bloodstained hypodermic inside. 'We found this beside the body. It could have been thrown in by some junkie but the man has an injection site inside the crook of his left arm.'

'Self-administered?' asked Mark Brett.

'Not when you have half your fingernails missing and three broken fingers. Somebody else gave him the injection. Forensics are now checking the areas for fingerprints.'

The body was being carefully lifted out of the bin and placed on a gurney. A small crowd had gathered to watch. A morning's entertainment before they went for their Sunday brunches and avocado toast.

'I'll know more after I complete the post-mortem this afternoon.'

'Could you send me the results?' asked Ridpath.

'I'll check with the North Manchester coroner, but I'm sure it will be OK.'

'Anything else, Doctor?' asked Mark Brett, eager to get away.

'One other thing. The man is missing at least four teeth.'

'That's normal, isn't it?' said Brett.

'You misunderstand, Detective, the wounds on the gums are still fresh. This man has had his teeth removed recently. In the last day or so, I would think. Now, if you'll excuse me, my body is waiting.'

The gurney had been placed in a mortuary van with the driver and his assistant patiently waiting for the signal they could leave.

As Schofield left them, Mark Brett turned to Ridpath. 'Somebody didn't like Garry Abbott very much.'

Ridpath ran his fingers through his thinning hair. 'It's the fourth person who has died in this case. First it was Ben Holdsworth, then the detention officer, Lucas Harvey. The custody sergeant supposedly killed himself last week and now this man, the key witness in the case. Without his testimony, I have nothing, just a bunch of coincidences, anomalies and far too many dead people.'

'We're checking the local traffic cameras to see if we can find out how Garry Abbott was dumped here. We might get lucky and get a hit.'

'And pigs might fly.'

Ridpath remembered the lip-reader's submission from yesterday. He opened his folder. 'In the interests of transparency, we asked a lip-reader to work out what PC 2568, your Trevor Sinclair, said to Lucas Harvey in the station.'

Ridpath handed Brett the transcript. After reading it, he whistled. 'Is this what I think it is?'

'The footage was taken just before the murder. He seems to be asking to go into a cell. But we don't know if it's Ben Holdsworth's.'

'It has to be. Why else would he be talking to Lucas Harvey?'

'But it's not proof. A clever barrister would argue he wants to check the cells out, but not necessarily Ben Holdsworth's cell. And that is if they accept the lip-reader's testimony at all. It's not an exact science.'

'I'm intrigued by the line, "It's all sorted... unintelligible... will handle it." What do you think he means?'

'I wish I knew. If, as you say, Sinclair is a hired gun, is he talking about someone higher up in the food chain?'

'Someone in an OCG? It would make sense. Ben Holdsworth was desperate to tell me something. What are you going to do next?'

Ridpath's shoulders slumped. 'In the absence of any witness, I'm going to take my boss's advice and let the jury decide whether this was an accident or an unlawful killing. The inquest starts tomorrow and I can't prove Ben Holdsworth was murdered, even though I know he was.'

'If it's any consolation, my boss approved us letting you know about Garry Abbott. We're actively looking for Trevor Sinclair as we speak. Don't know if we'll find him but, with your work, we reckon we've got a chance. He could be vital in cracking our case too.'

'I think he's murdered at least three people – probably four.'

Mark Brett nodded towards the blue rubbish bin, now being fussed over by a team of CSOs. 'You think he did Garry Abbott?'

'Certain of it, but I can't prove anything.'

Chapter Eighty-Eight

Emily Parkinson finally received the footage from the car park company at four o'clock in the afternoon. She stayed in to wait for it, ringing their office three times without getting an answer. She worried the girl had cold feet or had rung one of her bosses to check. But apparently, that wasn't the problem. It was simply that the server was down so she'd sent it from home.

Before downloading the footage from the three cameras, Emily logged into her police email and deleted the message. The last thing she needed was Turnbull snooping around.

She opened the first camera and played the footage. The car park was very busy, with a regular flow of cars in and out as people visited relatives at the hospital. Just after five o'clock, she recognised Turnbull's bald head as it bobbed its way through the parked vehicles to his car. He was just about to open the door when he turned round to talk to somebody.

Emily couldn't see who; the person was standing right at the edge of the camera's field. After a couple of minutes of conversation, the person suddenly walked up to Turnbull and punched him in the face.

To Turnbull's credit, he didn't fight back, simply standing there until the second blow knocked him back onto the bonnet of the car. The person then helped him to stand up on his feet and Turnbull wandered off towards the A&E entrance of the hospital, blood streaming down his face.

Why hadn't Turnbull fought back? And why had the assailant helped him to his feet?

Emily rewound the footage. The camera's quality wasn't very good, either that or the lens hadn't been cleaned in a million years. She could make out a face but couldn't see who it was.

Was it Ridpath?

The size and height were about right, but the build wasn't. This man seemed stockier, beefier than Ridpath.

She played the footage from the other two cameras. One was completely useless. It was focused at number-plate level to catch drivers who had overstayed or not paid the correct fee. All Emily could see were legs.

The last camera was better, but not by much. The footage showed the fight, but it was totally out of focus. Why have a CCTV system if you don't maintain it properly?

She sat back in her chair and tapped the desk. Was it Ridpath in the footage? She really didn't know.

Somebody had definitely attacked Turnbull as he went back to get his car. But who? And what had they spent two minutes talking about before the attack?

She needed clearer pictures, and she knew exactly who could get them from even the worst images. Len Gorman.

She grimaced. He'd asked her for a date a couple of times and, on each occasion, she had found a good reason to say no. But if he was going to do a favour for her, she could hardly refuse him again.

Bloody Ridpath. She hoped he realised the sacrifices she was making for him.

Chapter Eighty-Nine

After leaving Mark Brett, Ridpath had gone back to Stockfield to let the coroner know what had happened and check if she needed anything else.

She held up the case summary they had prepared. 'This is all I need. The rest is up to me to ensure each witness presents his testimony truthfully and directly. I am confident they will reach the correct conclusion. Never underestimate the common sense of the great British public.'

He had stayed quiet through her words of advice, suddenly feeling immensely tired. She seemed to recognise it immediately.

'You've done enough. Go home, and I'll see you at the inquest tomorrow.'

'You might need something, Mrs Challinor.'

'If I do, I'm sure Sophia will be able to find it for me. I will call you if she can't.'

He received the same message from Sophia when he saw her, but delivered rather more bluntly.

'You look terrible, why don't you go home and go to bed.'

He finally listened and went to pick up Eve, going to a McDonald's drive thru on the way back to pick up dinner. She was the third person to reiterate the message.

'You look awful, Dad, when was the last time you slept properly?'

He couldn't remember. Time, and the case, seemed to have blended together into one giant, amorphous mass.

They'd eaten in near silence. Eve had gone upstairs and was doing her homework. Ridpath found himself sitting in front of the TV, not really watching or listening, his mind going over the case again and again.

He felt nothing but an abject sense of failure. At least two people had died while he had been investigating, and he hadn't been able to do anything to prevent their deaths.

He hadn't even found the concrete evidence to prove that a crime, not an accident, had led to the death of Ben Holdsworth.

He remembered the words of Maureen Holdsworth about her son, spoken in what felt like the far-distant reaches of time but was actually less than a week ago. 'I think I was the only person who cared about him in the whole world.'

A deep sense of failure and tiredness gripped his body. He'd let her down too.

Slowly, he climbed to his feet and switched off the light.

He would spend the whole night lying on his bed, staring up at the ceiling, thinking of all the mistakes he had made.

November 8, 2021

Chapter Ninety

The following morning on the dot of 9.30, Mrs Challinor walked from her room and entered the court.

Ridpath saw everybody rise as she entered. All the witnesses they had invited had turned up. Chris Carter, the PC who had arrested Ben Holdsworth, was in full uniform, as was Bob French. Dr Bourke was sitting next to John Schofield, both of them no doubt talking shop. Terry Rodgers was on the front row, looking very glum and staring angrily at Ridpath. Apparently, according to Jenny, the coroner had decided he wouldn't be called until this afternoon.

Behind him sat the DUI from that night, Neil Mallender, looking positively the worse for wear. Ridpath felt sorry for him; he had obviously fallen off the wagon since they last met. Next to him was Steven Fellows, the head of the security firm, nervously tapping his foot on the chair in front. Of everybody here, he had the most to lose.

Mrs Maureen Holdsworth was at the front on the family table, close to the coroner. Next to her, Ronald Davies, the solicitor, was whispering in her ear, probably explaining what was going to happen. Opposite him, a bank of barristers and solicitors representing the police, the IOPC and the CPS, had been arrayed across two tables, both of which were heavy with legal texts.

Missing of course were three other witnesses who were no longer alive; Lucas Harvey, Tony Saunders and Garry Abbott. The people who actually knew what had happened on that cold, wet February night.

'Please sit,' shouted Jenny.

Ridpath closed the doors and stood in front of them, his arms behind his back.

'Ladies and gentlemen of the jury, today we will begin the inquest into the death of Mr Ben Holdsworth at Redbury Police Station in the early hours of February 21, 2018. You may have read some articles on this case in the past. I want you to immediately disregard them. It is up to this inquest and you the jury to decide what happened on the day, nobody else. To put it simply, your job over the next couple of days is to come to a conclusion about when and how Mr Holdsworth died. It is not our job to assign blame; we are not a court of law. However, if, after listening to the witnesses, you should wish to give a more detailed narrative verdict, I will advise you beforehand of the possibilities in front of you.'

Ridpath glanced at the jury members; all of them seemed to be nodding along with Mrs Challinor, listening intently to her words.

'Over the next few days, we will listen to witnesses describing what happened from their viewpoint. They will be questioned by myself, Mr Davies, the solicitor for the family and Mr Hargreaves, the barrister for the police. But please remember, unlike the Courts of Justice, the coronial system is not adversarial. It's our task is to discover the truth, not ascribe guilt or innocence.'

She scanned the room, finally looking at Davies and Mrs Holdsworth, before saying, 'Jenny, can you call our first witness please.'

'Will PC 4396, Mr Christopher Carter, please come to the witness stand and take the oath?'

Ridpath saw the barrister for the police visibly wince as the policeman's name was read out in open court. The burly policeman took his seat in the witness box and began reading the oath. 'I swear...'

As he did, Ridpath's phone began ringing. In his hurry to take Eve to school this morning, he'd forgotten to switch it off. Mrs Challinor stared at him.

He checked the screen. It was Mark Brett. What did he want this time?

Ridpath backed out through the doors into the reception area. 'What do you want? We've just begun the inquest.'

'I'm going to do you a favour, Ridpath.'

'What?'

'We've found him.' Brett's voice was excited.

'Found who?'

'Trevor Sinclair. We did a check of all the hotels in the northern district and he's staying at the Crowne Plaza. Even better, the next-door room is rented to a Mr Arthur Delaney.'

'The crime boss? MIT have been after him for years.'

'He was one of those who escaped our net in 2019. Did a runner to Cyprus, but must have come back for some reason.'

'Did he order the death of Garry Abbott?'

'One of Delaney's MOs when he was an up-and-coming thug in the Hewitt gang was removing the teeth of those who had offended him. He didn't bother with anaesthetic.'

'Garry Abbott was missing teeth.'

'You've got it in one, Lone Ranger. The boss has given me the go-ahead to take both of them down. We've got eyes on them at the moment and in ten minutes we're going in.'

'Wait for me.'

'Sorry, no can do.'

'I'm coming anyway.'

'Please yourself. Officially, this is a local CID arrest and they're taking him into custody.'

Ridpath ended the call and tore a sheet of paper from his notebook, scribbling a quick message to Mrs Challinor.

Urgent developments. Will be back soon.

He went back into the courtroom and strode up to Mrs Challinor's desk, handing up the note.

Chris Carter was just detailing how he had arrested Ben Holdsworth and found ten sachets of crack cocaine on the front seat of the car. He stopped, watching Ridpath and the coroner.

She read the message and stared at him, nodding slightly.

'Please carry on, PC Carter,' she said, as Ridpath hurried out of the court.

Chapter Ninety-One

Emily Parkinson knocked on the door of the digital forensics room. Len Gorman was sitting behind the console with an array of mixers, screen, wires, cameras, editors and assorted glowing and buzzing bits of kit in front of him.

It looked exactly like something out of *Star Wars*. Unfortunately Gorman was no Han Solo; he didn't even have the sophistication of a Chewbacca. He saw himself as the lothario of Police HQ. A uniformed Don Juan, ready to set the heart of any poor WPC's heart ablaze with the promise of beautiful portrait photography in the comfort of his home. His one saving grace, and his only one, was he was very good at his job, doing it quickly, efficiently and without error.

'Did you get the footage I sent you?'

'Good morning, the lovely Emily Parkinson, where have you been all my life?'

'Downstairs in MIT. Did you get the footage?'

He pressed a button in front of him and the image of the car park appeared on one of the monitors. 'You know, their maintenance of these things is getting worse. They should be recalibrated at least once a month. Most companies do it once a year. And this one looks like a spider may have built its web across the lens. Yuck.'

She approached his console, staying just out of reach. 'Can you clean it up?'

'Can an elephant dance the tango? Can the pope walk on water? Can Bono live with or without you?'

'Yes, Len, but can you clean it up?'

'No problem. This little baby can do anything.' He touched the machine to his left reverently. 'We use a combination of deconvolution: the improvement of the resolution of images by a mathematical algorithm to separate the information from any defects in the instruments used to collect it...'

One of Gorman's other problems was his need to explain what he was doing to anybody who would listen.

'...But this little baby goes one better, using AI to reassemble the images into what they should have been rather than what you gave me. Sweet, huh?'

Emily nodded her head. 'Can you just do it?'

'Be patient, the wonderful DS Parkinson, only a few more seconds.'

From the machine came a tiny beep as if it had burped.

'We're ready to rock and roll, Emily.' He pressed another button and a camera pre-roll began a countdown from 10.

10
9
8
7
6
5
4
3
2
1

The familiar bald head wove through the parked cars.

'Hang on,' said Gorman, 'I recognise him; that's DCI Turnbull.'

Once again, he stopped just before opening his car door and spoke to someone at the edge of the camera.

'This isn't what I think it is, is it? Footage of the attack on him on Friday?'

Emily didn't answer, staring at the screen. Once again, the man launched himself at DCI Turnbull, who didn't defend himself from the blows.

The attacker's head came up for a moment.

'Freeze it now,' she ordered.

Without thinking, Gorman paused the footage.

There was no blur. No shake. No judder of the image.

It was as sharp as a surgeon's scalpel.

Gorman sat forward. 'But that's not DI Ridpath.'

Emily recognised who it was immediately. But why had he attacked Turnbull?

And more importantly, why had Turnbull said it was Ridpath?

Chapter Ninety-Two

Hampered by the early morning traffic, it was past ten o'clock by the time Ridpath arrived near the hotel. A police cordon had already been placed, blocking off Swan Street and Rochdale Road.

As he was finding somewhere to park, his phone rang. It was Emily.

He ignored the call, squeezing the car in a small on-street space he found. He grabbed his phone and ran down the road, forcing his way through the crowd and reaching into his inside pocket for his warrant card.

It wasn't there – Claire Trent had taken it.

A young constable was standing on the other side, preventing people from getting closer.

'DI Ridpath, let me through.'

'ID, sir.'

'I've left it at the station. It's important you let me through.'

'Sorry, sir, no ID, no entry. You know the rules.'

He saw Mark Brett standing to one side, surrounded by a group of plain-clothes officers. Ridpath raised his arm and waved.

Brett noticed him and hurried over.

'No worries, officer, I'll vouch for DI Ridpath.'

'Yes, sir.' He raised the blue and white police tape for Ridpath to duck under, saying, 'You're supposed to carry your warrant card at all times, sir.'

Ridpath turned back to reprimand the pompous, snot-nosed trainee fresh out of Edgeley Park, but then thought better of it and smiled. 'You're exactly right, next time I'll make sure it's never out of my pocket.'

Brett took his arm.

'The Tacticals have just gone in. They're making their way up the stairs as we speak.'

None of the officers who were circled around a single radio tuned to the tactical officers' frequency looked up as Ridpath joined their group.

The radio squawked.

'Team One in position?'

'Roger, Team Leader.'

'Team Two, on my orders. Go.'

Ridpath heard footfalls along a corridor, followed by a moment's silence and then a loud banging in the door. 'Police, open up. Police, open up.'

Another moment's silence.

The crash of a battering ram against the door, followed by shouts of 'In, in, in.'

Muffled sounds of a woman shrieking, a man's raised voice and more police shouts of 'Get down on the floor, arms out. GET DOWN ON THE FLOOR.'

The same sounds were replicated for Team One. This time, Ridpath heard the noise of a struggle as the man refused to comply with the orders.

'Team Two, situation and prisoner secured, over.'

'Roger that, Team Two. Team One, situation, over?'

A breathless voice. 'Prisoner and situation secured. Over.'

The coppers around the radio high-fived each other. For the first time, Ridpath saw Mark Brett smile.

Three minutes later, both Trevor Sinclair and Arthur Delaney were led through the lobby of the hotel to a waiting Black Maria, their arms handcuffed behind them. Their two female companions, both draped in hotel blankets, followed them, loudly protesting their innocence.

In front of the Black Maria, Trevor Sinclair stopped and stared at Ridpath. He leant forward and whispered, 'You were next, you know. You and your daughter.'

Ridpath didn't know what to say. How did the thug know who he was?

One of the policemen shoved Sinclair in the back, forcing him into the van.

Ridpath tried to follow him, but was stopped by a large tactical officer.

'What do you mean, I was next?' he shouted.

Sinclair just smiled back at him through the tinted glass.

Ridpath banged on the window. 'What do you mean?'

As he shouted his question, the Black Maria accelerated away from the kerb in a cloud of blue smoke.

Ridpath started to run after it before realising how pointless it was. He ran back to Mark Brett.

'Where are they being taken?'

'I dunno. Longsight nick, I think.'

'I need to question Sinclair. How does he know I have a daughter?'

Brett nodded towards the group of plain-clothes officers. 'They're not going to let you anywhere near him. It's their collar. My boss can't even get to see Sinclair... yet.'

'But I have to, he just threatened my daughter.'

'He can't do anything now.'

Ridpath's phone rang. He answered it immediately.

'Ridpath, it's Claire Trent. I need you at MIT.'

'I can't come, I'm busy. Sinclair, he...'

'That is a direct order, Ridpath. You are to come to MIT now. Understand?'

What did Claire Trent want? He'd already been suspended and Professional Standards were after him. Was she going to stick the boot in again? 'I...'

'Understand, Ridpath?'

He couldn't see the point of arguing any more. He just replied quietly, 'Yes, boss.'

'When will you get here?'

It was a straight drive up the Oldham Road from here. 'Fifteen minutes.'

'Good. Don't be late.'

The call ended and Ridpath was left holding the dead phone to his ear.

What had he done wrong now?

Chapter Ninety-Three

As he entered MIT, the detectives behind their desks and computers all looked up.

There wasn't a welcoming face among them.

He looked for Emily Parkinson, but she wasn't there. Neither was Chrissy. Had Turnbull finally got rid of both of them?

He strode through the room with his head held high. These people weren't going to intimidate him. If he was going to get the chop, he wouldn't let them see it affected him. Afterwards, he would go and pick up his daughter, take her out of school on the pretext of seeing the dentist, and they could spend the afternoon together, eating something good, going for a walk or just hanging out.

Sod the police.

Sod MIT.

Sod the whole lot of them.

He knocked on Claire Trent's door and heard a crisp 'Enter.'

He went in and was surprised to see Emily, Chrissy and one of Turnbull's lieutenants, Alan Butcher, sitting in front of Claire Trent's desk.

'Ah, Ridpath, come in and sit down.'

'What's going on?'

'Come in and sit down, Ridpath.' She pointed to a free chair beside Emily Parkinson. 'DS Butcher has something to tell you.'

Alan Butcher didn't look at him as he began to speak. 'It's like this. I was with DCI Turnbull the day he went to the post-mortem on Tony Saunders.'

Ridpath frowned. 'I didn't see you there.'

'I didn't go in. I can't stand post-mortems. Too much blood and guts for me. So I went for a coffee while DCI Turnbull went in.'

'Yes, I saw him there.'

'He came out and I met him at the car. He said you two had an argument in the mortuary room. You nearly punched him.'

'I wanted to, but I didn't. He accused me of...'

Claire Trent leant forward. 'Please don't interrupt DS Butcher, Ridpath.'

'As we were standing at the car, he ordered me to hit him.'

'What?'

'He wanted me to hit him, causing bruises. He said he was going to accuse you of jumping him after your argument.'

'What? Impossible. Not even Turnbull would do anything so stupid.'

'You don't understand how much he hates you. For him, you're all that's wrong about policing. You're not a team player, Ridpath, you're a maverick, you go it alone and don't listen to anybody. The last straw was investigating another copper. A man who killed himself after you had interviewed him. Saunders was one of Turnbull's few friends in the force.'

'I don't believe you; he wouldn't be so stupid.'

'Show him the CCTV footage, Emily.'

The police detective turned her laptop towards Ridpath and entered the password.

As she did so, a strange feeling of déjà vu slipped through Ridpath's brain. There was something important he had missed, an idea which had floated briefly in his mind and vanished as quickly as it had appeared.

His thoughts were stopped as the footage began to play. They all watched in silence as Alan Butcher began throwing punches at his boss and then helped him into A&E.

'Thank you, Alan. I'll deal with you later.'

'I was ordered to do it, boss. I had no choice.'

'I said I'll deal with you later.' Claire Trent nodded towards the door.

Alan Butcher took the not-so-subtle hint and got up slowly to leave the office, his head down all the time.

When the door had finally shut, Claire Trent simply said, 'He's toast. Stupid bugger.'

'I don't think you should sack him, boss; he was ordered to do it.' Ridpath tried to defend the young detective sergeant.

'There's a time to obey orders and a time to disregard them. He made the wrong decision. And if you ever quote those words back to me, Ridpath, I'll make sure you never speak again. Understood?'

'Understood, boss. What about Turnbull?'

Claire Trent stared out of the window. 'Let me handle him. He's still on medical leave at the moment, and it's where he'll stay. He's a senior officer; we don't wash our dirty linen in public. But you're not in the clear, Ridpath; you still have the charge of misuse of confidential data hanging over you. However, given today's events, I'm sure a verbal caution should be sufficient punishment.'

'Thank you, boss.'

'Don't thank me, thank Emily and Chrissy here for showing me the footage. Without it, you didn't have a leg to stand on.'

Ridpath nodded at them both. He knew he didn't have to say a word.

'That'll be two curries down in Levenshulme, Ridpath,' whispered Emily.

'A cheap price to pay, in my opinion,' added Claire Trent. 'And before it becomes public knowledge, you three should know I've just been promoted to detective chief superintendent.'

'Congratulations, boss,' all three said at the same time.

'Before you get any ideas, I'm not going anywhere. The thought of being some pen-pushing bureaucrat in a division out in nowhere has no appeal.' She spread her arms wide. 'Not when I have all this. The chief is going to need some wins over the next few months and I'm going to give them to him.' She coughed once and pressed her thin lips. 'I thought if the cat went away, the mouse would play. And he did. Turnbull's ambition got the better of him. I'm sorry for what he did to you but, if I'm honest, it makes it easier to get rid of him. His mates in the Masons won't be able to save him now even with a lodge full of funny handshakes and rolled-up trouser legs.' A slight pause. 'And if any of you ever repeat what I've just said, you'll spend the rest of your careers on crowd duty at City.'

Chrissy smiled and touched her scarf.

'But for you, Mrs Wright, I'll make sure it will be at Old Trafford.' She opened a file on her desk. 'Now, I'm sure you've got work to do. I have to start talking to HR and Professional Standards about Turnbull and Butcher.'

Chrissy snapped her fingers. 'Before I forget, Ridpath, I got the lads to do the financial audit you asked for on Tony Saunders and Lucas Harvey's accounts. Saunders was as clean as a whistle but Harvey's showed large payments going in and going out. He was obviously paying off large gambling debts.'

'I think he was the one who worked with Trevor Sinclair to kill Ben Holdsworth. We have them on one of the CCTV cameras talking together.'

'Who's Trevor Sinclair?'

'I believe he's the man who murdered Ben Holdsworth, Lucas Harvey and Tony Saunders.'

'What?' exclaimed Claire Trent.

'Longsight CID have just arrested him and Arthur Delaney…'

'Delaney, the name rings a bell. Wasn't he the gang leader who did a runner to Cyprus before the EncroChat busts?'

'He's back now and he's just been picked up. I think Trevor Sinclair was working for him, cleaning up a mess.'

'And there's one other thing you asked for. The original arrest reports for Ben Holdsworth's previous offences.' Chrissy handed him two files.

Ridpath stared at the reports, not believing his eyes.

Of course, why hadn't he worked it out before? It all made sense to him now. All the pieces fell into place one after the other like the end of a complicated jigsaw puzzle.

He took out his mobile and called Mark Brett. 'I'm returning this morning's favour. Get yourself down to the Coroner's Court in Stockfield asap.'

'What's going on, Ridpath?' asked Claire Trent.

'Just a minute, boss, I have one more thing for Chrissy to do.'

He explained what it was.

'Should be easy, I just need to check the servers.'

Claire Trent interrupted. 'Ridpath, tell me what's going on or you're going to be suspended for the second time in three days.'

'It's like this, boss…'

Chapter Ninety-Four

After explaining everything to Claire Trent and getting her approval, he'd rushed back to Stockfield just as the Coroner's Court was breaking for lunch.

The coroner was briefed at her desk.

'Are you sure, Ridpath?'

'Positive, Mrs Challinor, it's the only answer.'

The SMS had already come through from Chrissy. It was as terse as one of City's attacks.

Six o'clock.

'There's no other way of doing it.'

'Right, let's make it happen. Take me through the new witnesses and their evidence again.'

At precisely 1.30 p.m., Ridpath was in his usual place at the entrance to the court. He looked around once again. The jury had assembled in their box waiting for the proceedings to begin. All the witnesses were seated in the same places as in the morning, ready to give their evidence or to be called again if anything needed clarifying.

The new witness Ridpath had summoned took her seat on the far side, close to the witness stand. She looked slightly nervous at the prospect of answering questions in an open court.

The footage was cued up to the right place. Jenny knew exactly when to play it. Mark Brett and David Holder were in their places and Claire Trent was stationed outside ready to come in when she was summoned.

Sophia was standing next to him. 'Are you ready?'

'As I'll ever be.'

Ridpath nodded in the court bailiff's direction.

The stage was set. The players summoned. It was up to Jenny to start the proceedings.

'All rise for the senior district coroner, Mrs Margaret Challinor.'

The coroner entered from the back of the court and took her place at her desk.

On cue, everybody sat down.

'I'm afraid,' Mrs Challinor began, 'due to extenuating circumstances, there is a change in the witness schedule for this afternoon. I do hope you will bear with me as we introduce these new witnesses.'

There were hurried whispers among the legal team on the police bench. Mr Hargreaves stood up. 'We are not aware of, nor have we received testimony from, any new witnesses, Coroner.'

'I do apologise, Mr Hargreaves, but these matters have only just come to my attention. Please proceed, Jenny.'

'I must object to being sandbagged in such a manner.'

'Objection noted, Mr Hargraves. Call the first witness, Jenny.'

The barrister reluctantly sat down.

'I call Sophia Rahman,' shouted Jenny Oldfield.

'Wish me luck,' whispered Sophia as she left Ridpath's side, and walked towards the witness box.

'Which book would you like to use for your oath?'

'The Qur'an. I swear by Allah the evidence I shall give shall be the truth, the whole truth, and nothing but the truth.'

'Miss Rahman,' the coroner began, 'what is your profession?'

'I am the assistant to the coroner's officer, Mr Thomas Ridpath.' Sophia's voice was clear and confident.

'And in your job, do you often help him prepare evidence and witnesses for inquests?'

'I do.'

'For this inquest into the death of Mr Ben Holdsworth, did you help him prepare evidence?'

'I did.'

'Which evidence?'

'I helped him prepare CCTV footage from Redbury Police Station taken in the early hours of February 21, 2018.'

'Where did you get this footage?'

'It was given to us by Mr Steven Fellows, the owner of the CCTV company who installed the cameras in the police station.'

'Mr Fellows has already testified this morning. He gave you footage?'

'He did.'

'Is the footage now being shown on the monitor the same as the footage Mr Fellows gave you?'

A still image of PC 2568 entering a code at the rear door of Redbury station appeared.

'It is.'

'Please roll the footage, Jenny.'

The monitor showed the man entering the code and then quickly opening the door and vanishing from view.

'Can you tell us what is happening?'

'This is from the CCTV footage at Redbury Police Station given to us by Mr Fellows. It shows the rear door to the station at 4.20 in the morning. This man, PC 2568, keys in a code and enters the station.'

'Thank you, Ms Rahman. Please roll the next clip.'

A still image of Lucas Harvey and a policeman speaking appeared on the screen above Sophia's head.

Mr Hargreaves was on his feet. 'I must protest again, as I did this morning, Coroner. There is no chain of evidence for this footage and it was held illegally by Mr Fellows against the wishes and bylaws of the police.'

'But the police have lost the original footage, have they not, Mr Hargreaves?'

'No, Coroner, they have not lost it. They simply cannot find it at the moment. The original footage was given to both the internal investigation and the IOPC investigation.'

'And because the police can no longer find it, I have allowed this footage to be used in court in order to discover the truth of what happened. Please play it now, Jenny.'

'I object, Coroner, this is most irregular.'

Mrs Challinor ignored the barrister, simply stating, 'Noted, Mr Hargreaves.'

The whole court watched the images of Lucas Harvey and PC 2568 as they talked together. In total it lasted for less than thirty seconds. There was no sound but they could see the lips of the two men moving.

'Is this also the footage from the internal CCTV camera given to you by Mr Fellows?'

Sophia looked up at the monitor.

'It is taken later the same morning, at 5.55. The custody officer on the footage is Mr Lucas Harvey, now deceased. I do not know the identity of the police officer but he was the same one who entered the station through the rear door at 4.20 a.m.'

'His badge number is 2568.'

'It is, Mrs Challinor.'

'Surely you can identify him?'

'We checked the records and the number belonged to a policeman who retired in 2017. It has not been reissued.'

A buzz went round the court. The coroner called for silence before continuing her questioning of Sophia.

'There is no sound, why?'

'That particular camera doesn't record sound.'

'Did you find out what they were saying?'

'We did.'

'How?'

'We asked a lip-reader to look at it and tell us what they said.'

'Thank you, Miss Rahman, that is all. Any questions for the witness, Mr Davies?'

The solicitor stared at the screen and slowly shook his head.

'Mr Hargreaves?'

'I must reiterate my objections to this footage once again.'

'You have already done so, and it has been noted.' There was steel in Mrs Challinor's voice. 'I do not want to continually hear myself cover the same point over and over again once I have ruled. Is that clear, Mr Hargreaves?'

The barrister stood up again. 'Perfectly, Coroner.'

'Good. Please call the next witness, Jenny.'

'I call Ms Lucy Gilmour.'

Ridpath checked the court. It was going exactly as planned at the moment. He gave the nod to Mark Brett, who casually moved round to stand near the witnesses.

After she had taken the oath, Lucy Gilmour stood up straight in the dock, her head cocked slightly to one side. She was a thin, frail woman with grey hair cut close to the head.

'Ms Gilmour,' the coroner began. 'What is your profession?'

'I am a professional lip-reader for police forces, the Home Office and legal firms.'

'Have you seen this footage before?'

'I have, Coroner. I was approached by Ms Rahman and asked to read what the people were saying.'

'The footage is silent, but can you tell us what they said to each other?'

Mr Hargreaves was on his feet again. 'I object, Coroner. Lip-reading can't be an exact science. This witness cannot prove what she says is an accurate reading of their conversation.'

The witness answered, not the coroner.

'Mr Hargreaves, at the age of eighteen months, I became profoundly deaf after catching German measles. Speech therapists helped me develop my voice, and through training, I became an expert lip-reader. I graduated from Manchester University with a degree in political science and international affairs.' A slight pause. 'I cannot hear you or the coroner at the moment, but as long as I can see your lips, I can understand what you are saying and answer your questions. Have I shown how accurate I am?'

The barrister looked from her to Mrs Challinor and sat down.

'If we play the footage, can you tell us what everybody is saying?'

'It will be my pleasure, Coroner. Before I start, I should explain, if somebody turns their head so I can't see their lips, I have no chance of understanding them. I will tell you when that happens.'

On a nod from the coroner, Jenny played the footage.

'The policeman on the right says, "You going to open it or not?" And the man in the white shirt asks him, "What you going to do?" I can't see the first few words, but the policeman answers "...not your business, just open it up."'

As Lucy Gilmour was speaking, Ridpath could see the words matching the lip movements and expressions on the people on the screen.

'The man in white replies, "But I'll be blamed." The officer replies quickly, "It's all sorted..." then it becomes unintelligible as the policeman turns his head, but I can read his last line, "...will handle it. Open the bloody door..." After that, I can't see the rest of the conversation.'

'How accurate is your reading, Ms Gilmour?'

'According to my experience, it is very accurate. In this clip, the sentences are short and the lips are clearly seen.'

'Thank you, Ms Gilmour,' the coroner said. 'In the interests of time, I am going to move on to the next witness quickly.' She turned towards the jury. 'However, ladies and gentlemen, I would like to remind you of the last sentence read by Ms Gilmour, "It's all sorted... will handle it." We will attempt to show who the last line referred to. Call the next witness, Jenny.'

There was a stir in the court. The witnesses leant forward. The reporters stopped writing and watched the coroner intently. Mr Hargreaves half rose out of his chair to object, then sat back down again.

'Calling Mr Thomas Ridpath.'

Chapter Ninety-Five

'You are the coroner's officer for East Manchester, are you not, Mr Ridpath?'

'I have that honour, Mrs Challinor.'

'You were tasked with looking into the witnesses for this inquest?'

'I was.'

'What did you find?'

'Mr Ben Holdsworth died in Salford General Hospital, at 7.35 on February 21, 2018. Earlier, at 3.40 a.m., he had been arrested and placed in police custody at Redbury station. The police actions in the case seemed exemplary; all custodial and arrest procedures were followed to the letter. CCTV showed an apparent fall with nobody else present and the post-mortem carried out by the pathologist, Dr Harold Lardner, confirmed the death was the result of a subdural haematoma probably caused by the fall—'

'What is a subdural haematoma?' interrupted the coroner.

'Bleeding in the brain. Mr Holdsworth's death seemed to have been an unfortunate accident. Nobody's fault.'

'So why did you carry on investigating?'

'Because there were a number of anomalies in the case. An unnatural number of deaths seem to have taken place. Before I began investigating, the custody officer, Lucas Harvey, died in a car crash. During my investigations, the custody sergeant, Tony Saunders, was supposed to have died by suicide. And just yesterday, the body of the detainee in the next-door cell to Mr Holdsworth was found dead in a rubbish bin in New Islington. Too many deaths, in my opinion.'

Ridpath paused and checked that everybody was in place before continuing.

'It was suggested to me that the custody sergeant, Tony Saunders, knew the victim, Ben Holdsworth. I was shown two arrest sheets from 2014 and 2016 for Mr Holdsworth with Sergeant Saunders' signature at the bottom. As you can see, he was charged with possession of cannabis and driving without a functioning brake light.' Ridpath nodded at Jenny and she displayed the arrest logs on the monitors. 'There were even rumours that Mr Holdsworth may have been involved in the death of the sergeant's daughter from a drug overdose.'

He nodded one more time at Jenny and the arrest sheets disappeared, to be replaced by an image of Ben Holdsworth standing in front of the custody counter.

'But when I looked at and listened to the CCTV footage of the booking-in process from that night, neither man appeared to recognise each other.'

Hargreaves rose to his feet. 'Where is this going, Coroner?'

Ridpath answered. 'Please bear with me a little longer, sir, I hope I can make it clear.'

He stopped for a moment and glanced over at Bob French.

'When I checked the original logs from the old police computer system, not the ones that had been uploaded to iOPS, the new system, I saw a different signature at the bottom of the page.'

A new image appeared on the screens: the original arrest logs for Ben Holdsworth on charges of dealing cannabis and driving without a functioning brake light.

'The signature on the bottom of the page is not that of Sergeant Saunders, but it is this man's.'

He pointed directly at Bob French, who tried to jump up but found himself being pushed back in his chair by the heavy hand of Mark Brett.

'And remember the code to the rear of the station being entered by the bogus policeman? The problem was it became live at four a.m., but the code was only sent out at six a.m. as an SMS to serving police officers so the day shift could use it when they came to work that morning. The only person who could have given the code earlier to PC 2568 was Inspector French.'

The court erupted. The reporters stood up to see where Ridpath was pointing. The jury was craning forward in their seats. The police solicitors and barristers were all looking over their shoulders to see what was happening.

Bob French tried to stand up, struggling against Mark Brett's arms holding him down.

His face reddened and he snarled. 'You bastard, Ridpath. I'll get you and your daughter for this.'

Rich Holder brought a pair of handcuffs from his back pocket and snapped them over French's wrists.

'I'll get you, Ridpath.'

He was hustled out of the court, struggling every step of the way.

Claire Trent had walked up to the police legal team and was now talking to Hargreaves.

After a minute's discussion, Hargreaves turned to the coroner. 'The police request a Section 28 adjournment to this inquest pending further investigation of the case.'

He struggled to make himself heard against the mounting noise.

The coroner banged her desk loudly, causing people to stop and listen.

'Agreed, Mr Hargreaves, twenty-eight days' adjournment. Mr Davies, will you bring your client to my rooms and I will attempt to explain to her what has just happened.'

The tumult in the court began again.

Mr Davies stood up. 'Certainly, Coroner. I would like to know too.'

'The court is adjourned,' shouted Jenny.

For once, everybody ignored her.

Two Weeks Later

Chapter Ninety-Six

Ridpath settled himself into the small bar in the City Arms and ordered a pint of Titanic Plum Porter. It was one of his favourite old Victorian pubs in the centre of Manchester. It was another place he'd discovered when he was a young copper based in the city centre. Strange how, these days, he was returning more and more to the places he knew when he was just starting out in the police. Nostalgia for the good old days, when life was simpler?

He looked around as he drank his first gulps of the rich, dark ale. He noticed disapprovingly that even here had succumbed to fashion and now offered a gin bar with over twenty kinds of mother's ruin.

Mark Brett came in two minutes later.

'What are you having?' asked Ridpath immediately.

'A pint of lager.'

'Another pint of the plum porter,' he told the barmaid. 'When are you off?'

'Next week. After my cover was blown with the arrest of French, I couldn't stay here any longer. Time to go back to heaven, otherwise known as Guildford.'

The pint of beer arrived.

'Bit dark for lager, isn't it?'

'Northern lager, Mark, enjoy it.'

Ridpath took a deep swallow of the Titanic. 'Mother's milk.'

'You can stand a spoon up in it. Tastes OK, though.'

Ridpath drank again. He really didn't come here often enough. 'What's going on with French? Is he talking?'

'Quiet as a church mouse. We've checked his bank statements. Looks like he's been on the take for a while, about five years we think. At least one of the OCGs was paying him off, probably more. Seems to have been taking a cut of everything going on in Redbury.'

Just when his wife left him, thought Ridpath.

'The only time he does talk is when we ask him about the police. He's as bitter as this beer. Thinks he was hard done by.'

'Shame, he was a good copper once, back in the day.'

'A good copper gone bad.'

They both took another swallow of beer.

'This stuff grows on you,' said Mark Brett.

'Puts hairs on the inside of your throat,' answered Ridpath. As Brett was being open, he asked more. 'What about Sinclair and Delaney?'

'Didn't you hear? Sinclair was shanked in Winson Green two days ago. I bet he would have gone for a deal, giving everybody up. His DNA was all over the cigarette butt you had tested from the roof and there were two lovely fingerprints on the brick. We had him bang to rights and he knew it.' He shrugged his shoulders. 'But the bosses decided he'd killed a copper and it was a no go.'

'Can't say I blame them. It was Emily Parkinson who ordered the forensic work not me. What about Delaney?'

'I have a feeling he's going to get off.'

'What?'

'He's hired a good brief and most of what we have is circumstantial. The only real charges are coming from the EncroChat taps. He's saying the phone was his brother's.'

'Selling out his own family?'

'Delaney would sell his mother for a quid and an ice cream. And there's nothing linking him to the other deaths.'

'What about Garry Abbott's missing teeth?'

'No forensics, no DNA, plus Delaney has seven witnesses saying he was in Liverpool for a wedding that day.' Brett put his pint down and leant forward. 'Have you given any more thought about Saunders?'

'Not a lot.'

'You think he was involved?'

'I dunno. One part of me would like to think he was clean, or at least cleanish. He trained a lot of good people.'

'And the other part?'

'Well… the other part thinks he must have worked out what was going on. He was too smart not to. Emily Parkinson checked him out. He may have been the one who altered the arrest logs for Ben Holdsworth. He had access to both the old and new management systems when he was on restricted duties.'

'But why put his own name down as the arresting officer?'

'Your guess is as good as mine. I think French had some sort of hold over him. I don't know what, though, unless French tells us. I think Saunders was always supposed to be the fall guy for everything. He was French's backstop, in case the accident narrative fell apart. The plan was to blame everything on him. Dead men tell no tales.'

Brett raised his eyebrows. 'You're right, literally the fall guy.' He took another swallow from his pint. 'And how are you? Professional Standards still looking for your blood?'

'I'm fine. Got a verbal warning for the data breach but after French was nicked it was the most they could do. Plus Claire Trent and the coroner backed me all the way. They can't touch me for the moment.'

'And Turnbull?'

'On sick leave still, but he's toast. He'll be allowed to resign quietly and take his pension. I've heard through the grapevine, he's got some corporate security job with one of the bookies lined up. A big salary and an even bigger benefits package attached to it.'

'Shit always rises to the top.'

'Doesn't it just.' Ridpath took a long swallow from his pint, wiping his mouth afterwards.

'What about you? If you don't mind me saying, you look as if you've had a tough time...'

'It was the...', Ridpath stopped for a moment, uncertain whether to go on. 'It was the threats against my daughter. Both Sinclair and French made them. You didn't help, visiting my house.'

Brett held his hands up in surrender. 'Sorry, not my idea. I would have done nothing to hurt your family, Ridpath, you must understand that. And as for the other two, one of them is dead and the other ain't going nowhere for a long, long time.'

Ridpath stared into mid-air. 'I sent her to stay with her grandparents last week. She wasn't happy but I think it's the best place for her at the moment. At least she's safe there.'

'Sorry, mate, can't advise you. Been married, been divorced, won't go through that again. Luckily no kids.' Mark Brett finished his pint. 'You having another? This stuff's not bad, but you can't beat a cold pint of lager.'

You can take the man out of Guildford, but you can't take Guildford out of the man, thought Ridpath. But what he said was, 'Why not, the night is still young. And Eve is at her grandparents'.'

As Brett went to the bar to get the drinks, Ridpath was left alone with his thoughts.

How long could he keep doing this?

For the last two weeks, he'd been feeling totally drained and empty, as if the last drops of energy had been sucked from him. Risking his life, his daughter's life and his career, all for a bloody collar.

What was the point?

Even the elation of putting French away hadn't lasted long. There were thousands of others ready to take his place, to sell their souls for a fast buck. The world was just becoming more and more greedy.

What sort of life were they making for Eve, and millions like her? He honestly didn't know any more.

Could he keep going on like this?

Mark Brett returned with two more pints of Titanic. 'We could have some sushi afterwards.'

Ridpath's eyes rolled far back into his head. Not another one. Whatever happened to good old fish and chips? Or a greasy kebab?

'They do a great all-day English near here if you want some food. A full monty is perfect after a few pints of this.'

'Here's to northern cuisine.'

They clinked glasses.

'You'll miss it when you go back down south.'

'Like an extra arsehole.'

They both laughed.

Outside, Ridpath was smiling, but inside he felt totally empty. It was like he'd reached the end of a long winter's night and the dawn refused to break. But what else could he do? He was a good copper and an even better coroner's officer. He had two bosses who were supportive for the most part, and a job where he felt he made a difference to people's lives.

What more could he want?

He didn't have the answer right now, but he hoped he would soon.

He took another long swallow of the Titanic. What was the name of the movie about the sinking of the ship? *A Night to Remember*, that was it.

February 21 was a night to remember for Ben Holdsworth. Shame he wouldn't remember it any more.

'Penny for them?' asked Mark Brett.

'I was just thinking of *Titanic* movies, and those who starred in them,' lied Ridpath.

'Leonardo DiCaprio.'

'Kate Winslet.'

'Alec Guinness.'

Ridpath raised his eyebrows.

'He was in *Raise the Titanic*, came out in the early eighties. I love my films.'

'Kenneth More.'

'*A Night to Remember*. Also had the wonderful Honor Blackman and Ronald Allen.'

'You do know your movies. Now answer this, what was the first movie about the sinking of the *Titanic*?'

As he asked it, Ridpath was hoping that his own dark night of the soul would end soon, and the light would come on.

For his sake and for Eve's sake.

'I give in; what's the answer?'

He focused back on the present. '*Saved from the Titanic*, released only thirty-one days after the sinking and co-written by Dorothy Gibson, one of the survivors.'

'Nah, you're having me on.'

'Google it if you don't believe me. I learnt it in one of the pub quizzes.'

Mark Brett finished his second pint. 'Goes down easy, this stuff, just like its namesake. It's your round.'

Ridpath wandered off to the bar, clutching two empty glasses.

The night would end soon, wouldn't it?

Do you love crime fiction and are always on the lookout for brilliant authors?

Canelo Crime is home to some of the most exciting novels around. Thousands of readers are already enjoying our compulsive stories. Are you ready to find your new favourite writer?

Find out more and sign up to our newsletter at canelocrime.com